## SIGNET Mysteries You'll Enjoy

SIGNET MYSTERY

# THE GREAT DIAMOND ROBBERY

## JOHN MINAHAN

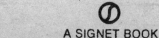

A SIGNET BOOK

NEW AMERICAN LIBRARY

NAL BOOKS ARE AVAILABLE AT QUANTITY DISCOUNTS WHEN USED TO PROMOTE PRODUCTS OR SERVICES. FOR INFORMATION PLEASE WRITE TO PREMIUM MARKETING DIVISION, NEW AMERICAN LIBRARY, 1633 BROADWAY, NEW YORK, NEW YORK 10019.

SIGNET TRADEMARK REG. U.S. PAT. OFF. AND FOREIGN COUNTRIES
REGISTERED TRADEMARK—MARCA REGISTRADA
HECHO EN CHICAGO, U.S.A.

SIGNET, SIGNET CLASSIC, MENTOR, PLUME, MERIDIAN AND NAL BOOKS are published by New American Library, 1633 Broadway, New York, New York 10019

First Signet Printing, July, 1985

1  2  3  4  5  6  7  8  9

PRINTED IN THE UNITED STATES OF AMERICA

## ACKNOWLEDGMENTS

I want to express my appreciation for the technical advice of John Gaulrapp, Brendan Tumulty, Happy Goday, Robert M. Cavallo, and the Police Department of the City of New York. A special note of gratitude goes to Chief Superintendent Les Clark of New Scotland Yard for cooperation far beyond the call of duty.

J.M.

*Beware, as long as you live,*
*of judging people by appearances.*

JEAN DE LA FONTAINE
*1621–1695*

# 1

ST.PATRICK'S DAY Wednesday, March 17, 1982, 1:45 P.M. All kinds of weird shenanigans going down, the Irish are looking to gross-out even last year's epic barfathon. Big John Daniels has the day off, he's marching in the gala parade up fifth, I'm working with Brendan Thomas today, old buddy of mine. Six-foot-four, about 220, comes from Wicklow, Ireland, talks with a slight brogue, has a trim mustache. Never drinks on St. Paddy's Day. Never. Says it'll be the dark night of his soul when he stoops to drinking with amateurs. Says it softly, with disdain. We're at the Chase Manhattan, Eighty-sixth and Second, we responded to a bank robbery with a bunch of other detectives and uniformed cops in the area. Now we get a call to go down to the Heritage Gallery, Madison and Seventy-second, to interview one Tara Alvarado regarding the possibility of a robbery. Whatever that means. Fact is, we're glad to be heading south, because the parade breaks up at Eighty-sixth and Third later this afternoon and nobody in his right mind wants to be caught anywhere near there.

Drive down to Heritage Gallery, double-park on Seventy-second, stick the orange ID card in the window stating we're on official police business. We've got a new four-door Chevy this year, black, tan upholstery. Heritage is seven stories of

severe neoclassic architecture; class gallery, one of the finest
in the city, on a par with Parke-Bernet just up the street. Go
inside, identify ourselves. Tara Alvarado turns out to be the
gallery photographer. Take the elevator to her office on the
second floor. Door's open. She's sitting behind a long table
cluttered with slides, prints, programs, brochures, shit like
that. Facing the window, studying a slide through a loupe in
her right eye. I knock on the door frame.

She keeps studying. "Yes?"

"Miss Alvarado?"

"Yes." Keeps studying.

"Detectives Rawlings and Thomas, Nineteenth Precinct."

Still at it. "Please come in."

We stroll in, glance around. Small room, wide window,
white walls covered with photographs in aluminum frames.
I'm not into artsy stuff, but I happen to know something
about photography. If this is her work, she's real good.
Concentration on general objects of art and gems with emphasis on capturing unusual refractions of light. Near the window
she's got a shot that I can only describe as dreamlike: A
jagged surrealistic mountain of jewels holding up an enormous deep-steel-blue diamond that refracts light like a prism.
Looks very much like a painting, a blue iceberg on another
planet.

Alvarado remains oblivious for a while, finally lowers the
loupe, gives us a glance. Kid looks to be in her mid-twenties.
Dark hair long and loose, dark eyes, high cheekbones, very
little makeup. Reminds me of Veronica Hamel, gal who plays
defense attorney Joyce Davenport in "Hill Street Blues."
Cool provocative confidence.

She stands, shakes my hand. "Detective—uh—?"

"I'm Rawlings, this is Thomas."

"Pleasure to meet you both. Please sit down." Eyes narrow as we sit. Walks around the table, goes to the door,
closes it. White silk blouse under a Calvin Klein denim
outfit, black Givenchy boots. Five-six, maybe 115, no-nonsense
walk. Sits down, glances at her small gold watch. "I met
with our chief of security yesterday, Jerry Donohoe, he's the
one who called Lieutenant Barnett. He suggested I tell you

the whole story. I've been approached by certain people and asked to supply certain information about an auction coming up here next month. Twelve diamonds are being auctioned. One of them is relatively well known, the North Star, seventy-two-point-four carats, valued at five million dollars. The total value of the twelve, about eleven-point-five million.''

Brendan and I exchange glances, take out our notebooks and pens, ask her to start at the beginning.

She walks to the window, props a boot on the ledge, gives us a thoughtful profile. Dark complexion, deep-set brown eyes, straight nose, full lips, strong chin. "It started senior year, University of Miami. I teamed up with another New Yorker in the class, kid by the name of Eddie Lopata. A big rawboned Polish kid from Queens. We broke a lot of bread together selling hash and pot.'' She smiles, shakes her head. "It was strictly platonic. We graduated, got back home, went separate ways. I lost track of him. I didn't see him again till last week, Monday. He called me at the office, we rapped a while, he said he had a good deal I might be interested in. We met at the Madison Avenue Pub that night, Monday night. We had a few drinks, he told me he's in a new business. He said he's in the jewelry business now. He's got good contacts in and out of the country for the right stuff. I asked him to get to the point. He wanted me to meet two buddies of his the next night. Neptune Diner on Queens Boulevard. In return for a small favor, I could retire for life. He said their names were Nick and Wally, that's all I'd need to know. He said he'd be in touch. The next night I went—''

Telephone rings. Pisses her off. Keeps staring out the window for a couple of rings. Whirls around, steps to the table, grabs the phone. "Yeah. Yeah, Jerry. Right. Right, they're here now. That's okay. Later, babe.'' Hangs up, massages the bridge of her nose.

"Next night,'' I cue.

"Yeah, right.'' But it's not that easy. She's got to find it again, get into it. Sits down, plants her boots carefully on the table. Sticks a Marlboro in her caps (educated guess), frowns as she lights up with a slim gold Dunhill. Inhales deeply, blows smoke toward the window, watches it flash into the shaft of light. "The next night, Tuesday night, I went to the Neptune Diner, eight o'clock. Nobody showed. I had dinner, left about nine-thirty, went to my car in the lot. Two guys pulled up in a white Eldorado. The guy in the passenger seat goes, 'Tara, I'm Wally; jump in.' I got in back. The driver introduced himself as Nick, said they're friends of Eddie, asked how Eddie was. I couldn't see either of their faces very well. We drove around in circles for a few blocks, parked in an empty lot.

"Nick turned around, he did most of the talking. The lights were off, I still couldn't see their faces. Nick goes, 'Saw in the paper about the auction coming up next month; very heavy jewelry.' He goes, 'We're talking eleven-point-five mill here, Tara, that right?' I told him yes. He goes, like, 'According to the paper, that one stone, the North Star, that's worth five mill alone.' I asked him to get to the point. He tells me, he goes, 'We want it all, Tara.' A real calm tone of voice. He goes, 'We want it all and we intend on getting it, but a person like you could make it a lot easier.' I ask how. He goes, 'We already browsed the place, but there're areas the public's not allowed.' He goes, 'Here's the deal, Tara: You get us copies of the floor plans, the alarm system circuitry, types and locations of safes, and as many pictures as you can snap of the areas involved.' He goes, 'We want a complete rundown on security, their schedules, if they're carrying while the stuff's in the gallery, all like that.' Now he goes, 'And for your trouble, Tara, six hundred thousand cash.'

"Okay, I didn't know what the hell to say, so I told him I'd have to think it over. Now Wally turns around, he goes, 'Listen, Tara, you know Eddie, he's solid, he's good people, you got no sweat of getting beat.' He goes, 'And don't worry, you'll get heavy bread before we move, to show good faith.' I told them I'd have to think it over and get back to them. Wally goes, 'No, Tara, we'll get back to you. Next week, say Monday.' They drove me back to my car, they took off. That's it."

"Nothing happened Monday?" I ask.

"I haven't heard from them since."

Brendan frowns, taps his pen on his notebook. "Miss Alvarado, you met these two men a week ago yesterday, Tuesday, right?"

"That's correct."

"And you say you reported it to your security man—what's his name?"

"Donohoe."

"Donohoe. You say you reported it to him just yesterday?"

"That's correct."

"So you waited a full week before telling anybody. Why's that?"

Alvarado takes a drag on her cigarette, inhales deeply, fixes her dark eyes on Brendan. "The truth? I was scared. I was afraid if I reported it to Donohoe he'd—he might suspect I was implicated in some way from the beginning. Dumb, I know, but what can I tell you? He's a security man, he's chief of security here, he thinks like that. I've had this job less than a year. It's a good job, it pays well. They're hard to find."

"Miss Alvarado," I say. "Forgive this question, but I feel obliged to ask it: Are you sure these men are absolutely serious?"

"Serious?" She considers it. "Yes. Why do you ask?"

"Follow my logic for just a minute. A robbery of this magnitude would probably be the biggest of its kind in history. Given the security involved—I'm sure it's elaborate—it's difficult to imagine that any group, however large or sophisticated, would attempt such a robbery."

She swings her boots off the table, sits up, stubs out her cigarette. "I know it sounds illogical. I know that. I realize that. All I'm telling you, they approached me, they seemed to know what they were talking about, they seemed very, very serious. That's all I know."

"Miss Alvarado," Brendan says quietly. "Apparently you've known this Eddie Lopata for some time now."

"Since college."

"Since college. Would you answer this question: Is he the type guy to pull practical jokes on his friends?"

"In college, sure. Of course. We moved in a fast crowd

down there. I haven't seen this guy in—we graduated in 'seventy-eight. So I haven't seen this guy in about four years. But I'll tell you this. When I saw Eddie last week, he wasn't kidding around. I can't prove it, I just know it, that's all. I know the guy. He was serious."

"The reason I ask," Brendan says, "we've investigated cases somewhat similar to this, where somebody—"

"Similar in what way?"

"Where somebody on the inside is approached, first by a friend, then by second parties. Discovered they were just very bad—sometimes very sick—practical jokes."

She's getting impatient. "Uh-huh. Look, I have a lot of work to do. Donohoe wanted me to tell you the whole thing, now I've told you. The ball's in your court."

Tough little lady. Give her our cards, arrange to meet her the following afternoon, ask her to bring a snapshot of Eddie Lopata.

Brendan and me, we can't help smiling on the way back to the car. Veronica Hamel City. Brendan's more or less convinced Eddie Lopata and his pals are playing a bad practical joke on this broad. He's seen it happen all too often: Offer a kid like this a cool $600,000 cash, her elevator pauses halfway to her brain. When it gets all the way up, if it ever does, now maybe she begins to think: Wait a minute; if the robbery actually comes off, these guys won't give me $600,000, they'll kill me. So now she blows the whistle. Concerned citizen. At least, that's what Brendan thinks.

Me, I'm not so sure. Something about this kid intrigues me.

Back to the precinct. Nineteenth Precinct, 153 East Sixty-seventh, between Lexington and Third. Second oldest in the city, built in 1887; Fifth Precinct is the oldest, 1881, but it's garbage compared to ours. Ours is now a Designated New York City Landmark; exterior can't be changed in any way. I'm glad. Love the place. Maybe that tells something about me, because most of the cops who work here don't exactly share my sentiments. I can understand why. No central air conditioning or heating, no elevators, no modern furniture, no bright color-coded antiseptic décor like most of the newer precincts. But this place has character, corny as that sounds. If that dates me, fine. Hell, I'm forty-eight years old, I've been in this department twenty-seven years now, eleven in this precinct alone. Don't get me wrong, I'm not against change, I'm all for it. On the other hand, I don't think a police station should look like a modern hospital, which a lot of the new ones do now. Come in and see the Nineteenth next time you're in the area, judge for yourself. Five floors of graceful, arched windows, intricate designs chiseled into the sandstone by craftsmen who obviously had a great deal of pride in their work. Step back and appreciate; you'll probably never see this kind of work put into a city building again. Or any other building.

Walk up the five front steps past the old iron boot-scrapers, pass under the vaulted entrance arch flanked by lamps that were once gaslight, it gives you a gut feel of history. This building was standing when the city still had a committee of police commissioners, before Teddy Roosevelt became president of the "police board" (1895-97). When Teddy first visited this precinct in 1895, he came in a horse-drawn carriage; automobiles didn't begin to appear in the city until 1898. Push open one of the heavy, three-inch-thick double doors, the big desk is off to your right, office of the commanding officer to the left. In 1977, some Spanish cuckoo strolls in here, walks up to the desk, pulls a .38 revolver, fires at the desk lieutenant, hits him twice in the chest; within seconds every cop on the floor opens up on this guy, who's shooting wildly now, they hit him twenty-three times before he finally goes down. Didn't hit a vital organ till the twenty-third shot. Bullet holes all over the walls, desk, blood spattered everywhere. Lieutenant was on the critical list for quite some time; finally recovered.

Little room up ahead to the right, looks like a box office at the old neighborhood movie house, that's where we keep our NCIC computer console now. Name the suspect, we'll have his complete rap sheet on the screen in seconds, if he has one. Now turn left, go up the reinforced but still rickety original wooden staircase, you're back to 1887 again. Creaks

like the door in "Inner Sanctum"; radio show, remember
that? No? Dating myself again, I know, but I'm not sensitive
about it. Didn't have TV when I was growing up on the
Lower East Side, had to use your imagination. Every time I
tell my son John about radio plays, he gives me this look.
*Radio* plays?!

Second floor, turn left, there's our squadroom straight
ahead. Hand-painted sign on the glass part of the door, "19th
Detective Squad," can't miss it, go right in, door's never
locked. Squadroom probably hasn't changed a whole lot in
ninety-five years. Low wooden gate leads to a relatively large
rectangular area filled with desks; lieutenant's office to the far
right, two sergeants' offices to the left. Old-fashioned steel
"holding cage" to the right of the door, extends all the way
up to the high ceiling, maybe fifteen feet. Why? Good question. Probably noticed kids were getting taller every year,
wanted to plan for the future, what do I know? Actually saw
a kid climb the cage once, real space cadet, got halfway up
before we coaxed him down. Maybe "coax" isn't the right
word. What we did, as I recall, Brendan and Big John
grabbed the cage and shook the piss out of the little sucker.
Cage is bare inside, about five feet square, nothing to sit on,
not even a john. I can imagine Teddy Roosevelt when he saw
it: "Bully! Let the baa-stids sit on the flaw like the dirty rats
they *ahh!*" Tough little guy, Teddy.

Tall windows with outside bars overlook the alley. Old
steam radiators in front of the windows. On the wall to the
right are the hand-painted individual wooden nameplates of
each man in the squad, nineteen now, probably less in the old
days. Ninety-five years of detectives, come and gone. Below,
a bulletin board with hundreds of the most recent "wanted"
posters. Ninety-five years of felons, come and gone. As the
man says, the more things change, the more they stay the
same.

Changes from the turn of the century include fluorescent
lights, many layers of green linoleum floors, untold layers of
blue paint on the walls, steel desks with dark-green bodies,
light-green tops, and rows of steel filing cabinets in almost
any condition and color you want. Luxury technological items

range from typewriters and telephones to electric fans and coffee-makers.

Brendan and I touch base with Lieutenant Barnett first, old-timer like us, short, lean, wiry, hair getting dangerously close to white; at least twice a year we leave a bottle of Grecian Formula 16 on his desk to no avail. Brief him on Alvarado's statement, then go to work. Brendan goes downstairs, has the computer guy run a make on Lopata, comes up empty; no arrest record. I make a call to the Office of the Registrar, University of Miami, Coral Gables. Edward Stanley Lopata graduated May 1978, B.S. Physical Education, Health and Recreation. Tara Maria Álvarado graduated May 1978, B.S. magna cum laude, School of Music. School of Music? Ask the clerk to double-check that. She does. School of Music. Magna cum laude. Ask for copies of both academic transcripts. They'll be in the mail today, ten-dollar handling fee, sorry about that, sir.

Going home on the Long Island Rail Road that evening, I glance through the *Post*, chuckle at centerfold shots of Mayor Koch and Governor Carey in the St. Patrick's Day parade, check the sports pages, then light up a cigar and concentrate on the pre-spring suburban landscape of southern Nassau County. Familiar little towns click past in the soft twilight— Valley Stream, Lynbrook, Rockville Centre, Baldwin, Freeport. For some reason my mind keeps returning to Tara Alvarado. Attractive young lady, soft spoken, obviously quite bright, apparently a music scholar and/or musician, talented enough photographer to land a full-time job with one of the best galleries in Manhattan. Intrigues me. By her own easy admission, this kid's no angel, pushed pot and hash with Eddie Lopata in Miami. Industrious couple. Strictly platonic? Now Eddie shows up four years later, scouts her out on the possibility of jumping straight from Class B to the bigs. Calmly throws a major-league knuckleball, she steps into it, base hit. One for one. Next he brings in a couple of veteran relievers, Nick and Wally. Bing-bing, no problem. Three for three. Kid looks like she's ready. Full week passes. No call, no contract, no bonus, no $600,000 salary. Decides to blow the whistle on them. Why? Basically honest? Can't quite buy it after a week. Scared she'd lose her job? Cute, but somehow I can't see it. Hell has no fury like a woman scorned? Doesn't play. What's left? Don't really know. Pieces of the puzzle are missing.

Train arrives at Bellmore 6:35, more or less on time. Already getting dark and chilly. In warm weather I usually walk home from the station, pleasant six-minute stroll, but Catherine and little John meet me when it's cold like tonight, if it's not too late; I always call from Penn Station. From the elevated platform I can see our car double-parked with a lot of others, motor running, headlights on, 1981 Cadillac DeVille, black, with V8-6-4 fuel injection. When I bought it new last year, a friend of mine, detective who lives in Merrick, he says, "John, don't let any of the brass see that thing." I says, "Why not?" He says, "You know why not. Doesn't look good, cop driving around in a new Caddy." I told him, I says, "That's bullshit, Charley." I says, "That's total bullshit." That's how I feel. If you're a successful executive and you own a luxury car, people say, "Well, of course, why not?" If you're a cop and you own one, certain people raise an eyebrow: Guy must be on the take, right? Doesn't seem to matter that you've worked twenty-odd years at your profession and can easily afford the car. Argument is, it just doesn't *look* good. I could understand if we were talking about, say, a Ferrari or a Jag or a Rolls, something in that category. But a Caddy DeVille? No way.

Same with the house, 117 Shore Drive, Bellmore, we worked our way up to it over twenty-five years of marriage. Nothing conspicuous, two stories of natural cedar shingles, quiet tree-lined street across from a small lake. Neighbors are mostly professional people, small families. We're very proud of our place. Four bedrooms, two baths, living room, dining room, family room with a fireplace, one-car garage. Patio in back has one of our few genuine luxuries, a free-form swimming pool, seventeen-by-thirty-six feet, diving board and all. We figure it was well worth the extra expense because John's six

years old now, right in the age range when he and his friends
can really enjoy it most; they're in that thing mid-June through
September. John's our only child, we had to wait almost
twenty years for him, nearly gave up. He's not John, Jr., he's
John Christopher; I'm John Phillip. Kid's much smarter than
I was at his age. That's no hype. Front of our refrigerator's
plastered with gold-starred exam papers—reading, writing,
math, history, geography—all marked "100" at the top in
heavy red pencil. He's written two short "books" on his own
this year, *Monsters* and *Ghosts*, both illustrated in color.
When I was his age, so I'm told, I couldn't even tie my
shoelaces. I was a dumb kid in comparison, but so was
everybody else back then, what can I tell you?

Well, not everybody. Not Catherine. She was something
else, she was a gifted child. Even her sister Eileen, who lives
with us now, admits that. So John lucked out. Television and
school play a significant role in his development, of course,
but the overwhelming influence in his education at this point
is Catherine. She's one of those people who seem to be
natural teachers. So, for all practical purposes, John's had the
equivalent of a private tutor. On average, I'd say Catherine
reads probably ten times as many books per year as I do—and
I enjoy reading. She's been a prodigious reader as long as
I've known her, and we started dating in high school. I'm not
talking about romance novels and like that, I mean relatively
heavy stuff; she's very selective about it. For example, she
doesn't wait till Sunday to read the *New York Times Book
Review*, she subscribes to it separately, so it's delivered
in the mail every Tuesday, five days before its actual publication date. Saves every copy for a full year, fifty-two
issues; throws them away every New Year's Day, starts all
over.

Reason I mention this, tonight we're in the family room
after dinner, I remember something that turns out to be
important. It's about 8:15, Eileen and John are watching
"The Greatest American Hero," I'm reading Antonia Fra-
ser's new Jemima Shore mystery *Cool Repentance* (I'm hooked
on that series), and Catherine happens to be reading next
Sunday's *Times Book Review*. Pine logs are snapping in the

fireplace. Suddenly I stop reading, glance at Catherine. It's difficult for me to describe her with any real objectivity, but I suppose the dominant first impression you'd get is she doesn't look anywhere near her age (forty-seven) and doesn't act it either. As usual, she's not really "curled" up in that chair tonight, she's like "coiled," left hand resting on the top of her light brunette hair as if holding it down, bright blue eyes wide behind the tortoise-shell-framed glasses, lean face flickering in the firelight, figure skinny rather than slender, even in the sweater and jeans.

"Cathy, remember that book about diamonds?"

She lowers the review, frowns. "Diamonds?"

"Yeah. Read a review about it. Couple of weeks ago?"

"Oh, about the cartel. I think that was just last week."

I get up, go to the desk, get out her big file folder, flip through last week's *Book Review*. She's right, it's in this issue.

# Diamonds Are Not Forever

## THE RISE AND FALL OF DIAMONDS
*The Shattering of a Brilliant Illusion.*
*By Edward Jay Epstein.*
*310 pp. New York: Simon & Schuster. $14.50.*

### By PAUL ERDMAN

FIRST Bunker Hunt, then Ahmad Zaki Yamani, now Harry Oppenheimer: They are all finding out that the rich don't necessarily always get richer. This threesome was betting on the money trees of silver, oil and diamonds respectively. In each case, the man involved thought he could keep the price of "his" commodity rising by controlling the supply of that commodity available for purchase in the world market. All three have failed, to varying degrees, primarily for the same reason: They were defeated by their own success, or perhaps the word is avarice.

In a classic case of supply-side economics at work, the prices went high enough—to $45 an ounce for silver, $40 a barrel for oil and $60,000 a carat for the purest white ("D") flawless diamonds—that new supplies of silver, oil and diamonds came out of the woodwork, because of increased output or dishoarding or both. The three men could have sustained the supply cartels they controlled by using their cash reserves to buy in all of the new "unscheduled" supply and thus keep it out of the market. Or they could have reduced their own output by amounts sufficient to compensate for the new supplies entering the market and thus restore the previous market equilibrium.

Since Bunker Hunt did not have a cartel that controlled the silvermining industry, he had no choice but to try to save his neck by buying all the silver that was on offer. He blew a couple of billion trying—and failed. Silver went back down from $45 to its current level of approximately $6 an ounce, and Bunker Hunt went back to Texas. Petroleum Minister Yamani knew that even Saudi Arabia did not have enough cash to sop up the oil glut, so he chose to reduce drastically the "captive" output in Saudi Arabia proper, from 11 million barrels a day to 6.5 million. He essentially sacrificed half his nation's income in an attempt to prevent a collapse in the world oil price. Though the plunge in oil prices has been stopped, it remains to be seen if his solution will be workable in the long run.

According to Edward Jay Epstein's "The Rise and Fall of Diamonds," Harry Oppenheimer, the man who runs De Beers Consolidated Mines Ltd., is trying both approaches in a desperate effort to stave off the collapse of the worldwide diamond cartel. In August 1981, following Sheik Yamani's example, Mr. Oppenheimer reduced the sale of diamonds from De Beers' own mine output and stockpile by 95 percent, and now he is spending billions à la Hunt in an attempt to reduce the number of diamonds in the open market.

So far these efforts have produced little success: The price of that benchmark one-carat D-flawless diamond has fallen from $60,000 to approximately $16,500 within just 18 months. (And Mr. Oppenheimer has recently resigned as chairman of Anglo American Corporation, the parent company of De Beers.)

What all this proves is that cartels, like diamonds, are *not* forever. This is the theme of Mr. Epstein's truly fascinating book, which chronicles, as the subtitle indicates, "the shattering of a brilliant illusion."

The review continues, going into considerable detail, but I already have the information I want. Now I get the notebook I used this afternoon at the gallery, look up some facts and figures mentioned by Alvarado. As usual, I have difficulty reading my own writing (never learned shorthand), but here's what I make out at the top of the page:

> 3/17/82, 2:10 P.M., Heritage Gallery, Mad. & 72. Tara Alvarado, photog. Auction next month—12 diamonds. North Star (famous), 72.4 carats = $5M. Total value of 12 = $11.5M. . . .

Now I turn to a blank page, do some simple arithmetic. If, as the book claims, the purest-white D-flawless diamonds had a 1981 market value of $60,000 a carat, the North Star, at 72.4 carats, would have been worth about $4.3 million, not $5 million. Of course, I don't know shit about diamonds, so it's entirely possible that "famous" stones are valued according to different sets of criteria. Have to check that. In any event, if it's true that the market value has now fallen to $16,500 a carat, that would mean the value of the North Star has now dropped to a laughable $1.2 million, somewhere in that neighborhood, all things being equal. Obviously, a rock like the North Star must have special qualities that make the purest-white D-flawless diamonds look like glass. Have to do some homework on that. I make a note to ask Catherine to stop in the local library tomorrow, see what she can dig up.

Thursday, March 18, 8:35 A.M., Brendan and I meet with Assistant DA Arnold Grossman at his office, 155 Leonard, give him a complete rundown on Alvarado's story. Arnold's the only guy in the D.A.'s office I honestly like. Serious little guy, balding prematurely, wears modern steel-framed glasses, looks like a successful corporate executive. Thing about Arnold, he doesn't feel the need to constantly prove how bright he is. Know what I mean? That kind of confidence. Also, he obviously loves his work, he's not using the position as a stepping stone. Sits there this morning in his shirtsleeves, sips coffee, listens to us. Really listens. He's not waiting for you

to take a breath so he can jump in with authoratative legal
bullshit and buzzwords like all the other hotshots. This guy
shuts up, looks you in the eye, listens, absorbs. Excellent
memory too. Pleasure to work with him.

Now we're finished, he waits, turns his chair, looks out the
window, thinks about it. Turns back, speaks quietly. "She's
positive they're serious?"

"Absolutely," I tell him. "We put it to her bluntly, Brendan
did."

"Run a make on Lopata?"

"Snow White," Brendan says. "Myself, personally, I can't
believe they're serious. I really can't. I think the three of 'em
are taking the kid for a ride."

Arnold nods, waits. Then: "What gives you that impression? The job itself?"

"The job itself. It's just too big. I mean let's face it, you'd
need a fuckin' army to pull it off. You really would."

"Not necessarily," I say. "Remember a certain hotel job
last year?"

Gets a smile from both of them.

"Man's got a point," Brendan says. "Three guys and a
broad."

"Three-point-four million," I say.

"And only one had a record," Arnold adds. "In any
event, we have no choice in the matter, we'll have to
follow through. So how you want to play it?" He waits.
"John?"

I take out a cigar, bite off the end. "Like to work Alvarado
a little. Like to make her an informant."

"Brendan?"

"Sure. Fine with me."

"I have no problem with it," Arnold says. "Touch base
with Barnett first. No problem. Tell her this office is
considering—better yet, 'seriously considering'—a conspiracy case. Involving Lopata, Nick, Wally—and her. Then tell
her the good news, that the D.A. will probably let her slide if
she agrees to cooperate fully in the investigation. We can't
promise her anything, of course. But, for example, if she

meets with Nick and Wally again and we can establish who they are, it'll certainly help take the heat off her. We're compassionate people here."

I light my cigar, sit back, blow smoke toward the ceiling. "Promise her anything, Arnold. But give her Arpege."

Back to the precinct, touch base with Barnett, he loves the idea. Spend the rest of the morning catching up on paperwork of cases in progress. Grab a late lunch at Hal Kendig's Speak Easy Saloon. Nice afternoon for a change, sun's out, not too chilly, so we walk up to the gallery for our two o'clock with Alvarado.

When we tell her, the kid's face turns white. "*Conspiracy* case?! Holy *shit!* And I came to *you!*" Now we tell her the good news, da-da, da-da. Can't promise her anything, of course. She agrees to cooperate, but she's into a sulk. We ask her for Lopata's address. She's got it: 263 Lockwood Avenue, Yonkers. Ask if she remembered to bring the snapshot. She did. Taken when they were seniors in 1978. High-camp shot of them both leaning nonchalantly against a sleek new red Ferrari, both wearing the latest unisex craze: Black silklike windbreakers, white wing collars, and black bow ties. They're smoking obvious joints in matching holders. Lopata's hair, deep-set eyes, and mischievous-kid smile remind me of James Dean. Rebel without applause.

Now the three of us go to the third floor for a meeting with Jerry Donohoe, gallery's chief of security. Office about twice the size of Alvarado's, expensively furnished; these corporate security guys live high off the hog. Turns out to be relatively young for such a position, maybe late thirties, medium height, full head of dark hair, small mustache, easy smile. Looks like he lost weight recently; tan cord suit fits a bit loose. Marks high on the bridge of his nose tell me he wore glasses for quite a while. No sign of them now, not even for reading; probably has contacts. We rap a while, he's a good listener. Picks up the phone, briefs the gallery president, arranges a meeting on the spot.

Take the elevator to the top floor, Donohoe leads the way down this red-carpeted hall, Alvarado sulking behind, Brendan and me absorbing the museumlike ambiance. Dark paneled walls are heavy with individually lighted portraits of scowling old farts going back to high-starched-collar days. Now we proceed through paneled double doors into an elegantly appointed waiting room. Elegantly appointed executive secretary seems lost behind an enormous paneled desk. We're expected; go right in.

Positively gigantic corner office overlooking Madison and Seventy-second. Persian carpets, antique furniture, display cabinets filled with hundreds of art objects; track-lighted oil paintings galore: Boticelli, Tintoretto, Rembrandt, Velasquez, Goya, Monet, Cagney, you name it. Louis XV desk in the far corner, high-backed chair turned to the window. We follow Donohoe up to the desk.

"Mr. Exeter," he says quietly. "I'd like to introduce Detectives Rawlings and Thomas of the Nineteenth Precinct."

High-backed chair doesn't move. Pause. Traffic noises.

Donohoe clears his throat. "Mr. Exeter?"

Valium-calm voice from the darkened corner behind to our left: "Uh, gentlemen, I'm over here."

We turn. Lamp in that corner snaps on, revealing a slender figure in an armchair, legs crossed. Graying hair is matted, ashen face somewhat bloated at the jowels, dominated by eyes that open wide now, almost bulge, and positively sparkle as he smiles at us. Wears a very wrinkled gray suit, blue shirt, blue-and-white striped tie pulled a fraction down and away from the collar. Studied casualness. Holds a ballpoint pen under his chin, begins clicking the top button in and out rapidly as we approach.

Donohoe does the introductions. Exeter's first name turns out to be Phillip. We follow him to four Queen Anne chairs situated around an ancient coffee table holding an array of ancient glass paperweights, snuff bottles, silver cigarette boxes, other brick-a-brac.

"Mr. Exeter," Brendan says. "Please forgive this question, but are you connected with the Phillip Exeter prep school?"

Exeter winces just perceptibly; an old wound has obviously

been touched. Closes his eyes, opens them, manages a thin smile. "Detective, uh, Detective—Thomas, is it?"

"Yes, sir. Sorry, I was just—"

"Not at all, Detective, uh, Detective Thomas. In point of fact, my name is Phil-*lip* Exeter. I expect you're thinking of the Phil-*lips* Exeter Academy in Exeter, New Hampshire, are you not?"

"Oh, yeah, that's right. Sorry about that, sir."

"Not at all. Now, gentlemen, as I—"

"You go there?" Brendan asks.

Exeter presses two fingers to his left temple. "Uh, no. No, I didn't attend the, uh, the Phillips Exeter Academy. For reasons that I used to assume were rather, uh, rather transparently obvious." He dismisses the subject with an unexpected, eye-bulging smile, turns to me. "Detective, uh, Detective Rawlings." Looks at the yellow legal pad on a clipboard in his lap. "As I understand it from Mr., uh, Mr. Donohoe, we appear to have something of an embryonic problem here."

"Yes, sir."

He clicks his pen. "To be specific, as I understand it, the district attorney's office is in fact seriously considering a con*spir*acy case involving one, uh, 'Eddie' Lopata, his two—what might one call them?—conspira*tors*, I believe, known to us only as, uh, 'Wally' and 'Nick,' and of course our own lady-errant, as it were, Ms., uh, Ms. Alvarado. Would you say that's essentially correct, sir?"

"Yes, sir."

"Yes indeed. And Detective, uh, Detective Rawlings, sir." Consults his notes again. "Would it be an accurate assumption that your office, as well as that of the district attorney, I gather, would like Ms., uh, Ms. Alvarado to indeed col*lab* orate with these, uh, these gentlemen; that is to say, sir, that you desire her to become—in the jargon of your, uh, your trade—an in*for*mant, if you will?"

Goes like that. Amid pen clicks, eye bulges, and ear-moving, forehead-flattening, charm-your-tits-off smiles. Bottom line, we stress the fact that, based on experience, if these people are in fact serious about pulling this job, there's a high probability they'll do it with or without inside help. Exeter pledges his complete cooperation, as well as that of Alvarado: "Indeed," he tells us, "I believe it was, uh, *Plu*tarch who admonished us: 'If all the world were just, there would be no need of uh, of *val*or.' "

# 2

MONDAY, MARCH 22, 10:18 A.M., we're in the squadroom when
we get a call from Alvarado. Wally just phoned and wants to
meet her at noon today, southwest corner of Park and Eighty-
sixth. Now we have to move fast. Brendan and I grab one of
the motor pool Checker cabs, pick up Alvarado at Madison
and Sixty-eighth, rush her down to the Intelligence Unit at
headquarters, have her wired with a micro. Haven't seen
Chief Vadney for almost a year now, I'm tempted to go up
and lay this one on him. Hey, Chief, how you doin'? Not
bad, Rawlings, what's new? Nothing much, Chief, same old
shit, laying bait for a bunch of clowns who plan to snatch
eleven million in diamonds. Ul-uleven million in diamonds,
Rawlings? Eleven-point-five, to be exact, Chief, probably the
biggest diamond robbery in history, if they get away with it,
ha-ha. I'm tempted, but I just don't have time right now.
Actually, it's standard operating procedure that Chief Vadney
be briefed on all robbery investigations involving $1 million
or more, for possible special assignment of personnel, but
this one hasn't even progressed to the stage of prima facie
evidence of intent, so we have a loophole here.

When Alvarado's wired, Brendan signs out for the appropriate transmission-recording gear, drives her up to the precinct in our cab. I sign out for two Nikons with 200-millimeter

lenses, plus a surveillance van with one-way windows, meet them in the squadroom about 11:30. Lieutenant Barnett gives us the green light to use four other detectives from the squad: Nuzhat Idrissi and Roger Stephenson in the van (they're excellent with cameras); Big John Daniels and Happy Goday in one of the Chevy cabs from the motor pool. Brendan and I take the Checker cab, him driving, Alvarado and me in back.

Off we go. Drop Alvarado at Eighty-fifth and Fifth, 11:53. She walks to the meet. Idrissi double-parks the surveillance van at the northeast corner of Park and Eighty-sixth; Goday double-parks his cab on Eighty-sixth between Madison and Park, headed east; we double-park ours on Eighty-sixth between Park and Lex, heading west. We're all in radio contact, of course.

Exactly 12:06 Alvarado's approached by a white male Caucasian, mid-thirties, about five-eleven, maybe 160, medium build, mod-cut dark hair, tan leather jacket, could be suede, dark trousers, dark shoes. Idrissi and Stephenson start photographing, I start recording. Conversation is somewhat garbled because of the traffic noises:

WALLY:   How y'doin', Tara?
TARA:    Okay, I guess.
WALLY:   Thought about the deal?
TARA:    Yeah, but I got (unintelligible). I want insurance. I like (unintelligible) who I'm working with.
WALLY:   You know Eddie good, you scored with (unintelligible). He ever give you a fast shuffle?
TARA:    No.
WALLY:   There's your insurance. Look, all (unintelligible) for now, are you in? Then we can all sit down and talk.
TARA:    Okay, okay. When?
WALLY:   Nicky's out of town on business. Be back Wednesday. I'll tell him you're in, we'll (unintelligible), we'll set it up. And Tara, no names, no telephone conversations, understand?
TARA:    Right.
WALLY:   We'll be in touch. Take care.

Wally walks east across Park, north across Eighty-sixth, heads
east on Eighty-sixth toward Lex, passes our double-parked
cab in a crowd. We turn and watch. About halfway down the
block he steps into the street, opens the door of a red 1982
Pontiac Trans Am. Young girl at the wheel slides over. He
pulls out carefully, heads west, passes us. New York plates
188 ADZ. Waits for the light at Park, hangs a right. Idrissi
moves out, several cars behind, followed by Goday, then us.
North on Park all the way to 127th, hangs a right. Idrissi
radios he'd better drop his van back now; Goday passes him,
we pass him, move up two cars behind Goday. Wally takes a
left on Third, crosses the Third Avenue Bridge, gets on the
Major Deegan. Goday decides to drop back now; we pass
him. Wally gets off the Deegan at 179th in relatively heavy
traffic. When he stops for a red light, we move alongside on
his right. Can't see the girl with him. Brendan's driving, me
in back, he takes a casual glance in Wally's car. Light
changes, Wally takes off, Brendan doesn't move for a couple
of seconds.

   "Jesus, Mary, and Joseph," he says softly. "Lady friend's
doin' a number on his naughty."

   In broad daylight, as they say. In heavy traffic. Nice kids.
Now we speed up, we hear a siren in the distance behind us.
White BMW flashes past on our left, four male blacks inside,
kids. We continue to stay with Wally. Up around Arthur
Avenue and 184th, BMW cuts in front of the car directly
ahead of us, hits the brakes, skids, fishtails; car ahead hits the
brakes, Brendan hits ours, we skid sideways, burning rubber,
ditto cars ahead and behind. BMW spins in a circle, stops,
four doors open, four black teen-agers jump out, split in
different directions; car radio's blasting hard rock. Squad car
screeches up on our left, two uniformed cops jump out, sprint
after the kids. In broad daylight, as they say. Now both lanes
are blocked, horns blaring.

   Brendan turns around to me, cigar stub stuck in his puss,
looks every inch a cabbie. "Ah, Jesus, I'm tellin' ya," he
says philosophically. "Ya believe that, Johnny? Doin' a number on his naughty."

   While we're waiting, Brendan gets on the radio, asks for a

DMV check on the plate 188 ADZ. Traffic's moving again by the time we get a reply: 1982 Pontiac Trans Am's registered to one Cynthia Caravetta, 269 Morris Park Avenue, Bronx. Girlfriend. Back to square one.

Tuesday, March 23, third day of spring. This morning's temperature, 36°F. Idrissi and Stephenson come in from the Photo Unit about 9:15 with twenty-three B/W blowups of subject Wally, all tight closeups, various angles. We stick them up on two walls of Big John's office, ask the troops in the squadroom to take a look. Negative. Nobody ever laid eyes on this guy. We play the taped conversation for Barnett, transcribe it verbatim for the file, pick up Alvarado, take her down to BCI to view mug shots. Negative. After an hour she's so punchy she wouldn't recognize Wally or Nick if they walked in the room.

At 2:15 Brendan and I drive the surveillance van up to the Bronx, make a pass at 269 Morris Park Avenue. Red Trans Am's in the driveway. Modest little two-story house, gray, badly in need of a paint job. We park about a block away, take turns with the binoculars. Subject Cynthia Caravetta comes out about 3:35 wheeling a small baby carriage. Surprises us. According to DMV she's nineteen and single. Five-eight, 120, brown hair, brown eyes. Wheels the carriage in our direction, opposite side of the street. Vital stats are often misleading. This kid looks to be in her mid-twenties. Very attractive. Stacked. Goes to a drugstore up the street, comes back, goes inside.

We hang around. At 4:55, a black 1981 Jaguar XJ6 swoops up, parks out front, New York license 593 FOG. Out hops Wally, in he goes. Brendan gets on the radio. Jag's registered to one Peter Kwapniewski, 32-95 Twenty-ninth Avenue, Flushing, Queens. Now we ask for a make on the NCIC computer. Negative. No arrest record.

Wednesday, March 24, 10:25 A.M., we're at the Taxi & Limousine Commission office, 67 Wall Street, Investigations Unit, digging deeper on Peter Kwapniewski. Guy by that name was printed and photographed for a hack license September 9, 1979. Compare the photo with one of our full-face surveillance shots. Not the same guy, but the resemblance is too strong to be coincidental; Jag must be owned by a brother. Drive over to BCI, check the mug shot files under the name *Wally* Kwapniewski. Find a Wally. Compare it with the surveillance shot. Positive ID. Rap sheet shows three arrests: (1) Possession of a loaded firearm, age sixteen, probation; (2) felonious assault (pipe) on police officer, age twenty, pulls eighteen months in Greenhaven Correctional Facility; (3) burglary, possession of a loaded firearm, age twenty-six, pulls four to seven years in Dannemora Prison; released April 1981. Accomplice in burglary: Leroy Cupola, white male, thirty-one, five-eleven, 175, brown hair, blue eyes, mustache.

Pull the duplicate mug shots of Kwapniewski and Cupola, drive up to the Heritage Gallery, show them to Alvarado. Positive ID on Kwapniewski. Negative on Cupola; he's definitely not subject Nick. Alvarado hasn't heard from either man about the meeting.

Rap sheet on Kwapniewski makes us believers. Odds-on this is no practical joke. Still, Wally's been a bush-league ground ball up to this point in his career and that gives us pause. Must've met some heavy hitters in Dannemora. Often happens. Time to tell the chief? Brendan and I discuss it with Barnett. He wants us to keep digging on Nick, see if we can come up with another positive ID. We've only been on the case a week and the robbery isn't scheduled until the auction, April 19-20. If this plan's on the level, let's show the brass some hard evidence based on first-class investigative work. Good advice.

Thursday, March 25, 9:15 A.M., we're at the executive offices of the New York Telephone Company, 1095 Avenue of the Americas. Meet with Andy Bradley in Security, request copies of Kwapniewski's phone bills for the past three months. While he's getting the information, we call Alvarado. No word from Wally or Nick. We study the phone bills, December through February. Average of about thirty-five toll calls per month, primarily Chicago, Detroit, Miami. However, between January 5 and February 23, he makes a total of seven-

teen calls to a number in Connecticut: (203) 966-7757. Bradley
checks it for us. Number's listed under the name of Nicholas
Mize, 377 Pinney Road, New Canaan.

Back to the precinct. More spadework, lots of calls. Brendan makes one to a state correction officer he knows at
Dannemora; we get a break: Wally Kwapniewski and Nick
Mize were cellmates for two years prior to Wally's release in
April 1981; Mize was released September 1981. Boom, down
to BCI, pull Mize's rap sheet and mug shot. White male,
thirty-seven, five-nine, 155, blond hair, blue eyes. Two pre-
vious arrests: (1) Burglary (safe), savings and loan associa-
tion, age twenty-four, two years in Sing Sing; (2) burglary
(safe), jewelry exchange, age twenty-nine, four to seven
years in Dannemora. No accomplices on either job. Take a
duplicate mug shot up to the gallery, show Alvarado. Bingo.
Positive ID. Now we got a make on all three of these clowns.

Discuss it with Barnett that afternoon. For a projected
robbery of this magnitude, it's obvious that many more than
three people are involved. Alvarado will undoubtedly be
contacted soon and we'll need more manpower. Barnett picks
up the phone, calls headquarters. Chief Vadney will see
Brendan and me in his office tomorrow morning, 8:30 sharp.

We knock off early today. Need to be bright-eyed and
quick-witted tomorrow morning. Isn't every day precinct detectives get to lock intellects with one of the sharpest minds
in enforcement. Man almost single-handedly broke the famed
Champs-Elysées case in 1981, biggest hotel robbery in American history. Hell, they wrote a book about that case. Talk
about celebrity. Ever since he appeared on "60 Minutes"
with Mike Wallace, the chiefs been deluged with pleas to
appear on virtually every major TV talk show in the country.
Turned them all down. Press Relations begged him to make a
few exceptions for the good of the department. Reluctantly
appeared on Johnny Carson, Merv Griffin, and Phil Donahue.
Said he did it "as a public-spirited gesture to assure crime-
conscious America that the Big Apple is still where it's all
happening."

Ed Koch had a shit hemorrhage.

*        *        *

Tonight I start reading two books Catherine got for me at the library, *The Rise and Fall of Diamonds*, by Edward Jay Epstein (the one I'd read the review about), and *Great Diamonds of the World*, by Dan Rogers Davis, this one published in 1981, complete with color illustrations.

Begin the Epstein book after dinner, and right off the bat I learn what I suspected from the review, the value of the relatively few "large cut" diamonds in private hands depends on various subjective as well as objective criteria. For example, get a load of this:

> . . . The legend created around the so-called "Elizabeth Taylor" diamond is a case in point. This pear-shaped diamond, which weighed 69.42 carats after it had been cut and polished, was the fifty-sixth largest diamond in the world, and one of the few large cut diamonds in private hands. Except for the fact that it was a diamond, it had little in common with the millions of small stones that are mass-marketed each year in engagement rings and other jewelry. When Harry Winston originally bought the diamond from De Beers, it weighed over 100 carats. Winston had it cut into a fifty-eight-faceted jewel, which he sold in 1967 to Harriet Annenberg Ames, the daughter of publisher Moses Annenberg, for $500,000. Mrs. Ames found it, however, extremely costly to maintain: the insurance premium just for keeping it in her safe was $30,000 a year. After keeping it for two years, she decided to resell it and brought it back to Harry Winston.
>
> Winston advised Mrs. Ames that he could not buy it back for the price for which she had purchased it from him, and suggested that she might do better auctioning the diamond at Parke-Bernet. She called Ward Landrigan, the head of Parke-Bernet's jewelry department, and explained that because she did not want any publicity, the diamond should be auctioned without her family's name attached to it.
>
> This caveat gave the publicist that Parke-Bernet retained for the auction the idea for a brilliant gambit. The huge diamond, which would appear on the cover of the catalogue, would be called "The No Name Diamond," and the buyer would have the right to rechristen it. In August of 1969, Ward Landrigan brought the diamond to Elizabeth Taylor's chalet in Gstaad, Switzerland, and assured her that it was the finest diamond then available on the market. She expressed interest in it, and

shortly thereafter items were planted in gossip columns suggesting that Elizabeth Taylor planned to bid up to a million dollars for the No Name Diamond.

At that point, Robert H. Kenmore, whose conglomerate had just acquired Cartier in New York, saw the possibility of gaining considerable publicity for Cartier by buying the No Name Diamond, renaming it the Cartier Diamond and reselling it to Elizabeth Taylor. He preferred to pay a million dollars for it, so that the sale would be indelibly impressed on the public's mind as the most expensive diamond ever purchased. He arranged to borrow the million dollars from a bank, and took the $60,000 interest cost on the loan out of his conglomerate's public relations budget.

The auction was held on October 23, 1969, and after sixty seconds of excited bidding, the diamond was sold to Cartier for $1,050,000. Harriet Ames received from Parke-Bernet, after paying their commission and sales tax, $868,600, and Cartier received the diamond. Four days later, Elizabeth Taylor and her husband, Richard Burton, bought the diamond from Cartier for $1,100,000 (which meant that Cartier took a slight loss on the interest charge), and a few days later the diamond was transferred to Elizabeth Taylor's representative on an international airliner flying over the Mediterranean to avoid any further sales tax on the diamond.

Some ten years later, when she was married to John Warner, the United States senator from Virginia, Elizabeth Taylor decided to sell this well-publicized diamond. She announced that the minimum price was four million dollars, and to cover the insurance costs for showing it to prospective buyers, she further asked to be paid $2,000 for each viewing of the diamond. At this price, however, there were no buyers. Finally in 1980 she agreed to sell the diamond for a reported $2 million to a New York diamond dealer named Henry Lambert who, in turn, planned to sell the stone to an Arabian client. The profit Miss Taylor received from the transaction, after paying sales taxes and other charges, was barely enough to cover the eleven years of insurance premiums on the diamond; and if inflation were taken into account, and the return Miss Taylor received calculated in 1969 dollars, she suffered a considerable loss on buying and holding the fifty-sixth largest diamond in the world for over a decade.

Interesting. Catherine's reading the other book, we're getting
a liberal education in diamonds tonight. It's about 10:45,
we're sitting up in bed by now, little John's long since asleep
across the hall, ditto Eileen in the next room, so we keep our
conversation to a minimum.

Catherine yawns, she's about ready to call it a night now.
"What's the name of that big diamond being auctioned?"

"The North Star."

She looks it up in the index, flips to the story, begins
reading. Couple of minutes later she says, "What a history."
Very softly.

"What?"

"Read this." She hands me the book.

Left-hand page has a black-and-white photograph of a very
large, rectangular-shaped diamond of obviously superb bril-
liance and clarity. Right-hand page reads:

## THE NORTH STAR

### 72.41 Carats

Among the most celebrated diamonds in private ownership
today, the North Star has the extremely rare distinction of
having been cut from the legendary Pretoria, the largest diamond ever found. Named after Sir Charles Pretoria, chairman
of the mining company that discovered it in the Pretoria Mine,
Transvaal province of South Africa, in 1905, the uncut Pretoria weighed 3,106 metric carats (1.3 pounds or 0.60 kilo-
grams) and measured 4½ by 2½ by 2 inches. It was cut
into two large stones, seven medium sized, and ninety-six
smaller stones. The biggest of these, the Star of Africa, at
530.21 carats, is the largest cut diamond in the world and
resides in the Royal Sceptre among the British Crown Jewels
in the Tower of London.

Although the North Star was one of the seven so-called
"medium-sized" stones cut from the Pretoria, it is, at 72.41
carats, the thirty-eighth largest diamond in the world, and one
of only sixteen large cut diamonds remaining in private ownership. Its fascinating history easily rivals that of such illustrious diamonds as the Jubilee (245.3 carats), the Kohinoor (106
carats), the Idol's Eye (70.2 carats), the Cartier (69.42 carats), or even the storied steel-blue Hope (44.5 carats).

The North Star was the only diamond of the 105 cut from the original to be retained by Sir Charles Pretoria himself. In *Pretoria and the North Star* (Oxford University Press, 1980), British biographer Aubrey Davis offered very rare glimpses into the man's private life, revelations that received wide publicity in the British press and uncovered a scandal that had been a rather well-kept secret among the aristocracy for nearly forty-four years.

Born in Johannesburg, South Africa, in 1872, the son of working-class British subjects, Charles W. Pretoria was a bricklayer by trade before he discovered the Pretoria Mine in 1904, approximately 900 miles north of De Beers' famous Big Hole in the Kimberley area. When the huge diamond that was to bear his name was found in 1905, Pretoria became wealthy and famous at the age of only thirty-three, dividing his time between South Africa and England. After presenting the two largest portions of the diamond to Edward VII, he was knighted and generally accepted by the aristocracy.

In 1917, at the age of forty-five, Sir Charles met a hauntingly beautiful British girl named Phyllis Waring, a seventeen-year-old hairdresser. Although he had been married for some twenty-two years and had children older than Miss Waring, they fell deeply in love. Miss Waring became his mistress, an arrangement that was *de riguer* in British society at the time, and the relationship lasted twenty-one years, until his death in 1938 at the age of sixty-six.

In his will, Sir Charles left the bulk of his estate (estimated to be in excess of £17 million) to his wife and heirs. However, he had added a codicil in 1927, unknown to his family, bequeathing: (1) his twenty-two-room Victorian "summer" mansion in Epping Forest, northeast of London, to Miss Waring; (2) the sum of £1 million cash to Miss Waring; (3) two trust funds in the amount of £100,000 each for Miss Waring's two daughters, then aged ten and four (allegedly fathered by him but not recognized as legal heirs), to be held until each had reached the age of twenty-one; and (4) outright legal ownership of the North Star Diamond, then valued at £855,000, plus trustee-account insurance on the diamond through Lloyd's of London in the amount of £250,000 to cover premiums of £5,000 per year for fifty years.

Biographer Davis notes that Miss Waring celebrated her eightieth birthday on March 30, 1980. Although Davis had not been permitted to interview Miss Waring or her two daughters, reliable sources have assured him that Miss Waring has resided in Sir Charles's magnificent "summer" mansion for the past forty-two years. Since the marriage of her younger daughter in 1957, she has lived there alone.

Due in no small measure to the enormous public notoriety ignited by Davis's revelations, the North Star is far more celebrated in England today than ever before. When the biography was published in the spring of 1980 and became an immediate sensation (Number 1 on *The Times* best-seller list in its very first week), tabloids all over the country made the love affair front-page news, a romantic cause célèbre, replete with long-ago photographs of the couple (taken individually, never together), "star-crossed lovers," as the *Daily Mail* dubbed them: the ruggedly handsome Sir Charles in his mid-thirties, already wealthy and famous; the strikingly beautiful Miss Waring in her early twenties, reminding millions of Vivien Leigh in *Gone With the Wind;* and of course the diamond, large, brilliant, flawless, the unchanging symbol of their love.

Despite the hoopla, much of it in the worst possible taste, the fact remains that the North Star, one of the rarest diamonds in private ownership today, cut from the greatest of them all, has not been seen in public since 1938.

And, judging by the unusually conservative personality of its owner, who has always shunned publicity of any kind, it is indeed possible that the diamond will never be seen in public again.

Friday, March 26, 8:22 A.M., we're at headquarters, 1 Police Plaza, this place is straight out of *Star Trek III*. Squats there in the plaza ready to lift off: Fourteen floors of recessed windows, each floor color-coded for maximum hospital-type efficiency. At the security desk in the lobby, Brendan and I get red plastic passes clipped to our lapels, restricting admission to that floor only, which happens to be fourteen, penthouse suite, known affectionately to most as the Psychiatric Ward. Chief has a big corner office, of course. We wait in the reception area with his assistant (secretary) Steve Adair, nice kid, bit flaky, but he types real good. Precisely 8:29, chief's voice comes over the intercom box: "Show 'em in." Steve shows us in. Chief's sitting in the familiar high-backed

leather chair behind the polished wooden desk that's so free
of clutter we can actually see his face in it: He's leaning
forward, sort of biting his tongue as he laboriously writes on
a yellow legal pad with a thick felt-tipped pen. Glances up
now. Brow-knitted Duke Wayne expression of bewilderment
over who the hell we are finally gives way to the boyish
left-sided molar display as he recognizes me.

"Rawlings!"

"Yes, sir."

"How y'doin', buddy?"

"Can't complain, Chief. Like to introduce Detective Brendan Thomas."

Chief stands, reaches across the big desk, shirtsleeves rolled
to the elbows, grabs Brendan's hand. "Nice to meet ya,
Thomas."

"Pleasure to meet you, sir."

First thing I do when we sit down is nonchalantly reach
under the seat of my chair and feel for the chief's Sony
TCM-600 tape recorder. Brendan does the same; I've long
since alerted him. My chair's clean. Brendan clears his throat,
fist to mouth, the signal that it's under his seat. Naturally, we
choose our words with some degree of care. Since I know
from experience how the chief's special high-fidelity, auto-
sensor, low-noise cassettes capture the strength and delicacy
of every sound, I'm hoping Brendan doesn't relax and try to
sneak one of his precinct-famous silent farts. Chief would
consider it a personal affront, especially if it's on the sly.
Intentional disrespect. I do most of the talking at first, bring
the chief strictly up to date on the progress of the case. He's
totally fascinated, hardly says a word. When I'm finished, he
waits a beat or two, shakes his head, leans forward. Forehead
wrinkles disappear an instant before we see the left-sided
molars.

"Rawlings, you got a—you sure got a way of stumblin'
into the biggies."

"Yes, sir."

"This gets special assignment immediately," he tells us.
"I want a team of heavyweights on this case. Why isn't Big
John Daniels in on this?"

"Had the day off when it started."

"Lieutenant Barnett assigned us," Brendan says. "We did all the spadework, sir."

Chief narrows his eyes. "You did all the——? Thomas, how long you been in the department?"

"Me? Joined in April, nineteen sixty-four, sir."

"That a fact? How old're you, son?"

"How old? Forty-three, sir. Be forty-four in May."

"Where you from—Ireland or what?"

"Yes, sir. Wicklow, Ireland. Born there."

"And what're you—naturalized or what?"

"Yes, sir."

"Give me a quick rundown on yourself, Thomas."

"A quick rundown?" Brendan sits forward, touches his trim mustache. Cuts a handsome figure this morning: Dark hair thick and neatly combed, serious expression, bull-like neck made civilized by a clean blue shirt, red tie; looks lean and hard in a dark Paul Stuart three-piece with pinstripes; black shoes have a spit-polish shine. "Well, sir, I started out, I played Gaelic football in Ireland. Moved to England to play pro football when I was nineteen. Didn't like it there. Came to New York with my brother in nineteen fifty-seven, worked as a longshoreman. Played on the all-star Gaelic football team here, made trips back to Ireland every year. Joined the department when I was twenty-eight."

Chief looks confused. "Wait a minute. Let me get something straight here. You come over here, you're a Gaelic football jock working on the docks. Don't get me wrong now, but I'm curious. How in hell you ever pass the department exam with that kind of background?"

"Well, sir, my father was a cop in Ireland for thirty-five years."

"A detective?"

"No, sir, he was what they called a *garda siochana,* a peace officer. He was the type of man, he made seven arrests in thirty-five years. He was that type of man, always helping his fellow—"

"You say *seven* arrests?"

"Seven; yes, sir."

"In thirty-five *years?*"

"Yes, sir, and it was usually for somebody with no light on his bicycle, that kind of thing, y'know."

"Somebody with no light on his *bicycle!?*"

"Yes, sir."

"What the hell kind of cop is *that?*"

Brendan touches his mustache, speaks softly. "My father was the best cop I ever knew, sir. The very best."

"All right, Thomas, don't get—don't get *touchy* now. I'm cognizant things are done a little differently over in the bogs."

"Bogs, sir?"

"Figure of speech, Thomas, didn't mean it in any derogatory sense. Go ahead. Interesting background."

"Graduated from the Police Academy in April, nineteen sixty-four, just in time for the Harlem riots. Assigned to the Tactical Patrol Force, spent two years—"

"You were assigned to TPF right out of the Academy?"

"Yes, sir, I was."

"At what age?"

"Twenty-eight."

"Very impressive, Thomas. As I remember it, TPF, they were the elite commandos of the whole department back then."

"Yes, sir, they were. Spent two years in TPF working high-crime areas of Harlem and the South Bronx. Became a detective in April, nineteen sixty-six. Went from Bronx Borough Detectives to Manhattan North Burglary Squad. From there to Sixth District Homicide Special Unit. In nineteen-seventy, I was assigned to the Fourth District Robbery Squad; that's where I met John here. In the reorganization of nineteen seventy-two, John and I were assigned to the Manhattan Area Robbery Squad."

"Which means you had to be ranked among the top five detectives in Fourth District Robbery."

"Yes, sir, we were one and two."

Chief glances at me. "Who was one and who was two?"

"John was number one," Brendan says.

Chief sits back. "All right, appreciate the rundown, Thomas.

Like to get to know my men. Effective immediately, I'm assigning the following six-man team to work the case full time: You two, Big John Daniels, Nuzhat Idrissi, Rick Telfian, Gene Thalheimer. Rawlings, you're team supervisor, pair 'em off any way you like. Report directly to me.''

Couple of minutes later, out in the code-red hallway, waiting for an elevator to take us back to civilization as we know it, Brendan smiles down at me from his eight-inch advantage. Big animal of a man, Brendan.

"First time I ever worked with the chief," he says happily. "Hear it's a holler."

"Better'n that."

"Yeah?"

"A scream, sometimes."

"Ah, Jesus, this case should be fun, Johnny." He hesitates, glances away. "One thing I wanted to ask you. See, being this early in the morning, and me being so nervous about the meeting, I just—well, I had an upset stomach in there."

"Uh-huh."

His eyes dart to me, then away. "Swear to God, I just— well, I couldn't help it in there. I dropped one."

"Oh, no."

"Yeah. Didn't get wind of it, did ya?"

"No, I didn't. When was this?"

"Toward the end, when he was talking. Just a little pip-squeak of a thing it was, shifted in my chair to cover it. Silent as they come."

I shake my head. "You ever drop one of those little pipsqueaks about one inch from a very sensitive microphone?"

He closes his eyes quickly, painfully.

"Know what it sounds like?" I ask.

"Don't. Don't tell me."

"Like a thirty-eight fired with a silencer. *Pffft!* Absolutely unmistakable sound."

"Don't. Please."

I glance at my watch. "He's probably listening to it now, studying it. Some people collect stamps, some people collect coins. Chief happens to collect farts blown in his presence.

Which he considers to be highly personal insults. What can I tell you?''

He gives me this hangdog look. "Christ, my big chance with the chief and I have to go and screw it up.''

"You didn't screw it up, Brendan.''

"No?''

"No. You just blew it.''

# 3

THAT MORNING we head for New Canaan, Connecticut. Nice day, pleasant drive, takes about an hour and forty-five. Get on the Hutchinson River Parkway in the Bronx, takes you north through quiet little towns like Pelham, Bronxville, Scarsdale, Purchase. Now you cross the state line, Hutchinson becomes the Merritt Parkway and you're into very cool, crisp, New England springtime countryside, wide-open spaces, still patches of snow on the frozen ground, many trees in bud, exits to sleepy towns like North Greenwich, Round Hill, Riverbank, Talmadge Hill. We get off at Exit 37, take Route 124 north into the center of town, South Avenue and Elm Street. No right turn on Elm, we hang a left, a right on Park, continue around the horn to Main. Pretty little town, New Canaan, very old, churches all over the place, quiet money. We park in front of City Hall. Two stories of clean red brick with white pillars, of course. Police Department's in the basement to the left, where else? Bob Curry's chief of police here, I've talked with him on the phone, never met him before. Seems young for the job, maybe thirty-five, bright, clean-cut, built like a lumberjack, arms like tree trunks.

"Nick Mize grew up in Norwalk," he tells us. "Norwalk High, class of 'sixty-two. Didn't know him personally, I went to Bridgeport, two years behind him. Played against him in football, sophomore year. He was their quarterback that year.''

"Any good?" Brendan asks.

"Average."

"Get to know much about him?" I ask.

"Not really. But, y'know, you live around here, you pick up on stuff. Kid had a reputation as a wise guy. Lost track of him after high school, heard he joined the Green Berets. Gets out, next thing I hear, he's nailed for burglary. Upstate New York, Schenectady, I think, savings and loan. Couple of years in Sing Sing. Next thing, jewelry store up in—think it was Albany this time. Pulls four in Dannemora.''

"When'd he move here?"

"Last year. September of last year, right after he got out. Rented a cottage up near the New York line. Reported to a parole officer in Stamford who got him a job. He's a phone installation man with Southern New England Telephone in Stamford now.''

Brendan laughs softly. "Great job for a burglar.''

"Made to order.''

We tell Curry we want to make a pass on Mize's place; he gives us directions to 377 Pinney Road.

We're in luck, because Pinney Road is actually a stretch of Route 124 and well marked. Road's called Oenoke Ridge most of the way, runs northwest out of town for maybe five miles. Homes around here are something else. Homes? Try mansions. Trees are still bare, so we get a clear view of what you obviously couldn't see in summer. Low rock walls along the road, typical New England boundary lines, then you see these gigantic old estates way back in there, English Gothic castles, multiple chimneys, some of them smoking this morning, adjoining greenhouses and guesthouses and stables, miles of white-graveled circular driveways, whole area looks to be zoned for a minimum of four acres per. Tell you what, you don't buy spreads like this, you inherit spreads like this, there's just no other way. If they were for sale, which they aren't, most of these suckers would have a price tag in the general neighborhood of a cool million. This isn't "quiet" money here, this is rock-walled, tree-hidden, Dobermanpatrolled, burglar-alarmed, coupon-clipped *Silent* money. Wonder what their taxes are? Must be tight-assed town-hallers, because this road we're on, Oenoke, Route 124, this has got to be one of the Forgotten Indian Trails of America. Potholes like bomb craters, you should see these mothers. Brendan's driving at a snail's pace now after we damn near lost our right front wheel, to say nothing of front teeth; he's snaking from one side to the other, we're still bouncing around, you could lose a kidney on this stretch of shit. This is a disgrace to WASP supremacy.

Finally there's a dogleg left, Oenoke suddenly becomes Pinney, potholes continue unabashed, only we're into hills now, signposted for deer crossings. They've got to be kidding. Deer wouldn't be dumb enough to challenge these potholes. Now we start looking at numbers on mailboxes. We're on a fairly straight stretch, 377 Pinney is the last house before the state line. Yellow mailbox, right-hand side, driveway goes down into a wooded area. Through the bare branches we can see a small white frame cottage way back from the road, yellow front door, open sundeck on the second floor. No garage. Car parked at the end of the drive is a white 1981 Caddy Eldorado, New York plates 133 YZN. Unless Mize took the day off, he must have another car. We continue across the state line. Ready for this? Road becomes brand-new black asphalt, bright white line down the center, smooth as silk, like driving into another century. Brendan and me, we're laughing out loud, we can't believe this. Good old New York, the Empire State, I'll never say another rotten thing about it. Hooray Hugh Carey! We're now in the clean little town of Scotts Corners. Brand-new shopping center off to the right. Ordinarily we'd turn around and make another pass on the way back, but not this time. We figure we're lucky our axle is still intact.

It's almost noon, so we stop at a clean-looking little Italian restaurant in Scotts Corners, have a couple of beers, share a cheese pizza. Before we leave, I call the precinct, talk to Big John.

"Got a call from your girlfriend Tara," he says.

"Yeah? What's happening?"

"Wouldn't tell me. Says she'll only speak to you or Brendan."

I ask Big John to run a check on Mize's plates through DMV, then I call Tara at the gallery.

"Wally phoned this morning," she tells me. "They set the meet for tomorrow afternoon, one-thirty, Rosie O'Grady's on Fifty-second."

Saturday morning, March 27, 10:15, Brendan and I pick up Alvarado in a cab near the gallery, take her down to the Intelligence Unit at headquarters, have her wired with another micro. Brendan drives her back. I drive up to the precinct in a new dark-blue surveillance van with the recording equipment and two cameras. Our six-man team meets in the squadroom, 11:25. Alvarado calls 11:39, says Nick just phoned, changed the time of the meet to three o'clock. Says he seemed very nervous; now she's apprehensive about wearing the micro. I tell her to cool it, I'll get right back to her. Discuss it with the guys, we decide to remove the micro, go in and bug the restaurant booth instead. Call Tara, tell her to take it off (no pun intended), explain the new plan: I'll call her at the gallery, 2:35, tell her exactly which booth to choose. Ask her to try and stall a little outside the restaurant after the meeting so we can get some photos. She doesn't buy that. Specifically, the kid tells me to kiss her left tit. Dangerous metaphor.

Rosie O'Grady's Restaurant-Pub occupies the northwest corner of Seventh Avenue and Fifty-second Street, same building that was once the House of Chan, remember that? O'Grady's, you couldn't miss this place if you were a Polish umpire. Only freshly painted shamrock-green joint for miles around. They got this canopy out front that must be fifteen feet square, extends way out over the sidewalk with the name in distinguished white capital letters two feet high. In case you miss that, there's this gigantic vertical sign hanging at the corner (red neon letters this time) that's a full two *floors* high. Irish in this town aren't noted for understatement.

Big John and Nuzhat go in the New York Sheraton Hotel directly across Seventh Avenue, speak to the assistant manager, tell him they want to photograph from a low-floor room overlooking O'Grady's. Assistant manager lets them set up in there, but he insists that a hotel security guy stay with them at all times. Combo of an Irishman and an Arab, does it every time. Citizen unrest. Telfian and Thalheimer, there's another good team, Armenian and Jew, they double-park the van with the recording equipment on Seventh near Fifty-third.

Brendan and I stroll in O'Grady's at 2:05, Saturday lunch crowd has thinned a bit. We've both been in here before, Brendan claims this is the closest thing to an authentic Irish pub he's seen this side of the water. Only difference, this joint has a lot more class. Whereas the old House of Chan had no ground-floor windows, O'Grady's has nothing but windows, nonstop wraparounds, you can actually see where you're going in here. Elliptical wooden bar straight ahead has a glass showcase overhead holding lighted flowers and stuff, surrounded by hundreds of hanging Irish beer mugs, every size and shape, pewter dominating. Dining room off to the right is a sea of pale-pink tablecloths lighted by chandeliers. Polished brass railing to the right separates the raised window-table area, tan banquette seats under Tiffany lamps, potted plants along the window ledge.

Brendan knows the maître d', guy by the name of Tumulty, asks for a quiet corner table in back. Tumulty shows us back there himself, another raised area set apart by brass railings, gives us a corner table for four to the far left, hands us two big green menus. We look around; nobody close to us. Wainscoted walls hold old Irish paintings and photographs; wooden ledge has a collection of ancient whiskey jugs, various sizes. Clever décor.

As I'm studying the menu, I plant the bug under the table. Now we talk normally, testing the bug for Telfian and Thalheimer in the van. Brendan's looking at the cover of the menu where there's a painting of Rosie O'Grady herself in a dress that's so low-cut it improves the appetite.

"Ah, Jesus," he says in his worst exaggerated Irish accent. "Seeing that painting of lovely Rosie O'Grady reminds me of an Armenian story. Seems this kid by the name of Rick Telfian, poor wretched soul that he is, he goes off to his first circus in Armenia, miserable woebegone land that it is. Bejeez, they got this bare-breasted Armenian dancing girl in one act, filthy-dirty pig that she is, mentally retarded like most of 'em. And for the finale of her act, she dances over to this flea-bitten stinkbag circus lion, y'see, stands right up to him she does. Now she grabs one of her boobs, one of her big, floppy, disgustin' dirtball boobs, and places it right in this poor lion's mouth. Tremendous ovation, the halfwit Armenians think this is real Barnum and Bailey stuff. Now the ringmaster grabs his bullhorn, he says, 'Are there any volunteers in the audience who'd like to try this thrilling experience?' Total silence falls over the crowd. Then, lo and behold, up stands Rick Telfian, who's just messed his knickers, by the way, pitiful creature that he is, up he stands, and he says, 'Yes, sir,' he says, 'I'd like to try, but I'm not sure I could fit it all in me mouth.' "

Goes like that. Quiet, intellectual conversation. We order beer and sandwiches, tell a couple more stories, enjoy our lunch. At 2:30, Brendan asks for the check; I go downstairs to the pay phone, call Rick and Gene to verify reception.

Rick answers. "Yeah."

"We coming through?"

"Yeah, give Brendan a message for me, will ya?"

"Sure thing."

"Tell him his secret's out. It's all over town. Everybody in the department knows, because I spread the word myself."

"What's the secret?"

"That he's such a fuckin' moron, he farts in the bathtub and bites the bubbles."

"I'll tell him."

"Big John called from the hotel. They're all set."

On the dot of 2:35, I call Alvarado, explain exactly where the table is, tell her we'll reserve that table in her name. She's on her way.

Brendan makes the reservation with Tumulty, asks him to seat the young lady personally, slips him a twenty-dollar bill. We leave O'Grady's at 2:45, go directly to the van at Seventh and Fifty-third.

Just our luck, a classy little meter maid is writing Thalheimer a ticket outside the double-parked van. Gene's not only a ladies' man, he's a cerebral-type ladies' man, good-looking, eloquent, likes to give them a hard time. Hasn't shown his shield yet, he's giving her some lip, seeing how long her fuse is. Brendan and I break it up, show the lady our gold, explain the situation. Kid rips the ticket off her pad, nonchalantly sticks it in Thalheimer's genuine Levi Strauss belt, puckers her lips and gives him a loud kiss-off as she leaves.

Inside, Brendan sits in front of the big one-way window in back, watches the army of bouncing tits cross the street. Telfian's glued to the radio. Short, dark-haired, muscular kid, about thirty-six, still plays a lot of semipro baseball. Short-stop, third base, arm like a .357 magnum. Varicose veins in his legs slow him up now. Still hits the ball a ton.

He's chewing gum, as usual. "Just picked up the voice of your waitress," he tells Brendan.

"Yeah? What'd she say? Loves me, right?"

"Must've collected your tip, because she mumbled something in Spanish."

"You speak Spanish, Rick," I tell him. "Translate."

"Rough translation, John, she has a bad cold. Says she's real glad she blew her nose in the tall gringo's sandwich bread."

Big John calls at 2:53: Alvarado just entered the restaurant. Calls again at 3:04. He's not certain, but he thinks Wally and Nick just went in. Turns out he's right. Greetings are loud and clear. Then:

| | |
|---|---|
| WALLY: | Tara, before we get down to business, I won-der if you'd mind taking a walk downstairs with us. |
| TARA: | Downstairs? What's downstairs? |
| WALLY: | Just another dining room. Always empty this time of day. I think we'd all feel more com-fortable knowing everyone was clean. |
| TARA: | In other words, you don't trust me. |
| NICK: | It's not that, Tara. We always take— |
| WAITRESS: | Good afternoon. Like to see the menu? |
| NICK: | No, thanks. We'd just like three cups of cof-fee, if that's all right. |

WAITRESS:   Coming right up.
NICK:       Come on, Tara. We always take this pre-
            caution, no matter who it is. Only take a
            minute, then we can all relax.
TARA:       Let's do it.

Chairs scrape on the bare wood floor; we hear them walking
away. Telfian gives a long, soft whistle, expressing the sentiments of all four of us. If Tara had remained wired, end of
ball game. She tells us later that Wally even searched the
lining of her clothes and the heels of her shoes. Not to be
outdone, she insists on searching them just as thoroughly.
Gives them both a good toss. Method actress, like her style.
They're gone maybe four or five minutes. We hear their cups
of coffee being served. Now they come back, laughing at
something.

NICK:       Okay, let's get to it. What've you got?
TARA:       Okay. President of the gallery, man by the
            name of Exeter, he's got the floor plans and
            the alarm system circuitry in a file cabinet in
            his office. It's locked, but the key's in the top
            drawer of his desk, which he doesn't lock.
            Total asshole. I was in his office late Thurs-
            day night after the cleaning crew left. It's just
            a matter of photographing the papers.
WALLY:      Do it. What about the safes?
TARA:       We have two large floor safes, a Mosler and a
            Diebold. Mosler's in the third-floor jewelry
            office; Diebold's in the accounting office,
            fourth floor.
WALLY:      When do the diamonds actually arrive?
TARA:       Okay. The auction takes place April nine-
            teenth and twentieth. Eleven diamonds arrive
            Saturday, April seventeenth, from Alistair Rod-
            ger Rare Jewels, Fifth and Seventy-first. Brinks
            armored truck. The North Star's coming from
            London. Scheduled to arrive Sunday, April
            eighteenth, commercial jet, two British secu-

rity guards. Brinks truck from JFK. I don't
know which safe they'll use yet, but I assume
it'll be the Mosler in the jewelry office.

NICK:        What's the story on security?

TARA:        Normally, right now, there's one man per
floor, daytime, and just two men for the whole
building at night. When the diamonds come
in, they'll beef it up plenty, of course, but I
don't have any details yet. Right now I'm
trying to get tight with the chief of security,
guy by the name of Donohoe. Takes time.

WALLY:       Okay, good. As soon as you know, check
times of shift changes, that's important. If
they're carrying, find out what type weapons.

NICK:        Now, just to fill you in, here's what we have
in mind, Tara. The day we go in, there'll be
three of us. You don't know the other man,
he's from out of town and he can handle any
type of alarm system. We can do the rest. We
have authentic telephone company uniforms,
equipment boxes, even worksheets. You have
to find a place where we can hide the tools
and ourselves when the gallery closes for the
day.

WALLY:       We want to do this as quietly as possible, but
we're ready for just about anything. We'll
have three forty-fives in the boxes, and your
buddy Eddie will be in the block with very
heavy weapons. We have excellent walkie-
talkies, state of the art, and we can change the
crystals for whatever police district we're in.
Nobody's going to sneak up on us.

TARA:        What if something goes wrong? What about
me?

NICK:        We don't know you, we never met you. But
don't think in those terms, Tara. We've done
this before with no problems, we know exactly what we're doing. If by some chance
they actually get a make on us, we're holding

on to the North Star for insurance. Nobody will ever do a day in the joint with that kind of bargaining power. When the time's right, we can ransom it back or unload it. We have plenty of contacts.

TARA: When would I get my cut?

NICK: All right. Tell you the truth up front, right? We can't do anything until we unload the stuff. Which—it won't take that long, we'll have it out of the country in twenty-four hours. But we can't do anything till it's fenced. What we can do, what we will do, is give you something heavy up front to show good faith. If that's acceptable to you.

TARA: Like what?

WALLY: We have good contacts with a Chevy dealer on the Island. If you want, we could get you a new Corvette like Eddie's. You see his 'Vette?

TARA: No.

WALLY: Brand-new, real beauty. That's a twenty-two thousand dollar automobile. We gave him that.

TARA: Yeah?

WALLY: Absolutely. We gave him that just for the introduction to you. You got a car?

TARA: You kidding? On my salary?

NICK: Saw one out there the other day you'd really go for. Just like Eddie's. White job, real black leather interior, it's loaded, you'd love it. Automatic transmission, air conditioned, power steering, power windows, the works. Tilt wheel, cruise control, stereo, tape deck, rally wheels.

TARA: (Laughs) What're you, a salesman?

NICK: (Laughs) Matter of fact, I used to be, yeah!

WALLY: That's twenty-wo thousand dollars, Tara. Up front. Be registered in your name, title of ownership, paid in full, you could sell it anytime you wanted. Think about it, huh? Let us know what you'd like. We'll get back to you next week.

Late that afternoon Brendan and me are back in the squad-room with Telfian and Thalheimer, transcribing the tape, preparing a progress report for the chief, getting periodic surveillance reports from Big John and Nuzhat. Now Nuzhat calls about seven, says Wally and Nick parked in a public garage on Fifty-eighth between Lex and Park, went into the Tatler Bar, 141 East Fifty-seventh. Tatler happens to be a known hangout for wise guys—gamblers, bookmakers, loan sharks, mob-connected people. I've always made it a point to go in there from time to time, have a couple of drinks, watch the games on TV, place a few bets. Good spot to be seen. Ginger, the bartender, knows me pretty good, takes my bets, kids around. Been going in there for years. I tell Nuzhat we'll be over to relieve them about 7:30.

We go over there, Big John and Nuzhat are double-parked just up the street from the bar. We park behind them, they take off. Brendan stays at the wheel, I go in, glance around, wait for my eyes to adjust. Good crowd for this early, but of course it's Saturday night. High-class hookers scattered around, guys at tables playing Liar's Poker with $100 bills, bimbos sniffing coke right at the bar, the usual. Wally and Nick are at the far end of the bar with a couple of very good-looking hookers. There's an empty stool four seats away. I go over, sit down, light up a cigar. Ginger spots me, walks over smiling, tough little blonde kid, probably mid-thirties. Grew up in the same general neighborhood as me, Lower East Side.

"Behavin' yourself, John?"

"Not if I can help it."

"Beefeater, twist, rocks?"

"Yeah, very dry, huh? Knicks on tonight?"

She pours the gin. "Yeah, Boston."

"I'll take the Celtics."

"Smart man." She serves my drink, picks up my fifty-dollar bill, pockets it, rings up my tab.

Now, I haven't glanced at Wally or Nick even once, there's no way I can know if they caught any of this, but my instincts tell me they did. Even in a joint like this, where the majority of hoods feel safe, they invariably make it a point to pick up on who's sitting near them. Not paranoid, just cautious. Later, when I glance over at them, I can see they're relaxed, rapping easily with the broads. Actually, Wally and Nick are fairly classy-looking guys. Expensive sport coats, ties, well groomed, definitely a cut above the average in here. Soft-spoken, too. Tell you the truth, I'm impressed. I figure, if you're planning the biggest diamond robbery in American history, the least you can do is look the part. Steinbrenner insists on having the Yankees wear coats and ties in public. Contends anything less is bush, especially when your average Yankee is making around half a million per.

Although I've studied good mug shots of these guys and listened to their voices, this is the first time I've had a chance to observe them at close range. Something about the two of them together strikes a familiar chord in my mind. Where have I seen them before? Wally Kwapniewski, thirty-four, five-eleven, about 160, mod-cut dark hair, brown eyes. Alumnus of Greenhaven and Dannemora, five-and-a-half years. Face, voice, and mannerisms remind me of Tom Brokaw, NBC News. Same fresh, self-assured style. Nick Mize is three years older, looks a lot more mature. Hair is blond, but it's a dirty kind of blond; in this light it seems almost brown. No mod cut for Nick, it's trimmed close and neat. Kid has a wholesome look about him, particularly when he smiles, like he's from a farm or something, I don't know. Graduate of Sing Sing and Dannemora, total of about five years. Some farms.

Knicks-Celtics game comes on at eight, I have another Beefeater, sit back, and try to concentrate. Wally and Nick are watching now, too, I can glance over more frequently. Where the hell have I seen these guys before? I get up, go to the men's room, come back, light up another cigar. I'm sitting there watching the game, bingo, it hits me. This kid Mize resembles Roger *Mudd*. Roger Mudd, co-anchor with Tom Brokaw of the "NBC Nightly News," which happens to be my favorite network news show. Question is, do these clowns really bear a strong resemblance to Brokaw and Mudd or is it my imagination? To me, they do. I make a mental note to ask Brendan and the others.

Bottom line, nothing much happens in the Tatler. Knicks

won, by the way. Lost my fifty dollars. Goes on the expense report. Chief won't like it, but it's perfectly legitimate. Life in the fast lane doesn't come cheap.

Wally and Nick start talking about leaving right after the game, around 11:15. I pay my tab, plunk down twenty dollars for Ginger. Outside, I walk toward Park, Brendan picks me up at the corner. We drive north on Park to Fifty-eighth, hang a right, double-park up the block from the garage. Couple of minutes later Wally goes in the garage alone, swoops out in his black 1981 Jaguar XJ6, New York plates 593 FOG, owned by his brother Peter. We follow him around the block, staying well back, he picks up Nick and the two young hookers in front of the Tatler.

Class act all the way.

# 4

CHIEF CALLS A STRATEGY MEETING at the gallery Monday, March 29, 2:30 P.M., Exeter's office. Since this is the first official conference of all major parties concerned, Exeter's choreographed the event appropriately: He presides in the high-backed leather chair behind his Louis XV desk, Chief Vadney is seated to the left of the desk, Chief of Security Jerry Donohoe to the right. This distinguished triumvirate faces all the rest of us, situated in two rows of neatly arranged Martha Washington chairs, five to a row. Front row, left to right from Exeter's viewpoint: Henry Sullivan (vice-president, jewelry department), Alexander Harkness (vice-president, finance), Tara Alvarado, yours truly, Brendan Thomas; back row, left to right: Big John Daniels, Nuzhat Idrissi, Gene Thalheimer, Rick Telfian, Chellie Powell (executive secretary to Exeter).

Naturally, the seating arrangements are far from fortuitous. When we enter the office, Ms. Powell hands each of us a clean white copy of what looks to be a typical corporate organizational chart, thirteen rectangular boxes arranged in a one-two-five-five chain of command. I assume it's a corporate chart for the Heritage Gallery before I look at the names. Full titles, too, this Exeter's not just a pretty face. Can't help smiling when I glance at his box on top, just a bit larger than the others:

> PHILLIP S. EXETER
> Chairman, President
> Chief Executive
> HERITAGE GALLERY

The fact that there's one leader and twelve disciples isn't entirely lost on me either. Now I know this meeting's got to be fun. Just before Exeter calls us all to order, I glance around, see no ashtrays in sight. I immediately take out a cigar, bite off the end, put it in my pocket, and light up in full view of my distinguished, mildly astonished colleagues. Pure joy.

Chief gives me a look. Exeter gives me an eye-bulge, signals to Ms. Powell. She gets up, hurries to the reception area, brings back a large ashtray, hands it to me with a smile. Kid's got a figure custom-built for a string bikini. I thank her kindly.

Now Exeter sits forward, consults the typed notes on his desk. He's a study in quietly elegant decadence today, dark two-piece Brooks not too wrinkled, white button-down loose enough to assuage the jowels. Striped tie is meticulously positioned a mere fraction of an inch down and away from the collar; just misses Yale casual-chic, nice try. Bulldog, bulldog.

"Uh, ladies and gentlemen," he begins, Valium-voiced. "Ms., uh, Ms. Powell will take notes of these proceedings, a verbatim transcript of which will be made available to those of you who so, uh, who so desire to receive one. Obviously, anything that's said here this afternoon should be considered highly confidential. Chief, uh, Chief Vadney has very graciously volunteered to deliver an introductory statement."

Must say, the chief looks like a million bucks. Best blue pinstriped two-piece for the occasion. Never wears a vest; his rawboned frame simply doesn't lend itself to such genteel fashions. We wait for him to begin, but he seems oblivious that he's been introduced. Happens to be reading the comprehensive progress report we gave him last Friday; file folder on his lap includes tape recordings, surveillance photographs, duplicate rap sheets, even the shot of Lopata and Alvarado at the U of M and their complete academic transcripts.

Exeter clears his throat softly. "Uh, Chief Vadney?"

Chief keeps reading. "Yeah."

"You wanted to make some introductory remarks, I believe."

"Oh, yeah, right." Looks up now, takes a swipe at his hair. Crosses his legs, gives just a hint of the shy, patented blue-eyed grin: Hell, puritans, I'm not very good at this, but here goes. "Ladies and gentlemen, I'm—I'm sure you all realize we have a potentially serious problem here. However, thanks to the cooperation of Miss Exeter, we've been able to identify—"

"Alvarado," Exeter prompts softly.

Chief turns. "Beg pardon?"

"Ms. Alvarado."

"What about her?"

Exeter's eyes sparkle-bulge as he smiles. "I believe you said 'Miss Exeter'; you meant Ms. Alvarado, obviously. Please go ahead."

"Oh, I beg your pardon." Chief turns to Alvarado now. "Sorry about that, Ms. Alvarado."

"That's quite all right."

Chief nods politely. "By the way, I wonder if you'd be kind enough to clear something up for me?"

"I'll try."

"Tell you the truth, I alway—I always kinda choke on the word 'Ms.' Know what I mean? I just—I dislike the sound of it, I dislike the connotation, the self-conscious feminist connotation: 'Maybe I'm married, maybe I'm not; it's none of your business.' That kinda thing."

Alvarado waits, then: "Uh-huh. What's your question?"

"I'm just curious. You prefer Ms. or Miss?"

"Personally, I prefer Miss."

Chief glances at Exeter, flashes a depreciatory grin. "Thought you might, Miss Alvarado. You're much too confident a lady to be saddled with a phony title. Some need it, some don't.''

Gets a few quiet chuckles from the crowd. Exeter sits back, gives Vadney the cold eye of a swordfish, begins clicking his ballpoint pen. Slowly. Very slowly.

Chief stands up, places his case file on the chair, shoves his hands in his pockets, walks in front of us as he continues. ''As I was sayin', thanks to the excellent cooperation of Miss Alvarado, we've been able to identify and follow the operations of two known felons, both highly experienced professionals. In my judgment, and in the judgment of Detective Rawlings, who's supervising the full-time surveillance team, these two conspirators, and a third party who's elected to maintain a low profile so far, probably represent the tip of the iceberg, so to speak. Front men in an obviously sophisticated international syndicate.''

Actually, that's *not* my opinion, we've seen no hard evidence to indicate anything like that, but I sit there poker-faced. I'm having too much fun. I puff on my cigar, the hell with him.

He turns, pauses, retraces his steps, head down in thought. ''Why do we believe that, you ask? I'll tell you why. For the simple reason that to assume otherwise, in a projected robbery of eleven-point-five million dollars in diamonds—to assume otherwise, ladies and gentlemen, would be injudicious. That's right. Injudicious and ultimately dangerous. Bottom line, we have a handle on this situation, a firm handle, thanks again primarily to Miss Alvarado. Who, by the way, in my judgment, and in the judgment of our entire team, has exhibited a very substantial amount of courage through all this. Practically all we know about this case so far can be directly or indirectly attributed to this young lady's cooperation.'' He turns, walks down the line of chairs again. ''All right, you ask, exactly where are we on this case, what's our strategy at this point? Answer: We know who some of 'em are, we know what they're planning, we're right on top of it. We're watching, we're waiting. We're giving these people rope, slack, running room, the illusion of open water, ladies and gentlemen. Very difficult illusion to create and maintain when you're dealing with seasoned professionals. When we decide we've got the hook in pretty good, when we decide we've implicated as many co-conspirators as possible, as far up the ladder as we can go, and when the DA's office agrees it'll wash in court, then we'll grab 'em. All of 'em. Fast. Just before the actual robbery attempt is made. Now, in the meantime, we need your full cooperation here at the gallery, your thoughts, your ideas, suggestions, whatever. Any questions so far?"

Everybody looks around. No questions from the gallery. Now Nuzhat Idrissi raises his hand. Heavyset Arab, dark complexion, trim mustache, terrific undercover man. He's got different frames on his bifocals this year, black steel instead of gold, aviator design, makes him look younger.

"Detective Idrissi?"

Nuzhat stands, checks his notebook. "Chief Vadney, I'd like an update on basic intelligence in three areas: One, transportation of the gems; two, safe to be used here; three, premises protection."

Chief turns. "Mr. Exeter?"

Exeter consults his typed notes, puts a curled index finger to his lips, clears his throat quietly. "On Saturday, April seventeen, a total of, uh, of eleven diamonds, some in bracelets, rings, and necklaces, will be transported by Brinks armored truck from, uh, from Alistair Rodger Rare Jewels to the gallery. Departure, two-fifteen P.M., arrival two-thirty. They were to be—they, uh, *were* to be secured in the Mosler safe, third-floor jewelry department. They will now be secured in the, uh, the Diebold safe, fourth-floor accounting office, per instructions from Mr., uh, Mr. Donohoe, following the suggestion of Detective Rawlings. The North Star will depart London Heathrow on Sunday, April eighteen, Pan Am flight one-oh-one, accompanied by two British security guards. Departure, eleven A.M., London time; ETA Kennedy, one thirty-five P.M., New York time. Transportation via Brinks armored truck from JFK to the gallery, ETA two forty-five. It, too, will be secured in the Diebold safe. Additional premises protection, April seventeen through twenty, will be provided by one of the top private security firms in the city, Paul T. Reilly Associates, who will have—"

"Excuse me, Mr. Exeter," the chief interrupts. "With your permission, I think I'd best take the ball at this point. Gets a little complicated from this point on out."

"Uh, Chief Vadney, sir. In all due respect to your, uh, your obviously superior expertise in these matters, I'm quite well aware of the complications that ensue at this juncture."

"I'm sure you are, sir." Chief checks his watch, turns abruptly to me. "Rawlings, I've got a three o'clock with Koch; remind me I've got to leave here at two forty-five sharp." Now, to all of us: "What I plan, ladies and gentlemen, is a decoy with a double-fail-safe backup. I've considered the feasibility of such an approach for several days now, but I haven't discussed it with anyone, not even my own special-assignment team. So I suggest you all listen very carefully."

Brendan and I exchange glances. Decoy with a double-fail-safe backup. Sounds impressive. Almost unconsciously, everybody seems to lean forward slightly. Everybody but Exeter. He sits back, his face is coloring now. By my own estimate, he's taken the equivalent of two quick slaps in the face, followed now, straight out of the blue, by a fast knee in the groin, all in full merciless view of his top disciples. If Pontius Pilate is so cruel, can the crown of thorns be far behind?

Chief stands there in his element, coat open, hands on hips. His eyes move to Tara, who holds the soft gaze easily. "Stage one, Miss Alvarado will be allowed to photograph the floor plans, the alarm system circuitry—after subtle alteration— the third-floor jewelry office with the Mosler safe, and one other place, which Miss Alvarado pointed out to me before this meeting: A little-used photography-equipment storage room on the second floor near her office, where the three suspects can hide safely. They'll be in that room when the gallery closes for business on Monday, April nineteenth, the only night they could logically attempt the robbery, in my judgment. Mark that date. Stage two, Mr. Donohoe will write a 'personal and confidential' memo to Mr. Exeter, today if possible, detailing gallery security procedures April seventeen through twenty. In it, he'll reveal that additional premises protection will be provided by the private security firm of Paul T. Reilly Associates, who will have two-man teams of armed guards on the third—repeat, *third*—floor in round-the-clock shifts, to wit: Eight in the morning to four in the afternoon; four to midnight; midnight to eight. They will be armed with thirty-eight-caliber revolvers. The only other guard on the premises will be the regular night watchman on the ground floor. Miss Alvarado will of course photograph this memo. Mr. Donohoe, do you have any problem with that?"

"No. No, I'll be glad to cooperate."

"Uh, Chief Vadney," Exeter says calmly. "Might I be permitted the luxury of a suggestion?"

"Sure."

"Thank you very much indeed." His charm-your-tits-off smile is directed at his two vice-presidents in the front row who alone grasp the dry humor here, both smiling broadly. "Uh, Chief Vadney, we all—I'm sure we all appreciate the, uh, the cloak-and-dagger element implicit in directing Ms. Alvarado to, uh, to photograph these documents. In my office, I gather, late at night, and so forth. I wonder if I might be permitted to suggest a more practical, albeit perhaps mundane, approach to this admittedly vital function?"

"Sure."

"We do have a Xerox machine on the premises, fully operational, last I heard."

"Where is it?"

"Second floor, last I heard."

"Second floor. And your office here, where you file all such documents, is the top floor, the seventh, is that correct?"

In the split-second hesitation, Exeter's eyes say it all: He's just stepped in another piece of shit. It's not his day, that's all.

Chief could nail him good, but, to his credit, he backs off on this one, glances at his watch, begins pacing again. "Stage three: In reality, our entire six-man team will be in the third-floor jewelry department when the gallery closes for business Monday, April nineteenth. All armed with shotguns and bulletproof vests, and personally commanded by me. As the first part of the double-fail-safe backup, the security guards from Paul T. Reilly Associates will in fact be stationed in the fourth-floor accounting office where all the jewels will actually be, in the Diebold safe. The three suspects will be allowed to move from the second-floor storage room up the back stairs to the third-floor jewelry office where the bust will be made. As the second part of the double-fail-safe backup, the outside of this building will be covered on all four sides by Emergency Service Division sharpshooters equipped with high-powered rifles. Security people in the adjoining buildings, as well as the buildings directly across Madison and Seventy-second streets, will be contacted to arrange advantageous positions for Emergency Service to cover the street, the side entrance of the gallery, and the loading area. At the appropriate time, I'll inform the Communications Bureau to keep all radio cars out of the immediate area. Emergency Service backup cars will be out of sight but within striking distance. I'll personally brief the Emergency Service commander on details, alerting him to the high probability that Eddie Lopata and his associates will be in the immediate vicinity with automatic weapons.''

Etcetera. Have to hand it to the chief, he's really given it some thought. Bet my eyeteeth he's already discussed the potential media coverage on a caper like this with Grady in Press Relations. Wonder if he's alerted Mike Wallace over at "60 Minutes"? Wouldn't surprise me.

Meeting breaks up shortly after the chief leaves at 2:45. We're standing out in the red-carpeted hallway waiting for the elevator and I'm rapping with my old buddy Big John Daniels. Impeccably dressed and groomed as usual, all six-two, 205 pounds of him, mirror-image of my favorite senator, Daniel Patrick Moynihan. We go back a long way, Big John and me, he's a sergeant now, been in the department twenty-five years. Elfin eyes always hold a certain sparkle of mischief.

"Need your astute opinion," I tell him.

"Hallucinations again?"

"No, no. Haven't had one in months, matter of fact."

"Out with it then, lad."

"You saw Nick and Wally together last Friday, right? After the meet at O'Grady's?"

"Photographed 'em outside."

"They remind you of anybody?"

Purses his lips. "No. No, can't say they do."

"I mean together, as a team."

"Into another of your look-alike fixations, are you?"

"No way. Not in the slightest."

"Last year it was Jimmy Cagney, Telly Savalas, Liz Taylor, David Stockman . . ."

"Well, they did, John. They really did. Even *you* admitted it."

"As I recall, you talked me into it."

"No way. You admitted it."

"Well, maybe you're right. So who's it this time?"

"That's my question. Wally and Nick together."

"Uh-huh. Gimme a hint at least."

"Anchormen."

"Anchormen. News anchormen, TV news?"

"Network."

Strokes his chin and cheeks, narrows his eyes. Now he smiles, laughs softly. "Hate to admit it, lad, but you got a point there. Son of a bitch, you got a point. Don't watch 'em that often, but there's a definite resemblance. Roger Mudd, and Tom what's-his-name."

"Brokaw. Tom Brokaw."

Shakes his head. "Jesus, I hate to admit it, but you're right this time. Probably never hear the end of it."

"Makes me feel better. Need reassurance now and then."

"Know what I'm gonna do for you, lad? Gonna see the department shrink and set up a Rorschach test for you. Y'know, the ink-blot designs? Jesus Christ, would that man get an earful. He'd be out the fuckin' window before you were half through."

"Took a series of those when I was a kid."

"Yeah? Reveal anything about your personality?"

"Yeah. Guy said I was definitely a breast man."

That night I drop in the Tatler for a drink about 7:30. Wally shows up solo at 8:12. Around 9:15 he's joined at the bar by a tall muscular kid, mid-twenties, blond hair, and two class broads. I'm too far away to hear what they're saying, but they're having a lot of laughs. Tall kid wears a smart blue blazer, white shirt, conservative tie, gold cufflinks, gold wristwatch. While I'm watching the Knicks, Wally and the kid approach a couple of regulars at a table, sit down and start playing Liar's Poker. At 11:10 the broads get their coats. I pay my tab, leave, Brendan picks me up, we drive to Fifty-eighth Street near the garage. All four subjects enter the garage 11:23. Exit Wally in his black Jag with one girl, followed by the kid in a 1982 white Corvette, New York plates 608 WHN. Logical assumption: Eddie Lopata.

Surprises me a little. It's late, I'm tired, I've had three or four drinks, but somehow it never occurred to me that this kid was Lopata. All I had to go on is that high-camp shot of him and Alvarado at the U of M in 1978, but his face reminded me instantly of James Dean in that shot. That was my first impression: Thick blond hair, deep-set eyes, mischievous-kid smile. Of course, that was four years ago when Lopata was a senior, about twenty-one, I suppose. Hair's much shorter, eyes are the same, but the mischievous smile's vanished, and he's at least a foot taller than Dean was.

We follow them to the Travelers' Motel, Queens Boulevard between Macy's and Alexander's near the Long Island Expressway. They check in. We call it a night.

Next morning I check the plates through DMV. Corvette's registered to Edward S. Lopata, 263 Lockwood Avenue, Yonkers. Brendan and I drive to the Yonkers Police Department, speak with Detective Lieutenant Lloyd Hudson, Intelligence Division. Although it's true Lopata has no record, he was one of several Yonkers residents under investigation in the illegal purchase of automatic weapons through Cubans in Miami during the summer of 1977. Four arrests were made, all Cubans. Insufficient evidence against Lopata. Hudson gives us directions to 263 Lockwood Avenue, we make a pass. Ten-story apartment house, garage under the building.

*        *        *

Wednesday, March 31, 2:15 P.M. Get a call from Alvarado at the gallery. Nick just phoned for an update. She tells him she has the photographs, suggests a meet for Thursday noon, entrance to the park on the southwest corner of Fifth and Seventy-ninth (as we designated), she'll try to get a bench. Wish all informants were was cool as this kid. At 2:45 we drive to the apartment building at 985 Fifth, southeast corner of Seventy-ninth, speak with the super, Gene McGlocklin, old friend of Brendan's. Apartment 6A facing the park is vacant and available to us at any time. We reserve it for 11:30 tomorrow morning. Back to the precinct, get another call from Alvarado 4:25. Nick just called, the meet's off till Friday same time. Wally's leaving town to see a friend about a problem.

Friday, April 2, 11:57 A.M. Excellent view from apartment 6A. Nice day for a change, temperature in the mid-fifties. Baseball season starts next week. Brendan and I have Nikons with 200-millimeter lenses focused on the lovely Tara, who's sitting on a park bench. Wish you could see this kid in medium closeup and living color. Sun gives her thick dark hair a healthy sheen, dark-brown eyes narrow as she scans our floor, not certain which windows we're in; actually, we're shooting through open venetian blinds, making it extremely difficult to spot us from her angle. Her tight-fitting black Courrèges jacket looks sleek in this light, ditto the matching handbag with white rope shoulder strap. She's holding a manila envelope with eight black-and-white glossy blowups. Places it on the bench now, reaches in the handbag, takes out a pack of Marlboro and her slim gold Dunhill. Lights up, quick small puff, then a long drag and a deep inhale as she turns to look north on Fifth.

We spot Nick and Wally, 12:11, walking south on Fifth. No hurry. Roger Mudd and Tom Brokaw strolling to the studio. Hi, Tara, how y'doin'? Sit on the bench next to her, she hands Wally the envelope. She's not wired. Brendan and I start clicking away. They take turns studying the blowups, asking questions. Tara's got questions of her own. We told her to ask for delivery of the new Corvette as soon as possible. At 12:39 Tara leaves. Wally and Nick remain, rap a while longer. They get up at 12:51, cross at the light, continue east on Seventy-ninth. Idrissi follows them on foot; Big John's parked near the gallery. We had a hunch they'd go to the gallery, check out what they could. We're right. They walk south on Madison in the heavy lunch-hour crowd, enter the gallery at 1:07. We have no men inside.

Back to the precinct. Alvarado calls us 2:19. Nick and Wally spent more than an hour observing the exhibit areas open to the public on floors one and two, five and six. Normal crowd for a Friday. Then, as Alvarado suggested at the meet, they managed to get "lost" looking for the men's room back on the second floor. Wandered into her wing of the floor, opened the door to the photographic-equipment storage room near her office, which she'd left unlocked, switched on the light, had a good gander. Next, they tried the fire-exit door at the end of the hall, cased the stairway. Finally they stood in the door to her office, asked directions to the elevator. Bottom line, everything's copacetic. They'll be in touch soon.

Monday, April 5, 9:05 A.M. Alvarado calls from her apartment, she has to see us immediately, something important; kid's voice is a bit shaky. Brendan and I drive up there fast, 200 East Eighty-fourth, southeast corner of Third, relatively fashionable neighborhood. Medium high-rise, brick exterior was once white, now more gray, hundreds of vertical black streaks from the air conditioner exhausts. New blue canopy spruces up the entrance. Doorman in a classy brown uniform and cap rings her on the intercom. We're expected, please go up, apartment 19D. Small lobby, worn furniture, two elevators. Up we go, closed-circuit TV camera in the corner, nice touch. Nineteen is the top floor. Get off, Tara's waiting for us in an open door to the far right, wearing a white short-sleeved jumpsuit, tight-fitting, zip fashionably low; red-lettered label on the breast pocket reads *Saint Germain.* Kid's eyes are red, hair's a mess, looks like she's been out all night.

Tell you what, for a gallery photographer, single, this kid's

got quite a pad here. Apartment occupies the whole north side
of the building overlooking Eighty-fourth. Huge tastefully
decorated living room with a skyline view of Yorkville,
pale-blue fitted carpet, matching drapes, black-and-white
marble-floored dining area to the left off the kitchen. She
leads us down the hall to the left past the kitchen, small for a
joint this size, turns right, and here's a room I can only
describe as a little world unto itself, a "music room," no
other term would fit. Big rectangular area, thick white fitted
carpet overlaid with what looks to be a red-and-gold Persian
rug, walls sound-proofed in thick squares of brown cork holding dozens of artistically arranged paintings, photographs,
drawings, lithographs, all in aluminum frames, all themed to
decidedly classical music, ranging from composers, musi-
cians, and orchestras to ancient sheet music, concert programs, and billboards. Focal point, full-sized grand piano
near the double windows, reflects the morning light like a
mirror. Elaborate stereo equipment on glass-and-chrome
shelves, tall speakers in two corners.

We sit on an elegant white three-seater couch against the
wall to the west; Tara sits on the piano bench next to the
window.

"You live here alone?" I ask.

She manages a weak smile. "Oh, God, no. I share with
another girl, stewardess with British Airways, she's on a trip.
I had to call in sick today; I was out till about three o'clock
this morning."

"Nice place," Brendan says.

"The rent takes the better half of our combined salaries,
plus help from home now and then. Can I get you a cup of
coffee or something?"

We tell her no thanks.

She lights a cigarette. "Go ahead and smoke if you want
to, there's an ashtray on the table there. I've got something a
little weird to tell you."

Brendan takes out his notebook and pen, I take out a cigar.

She inhales deeply, starts talking as she exhales smoke; her
voice has a slight shake now. "Eddie Lopata called me
yesterday afternoon, took me out to dinner last night. Couple

of drinks, he hits me with this. Says he had a meet Saturday night with Nick and Wally. He says, 'They got your car ready for you, they want you to pick it up on Tuesday.' I go, 'Oh, great.' He says, 'Only you're not gonna pick it up.' I look at him, I go, 'What the hell you talking about?' He says, 'Tara, we're friends, we been real good friends, you and me, we been through a lot together, that's why I'm here talking to you.' He says, 'The fact is, they don't need you anymore. You've given them all the information they need. They have everything.' He says, 'If something goes wrong and the cops grab you, they figure you're the weak link. They don't know you, they don't know what you can take, they figure you'd spill your guts.' He says, 'So they asked me to do the job.' I go, 'What job?' He looks at me, he says, 'Tara, they want me to hit you.' He says, 'And, y'know, we've done a lot of stuff together and I've done a lot of crazy things, but I never hit a friend.' I'm sitting there, I can't believe this is happening. I feel like somebody just punched me in the stomach. He says, like, 'So that's why I'm telling you.' Says he's done a lot of thinking about it. Says *he* won't do it, that's for fuckin' sure, but he knows these guys. He's not guessing about them, he *knows*. Says if he won't do it, *they* will.''

''Their records don't indicate that,'' I tell her quietly.

''No?''

''Nick Mize, strictly a small-time burglar. Never even been caught with a weapon on him. Kwapniewski, three arrests, each time he's had a weapon, but he's never been involved in a homicide.''

''To your knowledge,'' she says.

''True,'' Brendan says, ''but you'd be surprised, guys like this follow a pattern. Neither of these people has a record of violence.''

Tara nods, stubs out her half-smoked cigarette. 'I don't know what your records say, but Eddie told me Wally's known in the trade as a real bad nut-case. Says he beat the shit out of a *cop* with a *pipe* when he was still a teen-ager.''

''That's true,'' I tell her. ''That's on his record. Felonious assault on a police officer with a pipe. Age twenty. He pulled eighteen months for that.''

"Then what's all this *shit* you're telling me about them not being *violent!*"

"My fault," Brendan says. "Kwapniewski does have that on his record, I forgot about that."

I bite off the end of my cigar, toss it in the ashtray. "But, Miss Alvarado, keep in mind we're talking about the potential for murder here, not felonious assault. Sorry for interrupting. Please go ahead."

She straddles the piano bench now, squints out the window, and her voice drops. "God, what an asshole I was. What an *asshole* I was for ever getting *involved* in this."

In the pause, I light my cigar. Continual hum of traffic drifts up from Third Avenue.

Tara grabs another cigarette, lights it. "So Eddie tells me all this. I'm sitting there, I can hardly talk now, I'm shaking all over, I'm—I feel sick to my stomach. But I ask him, I go, 'So how'd you leave it, Eddie, what'd you tell 'em?' He shrugs, he says, 'I told 'em I'd do it.' Had no other choice, told 'em he'd do it, but in his own way, on his own schedule. Told 'em Tuesday was out of the question, forget it. First off, he told 'em they still *need* me. Security arrangements at the gallery could easily change over the next two weeks and they'd be in the dark. Second, if I just disappeared now, this close to the big auction, Jerry Donohoe's gonna shit green apples. If he does, you can *bet* he'll change things around. Okay, they buy his logic, they agree. He tells 'em he'll do the hit only after they're safe in that storage room. Late Monday afternoon, April nineteenth, soon as I get home from work. And they buy it all the way, both of 'em, they agree with the logic."

She stands, steps to the double windows, unlocks one, slides it open about two inches. Now she leans against the wall to the right, fingers the low upright collar of the jumpsuit, watches the traffic on Third. "Now he's had a couple of drinks, this clown goes off in another direction. He says, like, 'Fuck these humps, they're muck.' Spits out the words. He says, 'Never should've gone in with 'em.' He says, 'What I've been thinking, why not you and me, Tara?' I says, 'You and me *what?*' He says, first off, he's got connections.

Colombia. Drug connections. Big money, unlimited amounts
of money. They'd give anything to get their hands on stuff
like this. He says, 'We're talking eleven-and-a-half million?'
He says, 'I know I can get five. I know positively I can get
five. We whack it up between us, just the two of us.' I
go—I'm still shaking, but I'm relieved now. So I go, 'Keep
talking.' Now he asks me who has the—''

Loud siren cuts her off. Siren with earsplitting horn blasts,
definitely a fire engine, there's a station on Eighty-fifth between Lex and Third. I stand up, go around the piano to the
window. Big modern hook-and-ladder job roars east on Eighty-
fifth, wrong way on the one-way street, firemen running
ahead to clear the way, cars and cabs backing out into Third
against the light, total chaos. Fire truck hangs a wide left turn
into Third, fireman up in the rear seat turning his wheel like a
madman. Noise level is unbelievable. Off they go up Third,
through the red light at Eighty-sixth, followed by the fire
chiefs car, sirens, horns, tires squealing, the whole caterwaul
echoing in canyons of high-rise apartments. Must be nice at
two o'clock in the morning. When I turn to go back, I glance
at the piano keyboard. Steinway.

Tara remains leaning against the wall to the right of the
window, puffs calmly on her cigarette, waits for the noise to
diminish. Kid's got a classic profile, high cheekbones, straight
nose, sensuous mouth. Now she starts again, voice still has
that slight shake in it. "So I'm—I'm somewhat relieved, I
don't know where he's going with all this, but I tell him to
keep talking. He says, 'Who has the combination to the
Mosler safe?' I tell him Exeter for sure, probably Sullivan
too, vice-president of the jewelry department. He says, 'Does
Exeter have a family?' I go, 'Yeah, he's got a picture of the
wife and kids on his desk.' He says, 'Know where he lives?'
I go, 'Sure, One Sutton Place South, penthouse B. Why?'
Wants to know what time he gets in to work. I tell him real
early, it's like an office joke, he's always first in.''

Brendan utters a soft low whistle, keeps writing.

Tara steps to a table near the window, stubs out her
cigarette in the ashtray, sits on the piano bench again. She
closes the keyboard cover very carefully, runs her fingers

over the wood, inspects them for dust. "He says, 'All right, now listen, the timing's important on this.' He says, 'We'll dry-run this a couple of times, both of us will observe him leave the apartment a few mornings so I'll get to recognize him easily.' I'm listening to all this, it's like a bad dream, I can't—somehow I can't believe this is happening to me. He says he's got a uniform and an ID that'll get him into the apartment building. New York Telephone, real equipment belt, toolbox, worksheets, all that. He says he's done this kind of thing before, no real sweat. He says, okay, Monday morning, April nineteenth, he'll wait for Exeter to leave for work. Next, he goes over, identifies himself to the doorman, shows him the worksheet. Tells him Mr. Exeter ordered an extension for the terrace last week, this is the first chance he's had to install. Doorman rings Mrs. Exeter, tells her. Eddie says she'll do one of two things: Tell the doorman to send him up, or ask to speak to him. Either way, he says he's in, he can handle it, no problem. Goes up to penthouse B, rings the bell, he's admitted. Checks the place out, 'Where're your other extensions, bla-bla,' sees who's there. Now he pulls a gun, lines up the wife and kids, handcuffs, gags, blindfolds all of 'em. Calls me at the office, tells me it's okay. By now Exeter's at the gallery. Still very early in the morning, nobody else there but me, him, the two private security guards on the third floor—Eddie thinks it's the third floor, naturally—and the regular night watchman downstairs. Next, I'm supposed to go up to Exeter's office, I'm supposed to act almost hysterical, I just got a phone call from Eddie Lopata: 'He's in your apartment, he's got your wife and kids at gunpoint.' I'm hysterical, I give Exeter a rundown on what type of guy we're dealing with here: 'Lopata's a real psycho, I've seen him in action, I went to college with him.' Now Exeter calls home fast. Eddie answers, goes into his psycho act: 'Exeter, I'll kill 'em, I swear to God, I'll kill every one of 'em. I got 'em cuffed, gagged and blindfolded now, I'll blow their fuckin' brains out, starting with the youngest.' This sort of shit, y'know? Eddie's a consummate actor when he puts his mind to it: 'I got a gun against the head of this little fucker right now. Hear him trying to scream? Hear that?

Now tell me this, asshole, are twelve diamonds worth the lives of your whole family? Think about it. Here, wait a minute, here's your wife, I'll rip her gag off, she'll tell you exactly what those diamonds are worth.' On and on. He's acting the whole thing out for me. Incredible jerk. You get the general idea.''

I wait, then: "Okay. What happens next?"

Closes her eyes, massages the bridge of her nose. "The guy's just so—*spaced* is the only word. Never used to be like this. Used to be a lot of laughs. He actually—now that he's saved me from Nick and Wally, he actually believes he's doing me a big favor by getting me *actively* involved in the job. Risking my neck, right? Like I *owe* it to him, it's the *least* I can do. Makes me sick to talk about it.''

Again, I wait. Then: "What happens next?"

Glances down at the keyboard cover, rubs her fingers over it. Knows her eyes are bloodshot as hell, doesn't want us to see. "Okay, now he gives Exeter instructions on exactly what to do, instructions over the phone. First, Exeter's told to write down the combination of the Mosler safe and give it to me. Second, he tells Exeter to get his attaché case, and the two of us, Exeter and me, take the elevator down. Exeter gets off at the third-floor jewelry department. I continue down to the second floor, get off, wait by the elevator. Third, Exeter tells the two special guards it's time to set up the exhibit downstairs. He opens the safe, stands directly in front of it like he's placing the diamonds in his attaché case. Only he doesn't put anything in the case. Now he snaps it shut, locks it, closes the door of the safe, makes sure it's locked, spins the dial. Naturally, he asks the guards to escort him down to the ground-floor exhibit area. When I see the elevator pass my floor, I take the back stairs up to three fast, open the safe, take the diamonds out of their boxes, stick them in my handbag. I close the safe, take the elevator to the ground floor, go to the exhibit area where Exeter and the two guards are setting up the display cases. I go in, I tell Exeter his wife's on the phone upstairs. He instructs the guards to stop work and watch his attaché case till he gets back. He tells the regular night watchman at the door not to let anybody in, not even employees, till he gets back. Now he turns to me, asks if I'd please go out and get some coffee for him. Watchman unlocks the door, off I go. Exeter goes up in the elevator and calls home. Eddie tells him he's sitting pat on his family for exactly two hours. Pulls the psycho case on him again: If he blows the whistle before that, Eddie blows his whole family away. Now, what actually happens, Eddie takes the family in a bedroom, still cuffed, gagged, and blindfolded, sits them on the floor, pulls the telephone wire, closes the blinds and drapes, locks the bedroom door. He leaves the apartment, meets me around the corner in a cab. Boom, off to Newark Airport where he's got a chartered Lear jet to El Paso, yet. He's got friends on the border patrol, we'll be in Mexico before sundown. That's it. That's his plan.'' She folds her arms on the keyboard cover, rests her head on her arms.

"Miss Alvarado," I say. "One question. You tell him you're in?"

She looks up at me slowly with her red eyes. "We drank to it till three o'clock this morning. What the fuck else could I do? I'm in. I'm in this tub a shit up to my tits. Detective Rawlings. One question. How the hell you gonna get me *out?*"

# 5

---

CHIEF'S HAVING LUNCH AT HIS DESK when we finally get in to brief him about 12:45 that afternoon. Brendan and I haven't eaten yet, but after observing this gentleman's haute cuisine, our appetites are satiated. Picture this: We walk in, he doesn't look up, he's hunched over reading this morning's *Daily News* while simultaneously in mortal combat with a foot-long hero sandwich wedged in his jaws that's crammed with so much shit he's got to use both paws and every muscle in his neck to rip two inches from this sucker, sharklike. Delicate morsels of various meats, cheeses, onions, tomatoes, and pickles ooze in gobs of creamy mayonnaise from all sides of the soft sesame-seed roll and slip through his fingers to punctuate stories on pages two and three of the tabloid, spread like a charming tablecloth. Brendan and I mutter "Afternoon, Chief," words to that effect, and sit, Brendan in the chair I had during our first meeting, crafty devil. Chief keeps reading, chewing laboriously now, says, "Appaboom, mum," words to that effect.

I reach under my chair, fully expecting to feel the special plastic holder of his Sony TCM-600 Cassette-Corder. But no. Nothing. Brendan does the same, freezes, glances at me with a surprised, painful frown. Got to hand it to the chief, he anticipated us, switched chairs, clever son-of-a-bitch. Obviously, he's not through with Brendan by any means, the study continues. Routine's all part of a management course he took several years ago called Effective Retention of Verbal Communication. FBI course, Deputy Chief Mat Murphy took it with him. Strictly off the record, Mat told me the chief's got close to 300 tapes now, all neatly labeled and dated, carefully filed in the twenty-six steel-blue filing cabinets that surround his office. Arranged alphabetically, of course, securely locked, chief's got the only key. Idea's not as paranoid as it appears. What he's doing, according to Mat, he's systematically studying the verbal techniques of others, attempting to learn from them. Study ranges all the way from Mayor Koch and Commissioner Reilly down to common street detectives like us, guys who might be expected to pull dumb stunts like dropping a fart and simultaneously coughing in an utterly naïve attempt to cover it. No way. Clearly unsophisticated verbal technique. Could be interpreted as intentional disrespect, but not necessarily. Knowing the chief, I'm inclined to believe he'll give us the benefit of the doubt. Once. Twice, forget it. Bottom line, Brendan's sitting there somewhat rigidly now, tight-ass poised an inch from definitive judgment. Talk about pressure. Kid's career might very well hang in the balance. Words from the Good Book come to mind: "And he girded up his loins, and ran before Ahab." Remember that?

In any event, we've had time to prepare the brief on Alvarado the way the chief likes it. Brendan's notes are all typed up now, he places a copy on the desk, sits back. Chief munches slowly, reads the first few lines, nods at Brendan, says, "Weebit a-wowed."

Brendan clears his throat, begins reading softly, eloquently, pausing briefly in just the right places, giving just the right amount of stress to just the right key words. Slight brogue creeps in now and again, but I'm proud of his performance. After three or four minutes, the chief puts down his hero, uses a big paper napkin to wipe his mouth, chin, then each finger individually, gazing at Brendan with almost mesmerized attention.

Brendan turns to the final page. "At the conclusion of the

testimony, Detective Rawlings asked, quote: Miss Alvarado, one question. You tell him you're *in?* Close quote. To which Miss Alvarado replied, in part, quote: We drank to it till three o'clock this morning. I'm in. Detective Rawlings, one question. How the hell you gonna get me *out?* Close quote. End of report.''

Gets a slow left-sided molar display from the chief. Glances at me. ''Give her an answer?''

''No, sir.''

''Good man. All right, here's how we handle it. Number one, nobody else at the gallery gets hold of this intelligence. That goes double for Exeter, obviously. Don't want civilians getting nervous at this point in time. Still another, what, two weeks till the auction, right?''

''Right,'' Brendan says.

''Fewer people know about this new twist the better.'' Chief glances at the mutilated carcass of his hero, wraps it carefully in the *News,* drops it in his wastebasket, plunk. Opens the middle drawer of his desk, takes out a small plastic envelope, rips off one end, removes one of those wet paper towels with the fresh scent, begins wiping his hands. ''Number two, I want Alvarado to start playing both ends against the middle. Think she'll give you any static about it?''

''She might,'' I tell him.

''How come?''

''My opinion, the lady's getting scared now. Playing both ends against the middle puts her in a precarious position at best.''

Chief drops the wet towel into his wastebasket, plop, opens his middle drawer again, selects a toothpick, slides it out of the cellophane, has a go at his lower left molars first. ''Little John, you're a helluva good detective, but you got a lot to learn about women.'' Sucks out a choice little tidbit, savors it before swallowing. ''Precarious position? Hell, broads *love* this kinda action. Lies, deception, intrigue, seduction, it's instinctive to 'em, they get multiple orgasms just *thinkin'* about crap like this. Who was it said, 'The great aphrodisiac is death,' remember that?''

''Yeah,'' Brendan says.

"Who said it?" I ask.

"*I* don't know, Little John. What'm I, a walkin' fuckin' encyclopedia?"

"Sounds like Erich Fromm," I tell him.

"*Who?*"

"Erich Fromm. Played third base for Utica, Eastern League."

"Naw. No fuckin' Kraut jock would come up with a gem like that." Chief jams the toothpick into his upper right molars now, sucks hard, implodes a delectable chunk of something, gnaws it happily between his front teeth as he contemplates the riddle. Finally: "Don't know. Don't know who said it, but I'm convinced it was a broad."

Now we get what turns out to be a break. Alvarado calls us at the precinct about 2:15. Wally just called her, says there's a problem. His out-of-town friend has to take an unexpected vacation for a couple of years. However, he's got a few people in mind who might be interested in filling the slot. Also tells her the new Corvette will be available next weekend. He'll be in touch.

I update the chief by phone, his mind starts clicking on all five cylinders. Thinks now might be the ideal time for yours truly to go active undercover in an attempt to infiltrate this little group, since I've long since established myself at the Tatler.

First he sends me to Charley Katz at BCI who creates a rap sheet for me: I'm now Johnny Trumbo (who's actually doing five to ten years in a federal penitentiary in Arkansas). Trumbo's an alarm system specialist, real line-drive type guy who never quite made the bigs, originally from Philly, took collars in Atlanta, Miami, and D.C. Katz even puts out a wanted on me for jumping bail in D.C. Next I go to the Photo Unit for mug shots. Photographer says I look more like a murderer than an alarm man. Steel-blue killer eyes. Chief finally sends me to Continental Alarm Systems, 888 Seventh Avenue, to begin a crash course in basics and technical lingo in case I have to discuss the subject with Wally or Nick. This is the outfit that originally wired and still monitors the gallery. Arrive at 4:10,

I'm assigned a private tutor, kid by the name of Louis Carlino, electronics whiz, terrific teacher. Starts by pulling a copy of the gallery's alarm system circuitry. In fifty-five minutes he gives me a comprehensive rundown on state-of-the-art commercial computerized alarms, everything from infra-red thermal intrusion detectors to ultrasonic, microwave, photoelectric, beepers, Chapman locks, Ungo boxes, and a complete range of CCTV video equipment. Even gives me homework, first day: Seventeen index cards, each with a technical buzzword on one side and a one-line definition on the reverse. Next class 4:15 tomorrow, be prepared for a multiple-guess quiz. Me, I always liked shit like this, I'm looking for a gold star. Runs in the family, what can I tell you?

Start undercover work at the Tatler that night, 8:20, no rest for the weary, but tonight I'm with a girl, Sandi Hooper, very attractive undercover detective from the Major Crimes Unit, personally selected by the chief. Brunette, late twenties, viva-cious, has all the moves. We rap with Ginger, lay a couple of bets, watch the Rangers on TV. Wally and Nick don't show. Have to make a fast exit about 10:25 when I spot a guy I busted a few years back. Doesn't see me, looks like he just dropped in to use the pay phone, but why take a chance?

Tuesday night, April 6, I'm in the Tatler with another girl, Terri Krzczek (pronounced Cris-chick), detective from our own precinct, a real looker, early twenties. Light brunette hair, brown eyes, five-six, maybe 110, worked with her before, like her style. Nick shows solo around 9:45, has a martini, watches the game. Half-hour later, Wally strolls in alone. They sit at the bar, lay some bets with Ginger, pick up on Terri. Especially Kwapniewski, can't seem to take his eyes off Terri, knows a good Polish girl when he sees one. Peaches-and-cream, ultrafeminine voice and laugh, looks like she stepped out of a Pepsi ad. Just before we leave she casually sniffs something that looks like coke. Irony isn't lost on Wally.

Early Wednesday evening we get things moving. Thal-heimer and Telfian go in the Tatler about 6:15, long before most of the regulars, identify themselves to Ginger, who's just come on duty, show her my mug shots. Says she never saw me before to her knowledge, asks who it is. Johnny Trumbo, alarm expert, has an arrest warrant outstanding. Known to be in the general vicinity. They leave her a card, ask her to call if she has anything. Sure thing. About two hours later I come in with Terri, we sit at the bar, order drinks. Terri goes to the ladies' room. Boom, Ginger comes over, tells me quietly about the two cops flashing my photo around. I slip her a fifty-dollar bill for the information, tell her it's much appreciated. Nick and Wally don't show tonight.

Ordinarily, things don't move too fast in this type con; takes a lot of patience. Meantime, Terri and I have a lot of fun, we're on the same wavelength. Thursday and Friday nights, Wally and Nick drop in late, no dates, have some drinks, watch TV, kid around with Ginger, the usual. Wally's still eyeing Terri, who makes it obvious she doesn't mind. I go to the men's room maybe a little more than normal, figure I'll give him a shot if he wants it. No action. But late Friday night—actually, it's well past midnight—both of these guys start glancing at me in a slightly different way. They're not fags, so obviously Ginger's been rapping in my absence. It's happening a bit faster than we expected, but these gentlemen have a deadline that's only ten days away at this point and experienced alarm men don't grow on trees, even in Fun City.

Terri and I discuss it when I drive her home that night. She still still lives at the YWCA, 135 East Fifty-second; can't really afford the kind of apartment she wants yet, and this is a good place, relatively close to the precinct. We both have a gut feeling Wally and/or Nick will make some kind of oblique move within the next few nights.

We're right. Late Saturday night, April 10, Tatler's jammed, we've both had quite a few drinks, ditto Wally and Nick, both at the bar with dates. Around 1:30, Wally comes over, smiles, leans on the bar next to me. I'm wired:

"Name's Wally. Talk to you for a minute?"

"What about?"

"Don't think the lady'd be interested. There's a table in back. Won't take a minute."

I ask Terri to order me another Beefeater, tell her to hold the fort. Wally leads me through the crowd to a corner table way in back near the kitchen. Nick's sitting there smoking, holding a drink, face illuminated by a candlelamp. Roger Mudd on special assignment. We sit down.

Wally's formal now. "Nick, like you to meet Johnny Trumbo."

Nick sticks his hand out. "Johnny."

I ignore the hand. "What the fuck is this? Who're you guys?"

"Okay. I'm Nick Mize, this is Wally Kwapniewski."

"What can I do for you?"

Nick lowers his hand. "Buy you a drink, Johnny?"

"Don't drink with strangers. State your business."

Wally takes over. "Hear you know your alarms."

I look at him. "What?"

"We hear you know—"

"Listen, friend, go fuck yourself, huh? Both a ya. Who the fuck you think you are, comin' up to me? I don't like strangers comin' up to me." I start to get up.

"Relax, Johnny," Nick says. "We're not exactly strangers, you see us in here practically every night."

I'm on the edge of my chair. "So?"

"It's just we're in the same business," Wally says.

"Same business? What business is that?"

They hesitate, blink at me in the candlelight. Mudd and Brokaw stuck for an answer. Love it.

Nick stubs out his cigarette. "Okay, cards on the table. We spent a little bread checking you out. We know your background, that's why we're sitting here. We need your opinion and we're prepared to pay for it."

"My opinion?"

"We got something big in mind," Nick says. "Something that could include a guy with your expertise. Of course, we'd have to get better acquainted, know a lot more about each other."

I sit back, take out a cigar, bite off the end. "Got my own problems right now. Don't need yours."

"Would a hundred grand change your mind?"

I light the cigar. "Nick, look. Without the birdseed, huh?"

He looks me in the eye. "All you'd have to do is bypass a few systems for us. We can handle the rest."

"I don't work that way. Never have. I don't open doors unless I know what's behind them. Then it's down the middle."

"Tell you what," Nick says. "Why don't we meet here tomorrow night and talk it over a little more?"

"Sorry, I got other plans."

"How about Monday night then?"

I shrug. "I'll probably be here, but not to talk nickels and dimes. Meantime I'll do a little checking myself."

"You do that," Wally says.

Sunday, April 11, 2:20 P.M. Alvarado calls me at home. Wally phoned, says her new Corvette is ready for her at the dealership in Forest Hills, Queens. I tell her to pick it up. At 4:10 she calls me from the dealership. It's all legal, registered in her name, paid in full, straight cash deal. I tell her to drive it home, happy motoring.

Monday, April 12, only one week away from the auction. Spend three hours this afternoon with Louis Carlino at Continental Alarm Systems, sixth day of my crash course. Today we concentrate on three specific—and very complicated—techniques for bypassing the gallery's alarm circuitry, third-floor jewelry department only. By the end of this session I've got most of the theoretical problems licked, I need on-the-job training at the gallery. Carlino gets on the horn with Jerry Donohoe, sets up a dry run for tomorrow afternoon at five.

Tonight I waltz in the Tatler solo at 8:05, Nick and Wally are waiting for me at the bar. Not too crowded tonight, we manage to get a quiet corner table in back, away from the kitchen. Tonight I'm not wired, of course, I know what's coming. Before we get down to business, boom, they ask me to accompany them to the men's room, that whole routine. I insist on frisking them first and I do it thoroughly, each one alone inside a locked stall. Men are coming and going, all pissers, fortunately. Now Nick gives me a good toss, also inside a stall, even examines my wallet. Thanks to BCI, I'm loaded with John A. Trumbo IDs.

Back to the table. Drinks, small talk, during which I mention a few choice points about their illustrious backgrounds to prove I did my homework. Finally Nick hands me a dog-eared Xerox copy of an alarm circuit. It's not the gallery's system. I study it in the yellow glow of the candlelamp, point out a few things, toss in a couple of technical buzzwords to test their reaction. They nod, they go, "Uh-huh," they look fascinated, but I'm convinced they don't have a clue what I'm talking about. Doesn't surprise me. Fact is, the overwhelming majority of professional crooks today are specialists. Scared to death of anything outside their particular area of expertise; fear of the unknown. Most work in teams, even on relatively small jobs, because they need to combine talents. Now, if these two clowns were teen-agers today, weaned and honed and hooked on the latest gee-whiz electronic gadgetry, they probably wouldn't be so intimidated by burglar alarms, and they wouldn't necessarily need the high-priced services of hard-ons like Johnny Trumbo. Fear is a dreadful emotion.

Truth is, most alarm systems, commercial, industrial, residential, are basically simple, once you get past the fifty-cent technical terminology. Just to give you a brief rundown, so you'll know what I'm into, alarm systems break down to two general categories, perimeter and interior. Most widely used types of commercial perimeter sensing devices are magnetic contacts, plunger contacts, metallic foil, and vibration detectors. Not all that complicated. Magnetic contacts are just electromechanical units with a simple switching mechanism attached to doors, windows, transoms, what have you; when the access is opened, the magnet moves away from the switch, triggering the alarm. Plunger contacts are similar, but primarily limited to doors; they operate like the hidden light switch in a refrigerator door. Metallic foil, usually in the form of tape, is applied to various access points; when an attempt is made to gain entry, the foil breaks, activating the alarm. Vibration detectors are small electronic sensors attached to doors, walls, and especially windows, calibrated to detect vibrations of a given magnitude and set off the alarm.

Interior sensing devices can get just a bit more sophisticated, depending on how much your firm wants to spend, but the most popular in commercial use are pressure mats, photoelectric beams, passive infrared systems, and motion detectors. Pressure mats are essentially flat switches, generally used under rugs or carpets, that react to pressure from footsteps. Photoelectric units are often designed to resemble standard electrical outlets; they cast invisible infrared light beams across hallways, rooms, stairs, whatever, and of course the alarm is activated when a beam is broken. Passive infrared systems measure the degree of infrared heat generated within a protected area; the body heat of an individual passing through this area will trigger the alarm. Motion detectors, called "ultrasonics" and "microwaves" in the trade, operate by filling an area with sound waves far above the audio-frequency range, or electromagnetic waves of extremely high frequency, that are programmed in a specific pattern; anything entering the pattern in sustained motion changes the pattern and trips the alarm. Needless to say, there are variations on all these themes, depending on the manufacturer and the special requirements of the client, but this gives you the basics.

So now I'm studying the alarm circuitry given to me by Mudd and Brokaw, and it's a modern, sophisticated, obviously expensive system covering a large single-floor area. Finally I look up, shake my head. "What're you guys tapping into here, a miniature Fort Knox?"

Gets a grin out of Wally. "In a way, yeah, you might say that."

"Can you handle it?" Nick asks.

I give him a long look. "What?"

"Now don't get hyper, Johnny, huh? All I'm asking—"

"I heard the question." I glance away in disdain, take out a cigar, bite off the end real fast, spit it on the floor. "Listen, friend, let's get one fuckin' thing straight right now. Don't insult my intelligence, I won't insult yours. You got that?"

Nick nods, takes a fast swallow of Scotch. "Y'know, this is—this is getting ridiculous, it really is. If we're gonna work together here, we've gotta talk to each other. All I'm asking—you mention Fort Knox and that—all I'm asking, is this thing supercomplicated or what? We got problems? That's all I'm asking."

I light the cigar, blow smoke at the ceiling, take my time in explaining an adult concept to children. "As usual, you got a number of knowns and unknowns here, okay?" I glance at the circuitry. "Okay, let's start with the knowns. Perimeter, they got plunger contacts on all three doors, vibration detectors on all eleven windows. Interior, photoelectric units in four hallways, plus a series of six ultrasonic devices in just one fairly small room. Question: What the fuck's in that room?"

"Tell you later," Wally says. "Go ahead."

"You must be deaf," I say quietly. "Told you the other night, I don't open doors unless I know what's behind them. Remember that?"

"Yeah."

"What's behind that door?"

He glances at Nick to see if it's okay. Then: "Gold."

"Gold."

"Dental gold," Nick says. "Very high quality. Place is a dental-supply house. Gold's in a safe in that room. Go ahead."

Back to condescension. "Known: They got a fail-safe system. Normally it operates on electric current; if we shut the power off, it automatically switches to emergency batteries. Known: Since the schematic doesn't indicate any actual alarms, inside or out, it's obvious they're hooked into a silent system, an off-premises monitor. Depending on what city this place is located in, the alarm's either transmitted directly to the police or to a private central monitoring station that contacts the police."

They nod, go, "Uh-huh."

"Well?"

"Well what?" Wally asks.

I raise my brows, glance away. "Jesus, I swear to Christ, I must be talkin' to that fuckin' *wall* over there."

"What's the question?" Nick asks.

"What *city* is this place in?"

"New York," he snaps. "Queens, not far from La Guardia."

"Thanks very much. Sorry to keep you guys up. In that case, the alarm's transmitted to a private central monitoring station. Which leads to some unknowns: Is it monitored by tape or live personnel? If it's monitored by personnel, how fast is the reaction time?"

"What's the difference?" Wally asks. "It won't go off, that's what we're paying you for."

"Nick, where'd you find this guy? Day-care center?"

"Okay, let's all cool it," Nick says.

I tug at my collar, flick my ashes on the floor. "There's *always* a possibility these fuckers'll go off, asshole. Most of this new equipment's so sensitive, *air* conditioners can trigger 'em, *heat* vents, *telephones,* loose-fitting *windows.* Rats, mice, *cock*roaches, for Christ's sake. So sensitive they cause hundreds of false alarms in this city every fuckin' *day.* Over twenty-one thousand last year alone. That's why the cops won't touch 'em, they'd need a fuckin' army on any given *night.*"

"Okay, okay," Nick says. "Point made. Let's all cool it."

"And it's near *La Guardia?*" I ask. "Good luck. Vibration detectors and ultrasonics in the vicinity of La Guardia. Jets taking off every three minutes, seven days a week. Beautiful. 'What's the difference—won't go off, will it?' Why's it I get the feeling this is shaping up as Amateur Night?"

Nick takes a swallow, lights a cigarette. "Let me give you a rundown on what's what. Place is a relatively new dental-supply outfit, Ditmars Boulevard, Astoria. We have inside help, guy who works there. We're talking high-quality gold, mostly eighteen carat. Wholesale value, at least a hundred and twenty-five grand. We have excellent connections, we can unload it for seventy-five easy."

"Okay," I tell him, "I want it down the middle, plus a chunk of faith up front."

"Johnny, I'll level with you," Nick says very sincerely. "We can't do anything in the way of cash till we unload the stuff. But what we *can* do is give—"

"I'm gonna walk out that fuckin' door."

"Just hear me out, okay?"

"I should have my *head* examined for wastin' *time* with you assholes." I stub out my cigar hard, push my chair back.

"Johnny, just hear me *out*."

I glance at my watch. "Make it fast. Bottom line. Now."

"What we *can* do, we have good contacts with one of the biggest Chevy dealers on the Island. We can give you a brand-new Corvette, retail value twenty-two thousand dollars."

I damn near laugh out loud, have to take a fast drink to cover it. Déjà vu, these clowns got the script memorized.

"You got a car?" Wally asks.

"Yeah, I got a car."

"Sports car?"

"Don't *want* a sports car, asshole."

"Just hear me out," Nick says. "Pull in your chair, listen to the rest of it. You won't be sorry, I guarantee it."

I pull it in. "One line of bullshit, I'm out the door."

"Brand-new from the factory, registered in your name, title of ownership, you can go out and sell it tomorrow."

"Tell you what, *you* go out and sell it. Me, I don't want to know from no fuckin' *car,* understand? I'll take twenty-five cash up front, then straight down the middle. Period."

Nick sips his drink, thinks on it. Takes a legal-size envelope from his left inside breast pocket, a ballpoint pen from the inside right. Now he's into some fast figuring. I light another cigar, glance around the room, wish to Christ I was wired for all this. Chief would love this shit. "Little John, you can *act,* buddy-boy, you got it *down,* we're puttin' you in deep *cover* from here on out." All I'd need.

Brokaw turns on the charm. "Want another drink?"

"No, thanks, asshole."

Nick finally looks up from his figures. "All right, here's— here's what we can do. All right, twenty-five cash up front, you got it. Now. We're talking—the thing is, we're only talking seventy-five for the job itself, seventy-five tops.'' Consults his envelope. ''We split that down the middle with you, leaves us thirty-seven-five total. Whack that in half, Wally and me end up with eighteen-seven each. You walk away with—counting your twenty-five up front—you walk away with sixty-two-five. More than triple what Wally and me get. That's—in my opinion, that's out of line, Johnny. Wouldn't you agree with that?''

I shrug. ''You came to me, pal.''

''We came to you,'' Wally says, ''but we set the whole job up. We did all the head work, Johnny.''

I look at him. ''Hey, Wally. Go fuck yourself, huh?''

''It's the truth,'' he says. ''We put one hell of a lot of work into this job.''

''Yeah? Wally, do me a favor, huh? Go pull your pud.''

''All right,'' Nick says. ''Here's what we can do, Johnny. Didn't want to tell you this until after, but here it is: We got another job lined up. And this thing, I mean, I'm telling you, this thing'll make the dental job look like pin money. If you're willing to be a little more flexible on this first one, we'll make you an equal partner on the big one. We'll go in as a team. Interested?''

I yawn, fist to mouth, check my watch.

He puts the envelope back in his pocket, leans toward me, lowers his voice. ''This is no bullshit, this is straight, Johnny. You play ball with us on this one, I'll personally guarantee you one million dollars. One million dollars cash.''

I laugh softly. ''You guys, you're in the wrong business here. You should be in the confidence game, you'd make a fortune.''

Here's a frown from Tom Brokaw. ''Johnny, this is straight.''

''Yeah? Prove it, asshole.''

''We will,'' Nick says. ''We'll give you all the proof you want. Make a deal with you, Johnny. You agree to take twenty-five up front on this first one, plus a *third* when we unload, I'll personally prove it to you. To your satisfaction. No ifs, ands, or buts. Then, you're still not convinced, you don't buy it, okay. Back to your original demand, twenty-five and straight down the middle. Deal?''

I puff on the cigar, hold his gaze. "Yeah. Deal."

"I'll bring the proof tomorrow night."

"I'll be here. One question: You got any kind of timetable for the dental job?''

"Yeah." Nick picks up his glass, sees it's empty, looks for the waiter. "Yeah, probably next Saturday."

Obviously, something doesn't ring true here. If you're going after $11.5 million in diamonds and the *Guinness Book of World Records*, why screw around with a bush-league dental-gold job just two days before? Three possible answers come to mind: (1) They're nervous, they need a minimum-risk job to check my talent; (2) they figure we all need a warmup as a team to get sharp for the big one—which, by the way, is a fairly common practice among pros; (3) they haven't worked a job in months, they need fast capital to finance the big one. I'm inclined to number three.

I leave the Tatler about 11:35; Wally and Nick go to the bar for another drink. It's a cool night, Monday night, not much traffic on Fifty-seventh, the air smells good for a change. Surprise, Brendan's managed to find a legit parking space about halfway up the block. As I get closer and see him sitting up straight at the wheel, smoking his cigar, watching me, it gives me a feeling that's difficult to describe. I consider myself very fortunate to have Brendan as a partner. Man's a genuine professional, as dependable as they come. Think it's easy to sit alone in a parked car at night for hours at a clip, keep your eyes on the entrance to a bar half a block away—and remain alert? Try it. In my judgment, and in the judgment of most veteran cops, this is one of the hardest, loneliest, most frustrating—and often most important—jobs any detective must learn to master. Physically and psychologically you're fighting formidable odds: Fatigue, boredom, distraction, frequently hunger or thirst, sometimes extremes of cold or heat, all too often the need to urinate, and almost always the involuntary tendency of the mind to wander. There are tricks to control all of the above, of course, not the least of which is to prepare for physical necessities whenever possible, but the primary stimulus to maintain concentration is basic: The life of your partner may very well depend on your ability to remain alert.

I get in the car, close the door.

"So how'd it go?" he asks quietly.

"Pay dirt. Johnny Trumbo's got a job."

# 6

REPORT TO THE PRECINCT AT NOON, brief the troops, call the chief; I'm told he's having lunch at his desk, can't talk, he'll return my call. Hero sandwiches have a way of inhibiting conversation. Don't know the name of the dental-supply firm yet, so like any good detective I let my fingers do the walking through the Queens Yellow Pages. Here we are, Dental Equipment & Supplies, quite a few outfits, but only one in Astoria: James A. Travino & Sons, 10257 Ditmars Boulevard. Since this is an inside job, Big John and Nuzhat volunteer to pay a visit to James A. Travino at his home around six o'clock, tell him what may or may not be in the wind, explain that we'll have it covered upside-down and backwards, alert him to the possibility that he may or may not have a bad cavity in his employ, caution him to keep the matter strictly confidential. Next I call Carlino at Continental Alarm Systems and Donohoe at the gallery, cancel the dry run scheduled for five, tell them I'll explain later.

Chief calls back at 1:05, I give him a brief synopsis of last night's developments, tell him I'm typing the report now. To say he's delighted at the progress is an understatement; he's positively ecstatic, particularly because the infiltration gig was his own original idea. Decides to call a major strategy meeting, his office, four o'clock sharp. Present will be Emer-

gency Service Division Commander Jim Mairs, Deputy Chief
Mat Murphy, Press Relations Director Jerry Grady, and the
entire special-assignment team.

"Counting me, that's ten men," the chief says. "I want
ten—and only ten—clean copies of the report ready to hand
out. And I mean clean, clear, readable copies, Little John,
double-spaced, strict margins. Title page, heads, subheads, all
that. Introduction with brief background update, comprehensive blow-by-blow of last night's encounter, conclusion, sum-
mary. Facts, figures, dates, times. Understood?"

"Understood."

"Neatly typed, three-hole punched, put 'em all in those
blue presentation folders we use at headquarters now. Got
any of those?"

"Blue presentation—?"

"Naw, you probably don't have 'em yet. Got a pencil?"

"Yes, sir."

"Take this down: Duo Tang, that's D-u-o space T-a-n-g,
that's the brand name, Duo Tang five-dash-three-five-five-
eight. Size nine-by-eleven-and-a-half. Color, blue. NYPD
blue. Get 'em at any stationery store. If they don't have 'em,
here's the alternate choice, take this down: Acco, that's
A-c-c-o, Acco two-five-oh-seven-three. Same size, same color.
Send one of the team out. Now, how's your copying machine
there?"

"Well, you saw Brendan's report yesterday."

"Oh, yeah. Lousy. Good report, lousy copy. What the
fuck kinda machine you got there?"

"You mean the actual—?"

"Brand name, yeah. Xerox? Naw, couldn't be Xerox."

"Doubt it, Chief. It's just an old beat-up—"

"Be here three-thirty sharp with the original. Give it to
Adair, he'll take care of it. Duplicating here's got a brand-
new Xerox thirty-four-fifty, top of the small-line models.
Well, no, guess it's not brand-new, we got it on sale. Sucker
retailed for thirteen thousand nine-ninety-five, we got it for
ten. Either remanufactured or reconditioned. Feeds itself special three-hole punched paper, comes out cleaner than the

original, collates, all that shit. Forget the blue folders, we'll
use our own. Presentation counts almost as much as content
at this level, Little John, we've got a whole new streamlined
system starting around here. No more slipshod, old-line,
Rube Goldberg administrative practices around here, you're
probably not aware of it, hasn't filtered down to precinct
level yet, right?''

"Not that I've noticed, no."

"It will, buddy-boy, it's *got* to. Know what the basic
problem is? Administrative *inertia*. That's right. Know what
that means, inertia? That's a fancy business-school term for
*laziness*. Administrative laziness. Doin' things the old way.
Took an advanced-management course in January called
'Psychology of Effective Written Communication,' FBI course,
Mat took it with me. Fascinatin' shit, tell you about it some-
time. Now, agenda for the meeting: One, you lead off, read
your report aloud, we follow; two, group discussion of salient
considerations; three, synergistic strategy decisions from me,
from Commander Mairs—that's pronounced *Mars,* by the
way, like the planet, make a note of it—and from Grady; last
order of business, question-and-answer session. What we got
here is a *synectics* group, Little John, understand what that
means?''

"Uh, no, sir, I don't."

Sounds memorized: "Group of guys from various backgrounds and disciplines who meet in an attempt to find
creative solutions to problems through the unrestricted exercise of imagination and the correlation of somewhat disparate
elements."

"I see."

"One more thing. How's your typing, John?"

"Typing? Matter of fact—"

"Hunt 'n' peck, huh?"

"No, sir. Matter of fact, it's excellent. Took a course
in it, senior year in high school. Called 'Introduction to
Typing.'"

Chief hesitates. Wish I could see his face. Eyes undoubtedly narrowing now, trying to decide if he's been insulted.

Naw. "Good for you, Little John, should've known it. Like
your style, always have. Now, listen up. No need to hurry
this thing; take your time in there. No typos, huh? Can't
stand typos. Don't suppose you got an IBM Correcting Selectric
around the squadroom, do you?"

"No, sir."

"What y'got?"

"An old Royal manual, sir, but it's a good—"

"Oh, Jesus, one of *them*, huh? Shit, I had one of them
fuckers twenty-five *years* ago. Longer'n that, let's see. Twenty-
nine years in the department, first three in uniform, South
Bronx. Detective in February of 'fifty-six. Old Fifth Precinct
down on Elizabeth Street, Lower East Side. Oldest precinct
in the city, eighteen-eighty-one, y'realize that, John?"

"Yes, sir."

"Christ, I was—I was just twenty-four years old. Had an
old tin desk with an ancient Royal manual attached to the
side. Type faces kept gettin' all clogged up with black shit,
y'know, like the 'o' and the 'e,' sometimes the 'g.' Had to
clean 'em out with—"

"The 'a' too."

"That's right, Little John, the—had to clean 'em out with
a toothpick back then. Later on they came up with a special
type face cleaning fluid. That what you use now?"

"No, sir. Ran out of it about—oh, two years ago, I
guess."

"Two *years* ago!? What the hell ya use *now?*"

"End of a paper clip."

"End of a—?! Jesus *Christ*, Rawlings, that's just what I
was talkin' about before: *Inertia!* Administrative *laziness!*
Who's responsible for ordering supplies there, Barnett?"

"Yes, sir, but it's not his fault."

"Not his *fault?* Whose fault *is* it?"

"Whole squad, sir. Nobody here wants the cleaning fluid."

"Why the fuck not?"

"Too messy, sir. Got all over our—"

"Comes with an *applicator!*"

"Yeah, but it—major reason, sir, if you really want to
know—see, it stunk."

"Stunk?"

"Stunk. Stunk the place up. Everybody here was always holding their noses when somebody used it, y'know, which was all the time. Stunk like hell."

"*Mine* never stunk."

"Yeah? Must've been a different brand. Ours stunk like—if you'll excuse the analogy, sir, ours stunk like stale piss."

"Stale *piss?*"

"Exactly like stale piss. Y'know, like when you can't flush the toilet sometimes and it just mounts up in there? Ever smell that?"

Short pause. Then, softly: "Rawlings, I just finished lunch."

"Sorry, sir. Anyway, that's the real reason. We all use paper clips now. Does the job faster and cleaner. Cost efficient, too."

"*Cost* efficient? Ever think of the man-hours lost in diggin' out that crap? I could prove you wrong on that, Little John, but I don't have the time. Or the budget. I could run a time-and-motion study that'd prove you dead wrong. Definitely not cost efficient. Plus the fact—maybe this might sound esoteric to you, but it—well, fact of the matter is, it just doesn't *look* good. To the public, I'm talkin'. Civilians hangin' around the squadroom there, they see New York's finest detectives hunched over their typewriters, pickin' crud outa type faces with fuckin' *paper* clips. Now, how's that look, huh? How's that look to civilians, ever think of that? Looks like a hicktown Rube Goldberg operation. Makes the whole department look bad. Know what else? Reflects badly on *me*, John. That's right. *Me*. I'm supposed to be runnin' a modern, sophisticated, high-technology shop here. How's it make *me* look?"

"There's a solution, sir."

"Yeah? What's that?"

"Don't mean right away, I know we can't afford it, at least not this year, but there's a logical solution that'd make you, us, the whole department look good."

"Yeah? What's that?"

"Buy us all IBM Correcting Selectrics."

There's a long pause, then a series of slow, painful, staccato sounds from deep in his throat, like rumbling belches.

"Chief? You okay?"

Couple of gurgles, then: "Indigestion, John. Been wolfin' down my lunch lately. Acid indigestion."

"Know how to spell relief? R-o-l—"

"No, no. R-*e*-l-i-e-f. Why the fuck y'wanna spell *that?* What's your *point*, John?"

"I was—it'd take too long to explain."

"You have a coupla belts at lunch?"

"No, sir. Not a drop."

"Okay, okay. Don't get *touchy*, Little John. It's just y'sound a little off the wall today, buddy-boy. Now, as for your, uh, your suggestion. IBM Correcting Selectrics, huh? Y'got any idea what those fuckers *cost*, John?"

"No, sir, Afraid that's out of my league."

"In more ways than one, pal. Those fuckers happen to retail in the neighborhood of a thousand bucks each."

"Wow. Okay, well, maybe we could get *used* ones, huh?"

"Rawlings, look, I'll be candid with ya. I don't have time to blow on idiocy, however well meaning, okay? Back to your report now. And no typos, huh? Use Liquid Paper correction fluid, terrific stuff." He hesitates. "Got a bottle of that?"

"Right on my desk."

"Knew you would. Knew it. Like your style, John. Get one of the team to proofread for ya, huh? Somebody who can *spell*, y'read me?"

"Loud and clear."

"I'll instruct Adair to reserve the Xerox thirty-four-fifty for exactly three-thirty. Better be here about three-fifteen."

*Bang!* Hangs up. Always does that, just like on TV, never fails. No "Bye," no "See ya," not even a "Take care." Nothing. *Bang!* Right in your ear. Television writers knock me out with that shit. Sitcoms, dramas, sagas, you name it. *Bang!* Breaks me up every time. Writers know that's not the way 99.9 percent of the people in this country end conversations, but they think it's more dramatic. They're right, of course. Phony as hell, but more dramatic. What they don't know, what they can't know, is the ripple effect, the untold millions of people out there watching people hang up on people. Night after night, ad nauseam, almost never an exception. *Bang!* So what happens? Right the first time. Now it begins to penetrate the collective consciousness of macho types: "I mean, hey, this is obviously the chic fast-lane tony way to go." Today it's gaining popularity in New York, of course, you're not a six-figure powerhouse MBA corporate prick unless you got the balls to do it. Infuriated me at first, now I laugh at it. Deep down, I love New York, always have, always will, even though it's true this city's got more certifiable total assholes per square inch than any other city in the country, with the possible exception of L.A. Difference is, when assholes hang up on people in L.A., they do it with a smile and a fart; in New York, they do it with a frown and a belch. Question of life-styles.

Last-minute change: Meeting takes place in the office of Emergency Service Division Commander Jim Mairs, same floor, just down the hall, four o'clock. Reason, ESD's in the middle of a routine emergency now, there's a jumper on the roof of the Pan Am Building, Mairs has to stay close to his phone. I've worked with this guy before, he's a real pro, that's the best compliment I can give anybody in this racket, especially the brass. We go in his office, it's just about the diametric opposite of the chief's. Desk always piled high with letters, memos, reports, books, but not in disarray; he knows exactly which pile contains what. Three walls of floor-to-ceiling bookshelves crammed with hundreds of hardcovers and paperbacks, interspersed with collectibles like scale-model vintage locomotives and classic cars (Ferrari dominating), unopened Olympia beer cans, photographs, and several distinctly weird items: A preserved frog that was completely flattened by a car; a preserved bat hanging upside-down from the limb of a half-dead plant; and, in a tiny wire cage hanging from a plant near the windows, a live cockroach named Quint II. This is no shit, this is straight. Original cockroach named

Quint, who laid eggs in the cage, died of some unknown malady. Quint II, who I assume is Quint's sole surviving progeny, although I never asked, looks bright-eyed, slime-backed, and hairy-legged, diets on crackers and almost anything else you care to toss in the cage, and gets a cup of fresh water every day. Lots of potted plants around the office seem to be expiring from lack of water, but not ol' Quint II, this little sucker's got it made.

Judging by his office, maybe you expect Jim Mairs to be Commander Cuckoo, right? Never judge a man by his pets. This guy happens to be one of the brightest and most talented cops in the department. That's not just my opinion, that's the consensus opinion of virtually everybody who's ever worked with him, from the mayor and the commissioner on down. Hails from Minneapolis, graduated from Dartmouth, entered the Police Academy at twenty-one, finished first in his class, just like yours truly, only this guy's got an IQ that'd blow your doors. Mid-forties now, looks like a college professor, high forehead, receding brown hair, lean face dominated by penetrating green eyes, about five-eight, 145, wiry build, does a lot of jogging. Spare time, he collects and rebuilds organs. Yeah, *organs*. First time I hear that, after seeing the weird shit in his office, it gives me pause. Couple of years ago I go to a party at his apartment down on East Sixteenth Street, I'm relieved. We're talking *musical* organs here. Got at least one in every room in the joint, all sizes, all shapes, pipe organs, reed organs, even an electronic job with fancy synthesizers. Plays 'em all, too. Gets a couple of drinks in him, sits down and belts out Bach's Toccata and Fugue in D Minor, no sweat, E. Power Biggs. Fortunately, he lives on the top floor.

Just before the meeting today, mid-emergency, he sits calmly behind his desk, shirtsleeves, conservative tie, speaks softly to one of his ESD officers who's on the top floor of the Pan Am Building. Explains precisely how he wants the net rigged, cantilever style, out from the little terrace on the forty-sixth floor, west side, four floors below the jumper, a middle-aged white male, who's now sitting on the ledge. Answers a few questions about crowd control on Vanderbilt

Avenue, tells the guy to keep in constant touch. Says, "Thanks, Paul, take care," before he hangs up. Says it like he means it. But quietly. Class guy. Don't care if he has fifty cockroaches.

Meeting starts promptly at four. Chief's got his Sony TCM-600 Cassette-Corder right out in plain sight on the edge of Jim's desk. Only two visitors' chairs in the office, chief's got one, Mat Murphy's got the other; Jerry Grady and our six-man team stand. I start to lean against the bookshelves, stop instantly, glance back to make sure nothing's crawling around in there. Animal instinct, what can I tell you? We're all holding a clean copy of my report, eleven pages neatly typed, double-spaced, strict margins, three-hole punched, looking very official in NYPD blue Duo Tang 5-3558 presentation folders. Chief gives me a brief introduction, I lead off, read aloud, all follow. Next, group discussion of salient considerations, orchestrated by the chief. Next, synergistic strategy decisions initially dominated by the chief, gradually taken over by Jim Mairs.

"You're seeing Travino tonight?" Jim asks Big John.

"At his home, right."

"I'd suggest you ask him to draw you a floor plan."

"Will do."

Mairs lights a cigarette, makes eye contact with each of us as he talks. "Six o'clock Thursday morning we'll use the chopper, take some shots of Travino's physical plant and the immediate surrounding area. That afternoon I'll have a man scout the surrounding buildings, get the names and addresses of the companies in closest proximity that could give us strategic positioning. Friday afternoon we'll speak to the appropriate individual in each of the firms, arrange to have sharpshooters admitted to the buildings in gradual stages late Saturday afternoon. Walt, you want help inside Travino's?"

"We'll have six men plus me, Jim. Should be sufficient."

"How you getting in?"

Chief glances at Big John. "When you see this guy tonight, tell him he'll have to admit us himself early Saturday evening. Soon's Little John finds out the timetable, we'll pass it on to him, he'll be expected to let us in at least an hour before the hit. At least an hour. He's gotta shut off the alarm, get us in through the back, show us around. Then he splits. Turns the alarm back on and splits."

"Can't turn the alarm back on again," I tell the chief.

"Why not?"

"Six ultrasonic devices in—"

"Ya tellin' me ya can't handle the *alarm*, Little John?!"

"No, sir, I'm just—"

"After a whole *week* of special *trainin'?*"

"Chief, the man's got six ultrasonic devices in the room with the safe. Plus photoelectric units in four hallways."

"So? Should be a piece a *cake* for ya now."

"Chief, can I point out one small detail?"

"Shoot. That's what we're here for."

"You and the rest of the team, you'll be *inside* the building long before we arrive."

"Fuckin'-A right."

"And I assume you'll position at least two men inside the room with the safe, is that correct?"

"Fuckin'-A well. Flat against the wall by the door."

"Okay. All I'm pointing out, since ultrasonic devices are essentially motion detectors, extremely sensitive ones, here's what you'd have to do. Soon as Travino turns the alarm back on, the two men in that room would have to hold their breath and remain absolutely, positively, totally motionless until I arrive with—"

Chief clears his throat loudly. "Point well taken, Little John. Alarm stays off."

I smile, shrug. "Don't need it anyway. Got the place covered."

"Point well taken. Naturally, you'll have to fake the by-pass operation in front of Kwapniewski and Mize, make it look real good."

Mairs's assistant appears at the door, very attractive young lady with glasses, blonde, mid-twenties, fashionably dressed, bright as they come. "Sorry, it's important. Paul's on the line."

Jim picks up. "Yes, Paul."

Goes like that. Interrupted on the average of once every five minutes. Chief reserves the most important part of the meeting for last, Jerry Grady's strategy for effective press relations. You'd love Jerry, always reminds me of Jack Lemmon for some reason. In the wake of all the media hype generated by the Hotel Champs-Elysées robbery last year, he's worked with the chief to create a new "NYPD Press Package" for all important cases, especially those in which the chief personally participates, and this mother's nothing short of a modern media man's dream: Blue Duo Tang 5-3558 presentation folder with NYPD insignia on the front holds neatly typed Xerox copies of (a) hard-news press release; (b) background information on case development; (c) brief biographical sketches of the accused; (d) quoted statements from appropriate NYPD authorities, in the vernacular whenever possible; (e) quoted statements from victim(s) of the crime, in the vernacular whenever possible; plus (f) variety of 8"-x-10" B/W glossy photographs of the accused, the victim(s), and the arresting officer (if not a detective). In this particular case the package will include a selection of candid shots of the chief escorting Nick and Wally from the scene of the crime, flanked by ESD officers in standard emergency gear. Photos taken and developed by Press Relations. Captions attached. To nobody's surprise, Grady's already started an off-the-record countdown with all segments of the media: Major press conference scheduled for Sunday, April 18, 10:00 A.M., headquarters auditorium.

Chief's delighted. "Timing's perfect. Ali shuffle, rope-a-dope, then a one-two combination that'll knock their socks off. Collar Mize and Kwapniewski late Saturday night, Astoria; press conference Sunday morning. With them out of action, Lopata's got green lights all the way for the hostage caper Monday morning. Collar him at Exeter's apartment, call a press conference at the gallery Monday afternoon, show the diamonds in all their splendor, explain the whole scam. Absolutely first-class investigative work. 'Cops Foil Biggest Gem Heist!' Huh? Still showin' 'em who's *boss*, still kickin' 'em in the *ass*, still bringin' home the *bacon!*'' Words to that effect.

Tonight I drop in the Tatler about 7:45, meet Wally and Nick at the bar, they have a table reserved in back. I'm not wired. Before we sit down I insist on frisking them both in the men's room; Nick's got an attaché case with him tonight, locked. I demand he opens it. He does. Here's Tara's manila envelope filled with her black-and-white glossy blowups, plus two newspaper clippings. Alongside is a smaller manila envelope, legal size, very fat, sealed, stuffed with something that feels like cash. Close the case, hand it back. Now Wally searches me.

Back to the table, order drinks, get down to business. Best defense is attack, so I immediately ask Nick for the promised proof of the big job. He unlocks the attaché, takes out Tara's envelope, removes the two news clippings, places them in front of me.

"Read these first."

I squint in the light of the candlelamp. One on top is from the *News*, April 10, relatively short, no photos, headed: "Biggest Diamond Auction, Apr. 19-20." I've already read this one, but I glance through it anyway, poker face, toss it aside, start on the other. This one's from the *Times*, April 12 (yesterday), which I've also read, longer, no photos, headed: "Heritage to Auction 12 Diamonds Valued at $II.5 Million." Again I go through the motions. Our drinks arrive shortly before I finish.

I toss the article back at Nick. "You gotta be kiddin'."

"No way." He reaches in the envelope, takes out the glossy blowups, places them in front of me. "Keep reading."

Photo on top is the "personal and confidential" memo from Donohoe to Exeter detailing gallery security procedures April 17-20; nice job, looks very official. I take out a cigar as I read, bite off the end, drop it in the ashtray, light up. Following photos are arranged like a story: Schematic of the second floor; interior shot of the second-floor photographic equipment storage room; interior of the fire exit stairway to the third floor; schematic of the third-floor jewelry office;

medium shot of the area with the Mosler safe; closeup of the safe's combination dial; lastly, a schematic (slightly altered) of the jewelry office's alarm system circuitry. I take a drink, puff on the cigar, study this last photo.

"You wanted proof," Wally says. "You got it."

I ignore him, push the photos back to Nick. "I don't know what half this shit's all about, but I assume you got somebody on the inside."

"Believe it. Deep inside. Everything's planned to the smallest detail. We got a deal?"

"Not till I see the chunk up front."

Nick picks up the photos and clippings, puts them back in Tara's envelope, returns it to the attaché, takes out the sealed legal-size envelope, hands it to me.

I tuck it in my inside breast pocket, stick my cigar in the ashtray, stand up, walk to the men's room. Only one guy's inside, taking a leak. I go in a stall, close and lock the door, sit on the john, open the envelope, start counting. First seventy-five are $100 bills, followed by a hundred $50 bills. That's it, $12,500. I laugh out loud at these clowns. Can't help it.

Walk back to them poker faced, toss the envelope on the table, keep going toward the bar area. Nick's after me like a shot.

"Johnny! Wait a minute! Will ya *wait* a minute?!"

Continue through the crowded bar straight toward the front door, Nick in pursuit. As I'm opening the door, he grabs my arm.

"Just hear me out, huh?"

I stop dead, glance at his hand, lift my gaze fast, speak very softly. "Get your fuckin' hand off me."

"Will you just wait and hear me out?"

"Get your fuckin' *hand* off me."

Takes his hand away. I open the door, walk outside, he's right behind me. Cool April night, air smells fresh compared to inside. Walk west on Fifty-seventh toward Park, opposite direction from where Brendan's parked. Nick's right at my side now, Roger Mudd in a rare fluster.

"I *got* the other half." Pats his breast pocket hard. "Y'want it *now*, okay, fine."

I keep walking, don't even glance at him.

"Johnny, for Christ's sake, come *on*. We *always* do it this way. Half now, half before we actually go in."

"Take a fuckin' hike, will ya?"

"Y'want it now, y'*got* it, no problem."

I stop, look at him. "Listen, friend, I don't play *games*. You understand that? I don't play fuckin' *games* with anybody."

"All right. I understand."

"Then understand this, too, asshole. That little game's gonna cost you. You still want to do business, I go back to my original deal. Twenty-five front, plus *half*. Take it or leave it."

"You don't want in on the big one?"

I glance away, then back, Brando style. "Tell you what, asshole. Depends. Depends on how you two clowns check out. Pull another stunt like this, I'm gone."

"Okay, fair enough. Head back?"

I think about it, finally turn, walk slowly. "Another thing. I want to see everything you pull out of that fuckin' safe. Everything. Matter of fact, I'm appointing myself swag man on this. Got any problem with that?"

"No problem. Tell you exactly what to expect right now. Ever see dental gold?"

"Only in my teeth."

Gestures with his fingers. "It comes in little thin squares, looks like Wheat Thins, only thinner. Now, each square is a pennyweight measure, twenty-four grains, one-twentieth of an ounce. Wholesale, costs around five hundred an ounce. Any given day, this guy's got about two hundred and fifty ounces in stock. At five hundred an ounce, that's a hundred and twenty-five grand. Comes six squares to a box. So we're talking in the neighborhood of two hundred and eight boxes, very small boxes, okay? Twelve hundred and fifty squares, total. Our guy says it weighs just about fifteen and a half pounds. Carry it out in a single toolbox."

"Toolbox?"

He smiles, shrugs. "We're going in uniform, Johnny. New York Telephone Company. Uniforms, equipment belts, tool-boxes, we'll even have a truck by Saturday night. Park right out front, we got a key to the front door. First class all the way. Short-wave radio for police calls. Wally's wheel man, he stays in the truck, stays tuned. We got walkie-talkies, anything's happening on the radio, we know it fast."

I pause in front of the Tatler. "You got a key to the front door?"

He hesitates. "Yeah."

"You playing games again?"

"No. What games?"

"You know fuckin' *well* what games, Nick. If you got a key to the front door, you know fuckin' well you can walk right in, the alarm's undoubtedly got a time delay, almost all of 'em do, anything from thirty to forty-five seconds. You can turn the alarm off *yourself*. What the fuck you need *me* for?"

Looks like a kid caught in a lie. "Okay, okay. Calm down and hear me out. You're right. I didn't—we didn't plan to tell you about the key until Saturday night, okay? Reason, sim-ple. We had to check you out, Johnny. We had to, that's the God's honest truth, we never worked with you before. We had to be sure for the big one."

"So you were gonna watch me sweat my balls off to deactivate the alarm systems, then calmly walk in the front door."

Glances down and away. "We should've told you. I admit it. It looked like such an easy job, we figured it'd give us all a tune-up for the big one. Working as a team, y'know?"

"You're a pisser, Nick. Y'know that?"

He looks up, sees me smiling.

"You guys missed your calling."

"I know." He's smiling now too. "Shoulda been con men."

"Woulda made a fortune."

"Want to do it anyway?"

"Why not?"

We go inside laughing. Actually, he's right about needing

THE GREAT DIAMOND ROBBERY

a tune-up, working together as a team. Opening Day in the majors is one thing if you're a rookie with the Cubs. Stepping to the plate in pinstripes at Yankee Stadium in the seventh game of the World Series with the bases loaded and two outs in the last of the ninth is something else again. R-o-l-a-i-d-s.

# 7

SATURDAY NIGHT, APRIL 17, we pull up in front of James A. Travino & Sons just about on schedule, 8:45. We're in a New York Telephone Company van that Wally borrowed from Ma Bell's Westchester regional headquarters lot in White Plains less than an hour ago, and we're wearing authentic New York Telephone Company jumpsuits Wally acquired from the manufacturer several years ago. Our equipment belts and toolboxes were obtained from Nick's present employer, Southern New England Telephone. Inside each toolbox is a Colt .45 automatic, courtesy of Wally. Inside my jumpsuit, stuck in the belt of my jeans, is my service revolver, a Smith & Wesson snubnosed .38 Chief's Special. Inside the chamber of that revolver are five friends with certain characteristics that happen to be frowned upon by NYPD. Matter of fact, these particular characteristics are unauthorized. Not illegal, mind you, just unauthorized by the department. Simple translation: If I got caught carrying these five friends while on duty, I'd be subject to a slap on the wrist—at least several days' suspension without pay.

Why, you ask, after twenty-seven years in the department, do I insist on carrying unauthorized friends? Only one reason comes to mind: I want to stay alive. Typical NYPD-authorized ammo happens to be .38 Special, 158-grain, copper-jacketed soft-points. Sound impressive? I've seen those suckers actually bounce off leather jackets from certain angles. This is no shit, I've seen them immobilized by the linings of sheepskin jackets and heavy topcoats. Reason? Relativey low muzzle velocity (775 feet per second) and muzzle energy (200 footpounds). Now, when you combine this with the fact that your fashionable New York felon today routinely carries automatic weapons like Colt .45s and 9-mm. Parabellums that have magazine capacities of seven and nine rounds respectively and fire "hot-loads" like .45 Auto, 185-grain, silvertip hollow-points (1,000 fps and 411 fp) and 9-mm. Parabellum, 115-grain, silvertip hollow-points (1,475 fps and 556 fp), you begin to see the broad outlines of the problem. That's why I choose my friends with extreme care: Winchester-Western .38 Special Super-X + P, 158-grain, copper-jacketed hollow-points (1,100 fps and 255 fp). Not as hot a hot-load as some I've faced, but just about the hottest my weapon can safely fire. Department particularly frowns on hollow-point friends because they have a distinct tendency to fan out when they hit a party. Fact is, they can stop a party cold. Beauty of 'em, after they've fanned out and stopped the party, even a ballistics expert can't tell they were hollow-points. Bottom line, I get caught in a split-second situation where deadly physical force is being used against me, I want five friends I can depend on to be as deadly and physical as possible. And I make no apologies to anybody.

Back to the van. We park in front near a streetlight, Wally's at the wheel, me in the middle, Nick to my right. This section of Ditmars Boulevard is commercially zoned, mostly small buildings, not much doing, light traffic. Travino's place looks relatively modern in the glow of the streetlight, one story of dirty-white brick, three long rectangular windows situated up near the flat roof. Dark-blue steel door holds a big white sign with bold black letters:

JAMES A. TRAVINO & SONS
Dental Equipment & Supplies
(Wholesale Only)
10257

Nick reaches behind our seat, grabs a Sony short-wave radio
in a black plastic carrying case, pulls up the antenna, switches
it on. It's already set at the police frequency for the area. Lots
of static; all radio cars have long since been ordered out of
the vicinity. He studies the dial, hands it past me to Wally.
Next he leans back to grab the two walkie-talkies, hands them
to me, I pass one on to Wally. Now Nick opens the door,
steps out, I hand him the other walkie-talkie, reach back for
the two heavy equipment belts, hand them out, then two of
the three toolboxes. All this without a word. I get out, close
the door, Nick and I put on our belts, pick up the toolboxes,
and walk calmly to the front door. Cool, quiet Saturday
night, air smells of spring. Now a jet takes off from La
Guardia, roars north toward Rikers Island.

Naturally, we're omitting the whole alarm-bypass routine,
no need to play games that might backfire, my role's swag
man for this one. We reach the cement stoop, I put down my
toolbox, open it, remove a flashlight, glance at the Colt .45
as I close the lid. Nick sticks his duplicate key into the
Medeco deadbolt lock that's surrounded by a big steel plate.
*Click.* He opens the door, I step in, turn on the flashlight,
walk quickly to the time-delay alarm switch on the wall
straight ahead. Lever's in the "off" position, Nick can't see
it, he's closing the door, but I make the appropriate motions
before turning to him. I play the beam of my flashlight on
him as he places his toolbox on the floor, snaps it open,
removes his flashlight first, turns it on, then removes his
.45 carefully. Thumbs the safety off, draws the slide to the
rear, cocking the hammer. Toolbox is loaded with state-of-
the-art electronic locksmith's gear. Closes the lid, stands,
.45 in his right hand, toolbox and flashlight in the other.
Off we go.

We know the layout by heart, of course. Room with the
safe is Travino's office at the end of a short hallway to the
left. Nick leads the way, heels sounding hollow on the linoleum, keeps his beam low. I follow at a distance of maybe
five feet. Office door is open. Needless to say, I know
exactly where our men are positioned: Chief and Nuzhat
Idrissi are in the office, flat against the wall on either side of

the door, both wearing bulletproof vests and holding cocked twenty-gauge Ithaca pump-action shotguns with five rounds of double-O buck each. Other four men are deployed at strategic points in the building, all wearing vests, revolvers drawn: Big John's in the adjoining office, Brendan's covering one of the two back doors, Telfian's got the other, Thalheimer's somewhere near the front door now, ready to block that. There's no way out. Emergency Service Division sharpshooters are poised in windows of surrounding buildings; ESD radio cars with special frequencies are in reasonably close proximity to Wally's van, ready to block him forward and rear. Price of gold is high.

Nick enters the office, plays his beam on the big Chubb floor safe, walks to it quickly. Following the chief's game plan, I stand in the doorway, pull the zip on my jumpsuit, grab my revolver, shine my light on Nick's back.

"Hey, Nick," I say softly.

"Yeah." Doesn't even give me a glance.

"You just bought it."

He turns, sees me in a combat crouch with the gun. Everything happens so fast I can only recall it in flashes: *Blam!—blam!—blam!* Fires at me wildly as he leaps behind Travino's desk, I hit the floor fast; instantly, shotguns explode from both sides of the door: Ka-*BOOM!* Ka-*BOOM!* Pellets ricochet off the desk and walls, I'm shaking, I'm squirming around like everybody else, adrenaline pumping like crazy. Nick's flashlight's rolling on the floor, I've still got mine, I snap it off immediately.

Chief's voice from the far left side: "*Police!* Give *up!* —you're *surrounded!*"

Outside, tires burn and squeal, high-powered rifles sound like machine guns: *Pow!—pow!—pow!—pow!—pow!* Split-second later, screech of tires followed by a sickening heavy crash of steel and glass. Inside, Nick's at it again from the left side of the desk: *Blam!—blam!* Nuzhat, from the right: Ka-*BOOM!* Ka-*BOOM!* Ka-*BOOM!* Whole room shakes, pellets ping off the desk, walls, floor, two men start yelling:

"*Hold* it, I'm *hit! Hold* it!"

"Hold your *fire*, I'm *hit*, I'm *hit!*"

I snap on my flashlight. Heavy smoke fills the room now, I'm choking, my eyes sting, it's hard to see, smell of gunpowder is awful. Nuzhat turns on the overhead lights. Chief's on the floor to the left behind a chair, groaning, legs moving slowly, in obvious pain. I drop the flash, stand up, approach the desk in a crouch, gun in two-hand combat position. Nick's on the floor by the wall, writhing in pain, jumpsuit spattered in blood, .45 by his side. I move in, grab the gun.

It's over. Whole thing lasts maybe fifteen, twenty seconds. I'm standing there coughing in the smoke, legs shaking, heart pounding, gun in each hand, I can't believe what just happened. Happened so fast I didn't even get a chance to fire a shot. Nick's crying now, yelling, "*Help* me, *help* me!" I just stand there and look at him.

Next thing I know, room's full of people, everybody's talking, shouting, the chief's surrounded by Nuzhat, Big John, Brendan, Telfian. Less than a minute later, Thalheimer lets in a whole gang of people, Jim Mairs, Mat Murphy, four paramedics from Emergency Service, even Jerry Grady and a department photographer with a Nikon, strobe, battery-pack, motor-drive, this clown's already shooting—flash-click-whine! —people could be dying here, he's looking to get candid angles of it all. I give Jerry Grady my fisheye glare, he just shrugs.

So many people around the chief, it's hard to see what's going on, but two of the paramedics are working on him, they've got his vest off, they're cutting off his shirt and trousers quickly. Other two paramedics are with Nick, they've got his jumpsuit off, they're cutting off his T-shirt and jeans, he's bleeding badly from his left side and left arm. Place is bedlam. At this point Jim Mairs takes full command, gets on his walkie-talkie, orders an ambulance for Nick and Wally, a paramedic van for the chief, a tow truck for the damaged vehicles, what have you; only calm guy in the place.

Still can't see where the chief's been hit, his upper torso seems okay, thanks to the vest. Now two men bring in a stretcher, remove the two metal poles, slide the canvas part under him, cover him with a sheet and two heavy blankets.

His face is sweating, he's in considerable pain, but he asks to see Nick before going outside. They carry him over—flash-click-whine!—he sits bolt upright, looks Nick in the eye at fairly close range—flash-click-whine!

"Ya dumb fuck," chief says softly. Flash-click-whine!

Hustle him outside, street's alive with ESD officers, cars and trucks parked every which way, doors open, motors running, headlights crisscrossing, emergency lights coloring the whole area, short-wave radios booming. Just fifty yards away, the New York Telephone van's upside-down across the sidewalk, front smashed in, windshield shattered. Wally broadsided an ESD car that also looks totaled. No sign of injured officers, but Wally's lying on his back near the van, looks like he's hurt real bad; a paramedic's down on his knees giving mouth-to-mouth.

ESD van weaves its way through the other vehicles, jumps the curb, pulls up on the sidewalk in front of us. Two paramedics hop out, open the back doors, pull out a rolling stretcher, transfer the chief, roll him inside. One paramedic jumps in back, followed by Mairs, Brendan, Nuzhat and me, we sit on padded benches along the sides.

Away we go, full siren and lights, destination Bellevue Emergency. Elmhurst General's closer, but Mairs insists on Bellevue because of its superior facilities and staff. Mat Murphy, Jerry Grady, and his photographer are in a car directly behind. Route takes us northwest on Ditmars, southwest on Thirty-third, across the Queensboro Bridge, south on FDR Drive, west to First Avenue and Twenty-seventh. Chief's fully conscious, resting on his left side now, facing Nuzhat and Brendan. Young blond-haired paramedic takes his blood-pressure reading, gives him a shot of Demerol for the pain, then sits back between Mairs and me. Five minutes later, curiosity gets the best of me. I motion the paramedic to lean close, speak directly into his ear; he has trouble hearing because of the siren.

I raise my voice. "Where's he hit?"

"Lower right buttock, sir."

"Single slug?"

"Yes, sir."

"Forty-five?"

Kid hesitates. "Don't look like a forty-five, sir, the wound. Too small."

"Shrapnel?"

"Doubt it, sir. Too clean-cut."

"What's it look like?"

Hesitates again, glances at the chief's back. "I don't know, sir, I'm not a doctor."

"How many gunshot wounds you treated?"

"Me?" Shrugs, looks away. "Lots."

"Hundreds?"

"Yeah, easy."

"Take a guess on this one."

Licks his lips, leans closer. "Hate to say it, but it looks to me like a double-aught pellet wound, sir."

I close my eyes tightly, lean back, listen to the rapid staccato whine of the siren. Open my eyes, glance at Nuzhat now. Sits over there next to Brendan, stares straight ahead, reflections of passing headlights move across his face. Adjusts his aviator-style glasses, his trim mustache twitches just perceptibly, he's got his strand of white worry beads in hand, massaging slowly. Tonight he just might have something to worry about, ol' Nuz. Doesn't know it yet, but tonight he just might have been selected by the gods to become a Living Legend in NYPD: THE COP WHO SHOT THE CHIEF IN THE ASS. Ramifications stagger the imagination. Generations of cops as yet unborn might honor his Name and his Achievement. Thousands of cops who always considered him to be "that weird little A-rab from the Nineteenth" might be buying him drinks for years, begging him to tell the story just one more time, every detail, start to finish, "The Night the Duke Pooped Red." Who knows? Within hours, the *News* might start a new cartoon series, "The Arabian Knight"; within days, heavy-weight literary agents might sign him to collaborate with Jimmy Breslin on the shoo-in million-copy Number 1 best seller, *The Chief Who Couldn't Shit Straight;* within months, all the big studios might be bidding for film rights; within a few years, Nuzhat Idrissi might be a household name, winner of a Pulitzer, an Oscar, *Time*'s "Man of the Year," and *Playgirl*'s "Balls of the Decade."

What happens to his NYPD career is another story. You don't bang the chief in the bum and get promoted for it. A more charitable version of the circumstances would trace the blame to ricochet; unlikely, but one suspects this may be the official explanation. Fact is, it's not really Nuzhat's fault, the chief should've known better than to move that far away from his original position in almost total darkness. Violated one of the cardinal rules every raw rookie's taught in the academy: Avoid any possibility of cross fire. One thing I know for sure, catching one of those little suckers in the ass or anywhere else is no laughing matter. To give you an idea of the power involved, a single high-base shell of double-O buck contains nine pellets, each measuring .33 inches in diameter, which means one single shell delivers a payload equivalent to nine .33-caliber slugs fired simultaneously. Chief was only twelve to fifteen feet away when he caught it, so if it's not a ricochet, the thing's in pretty deep. Either case, he needs emergency surgery to dig it out, of course, and that's no piece of cake in any man's league.

Finally roar into the Bellevue ambulance entrance opposite the Municipal Yacht Basin. Bellevue complex actually extends all the way from Twenty-third to Thirty-fourth streets along the East River, includes a Veterans Administration Hospital, Bellevue Hospital, and the NYU Medical Center. Whole area's like home to me, I grew up in this neighborhood, 424 East Twenty-fourth, went to the Epiphany School on East Twenty-second, played stickball in the streets around here.

Pull up in front of the marquee marked EMERGENCY. Paramedic opens the double doors, we pile out. They slide the chief out carefully, we follow the rolling stretcher into a large green corridor; antiseptic odor's very strong. Overweight young intern in a green scrub suit comes over fast, talks to Mairs and the paramedics, now they transfer the chief to a rolling tablelike stretcher. Intern decides to skip the admissions process in the presence of such brass, figures we're a safe bet. Paramedics split, we follow the fat intern as he wheels the chief down a long green hallway; Mairs does all the talking, he's obviously used to this shit. Halfway down the hall we turn right, into another green hall that ends in windowed double doors; as they swing open, first thing we see is a green bulletin board with a clean white sign:

DONATE YOUR BLOOD
DONE SU SANGRE

Emergency Room hasn't changed that much over the years: Big, old, strictly utilitarian, separated into two sections by a thin green wooden partition, men left, broads right. High white ceiling holds ten very strong lights on long poles, five over each section, thick plaster walls have a fresh coat of green, white tile floor's sparkling clean. Sixteen modern hospital beds in here, eight to a side, each separated by a stainless-steel table, a wall-model Baumanometer, and an oxygen tank. Above each bed is a rectangular metal rod with a long pink draw-curtain. East end of the room, a raised platform overlooks both sections, has five or six people at desks with typewriters and telephones.

Intern wheels the chief to the left of the partition; first five beds are occupied, pink curtains drawn, dark silhouettes inside. Lots of people in motion here—doctors, interns, nurses, attendants—hustling to and from occupied beds. We stop in front of the sixth bed in the row, intern strips back the covers, motions to an attendant who helps him transfer the chief. We all stand back now, even Mairs. Two young nurses come over quickly, white dresses and caps, sensible white shoes. Intern gives them orders in a flat Bronx monotone:

"Doris, type and cross-match; Nan, have Dr. Samson paged, tell Scott to get a transfusion pole set up here, clean him up, huh?"

Girls split, intern goes to the Baumanometer, a blood pressure device. Straps the pressure-cuff around the chief's arm, pumps fast on the rubber bulb, watches the indicator on the wall that has a range from 0 to 300.

"What's normal?" the chief asks softly.

Looks at him like he's a moron. "Depends. One-twenty over eighty." Same flat Bronx monotone, never changes.

Now I see this intern up close, feel a little sorry for the kid. Poor devil's teeth are a grotesque glitter of silver braces straining to correct an occlusion that'd make simple buckteeth a blessing, looks like an expensive tangle of barbwire. Surprised he's overweight; surprised he can jam a forkful of anything through the wireworks. Probably sucks lots of spaghetti. Add insult to injury, kid's got a healthy crop of mean red zits on his chin and forehead, he's obviously been squeezing 'em out tonight. Hope he used surgical gloves; like to think the chief's in good hands here.

Nurse named Doris returns with equipment on a tray. Not unattractive brunette, late twenties, dark eyes. Swabs the chief's right arm, carefully inserts a needle, draws blood into a syringe.

Chief's eyes bulge. "Whaddaya *doin*', lady?"

"Have to get your blood type, sir."

"Have to get—? I'm type *A-positive!*"

"Why didn't you say so?"

"Why didn't—? Why didn't ya *ask?!*"

"I'm not a doctor, sir."

Chief groans, she swabs his arm again, sticks on a small bandage, leaves quickly. Loudspeaker comes on: "Dr. Chow, six twenty-two; Dr. Chow, six twenty-two. Dr. Samson, E.R. Dr. Samson, E.R." Seconds later, nurse named Nan returns pushing an aluminum rolling table with stacks of surgical gauze, a pan, several bottles. She's a brunette too, short hair, hazel eyes behind oversized glasses. Starts to pull back the blankets; chief clutches them at his waist.

"Whaddaya *doin*', lady?"

"I've been ordered to clean you up, sir."

Chief groans, sits up painfully. "Doc, for Christ's sake, what's goin' *on* here?"

"Standard preoperative procedure."

"Yeah, look, Doc, all I ask is a little—I'd like a little bit of dignity here, huh?"

Intern shrugs. "Sure. I'll draw the curtain."

Chief glances at us now, manages a weak left-sided molar-shower. "Look, Doc, huh? Can't ya get a *male* nurse to do this—*cleanin'* stuff?"

"Sorry, we don't have one on duty." Intern motions us to step back, starts to draw the pink curtain around the bed.

"Then *you* do it!" chief snaps.

"I'm not a nurse, sir, that's not my job here."

"Not your *job?!* What's your name, mister?"

Same flat Bronx monotone, never changes an octave: "My name is Dr. Delilah, sir. Dr. Donald T. Delilah. That's D-e-l-i-l-a-h."

"Don't get smart with *me*, mister! Who's your superior?"

"Dr. Stephen A. Samson, he's the resident surgeon on this shift here, he'll be here any minute."

Chief hesitates, narrows his eyes. "Samson and—*Delilah?* You puttin' me *on*, mister?"

Suddenly, the monotone vanishes with an angry flash of barbwire: "No, I'm *not* putting you on—mister! Those happen to be our *names*, our *real* names, and I'm sick of the adolescent connotations and innuendoes and dumb *jokes!*"

"All right, Doc, don't get—don't get *touchy* now, huh? All I asked—"

"For your information, *mister*, I've been trying to get trans*ferred* from this shift for three solid *months* now! To no avail, of course, because the juvenile bitches in Personnel, who put us together purposely in the *first* place, break *up* every time they hear the *names!*"

"All right, Doc, I get your—"

"Switchboard operators around here, they even have us *paged* together when they get *bored:* 'Doctors *Sam*son and De*lil*ah, Doctors *Sam*son and De*lil*ah'—that's the level of men*tal*ity I have to deal with in this day-care center!"

Chief lifts his hand in a calming gesture. "Okay, Doc, point well taken, I didn't—"

"Yeah, sure. Now *you* come in here, big macho chief of detectives with all your henchmen, throw your weight around, yell at the nurses here, demand to be washed by a *male*, take a cheap shot at my name, right? Let me tell *you* something, mister, I've *had* it with this shit!" Now he's moving around, pulling the curtains like a madman.

We're standing there, Brendan, Nuzhat, Maris, and me, we don't know to laugh or bark at this guy. Maybe he escaped from the psychiatric ward, they got a big one here, what do we know?

"You have to leave now," he tells us. "There's a waiting room just down the hall or you can go in the cafeteria."

"One minute." Mairs steps behind the curtain, becomes a dark silhouette next to the chief's. "Anything you need?"

"Just to get it over with."

"Want me to call your wife?"

"No. Later, huh?"

"Mat and Jerry should be here any minute, I'll handle it."

"Good man."

"We'll be in the cafeteria. We'll be around all night."

"No, Jim. You guys go on home, I'll be—"

"No way. Come on, lie back now, try and relax, huh? We'll be here. Anything you need, just get word to us."

Chief's silhouette lies back slowly. "Will do, buddy. Thanks."

Jim steps out, speaks to the intern. "Any idea when they'll operate?"

Kid looks at his watch, then glances at the double doors. A tall man with a trim beard has just entered the room, walks toward us quickly in a green scrub suit. Distinguished-looking guy, late forties.

"Here's Samson now," kid tells us.

"What've we got?" Samson asks softly.

"Gunshot, lower right buttock, he's stable, vital signs good."

They both go behind the curtain, Samson greets the chief, turns him over, takes a look. We follow Mairs out through the double doors, down the green hall, left down another hall into the big corridor near the ambulance entrance. Mat, Jerry, and the photographer are sitting on benches outside the Admissions Office. Jerry's filling out the chief's admission and insurance forms on a clipboard. We bring them up to date on what's happening, wait for Jerry to complete the forms and hand them in, then we all go to the cafeteria.

I figure it's only fair to brief Nuzhat on the physiological details of this thing so it won't come as a shock after the operation, so I take him aside at a table away from the others, explain what the paramedic told me in the van.

"Oh, boy," he says quietly.

"Remember, it's only a guess, Nuz."

"Ohboyohboy." It's really sinking in now.

"Could be a ricochet, y'know?"

Face is turning white. "Oh, boy." Adjusts his glasses, gets out his worry beads, starts massaging fast.

"Only a guess. Won't know till they dig it out."

"Ohboyohboyohboy."

"Important thing is, it wasn't your fault."

Drops of sweat on his forehead now. Looks at me with eyes like E.T. "John. John, if this is true what the man said, then what I have done, actually, I have shot the chief in his ass, John."

I stir my coffee, watch it whirl. "Accidentally. But yeah."

Mutters something in Arabic, then: "If this is true, my career, John. My career is ruined. My career is—how do you say it?"

"Shot in the—? No way, Nuz. Not true at all."

"Shot in the ass, John. After twenty-four years." Eyes well up now, chin trembles, sniffles turn to stifled sobs, removes his glasses, head goes down on the table, all like that. Me, I'm sitting there, I don't know what to do for this guy, hate to see a grown man cry, particularly an Arab. Glance over at the others, they're pretending not to look, but there's a sudden hush over there, y'know? Reach in my pocket, pull out a ratty handkerchief, poke it at his hand. Nuz grabs it like a drowning man, sits up in a hunch, wipes his cheeks, turns around, blows his nose—wham-*bam!* Sniffs, keeps his back turned, swings an arm around, holds out the wet snotrag. Must be an old Arab custom, I don't know. I tell him it's okay, he can keep it, I'm all heart tonight.

Two coffees and a stale ham-and-cheese sandwich later, Dr. Samson walks in the cafeteria in his scrub suit and cap, gives us the thumbs-up sign before he goes over to draw his coffee; in deference to other late diners, we give him a subdued round of applause. We're all at one big table now, we pull up a chair for him at the head. Comes over smiling but obviously tired. Beard is dark and trim, voice is soft and reassuring:

"Gentlemen, Chief Vadney's in post-op now, he's conscious, he's stable. I'm having him admitted to a private room, I want him under observation for at least twenty-four hours. It was a relatively simple operation, no complications." Reaches in his pocket, pulls out a double-O pellet, places it on the table. "I removed this shotgun pellet"—lowers his voice—"from his lower right buttock. I—I've spoken to the chief about this projectile. I'm aware of the potential problems this might present."

Silence. All seven officers lean forward. All eyes are fixed on the gleaming double-O .33-caliber pellet.

Dr. Samson glances left and right, speaks just above a whisper: "As I told the chief, I'm willing to cooperate with you people as much as I can within the law. By that I mean, specifically, my post-op report must be accurate as to the type of projectile removed. However, Chief Vadney tells me there's a press conference scheduled for ten o'clock tomorrow morning. Incidentally, before I forget it, he asked me to tell Detective Jerry Grady—which one of you is—?"

Grady lifts a forefinger, clears his throat.

"He asked me to tell you to reschedule the press conference. It's to be held here instead of at headquarters. I'll reserve one of the large conference rooms."

"Same time?" Grady asks.

"Yes, ten o'clock tomorrow morning. Barring complications in Chief Vadney's condition, he'll certainly be able to attend." Looks at the pellet again, frowns, keeps his voice very low. "But to get back to what I was saying. Although my post-op report must be completely accurate relative to type, caliber, and location of projectile removed, your press release—and my own statement to the press—can naturally be worded in such a manner as to—well, soften the counterproductive impact implicit in revealing the actual weapon used, and by whom, as well as the specific—Chief Vadney was emphatic about this—the specific location of the wound itself."

Silence again. All eyes are on the pellet.

Grady loosens his tie, comes up with his innocent Jack Lemmon grin. "Dr. Samson, could you give me some idea of how you expect to, uh, *word* the statement in question?"

"Carefully."

Gets a quick smile from Grady. "I know, but the thing is, I have to prepare the whole press package tonight."

Samson glances at his watch. "I'll give you a draft of my own statement within the hour."

"Excellent. Appreciate it."

Jim Mairs clears his throat. "Now that we have our own affairs in order, gentlemen, I have some other news. Jerry, I'll give you an update on this, it's still tentative. As you know, Kwapniewski and Mize were rushed to the nearest hospital in Queens, Elmhurst General, as their conditions were far more serious. Over the past hour, I've called the Emergency Room at Elmhurst four times, spoke to both Telfian and Thalheimer at some length. At this point, both suspects are listed as critical. Kwapniewski suffered a fractured skull and multiple internal injuries. Mize had a total of eight double-aught pellets removed from his left side and left arm. Both are now in the Intensive Care Unit. Attending physicians are giving us half-hourly reports. Jerry, I'll give you the number, you can get updates through the night."

"Question," Jerry says. "Sorry, but for the record, for the release, I need to know which detective actually shot Mize, if we know."

Mairs glances at Nuzhat, then me. "Nominations?"

I laugh softly. "And the winner is . . .?"

"Chief *Vadney*," Nuzhat says with absolute conviction. "No question about it, John and me were eyewitnesses. Furthermore, Jerry, I would like to go on record in the press release as saying that never in my twenty-four years in the department have I personally witnessed such—*courage*. You may quote me on that. Courage far above and beyond the call of duty. Putting his own *life* on the line to protect his fellow officers. Please, I would like you to quote me on that, Jerry. I will—in fact, I'll be only too glad to put it in writing for you."

Grady decides to write it down on the spot. So excited his

hand is shaking, hasn't had a statement this hot in years. I light up a cigar, lean back, glance at Nuzhat as he repeats the words slowly, massaging his worry beads under the table. Reminds me of an old Arab proverb: "Praise is music even to the ears of a deaf man."

# 8

PRESS CONFERENCE gets off to a noisy start. First thing, room's not big enough to comfortably—or uncomfortably—accommodate all the "legitimate" boys and girls of the media, to say nothing of the pervasive *paparazzi*. Television crews from CBS, NBC, ABC, CNN start jockeying for territorial imperatives as early as 9:15 A.M. and by 9:45 we have a real grunt-and-fart mass-media event here with isolated skirmishes among TV crews, hometown reporter-photographer teams from the *Times*, the *News*, the *Post*, the *Voice*, *Newsday*, *Time*, *Newsweek*, *U.S. News*, AP, UPI, and correspondents from at least a dozen out-of-town papers, Boston to L.A., Chicago to Miami. By 9:55 Grady's going nuts, he calculates we're trying to cram roughly fifty-five angry people into a conference room with exactly twenty-eight chairs and a lectern. Noise level is totally unbelievable, TV lights are rapidly turning the place into an oven, air in here is strictly pee-you, tempers are dangerously close to ignition. Although Grady seriously underestimated our wounded chief's drawing power on this obviously slow-news Sunday, there's one significant saving grace: His NYPD Press Package is a minor masterpiece of modern mass-media management. Also, we have enough copies to go around.

Of course, Grady was up all night pulling this shit together, ditto his intrepid photographer. Comprehensive? Each blue Duo Tang 5-3558 presentation folder, with NYPD insignia on the front, is at least one inch thick with neatly typed Xerox copies of everything your modern newsperson could unreasonably request: Obligatory hard-news press release; background intelligence on case development; brief biographical sketches of Mize and Kwapniewski; quoted statements from Jim Mairs and the chief; quoted statements from James A. Travino; plus a generous variety of 8"-x-10" B/W glossy photos: Chief on the floor of Travino's office, still in his bullet-proof vest, shotgun nearby; Mise on the floor in the corner, jumpsuit splattered with blood; chief sitting up in his stretcher exchanging pleasantries with Mize ("Ya dumb fuck"); Kwapniewski getting mouth-to-mouth from a paramedic on the street, upside-down telephone van in background; formal portrait shot of the chief, brows knitted slightly, left-sided grin, swear to Christ it looks like Duke Wayne impersonating him; formal mug shots of Wally and Nick, take away the numbers and you got Mudd and Brokaw on a bummer.

Get a load of the opening-page hard-news release, typed on official NYPD Press Relations stationery with Grady's personal IBM Correcting Selectric III:

**POLICE DEPARTMENT**
NEW YORK, N. Y. 10013

FOR IMMEDIATE RELEASE

CONTACT: DET. JERRY GRADY

PRESS RELATIONS
(212) 477-9777

CHIEF VADNEY WOUNDED IN QUEENS SHOOTOUT

NEW YORK, April 18—Chief of Detectives Walter Vadney, 52, was shot and wounded last night in a

dramatic gun battle with suspects alleged to be
burglarizing $125,000 in dental gold from a
dental equipment and supply company in the
Astoria section of Queens.

Chief Vadney, a 29-year veteran of NYPD, was
rushed to Bellevue Hospital where he underwent
emergency surger last night. A hospital
spokesman listed his condition as stable this
morning.

The two burglary suspects, both convicted felons,
were identified by police as Nicholas Mize, 37, of
New Canaan, CT, and Wally Kwapniewski, 32, of
Jackson Heights, Queens. Both sustained serious
injuries and received emergency surgery at
Elmhurst General Hospital, Queens, last night.

Hospital authorities revealed that Mize had eight
shotgun pellets removed from his upper left torso
and left arm; he was listed in critical condition this
morning. Kwapniewski, said by police to be the
driver of the getaway vehicle, a New York
Telephone Co. van allegedly stolen last night,
suffered a fractured skull and multiple internal
injuries when he reportedly collided with a police
Emergency Service vehicle in attempting to escape.
His condition was also listed as critical.

Deputy Chief of Detectives Mat Murphy stated
that Mize and Kwapniewski had been the
subjects of an intensive undercover investigation
for several weeks prior to the attempted
burglary.

According to Murphy, a team of detectives led by

Vadney was concealed in the office of the
dental-supply firm, James A. Travino & Sons,
10257 Ditmars Blvd., Queens, when Mize entered
the building illegally at approximately 8:45 last
night. Mize was reportedly wearing the uniform
of a New York Telephone Co. repairman; his
partner Kwapniewski waited in the stolen van
outside, Murphy said. Emergency Service Division
police were secreted in surrounding buildings
and streets to block all possible escape routes.

When confronted by Vadney and other detectives
inside, Mize opened fire with a .45-caliber
automatic pistol, Murphy said. Fire was returned
by Vadney and Detective Nuzhat Idrissi, 49, both
armed with shotguns. A total of ten shots were
exchanged in the battle, all in virtual darkness,
Murphy stated.

Although wounded in the upper right thigh and
bleeding profusely, Vadney charged Mize and
wounded him to end the wild melee, Murphy said.
No other detectives were injured.

Detective Idrissi, who was directly involved in
the shooting, said later about Vadney's actions:
"Never in my 24 years in the department have I
personally witnessed such courage."

Police Commissioner William B. Reilly, reached at
home late last night, stated that "under the
extraordinary circumstances, and pending the
official departmental investigation, Chief Vadney
would certainly appear to qualify as a candidate for

the NYPD Combat Medal," one of the highest
citations awarded by the department.

Dr. Stephen A. Samson, the resident surgeon at
Bellevue who operated on Vadney, defined the
injury as "a relatively deep wound in the lower
right region of the gluteus maximus muscles
above the iliotibial tract of the right thigh." Dr.
Samson added that the projectile had not touched
the femur bone; he expected Vadney to be
discharged from the hospital tonight or Monday
morning.

Part about the Combat Medal, that's a nifty little story in
itself, I ask Grady about that. Says it was the chief's idea,
thought the timing might be right on the money. He's so
right. Grady calls Commissioner Reilly two-fifteen this morning. Two-fifteen Sunday morning! Reilly's been out to some
chichi Irish bash, he's in bed, he's half asleep, he's still got
half a load on. Grady tape records the conversation, of course,
tells him the whole story, lays it on real thick, quotes Nuzhat
and all, roll up your pants. Now he starts offering helpful
suggestions: "Commissioner, don't you think—I mean, under the extraordinary circumstances, and pending the official
departmental investigation, don't you agree with all the detectives at the scene that Chief Vadney would certainly qualify
as a candidate for the Combat Medal?" Reilly's voice sounds
like it's coming from an open grave, full moon, New Year's
Eve: "Wha?" Grady goes, "All the detectives at the scene
agree he'd certainly qualify as a candidate, sir." Pause.
Reilly: "Yeah? Huh." Pause. Grady: "You agree with the
consensus opinion, sir?" Pause. Reilly: "Huh? Yeah." Pause.
"Zzzzzz." Click. That's how the chief gets nominated for
the-Combat Medal.

Ten o'clock sharp Grady stands behind the lectern in the

hot glare of the TV lights, leans toward the tangle of microphones taped before him, Jack Lemmon with bloodshot eyes: "Ladies and gentlemen," he lies. Noise level drops maybe half an octave, not bad. "Ladies and gentlemen, while you get readings on lights and voice levels here, I've got a brief introductory statement." Chaos becomes merely bedlam, I'm impressed: Whir-clack-buzz-beep-wham-flash-click-whine!—*"Down in front!"*—*"Speed!"*—*"Rolling!"*—*"DOWN IN FRONT!"*

Grady reads from a prepared statement now, voice hushed for an appropriate reaction: "In a now famous interview published in the *New Yorker*, November, nineteen twenty-nine, a young writer named Ernest Hemingway defined 'guts' in three words: 'Grace under pressure.' Last night over in Queens, in the darkened office of a dental-supply firm, in the heat of a close-range gunfight, Chief of Detectives Walter Vadney gave us all a superb practical example of exactly what 'grace under pressure' is all about. As chief, he could easily have delegated the responsibilities of front-line high-risk duty to others—younger, stronger men, specially trained for unusually hazardous police procedures. Chief Vadney didn't choose to do that. In twenty-nine years with the department, he's never chosen the easy way. Last night, in the split-seconds of initial gunfire, realizing officers under his command were in imminent danger, he elected to personally charge rather than take cover, wounded the gunman, and ended a conflict that could've resulted in many injuries, even fatalities. As we all know, he paid a price for that courage, a painful gunshot wound in the thigh. Chief Vadney considers it a small price to pay. He told me afterward, quote: Y'know, Jerry, sometimes a cop earns his week's salary in a couple of seconds, end quote. Ladies and gentlemen, I suggest to you that he earned far more than that last night. By his instantaneous, unselfish action, he earned not only the gratitude and respect of his fellow officers, but the gratitude and respect of everyone who resides or works in this city." Grady turns to his right, signals to a uniformed officer at the door, keeps his voice low: "Ladies and gentlemen, Chief of Detectives Walter Vadney."

All cameras and eyes focus on the door. Chief's pushed in slowly in a wheelchair by Dr. Samson. Boom, strobes flash like disco beats, motor-drives whine, videotapes whir. Brendan and me, we're way in back against the wall, he nudges me, starts to applaud, I join in automatically. Mairs, Idrissi, Telfian, Thalheimer, Grady, Big John, all start applauding. Loudly. Within seconds, the boys and girls of the press feel somehow obliged to join in. Suddenly, everybody's standing, clapping, yelling, even whistling, I can't believe this shit, I've never seen media people lose their detachment like this. Lasts maybe eight, ten seconds, then it's over abruptly. Nobody even has to shout "Down in front," they all squat fast except for the TV cameramen in back.

Any doubts about the chief's condition are wiped away when he stands up at the lectern, all six-foot-three, 175 pounds, towers over Grady and Samson. Sky-blue eyes narrow in the glare, left brow arches momentarily, then his forehead flattens and both ears jerk back as the left-sided grin takes twenty years off his face. Wears a dark-blue bathrobe over his hospital gown, plastic ID bracelet on his right wrist. Voice has just the right touch of gravel:

"Apologies for the wheelchair, ladies and gentlemen, hospital rules, y'know. Like you to meet Dr. Stephen A. Samson, the surgeon who performed the operation. Did a great job. He'll—I'm sure he'll be glad to answer any questions you have in a few minutes. All I've got to say, really, I feel okay this morning, I—I'm a little sore, but I feel okay, I'm anxious to get back to work. They're letting me out of here at noon today, so I'm—my wife and I are real pleased about that. Doc here, he wants me to—" he laughs softly, glances at Samson. "He wants me to use a *cane* for a coupla days, I—"

Gets a polite laugh.

"Guess I'll have to do what I'm told—till I get outa here, at least." Knits his brows, looks at the open door. "Ladies and gentlemen, like you to meet somebody else this morning. Somebody who keeps a very low profile, but who's always there behind the scenes: My wife Samantha."

Loud spontaneous applause as Samantha Vadney moves

through the crowd around the door, relatively short, heavyset blonde in a basic-black high-necked dress with a sleeveless white tunic. Gets up to the lectern, chief leans over, gives her a hug—flash-click-whine!—*"Hold it!"* Gives her a kiss— *"Hold that!"*—flash-click-whine!—*"Chief, one more!"* flash-click-whine!

Now Samantha stands there demurely behind the chief as he starts the question-and-answer session. Predictable questions, except for one guy from the *News* who asks nonchalantly: "Chief, could you tell us in layman's terms exactly *where* you were hit?" Samantha stiffens, Samson coughs, Grady looks like he squirted. Chief narrows his eyes, thinks on it, says slowly and deliberately: "The northeast corner of Mr. Travino's office, in relatively close proximity to a high-backed leather chair, approximately nine feet from the man's desk." Goes on to the next question fast. Samantha lights a cigarette at this point, nicely manicured nails, elegant gold lighter. Attractive lady, mid-forties, high forehead, bright eyes, strong chin, mouth I can only describe as sensuous. Obviously endowed with an extraordinary amount of "grace under pressure," or an unlimited supply of Valium, to live with a complicated, perfectionistic, workaholic yahoo like the chief all these years. Fact is, she was a policewoman when they first met at the old Police Academy shooting range some twenty-three years ago. Story goes, first date, he shows up at her apartment in his newest, most expensive, flashiest sports clothes, confidence personified, flowers in hand. Samantha opens the door, looks him up and down slowly, says, "Who picked out your wardrobe, Helen Keller?" Takes her to a posh restaurant, mulls over the question that night, comes in to work next morning, grabs one of the best-dressed detectives, says, "Who the fuck's Helen Keller?"

That afternoon Brendan and I drive the chief to Exeter's apartment so he can finally reveal the hostage plan and detail our strategy for collaring Lopata. One Sutton Place South is twelve stories of ultraconservative aristocratic opulence overlooking the East River at Fifty-third. Three graceful archways enclose the semicircular entrance drive, cement façade contin-

ues ceremoniously for two floors, gives way to dignified gray
brick for the remaining ten. Fifteen small ornamental balconies are spread across the upper three stories; penthouses are
not visible from the street. Only thirty-four apartments in this
block-long edifice, but they range from ten to fourteen rooms
each, all co-op of course, always have been. My opinion, for
what it's worth, of all the genuine haut monde addresses in
Manhattan, and there are plenty, One Sutton Place South is in
a class by itself. Today, like the hidden castles of New
Canaan, you don't buy into this joint, you inherit these
suckers. We're not talking apartments here, we're talking
about thirty-four family traditions, heirlooms, from *pied-à-
terre* to penthouse, they simply transcend the inherent vul-
garity of—dare I say it?—money. Tell you what, if the old
money of New Canaan is Silent, the ancient money of One
Sutton Place South is positively Ultrasonic. To put it another
way, George Steinbrenner's said to have confided to other
nouveau millionaires he'd kiss Reggie Jackson's ass, Times
Square, high noon, to get in this place. Forget it, George.

We pull in under the arches, distinguished silver-haired
doorman in banker's gray uniform and spotless white gloves
waits for us on the narrow sidewalk, opens our back door
first. Chief struggles out, using his cane.

"Good afternoon, gentlemen."

"Afternoon. Name's Vadney, we have—"

"Yes, sir, Mr. Exeter's expecting you, please go right in."

Chief leads the way, no grunts or groans, but it's obvious
he needs the cane. Doorman opens the heavy glass door, tips
his cap smartly. Distinguished silver-haired man in banker's
gray uniform and spotless white gloves greets us at the mahogany reception desk.

"Good afternoon, gentlemen."

"Afternoon. Name's Vadney, we—"

"Yes, sir, Mr. Exeter's expecting you, penthouse B. The
elevator's straight down the hall to your right."

Talk about class lobbies? Straight ahead, huge Windex-
clean glass doors span the rear, revealing an enormous sun-
dappled rectangular terrace, putting-green quality, bordered
to the north and south by wings of the building, to the east by

the river beyond a fence. Turn right, one of two mahogany-paneled elevators is waiting with a distinguished silver-haired operator in banker's gray uniform and spotless white gloves.

"Good afternoon, gentlemen."

"Afternoon. Name's—"

"Yes, sir, Mr. Exeter's expecting you, please step in."

Up we go, almost soundlessly, unobtrusive TV camera observing from a high neutral corner. Imagine writing annual Christmas checks for three shifts of distinguished silver-haired farts in banker's gray uniforms and spotless white gloves? Not to mention the distinguished super, crews of maintenance men, three shifts of security guards, all like that? All these distinguished guys finish shifts, must be a traffic jam outside with chauffered limos waiting to take them to their own humble abodes on Park and Fifth. Home, James, they're expecting me.

Elevator has front and rear doors, we exit the rear for PH-B, please watch your step. Plush red-carpeted hallway looks like a scale model of the long hall to his office at the gallery, only more personal: Dark paneled walls with twelve elaborately framed oil-painted portraits of family members, six to a side, all men, not even a token broad. Puritans with scowling puritanical expressions, bushy sideburns, George Washington-type collars and coats. Each frame holds a gold or brass nameplate below with inscriptions like: ELIHU WHITNEY EXETER IV, 1607-1648; WILBUR HAMILTON EXETER, 1629-1671; GRANVILLE ELIOT EXETER, 1654-1697; to name the elders. Fact is, they're all old-looking gents, although most passed on at early ages, typical for that century. As the chief rings the chimes, which actually sound like ancient church bells, I study the faces of some of these forefathers. Absolutely amazing resemblance to our own Phillip S. Exeter: Matted graying hair, ashen faces somewhat bloated at the jowls, dominated by bulging eyes that seem to hold a remarkably similar sparkle, as if collectively protecting a centuries-old private family joke, despite the uniformly disdainful down-turned lips. Wonder what the private family joke might be? At this level of society, it must be juicy. Would it be even remotely possible that, under the layers of exquisite brush strokes applied by cosmeticians at spas like Yale and the Hamptons and the Cape and even the Cap d'Antibes, the real faces were those of roughneck robber barons, rumrunners, coke smugglers, cool fantastic hustlers? Or much worse? Kinky weirdos in WASP clothing? Remember that shock-cut to the canvas in *The Picture of Dorian Gray?*

Church bells toll solemnly, peephole goes *pffft,* two Medeco deadbolts go *click-click,* mahogany-paneled door opens slowly. Exeter stands there like a little holographic projection of his ancestors in modern sailing attire: Wrinkled blue blazer with the insignia of the Southampton Yacht Club, white button-down Brooks, foulard ascot pulled a fraction down and away from the collar, white trousers, white deck shoes. Since their last meeting at the gallery, there's no love lost between Exeter and the chief, so we're deprived of the sparkle-bulge. Instead, an appropriate swordfish stare. Valium voice unchanged:

"Good afternoon, gentlemen."

"Afternoon." Chief glances at his stainless-steel Omega Astronaut Moon Watch. "Think we're right on the button, one-thirty."

Exeter glances at his eighteen-karat-gold Rolex Submariner Date Oyster with matching bracelet, pressure-proof to 660 feet. "Please come in, hope this won't take long, I have a sail at three."

Chief hobbles in. "Half an hour tops."

"What happened to your, uh, your leg?"

"Little skirmish last night, tell you about it later."

We follow him through the entry hall into a sunken mahogany-paneled living room with décor somewhat similar to his office: Aubusson carpets, antique furniture, display cabinets filled with art objects, two walls of floor-to-ceiling books, Coromandel screen in one corner, grandfather clock in another, gold and enamel Fabergé knickknacks on the mantel of a black marble fireplace, mirrors, chandeliers, Steinway grand piano near the picture window facing east. Oil paintings? Name an artist.

Now we're led through glass doors onto a huge patio that occupies the entire south side of the roof. Garden furniture,

statuettes, exotic plants, flowers, even small trees. Patio actually surrounds the place and this is a true penthouse, a
relatively large one-story "house" on the roof of the building. Penthouse A, separated by a black wrought-iron fence to
the north, takes up the remainder of the roof. Owing to the
fact we're only atop the twelfth floor, south and west vistas
are blocked by skyscrapers, but the east exposure is wide
open, of course, overlooking the river, the Queensboro Bridge,
all of Welfare Island, and much of Queens. Sunny Sunday
afternoon, I'd like to walk around for a better look, but
Exeter's all business, sits us in blue deck chairs in the shade
of the blue-and-white striped awning near the glass doors.

"I'll give you gentlemen an update first," he says quietly.
"Yesterday afternoon the eleven diamonds from, uh, from
Alistair Rodger Rare Jewels arrived at the gallery on schedule. They were immediately—Mr. Henry Sullivan, vice-
president of our jewelry department, immediately secured
them in the Diebold safe, fourth-floor accounting office. Two
armed guards from Paul T. Reilly Associates are on duty
in 'round-the-clock shifts, of course. This morning, Mr. Sullivan called to advise that the, uh, the North Star Diamond
departed London Heathrow on schedule, eleven A.M. London
time, Pan Am flight one-oh-one, accompanied by two British, uh, two British security guards. ETA Kennedy, one
thirty-five P.M. New York time." Glances at his watch. "Matter of fact, just several minutes from now, if it's on time.
Transportation from JFK to the, uh, to the gallery via Brinks,
ETA approximately two forty-five. Sullivan will of course be
there to secure it in the Diebold safe, then call me at the club
before we set sail at three."

Chief nods, narrows his eyes to the southeast. "Mr. Exeter, you recall our meeting in your office about—oh, three
weeks ago?"

"Yes, indeed."

"Okay. Now, as you recall—"

"Yes, indeed, I daresay I could scarcely forget it, Chief,
uh, Chief Vadney. Monday, March twenty-nine, to be precise. Sorry, go ahead."

"As you recall, at that time I outlined a basic strategy

plan. Decoy with a double-fail-safe backup. Remember that?"

"Yes, indeed."

"Uh-huh. Well, that's all changed now."

Exeter hesitates, blinks rapidly, finally treats us to at least the hint of a possible sparkle-bulge to come. Voice drops ominously low: "That's . . . all—"

"Yeah."

" . . . changed . . . now?"

"Yeah. Afraid so."

In the pause, I take out a cigar, I want to enjoy this. "Uh, excuse me, Mr. Exeter, mind if I smoke?"

Looks at me like he's suddenly aware I'm here. "What?"

"Mind if I smoke?"

"No. No, go right ahead."

I glance around. "Happen to have an ashtray?"

Swordfish eye. "Detective—uh—?"

"Rawlings. John Rawlings."

"Detective Rawlings, sir. Not that it matters in the slightest, but I'm sure you're at least marginally aware by now, as a trained observer, that I—discourage smoking in my presence. Ergo, the absence of ashtrays, particularly—"

"Sorry, I didn't—"

"—indoors, confined to a small area where I have no recourse, as it were, to avoid breathing contaminated air."

"Rawlings," the chief snaps. "Put it away, huh?"

"However, Detective Rawlings, not to worry, please. As my, uh, as my wife assiduously reminds me, perhaps no one on earth is more of a boor about smoking than a reformed smoker, which I have the, uh, the shabby honor of being."

"Rawlings, *stow* it, will ya!"

Exeter lifts his hand in solemn benediction. "No-no, I insist. Since we're outside, please do go ahead."

I look at him, the cigar, the chief. "No, I really don't—"

"I insist. I absolutely insist. Flick your, uh, your ashes on the tiles, it's quite all right, it just—blows away."

I'm aware of the chief's condescending stare, reformed smoker that he is. Brendan to the rescue, he whips out his own Dutch Masters panetela, bites off the end, lights up, casual as you please. Heat's off now, I follow his lead.

Chief shifts painfully. "As I was saying, Mr. Exeter, I'm afraid that initial strategy had to be changed. Now, subsequent to that meeting in your office. The following Friday, I believe, Miss Alvarado delivered the intelligence photographs to Mize and Kwapniewski, as you know. Everything they asked for and more, including the confidential security memo. They visited the gallery that afternoon, they checked things out, told her it was a go. At that point in time, we figured we had the hook in pretty good. Following Monday, Rawlings and Thomas received a call from Miss Alvarado, she had to see them immediately. Called in sick that day, maybe you remember."

"Vaguely."

"Monday, April fifth," Brendan says.

"Come to find out, she had a horror story for the boys here. Rawlings, tell him about it, make it brief, huh?"

Remove the cigar, clear my throat. "Turns out she has dinner with Eddie Lopata the night before, Sunday night. Lopata, he's met with Kwapniewski and Mize on Saturday, they tell him they have everything they need to pull the job. Now they're antsy about Alvarado, they figure she's the weak link in the chain between them and eleven-point-five million. Stakes are too high to gamble on unknown factors, they want the problem removed. So they ask Lopata to waste the kid."

Exeter blinks, frowns.

"To kill her," the chief translates softly.

Blinks, frowns. "To *kill* her? To kill Ms. *Alvarado?!*"

"Afraid so," chief says.

"Oh, no. You can't be—!"

"Afraid so," chief says. "Deadly serious."

"Oh, my God, that poor girl. What we've—put her through."

I nod, flick my ashes. "Not as bad as it sounds. Lopata, he's a long-time friend of hers, as you know. Went to school with her and all. Lopata won't have any part of it. *Tells* them he will, of course, *tells* them he'll hit her, but now he's turned off these guys. Comes up with a plan of his own. Tells her he wants to double-cross these clowns, pull the job himself. Wants her to help him do it.''

Chief sits forward, winces with pain. "Now it gets a little complicated, but I'll summarize for you.''

Exeter sits forward, frowns. "Why wasn't I *informed* of this?''

"Frankly,'' chief says softly, "we were getting into highly confidential areas at this point. Only a few selected individuals were told, and only on a 'need-to-know' basis.''

"Only on a—? *I* needed to know! For God's *sake*, man, I'm president of the *gallery*, I'm *responsible* for those gems!''

Chief narrows his eyes. "Hold on now. Hold that thought for a minute. You'll find out exactly why we couldn't tell you. First off, Mize and Kwapniewski are no longer in the picture. Both men are now in the hospital, under arrest. Caught 'em last night in the commission of a burglary unrelated to the gallery.''

Exeter's face and voice turn Valium calm again. "Last night? May I ask why I wasn't, uh, wasn't informed of this?''

"Highly confidential operation,'' chief says. "Didn't break the news till this morning, it's not in the papers yet, far as I know.'' Checks his watch. "Probably TV bulletins by now, radio, that's about it.''

"May I ask what happened?''

Chief's voice drops to a modest monotone. "Shootout last night. Queens.''

"Chief Vadney was wounded himself,'' I volunteer quietly. "Rushed to Bellevue, had an emergency operation last night. Took a slug in the thigh.''

"Rawlings, that's enough,'' chief says.

"He saved John's life,'' Brendan adds quickly. "Shot and critically wounded Nick Mize. Risked his life to protect five other detectives.''

Chief dismisses the subject with a wave of his hand. "That's enough about that, we're not here to discuss that. The primary reason we're here, Mr. Exeter, is to explain Lopata's plan for stealing the gems tomorrow and to detail our strategy for his apprehension.''

Easier said than done. Takes us a full half-hour just to

outline the hostage plan, one point at a time, in between outraged questions, furious denunciations, personal insults, and irrational threats ranging from lawsuits against the city to influential lobbies demanding the chief's immediate resignation for "reckless endangerment of innocent life." This guy's just totally flabbergasted, jumps out of his chair every two minutes, paces up and down, waves his arms in dramatic gestures, I'm nearly out of cigars watching this show. Calls the yacht club, cancels his sail, apologies to caterers, cast, and crew; calls his wife at their summer digs in Southampton, tells her to return to the city at once, emergency, can't explain now; calls his attorney, damn near throws a tantrum when he discovers the guy's out of town for the weekend.

Must say the chief more than lives up to his reputation for staying calm, cool, and logical in a crisis situation; with all his faults, this guy can piss ice water in a sauna. Finally gets a good belt of brandy into Exeter, concentrates on three solid points of psychological persuasion: (1) There's absolutely no physical danger involved for his wife or for him; (2) since his two teen-age sons are both away at prep school in Massachusetts, they're obviously out of harm's way; (3) apprehended in the act of committing a felony, Lopata poses no threat to Exeter or his family for the indefinite future; free—as he'll be without Exeter's cooperation—Lopata remains a frustrating potential threat indefinitely.

Time flies when you're having fun. Around two-thirty Exeter's finally worn down. Chief repeats the basics slowly, clearly, patiently: Early Monday morning the Emergency Service Division will have Exeter's apartment building covertly surrounded. He'll leave for work at the usual time, 6:45 A.M., arrive at the gallery via taxi about seven. We figure Lopata will approach the distinguished silver-haired doorman on that shift (who won't be alerted to anything) at approximately 6:50, wearing his telephone company uniform, carrying his toolbox and worksheet. When the distinguished silver-haired man at the reception desk rings, Mrs. Exeter will ask to speak to the telephone man, listen to him, tell him she didn't know her husband ordered another extension, but to please come up and install it; she'll then tell the reception man to send him

up. Chief and our entire six-man team will be in the penthouse waiting for him. DA's office says Lopata has to be
physically in the residence before we can make a solid case.
He will. We will. No fuss, no mess.

Before our meet breaks up, Exeter gets a call from Sullivan
at the gallery, who'd tried to reach him at the yacht club: The
North Star arrived on schedule about 2:45 via Brinks. Sullivan immediately placed it in the Diebold safe. All twelve
diamonds are now secured.

Hate to air dirty linens, as it were, but in the interests of
accuracy I should mention that when the chief tells Exeter
about the news conference at the gallery scheduled for Monday afternoon, we have reason to believe the veteran sailor
experienced an abrupt physiological discomfort. In any event,
he departs the patio quickly. When he comes back some five
minutes later, he seems Valium calm as ever:

"Chief, uh, Chief Vadney, sir. I should think it's *abun-
dantly* obvious that an institution such as the, uh, the Heritage
Gallery doesn't exactly encourage—nor indeed are we in any
urgent *need* of—such patently sensational publicity."

Chief looks confused. "Yeah? Gosh, Mr. Exeter, I'd planned
on you being the one to hold up the North Star for all the TV
cameras and all, y'know, maybe explain your role in the
whole thing."

They compromise. Chief assures him the conference won't
begin until 3:30 P.M., a full half-hour after the day's exhibit
ends. Only those with bona fide press credentials admitted;
security tight but discreet. Irish need not apply.

# 9

MONDAY, APRIL 19, 6:45 A.M., Exeter leaves the apartment on schedule, doorman hails him a cab. Emergency Service guys have the building covertly surrounded, poised for action, police radio cars have long since been ordered out of the area. Our team's in the apartment ready to welcome Eddie L., the friendly telephone man. Chief's on the phone with Grady making sure our photographer's in the immediate vicinity and set to go. Next he calls Jim Mairs, who's in the lobby of an apartment directly across the street: Nobody in sight at the moment, distinguished silver-haired doorman is reading the paper. Tell you what, Mrs. Exeter's very much in attendance here, I got to tell you about this little lady. Here she is, fresh in last evening from Southampton, tanned to a turn, straw-colored hair creatively coiffed. Tight-skinned face says maybe mid-thirties, hands tell another story despite the distraction of a rather large emerald-cut diamond and the obligatory Cartier diamond watch; ditto her neck despite the gold-chain glitter, but I don't want to get catty now, she's a real class-act broad all the way. Lean figure's packaged in a simple white pure-silk long-sleeved shirt, cream-colored raw-silk pants. Thing about her, at the risk of overstating the case, this lady gives the distinct impression she's giving a breakfast garden party of some kind. Out comes this young British maid in a dark uniform with a frilly white apron, she starts serving—this is no shit—she's serving us a selection of freshly baked crois- sants, coffee in Spode bone china with gold fleur-de-lis (I gauched-out and looked under my saucer), all from a sterling silver tray with matching silver coffee pot, sugar bowl, and tiny spoons.

So, what I'm saying, here we are, seven cops in bullet- proof vests, revolvers on our hips, chief with a shotgun in his mitts, we're trying hard to be polite and all, but in less than five minutes this charming hostess has got to open her front door to a big rawboned animal who might very well be indelicate enough to stick a gun in her puss. What happens then? We don't know. When you face this type situation enough times over the years and actually see some of the cuckoo stunts pulled by the Eddie Lopatas of this world, you tend to sweat more—not less—as the confrontation approaches. Any cop who claims otherwise is a liar or a psycho. But Mrs. Exeter? Amazing broad. Seems utterly fascinated with the whole routine, chattering away at the chief, musical voice with predictable marbles in the mouth. This is a thrilling new experience for her, she'll be telling this one to rapt audiences at cocktail soirees for years to come: "So then I opened the door, and *oh*. Oh, my God, there's this, this positively hulking Neanderthal man, a veritable survivor of the *Stone* Age, pointing this, this enormous *gun* at me! I *mean!* Well, naturally, I rose to the occasion, as any red-blooded New York lady *would* do. I threw up all *over* him!"

Not such a bad idea, if one could manage it. Lady who can toss her cookies at will, she's got a weapon there better than Mace. Unfortunately, as the critical seconds tick by—it's now 6:51 and no sign of Lopata—Mrs. Exeter betrays her first ostensible sign of stress. Announces blithefully to the chief that she has to excuse herself for a few minutes, be right back.

"Mrs. Exeter," he says softly, "I'm afraid that's out of the question right now."

"I—beg your pardon?"

"The man's due any second now."

"Chief Vadney, I don't think you understand. This happens to be somewhat—urgent."

"I understand. But the fact is, that intercom's due to ring any second. You've absolutely got to—"

"Are you—? Are you *ordering* me to—?!"

"All I'm saying, I'm terribly sorry, Mrs. Exeter, but at this particular point in time you'll have to—you'll just have to hold it *in* somehow."

Well, there's an abrupt silence, she stands there glaring at him. It's embarrassing for all of us, but she's suddenly reduced to the indignity of crossing her legs. At which point she calls him a name. Just above a whisper, but we can all hear. Calls him a "crypto-Nazi." Swear to God. Turns around, stiff-legs it to the bathroom. Some broad.

She's back by 6:56 and nothing's happening. At 6:58 the chief calls Jim Mairs again: One jogger, one elderly lady walking her dog, two cruising cabs, no sign of Lopata.

By 7:01 the chief's going nuts. "Rawlings, call the gallery, see if Exeter's arrived yet."

I call. Phone rings eight times.

"Hello."

"Mr. Exeter?"

"No, this is Johnson, private security."

"Detective Rawlings, NYPD. Exeter around?"

"Yes, sir, but he's—we're in the exhibit area, ground floor. The man's—I think he fainted. I think that's all it is. We're trying to bring him around now."

"What happened?"

"I don't really know, sir. He came in, greeted us, saw the attaché case we're guarding for Mr. Sullivan."

"Attaché case?"

"Yes, sir. Mr. Exeter asked us a couple of questions, then he collapsed. Fainted. Went down pretty hard, too."

"What'd you tell him?"

"Nothing unusual, to the best of my knowledge. Just that Mr. Sullivan came up to the fourth floor about six o'clock this morning. Said he had to set up the exhibit early so Miss Alvarado could photograph."

"Photograph?"

"Yes, sir. Mr. Sullivan took the diamonds out of the safe, put them in his attaché case, and we escorted him down to the exhibit area. While we were setting up all the display cases, Miss Alvarado came down—"

"And told Sullivan he had a call from his wife?"

"Yes, sir. How'd you—He's up in his office now. Guess he's still talking to her. How'd you—?"

"And Alvarado went out for coffee, right?"

"Yes, sir, Mr. Sullivan asked her to. She's not back yet. How'd you—?"

"Don't expect her back, Johnson."

"No? What happened to her?"

"She's just became famous."

"Famous?"

"Yeah. She just pulled the biggest diamond robbery in history."

There's still time to collar these kids, they've only got a forty-five minute head start at best. Chief barks orders, our team goes to work fast: Put out an immediate APB on both 1982 white Corvettes, plates, personal descriptions; alert the Port Authority Police at all terminals, tunnels, bridges; give detailed descriptions to airport police at Kennedy, La Guardia, Newark, ask the State Police to stake out Westchester and Teterboro airports. Big John and Nuzhat split to the gallery, speed Sullivan home, 400 West End Avenue, find his wife and nineteen-year-old daughter cuffed, gagged, and blindfolded in a bedroom; Alvarado was admitted to the apartment 11:35 last night on a ruse, pulled a gun, let Lopata in, they terrorized the family all night. Nice kids. On a long shot, Telfian and Thalheimer tear up to Yonkers, go to Lopata's pad with the local police; he's gone, of course, but we get one lead: His Corvette's not in the garage.

Brendan and I play another long one, drive up to Alvarado's apartment, 200 East Eighty-fourth, double-park on the southeast corner of Third. Short doorman in a brown uniform is standing under the new blue canopy exchanging greetings with tenants leaving for work; it's now 8:25. Show him our gold shields discreetly, ask to see the super. He takes us into the glassed-in foyer leading to the lobby, rings the super's apartment, gets the okay, escorts us through the lobby and up a short flight of stairs to the left. Super's waiting for us in his doorway, big friendly type guy, early fifties, about five-ten, at least 275, name of Manny Bizzari. Show him our gold, introduce ourselves, ask for the name of Miss Alvarado's roommate.

"Mrs. Hill," he says.

"*Mrs.* Hill?" I ask.

"Yeah. She's—I guess maybe she's divorced or separated, y'know?"

"Like to talk to her," I tell him.

"Sure, if she's in. Not in trouble, is she?"

"No," Brendan says. "No trouble at all, just want to ask her a couple of routine questions."

Bizzari closes his door, leads us down the short flight of stairs and through the lobby into the foyer. Picks up the intercom receiver, presses the button to 19D, waits, nods to a couple of passing tenants, presses the button again. "She's a stewardess, y'know, she's out of town a lot." Glances at his watch. "Miss Alvarado's probably left for work by now." On the stainless-steel panel above the buttons are two closed-circuit television screens showing the interiors of both elevators; one's crowded, on its way down, the other's empty, going up. Bizzari studies the people in the elevator, presses 19D one more time, finally shrugs and hangs up. "Nobody home."

"Thanks anyway," Brendan says. "Happen to know which airline Mrs. Hill works for?"

"Yeah, British Airways. She's an English girl, she's got a beautiful English accent. They're both nice kids, no wild parties or nothin' like that."

"One other thing," I say. "Miss Alvarado park her car in the garage here?"

He looks surprised. "Since just last week, yeah. Brand-new Corvette, she just bought it about a week ago."

"Could we see it?" Brendan asks.

"Sure thing, if it's there."

It's there. So at least we know there's a high probability they're using Lopata's car, or were, if they're still in the country. Not much to go on, but as the chief always says,

when you sleep on the floor you can't fall out of bed. Words
to that effect.

Next order of business, we need warrants to search both
apartments. It's now about 8:45, we haven't even seen the
morning papers yet, so on the way down to headquarters we
buy copies of the *News* and the *Times*. Front page of the
*News* has that unflattering shot of the chief sprawled on the
floor in his bulletproof vest, shotgun by his side, under the
bold head:

## TOP COP SHOT
## IN GOLD BUST

Unfortunate choice of words? Not when you consider that
Vinnie Casandra, managing editor of the *News*, doesn't happen to be one of Chief Vadney's most ardent admirers. Story
on page three looks like an exposé from the *Enquirer*. Team
of investigative reporters assigned by Casandra obviously did
some hard digging on Dr. Samson, instantly cut through the
medical jargon, then figured the logistical and physical odds
against Mize somehow managing to get a shot at the chief's
bum, but Casandra keeps his punches above the belt and his
butts between the lines. Here we have a cheesecake photo of
the chief in his bathrobe at Bellevue planting a big sloppy
kiss on Samantha, with the derring-do double-entendre head:

## SO WHO SHOT CHIEF VADNEY
## IN DAT WILD QUEENS BUST?

Doesn't take a literary genius to realize the simple insertion
of an apostrophe in "Queens" would've altered the whole
kaleidoscopic history of police-press relations in this city,
initiating an immediate libel suit the chief would unquestion-
ably have won. Dastardly defamation of character. Megabucks
out-of-court settlement. Samantha choked in diamonds, smoth-
ered in furs, oh. For the lack of an apostrophe, so near and
yet so far. Clever surgeon, Casandra, draws more blood with
a scalpel than the chief does with a meathook. Fued between

the two came to a head last year just after the big Champs-Elysées heist when the *News* stumbled into that outrageously popular cartoon series titled "How'm I doin'?" starring the chief and Mayor Koch. Talk of the town. Chief makes the fatal error of momentarily losing his cool, calls Casandra, demands the series be canceled at once "for the good of the department." Casandra pleads First Amendment. Rather heated name-calling session ensues. Real nasty exchange, story goes. Upshot, series continues in earnest, of course, till the case is ultimately closed. Smoldering hostility held in uneasy abeyance. So one can't help wondering what one's bloodshot eyes might behold in the pages of this fine tabloid when news of the biggest diamond robbery in history hits the streets, with in-depth investigative reportage on exactly how two kids could possibly have snatched $11.5 million in rare ice from directly under the nose of a special-assignment team of top detectives hand-picked and commanded by Chief Vadney for the specific purpose of preventing this specific crime. Ramifications stagger the imagining mind. Such stuff as Casandra's dreams are made of.

One interesting item in the gold-bust story, there's a hospital update on Mize and Kwapniewski. Both have been removed from the critical list and are now in serious but stable condition in the Intensive Care Unit at Elmhurst General. Glad to read that. No personal animosity against these guys, wish them a speedy recovery.

Tumultuous press conference, headquarters, noon, biggest mass-media event we've seen since the Champs-Elysées, Grady's in a state of hysterical collapse, the chief's in his total euphoric element, facing the same fifty-five angry boys and girls he sweet-talked yesterday morning at Bellevue, plus the *paparazzi*, plus a surprisingly large contingent of foreign correspondents, particularly from England. Fortunately, the staging's on our side today, we're in the ultramodern, air-conditioned, spacious headquarters auditorium. Hard-news release in the hastily revised NYPD Press Package neglects to mention the master-plan strategic stakeout of our entire special-assignment team in Exeter's apartment while the actual robbery was in progress, but we figure Grady's looking to let the more abrasive boys and girls dig for that angle on their own, which some of them will undoubtedly do sooner or later.

Chief stands tall behind the lectern on stage, cane long since discarded, shirtsleeves rolled up, tie yanked down, gleaming nickel-plated S&W .38 Chief's Special holstered back on the right hip, walkie-talkie on the left hip. No-nonsense attitude today, this is definitely world-class stuff in anybody's book, an international diamond robbery the likes of which has never been known before, lead-story material on TV news programs via satellite to major cities around the globe—think of it, London, Paris, Rome, Tokyo, maybe even Moscow—not to mention front-page attention via wire services to major newspapers throughout the civilized world. You look around at these faces, must be close to a hundred media people here, you know this one's a winner, you can feel the vibrations of excitement. Brendan and me, we stand against the wall way in back, as usual, light up our cigars, get set to enjoy the unfolding spectacle.

"Ladies and gentlemen," the chief says softly. "I have a brief opening statement here, after which I'll attempt to answer as many of your questions as possible." Suddenly, boom, can't believe it, almost total silence, first time in recent memory, presidential press-conference respect. Chief senses it, clears his throat, reads the prepared statement slowly, pauses after each sentence, glances up for maximum impact, nice touch. "Today, April nineteenth, at approximately six-fifteen A.M. New York time, the Heritage Gallery in Manhattan was robbed of twelve rare diamonds, including the famed North Star from the United Kingdom, one of the largest diamonds in private ownership. All twelve gems were scheduled to be exhibited and auctioned at the gallery today and tomorrow. Their combined estimated value has been placed officially at eleven-point-five million U.S. dollars. Phillip S. Exeter, chairman and president of the Heritage Gallery, confirmed to us, quote: In terms of monetary value, this is far and away the greatest diamond robbery of all time, unquote. It should be made clear from the outset that we have eyewitness testimony on the positive identifications of two prime suspects in this case. Arrest warrants have been issued for:

Edward Stanley Lopata of Yonkers, New York, white male Caucasian, twenty-six years old, six-foot-four, two hundred ten pounds, blond hair, blue eyes; and Tara Maria Alvarado of New York City, white female Caucasian, twenty-five years old, five-foot-six, one hundred fifteen pounds, dark-brown hair, dark-brown eyes, a former employee of the Heritage Gallery. Our investigation is well under way at this point. This morning I informed Police Commissioner William B. Reilly that I have selected a special-assignment team of forty detectives, chosen from all five boroughs of New York City, to work exclusively on this case and report directly to me.''

Goes on like that, gives a rundown on the hostage operation, whole nine yards, then opens it up to the Q/A session, at which time Brendan and I split, we have work to do. Find out later the chief appoints me supervisor of the big new team, I'm going up in the world. Appoints Brendan assistant supervisor, a stepping-stone position in the celestial hierarchy he accepts with enthusiastic humility tempered by cautious optimism: Has he actually passed the chief's acid test? Maybe, maybe not. Depends on a lot of variables now. I'm pulling for Brendan, I really am, long as he doesn't drop one at the wrong time I think he's got it made.

Early afternoon edition of the *Post* goes front page with the only photo we have of Alvarado and Lopata together, that one she'd given us herself back on March 18, taken when they were seniors at the University of Miami in 1978: Camp shot of them leaning against a new Ferrari, both wearing black silk windbreakers, white wing collars, black bow ties; smoking obvious joints in matching holders. Lopata's mischievous-kid smile reminds me of James Dean. Headline reads:

**BIGGEST**

**DIAMOND**

**ROBBERY**

---

Whiz Kids Grab $11.5M!

Turns out to be quite a day. Late that afternoon, Big John, Nuzhat, Brendan, and me are finishing the search of Alvarado's apartment when I get a call from Mat Murphy. Less than an hour ago officers from the Twenty-fourth Precinct discover a dead body in Riverside Park just off the Henry Hudson Parkway at 116th Street. White male Caucasian, mid-twenties, over six feet, blond hair, blue eyes. Single gunshot to the head.

"Oh, no," I tell Mat. "Couldn't be him."

"I think you'd better take a look, John."

"Lots of people meet that description, y'know?"

"You're the only one who's seen him up close. Take a look, just to be on the safe side. I told them not to move the body till you get there."

"On our way."

Six forty-five, twilight coming. Brendan drives, we take Eighty-sixth west through the park, stay on it all the way crosstown to Riverside Drive, north to Ninety-sixth, get on the parkway, north to 116th Street up near Columbia University. Squad car, unmarked car, and a van from the Medical Examiner's office are parked on the strip of grass between the southbound lanes and the river. We can't U-turn because of the divider, so we pull off on the grass to our right, get out, wait on the curb for a break in the traffic, then run across.

Detective Delehanty from the Twenty-fourth comes over, introduces himself, sharp-looking guy in a tweed sports jacket, mid-forties. Two uniformed officers and two men from ME stand near the dead body that's covered by a green plastic sheet. Delehanty pulls the sheet back from the face. Gives me a little shock, didn't really expect to be seeing this.

"Eddie Lopata," I hear myself say.

"Positive?" Delehanty asks.

"Positive." I get down on one knee, take a closer look, turn his head. Single gunshot wound, left temple, exists at an upward angle, takes off a small chunk of skull above the right ear. I glance at the guys from ME. "How long's he been dead?"

Shorter man shrugs. "Rough estimate, three to four hours."

"Broken bones?" I ask him. "Cuts, bruises, anything?"

"Not that we can see."

"No grass stains on his clothes," Delehanty says. "No dirt, nothing. Looks to me like he was dumped."

"Chief'll want an autopsy soon as possible," I tell the men. "This one gets top priority."

As they get him on a stretcher and into the van, I thank Delehanty and the two officers who discovered the body. Before leaving, Brendan and I walk along the grass toward the river.

It's about 7:20 and getting dark now. Large rocks along the shore are dry and the water's calm and high. We sit on one of the rocks, light our cigars, watch the last few minutes of sunset behind the high-rise apartments in Jersey. It's been a long day, we've been on the job since six this morning, we're tired, we've had it. So we sit there in silence for a while. Darkness comes quickly and the huge neon signs of the Jersey waterfront factories cast reflections across the river. In the distance to our right we can see the green lights along the spans of the George Washington Bridge. Behind us the parkway is well lighted and the cars rush by quickly, each breaking the air with a sharp sound. Our shadows are dim on the water.

Shock of seeing Eddie Lopata is the psychological turning point in the case for me. My instincts tell me something strange is going on here, this whole robbery just isn't what it seems on the surface. I begin to ask myself the following questions: Is it possible that Alvarado set everybody up from the beginning? Is it conceivable that she was the one who actually approached Lopata in the first place, asked him to join her and find accomplices? Did she then come to us with the invented story, knowing that our knee-jerk reaction would be to make her an informant, thereby guaranteeing that she could follow every move we made? Is it logical to assume that when she discovered Wally and Nick's "alarm man" had been collared out of town she suspected they'd back out or bungle the job, so she went to Lopata, invented the story that Wally and Nick planned to kill her, and switched to the hostage plan?

Keep in mind that, aside from the two taped conversations, we have only Alvarado's word about virtually everything that was happening. Would she be bright enough to create such an elaborate scheme? Would she be that talented an actress? Would she have the guts to kill a man in cold blood? After working a full month with this girl, the appalling truth of the matter is that we know relatively little about her. We'll have to find out fast.

No question that she's unusually bright and talented, but my gut feeling is that others are involved in both the robbery and murder. A key fact leads me to that conclusion: The North Star. If you study the history of important gems of this rank, you discover that eventually they almost all wind up in a permanent museum collection. Why? No market. Today, auctions are the only possible vehicles for the sale of famous stones and, in point of fact, few are actually sold.

I glance at Brendan's shadow on the water. "Think she planned it on her own?"

He gives it some thought, watches the lights of a large boat coming downriver toward us. "Could be. Could be, but I doubt it."

"Why would anybody want to steal the North Star?"

Keeps watching the big boat. "Don't know. Obviously, you can't fence anything that famous."

"Ransom? Ramsom it back to the insurance company? That make any sense?"

"Yeah, it might. It might, John, but in many ways that's even more of a hassle than stealing it."

"Of course, you could use it as a valuable chunk of plea-bargaining power if you were collared. But you'd still go to prison."

The boat comes closer, lights blazing across the water. It's a double-decked Circle Line sightseeing boat, last one of the day, finishing its swing around Manhattan and heading back to Pier 81 down at West Forty-second. We can see people all along the railings of both decks, but of course they can't see us. Loudspeaker comes on now, man's voice tells the tourists that the lighted dome above the trees is Grant's Tomb and the floodlighted Gothic spire is part of Riverside Church. When the boat moves directly in front of us, it cuts off the neon reflections from the factories, then it passes and the colors flash back on the water, bent by the wake.

"My guess," I say quietly, "if she'd planned the robbery on her own, she'd go for the eleven smaller stones, leave the famous one behind. Just can't believe she acted on her own."

Lights of the Circle Line boat move away in the distance. Loudspeaker comes on again but we can't make out the words. Wake's been moving in quietly, now it startles us when it splashes suddenly against our rock.

Brendan laughs softly. "We'd make good detectives."

"Think we need some liquid refreshment."

"Now you're talking." He stands up, stretches his arms to the sky. "Who the hell was it said: 'Beware, as long as you live, of judging people by appearances'?"

"Don't know."

"Sounds to me like a detective."

"Could be."

"Sounds to me like an Irish detective."

"Doubt it," I tell him. "The man has too much wisdom."

Next morning we do a lot more digging on Alvarado. Some highlights: Born in Manhattan (Upper West Side) in 1957, Tara Alvarado attended the School of Performing Arts where she was valedictorian of her graduating class in 1974. Big John and Nuzhat learn from one of her instructors that she was considered "an extraordinarily gifted pianist." Telfian and Thalheimer learn from her father, an associate professor of Spanish literature at Columbia's School of General Studies, that she turned down a scholarship at Juilliard to accept a similar offer from the University of Miami's School of Music, a decision he was never able to fully understand. After graduating magna cum laude in 1978, she returned to New York, told her father she considered a musical career a "waste of time." Promptly took a series of advanced photography courses at the Nikon School in Garden City, Long Island. Became a free-lance photographer in 1979, developed a portfolio that Exeter himself described as "clearly a work of genius." Hired by the Heritage Gallery when the position became available in January 1982.

Late that afternoon we ask Exeter's permission to conduct a comprehensive search of Alvarado's office before the stuff is moved out. Gives us carte blanche. Brendan and I turn the place inside out, even the photographic-equipment storage room which she also used as a darkroom. Finally I study her portfolio. More than 200 photographs, all sizes, shapes; color, black-and-white, absolutely dazzling work, I see what Exeter meant. Specializes in general objects of art and gems, emphasis on capturing unusual refractions of light. Toward the end she has a shot I've seen someplace before. Composition is brilliant, looks like an oil painting, a jagged surrealistic mountain of jewels holding up an enormous steel-blue diamond that refracts light like a prism; a blue iceberg on another planet. I sit back at her desk, try to recall where I've seen this shot before. Brendan's in the closet taking stuff down from the shelves.

I hold up the shot. "Ever see this before?"

Takes a quick look, frowns. Glances around the office. Now he points to one of the many aluminum-framed photos on the wall near the window. "Had teeth, it'd bitecha."

He's right. Identical photo. Caught my attention the very first time we walked in here, St. Patrick's Day. I place the loose photo in a manila envelope, get up, go to the door, pause with my hand on the knob.

"Brendan, me boy."

"Yeo."

"Who the hell was it said: 'Never overlook the obvious'?"

"Don't know."

"Sounds to me like a detective."

"Could be."

"Sounds to me like a German-Irish detective."

"Doubt it. Whaddaya got?"

I hold up the envelope. "A clue, lad. A clue so obvious it's bound to be overlooked. Bejeez, had teeth, it'd bitecha."

Off I go, take the elevator up to seven, stride down the red-carpeted hall, nod politely to the individually lighted portraits of old farts scowling down at me. Through the paneled double doors into the elegantly appointed waiting room. Elegantly appointed executive secretary nods politely:

"Detective Rawlings."

"Mrs. Powell. Like to see Mr. Exeter, it's important."

She smiles, buzzes him. "Detective Rawlings to see you, says it's important."

"I should hope so. Please send him in."

Off to the inner sanctum, fools rush in, da-da. Persian carpets, ancient antiques, chrome-and-class display cabinets, track-lighted priceless paintings. Louis XV desk in the far corner, innocent of clutter, high-backed chair turned to the window. Before committing myself, I glance at the darkened corner behind to my left; armchair's empty.

I address the high-backed chair with complete confidence. "Mr. Exeter?"

Slowly, very slowly, swivels around. He's engrossed in the thrilling best seller *Marco Polo, If You Can*, William F. Buckley, Jr., if you will, bulldog-bulldog. Snaps it shut with just the hint of a sparkle-bulge, glances at my manila envelope. "Yes, Detective Rawlings, what can I, uh, what can I do for you?"

Take the photo from the envelope, hand it to him. "Tell me anything about this photograph?"

"Please sit down." Gives the photo a quick glance, tosses it aside, rolls his eyes, closes them in disdain, opens them wide, almost smiles at the naïveté of it all. "Precisely what is it you'd, uh, you'd like to know?"

"Brief history will do."

"Brief—? Brief history. Yes. Dear God, I must be—I must be sinking into senility. Correct me if I'm wrong, Detective Rawlings, but somehow I seem to have acquired the preposterous idea that you wanted to see me about something *important*. Is that correct?"

"Yes, sir."

Leans forward, elbows on desk, gingerly places his fingertips to his forehead. "Forgive me, Detective Rawlings, I've had a—had a frightful headache all day. Brought about in no small measure by reading the papers this morning. The, uh, the photograph in question is of course the North Star, foremost of the diamonds you were entrusted to protect."

"I see."

Leans back now, opens the top drawer of his desk, takes out a stack of thin catalogues, tosses them across the desk. Cover shot is identical. Catalogue intended for the auction. "Take one, please. I've no further need of them."

"Mr. Exeter, happen to know when this photo was taken?"

"When it was—*taken?* Good God, man, I—I haven't the foggiest *notion* when it was taken."

"I see."

"Forgive me for asking, but what possible *difference* does it make?"

"Ever hear of a book called *Great Diamonds of the World?*"

"Yes. Published last year, I believe."

"Read it?"

Fingers to the forehead again. "Uh, no. No, I didn't read it. Simple fact of the matter, I'm not in the habit of reading 'coffee-table' books about diamonds, expressly targeted for the edification of the uninitiated—the lay public, as it were."

"Ever read *Pretoria and the North Star?*"

"Uh, no. Heard of it. Biography, wasn't it?"

"Yes. Point I'm making—"

"Yes, I do wish you'd get to it."

"Point I'm making, according to these books, the North Star hasn't been seen in public since nineteen thirty-eight."

Slowly, very slowly, he spreads the fingers on his forehead, looks at me through the slits. "What . . . what did you say?"

"Hasn't been seen in public since nineteen thirty-eight."

"You're . . . you're quite certain?"

"Quite. Matter of public record. As I'm sure you know, the owner's a recluse."

"Miss Waring, yes. I made all arrangements for the auction through her attorney. Never actually met the lady."

"Apparently, few people have. Eighty-two-year-old recluse. Always shunned publicity of any kind."

Eyes wide through the slits. "Then how . . .?"

"Exactly my question. Was this photogrph in Miss Alvarado's portfolio when she applied for the job?"

"Oh, my . . . God."

"That mean yes?"

Removes his fingers now, stares straight ahead. "Oh, my God. We saw that photograph in her portfolio as far back as last November."

"When was she hired?"

"January. First week in January."

"Recall when you started negotiations for the auction?"

"For the North Star? Yes. I believe Mrs. Waring's attorney, Mr. Cavallo, I believe he first contacted me with the proposition last autumn. October, November, as I recall."

"Uh-huh. One last question. Don't suppose you asked Miss Alvarado how she happened to get access to the diamond."

"Uh, no. No, I didn't. I was quite impressed with the photograph, of course, we all were. I suppose I assumed it was—I don't know, on *display* somewhere. Somewhere in England."

"Apparently it was."

"It was?"

"Yeah. For her eyes only." I stand, pick up the photograph and catalogue, put them in the envelope. "Well, that's all I wanted to see you about, Mr. Exeter. Much obliged."

He stands, looks flustered. "Well, what's—next? What're you going to, uh—to do *now?*"

"Me? I'm going to London. Never been there before. Hear it's a kick in the head."

# 10

ARMED WITH A FUGITIVE WARRANT and the chief's broken-record
pleas for action, *any* kind of action to get the *News* off his
back, Brendan and I get the green light for a trip to London.
Leave Sunday, April 25, 8:45 P.M., Pan Am flight 102,
scheduled to arrive Heathrow 8:25 A.M. Monday, London
time. Round-trip cabin class fare, $750 plus tax, but as the
chief points out to Commissioner Reilly, we're talking $11.5
million in diamonds here, right? We're not carrying guns, of
course, only Secret Service agents are permitted to bring
firearms into the U.K., and only when they're guarding the
president, vice-president, or secretary of state. First time in
our careers we're working a case unarmed. Vulnerable feeling, difficult to describe. However, there's a bright side:
Today, detectives from New Scotland Yard—and even selected uniformed policemen—are authorized to carry hand-
guns for specific major crime cases involving suspects known
to be armed and likely to be violent. Didn't know this till the
chief briefed us Friday afternoon, turns out he's a big fan of
New Scotland Yard, knows a lot of the brass over there.
Reaches proudly into his desk, hands us each an attractive
blue-and-white folder straight from the Yard titled "Facts
About the Metropolitan Police." Folder holds a stack of
color-coded information sheets with up-to-date intelligence on

twenty-seven major subjects. He tells us to know four of them cold before we arrive: "Organisation of the Metropolitan Police District" (they spell it with an s instead of a z); "Scotland Yard—its History and Role" (that's the most interesting); "Criminal Investigation Department" (commonly called the CID); and "Special Branch." Our contact at the Yard is an old friend of Vadney's, Chief Superintendent Ashley Kellogg, who's in charge of Cl, Serious Crime Branch, reports directly to the assistant commissioner in charge of C Department. Cl Branch has nine squads, including the celebrated Murder Squad. Apparently we'll also work with the mysterious Special Branch of C Department, the one that's frequently mentioned in spy novels and movies. Luckily, I brought my trench coat.

So here we are, Sunday night, aboard a crowded Pan Am 747, seats 47H and J (middle seat's empty), studying this classy Yard intelligence as we sip our first martinis. A few highlights:

Metropolitan Police District has approximately 25,000 police officers (compared to NYC's 1982 "beefed-up" 20,000) to cover Greater London's 7,111,500 residents (NYC has 7,071,030), spread out over an area of 787 square miles (NYC has 365 square miles). To make those 787 square miles manageable from a police standpoint, Greater London is divided into four Areas; each Area is divided again into six Districts, making a total of twenty-four, each identified by a letter of the alphabet. In turn, each District is divided into Divisions, Sub-Divisions, and Police Stations. Fortunately, they include a map.

Fact sheet on the history and role of Scotland Yard itself is fascinating stuff. If I tried to explain it in my own words, it'd suffer badly in the translation, so here's a quote:

As soon as Sir Robert Peel, Home Secretary, knew in 1829 that he was to provide, for the first time, a properly organised police force for London, he started to look for a building that would be suitable to act as the police headquarters. The building would have to be in a really central position and since the Home Secretary was to be the chief police authority, the building would have to be as near as possible to the Home Office.

Peel found the building he was searching for at 4 Whitehall Place. There was a large house here that backed onto an ancient court called 'Scotland Yard'. According to tradition, the buildings that had stood originally round this yard had formed part of the Old Royal Palace of Westminster and had been used principally to house the members of the Royal Family of Scotland or their representatives whenever they were visiting the English Court.

The boundaries of the Palace were defined in an Act of 1531 which referred to 'the croft or piece of land commonly called Scotland'. A plan of the Palace drawn in Stuart times shows a double court or yard named 'Scotland Yard'.

Although the official address of the new police headquarters was '4 Whitehall Place', behind the new headquarters, in Scotland Yard itself, was a separate building to which members of the public were referred which became the most frequently used entrance. Thus many people—and particularly those connected with the Press—came to refer to the Commissioner's headquarters as 'Scotland Yard' and it was not long before the unofficial address became the official one; even today the main entrance to the present building is known as 'the Back Hall'.

By the last quarter of the nineteenth century the Metropolitan Police had outgrown their original headquarters. There were more than 13,000 men on the Force by that time and the scope of their work and the administrative effort required had increased proportionately. New offices therefore became necessary.

There was a site on the recently constructed Embankment that had been earmarked for a grand opera house. Problems with the foundations of the building and financial mismanagement ruined these original plans and the site was acquired for the new police headquarters. The building was designed by the eminent architect Richard Norman Shaw. The lower floors of this building were faced with 2,500 tons of granite that had been quarried by the convicts of Dartmoor Prison.

By 1890 the Norman Shaw building overlooking the Thames was completed and all the departments were moved into it.

The name 'Scotland Yard' had become so familiar that the police authorities decided that the name should be retained and so the official title of the new headquarters became 'New Scotland Yard'. A few years later, another building—'Scotland House'—was put up just to the south of 'The Yard'. This block was used for housing the Receiver and his staff, responsible for the finances and supplies of the police.

In 1961 some further changes were made when the Receiver's Office was moved from Scotland House to Tintagel House, which is a tall building on the Albert Embankment on the south bank of the Thames. This made it possible for various police departments from The Yard or in other buildings in London to move into Scotland House.

In 1966 the Commissioner's and Receiver's offices were combined into a single office and, in 1967, moved to a modern building at Broadway, SW1, between St. James's Park Underground Station and Victoria Street and very close to the new Home Office building in Petty France. As before, the name of the old building was transferred to the new one and so 'Scotland Yard', the ancient name of the courtyard of an ancient palace, lives on as one of the most famous addresses in the world. Apart from the Information Room, Central Traffic Control, and the Criminal Record Office, etc., it is from here that the Commissioner and the Receiver run the world's largest police force and the many departments for which they are responsible. . . .

Goes into more detail, lists the fifteen principal headquarters departments, the officer in charge of each, general functions, and so on, but you get the basic flavor, or flavour, as the case may be. Brendan and I read the whole folder, total of forty-seven pages, then reread the four subjects we're supposed to know cold, finish up before dinner's served. Cabin class section must have at least 250 passengers, but the flight attendants manage to serve all the trays with a smile. On a scale of one to ten, I give the service a nine, the food an eight, the attitude of our particular attendant, Fran Werner—who happens to be British—a ten.

Now it's time for the film. We rent headsets ($3), slide down the window shades, settle back with an after-dinner brandy ($1.50), light up a cigarette (cigars not allowed), and watch *Buddy Buddy* with Jack Lemmon and Walter Matthau. Clipper class section gets *Absence of Malice* with Paul Newman and Sally Field; first class gets the same as us. Figures, because it's definitely a first-class film. Anytime I see Jack Lemmon and Walter Matthau together I can't help smiling.

This time they're in adjoining hotel rooms, Lemmon's trying to commit suicide because his wife doesn't love him, Matthau's a professional hit man with a high-powered rifle trying to bang some clown from the window. Half-hour into the film, I'm laughing, I'm feeling no pain, I glance over at Brendan in the window seat. He's asleep. Sound asleep with the stereo headset still blasting in his ears, full glass of brandy in his hand. Slowly, slowly, I reach over, relieve him of the brandy glass, pour it into mine. Candy from a baby. Now I toast to his generosity, take a nice long swallow. Hour or so later, I glance over again. Hasn't moved a muscle, looks like a wax dummy with earphones. Thought flicks through my mind, maybe he passed away. Naw.

Around eleven o'clock, film's reaching the big hilarious climax, Brendan begins snoring. Really driving 'em home, I can hear him over the music and dialogue, I can even feel the vibrations. I wait a few minutes, try to concentrate on the screen, I'm a patient man. ZZZzzzzz . . . ZZZzzzzz . . . ZZZzzzzz. Loud, rhythmic, unrelenting. I'm tempted to do something unkind. Sorely tempted. Try to resist, try to concentrate on the film. ZZZ—gup! —zzzzz . . . ZZZ—gup! —zzzzz. Temptation wins out. Slowly, slowly, I reach over to his right armrest, where the channel selector and volume control dials are located. Slowly, slowly, I turn up the volume, watching his face. Up, up, all the way to the end, full volume. Face remains motionless, mouth open slightly. I remove my own headset, lean close to his left ear, listen. This is no shit, music and dialogue are blasting into his head so loudly they'd wake the dead. Not Brendan. ZZZ—gup! —zzzzz—pop! Makes you wonder what's going on in his brain. I sit back, shake my head, sip the last of my double brandy, think unkind thoughts.

Wait a minute, hold on, got another idea. Reach into the seat pocket, pull out the inflight magazine *Pan Am Clipper*, flip to the back, study the audio entertainment guide. Music channels for every taste—classical, pop, country and western, jazz, all like that. Ah, here's the one I want, channel 5, Helen Reddy, entire channel devoted to her biggest hits. Happen to like Helen Reddy, terrific voice, unusual range, really knows how to belt 'em across. Reason I select her, this kid's got a high-C that'd shatter a brandy snifter at twenty yards. Slowly, slowly, I reach across to the channel selector in Brendan's armrest. Film's on channel 2. Channels 3 and 4 are classical and pop, respectively. Got to click past them fast. Pause with my fingertip on the dial, take a deep breath, turn the dial quickly—beep-beep—then *boom:* With my naked ear I can hear Reddy screeching into the finale of her biggie "I Am Woman!"

"*AHHH-EEE!*" Brendan sits bolt upright, bug-eyed, widemouthed, hair on end, snatches off the headset like he's been electrocuted. Instantly, people turn around, give him dirty looks.

Me, I'm sitting back, headset on, innocent eyes glued to the silver screen, face frozen in an expressionless cast. Brendan's staring at me with his precinct-famous Hurt Expression. Know it. Feel it. Burns through a man's soul, so they say. When I finally give him a quick, surprised glance, he motions for me to remove my headset. I do. Frowning, mildly irritated.

"What's the matter?"

Reproachfully: "Ah, Jesus, Johnny."

"What?"

"Ya got a wicked—"

"—mean streak in ya," I finish for him. "Doin' me like that."

He laughs softly. "Doin' me like that."

We're both laughing now. He knows exactly why I did it, his snoring's even more famous than his Hurt Expression.

"You'll sizzle in hell," he tells me.

"That I will, with all the Catholics from Wicklow."

Mere mention of the name makes his eyes go misty. "Round about eight o'clock in the morning, if we're on course, lad, you'll get your first unforgettable bird's-eye view. Wicklow, Garden of Ireland." Sits back, smiles, closes his eyes. "Situated on the gentle slopes of lovely Ballyguile Hill, overlooking the wide blue bay. Trimmed by a crescent curve of coast on the great Irish Sea."

Should've let him snore.

*    *    *

We both manage to get about three hours sleep after the film. Wake up, set our watches ahead five hours, breakfast is served at 7:30. Hits the spot. Stand in line for the bathroom, quick shave, brush my teeth, comb my hair, ready to go bear hunting with a buggy-whip. About 8:05 Brendan turns from the window with eyes all aglow, says, "Land-ho, lad." Now we switch seats, I look down, there it is, west coast of the Emerald Isle. Brendan points out Galway Bay, then we're over miles and miles of bright green countryside, a crazy-quilt of farmland across the Central Plain. He proudly points out the northern tip of Lough Derg, the little towns of Mountmellick, Portlaoighise, Athy, and finally: "There she is, John—*Wicklow!*" Glad I didn't blink. Tiny little town, but due north is a wide curving beach of sand and "clean shingle" (pebbles), backed by a stretch of "sward" (turf) that's been developed as a public promenade. I take a long look back as we head out over St. George's Channel. Have to admit it's a beautiful little seaside town. Now I know why he comes back here on vacation every year.

My own overseas experience is limited to Germany and Spain. Wouldn't really want to go back to either place. I was in the army in Germany during the Korean War. This was 1952–53, I was still just a kid. Funny thing happened on the way to the war. Took basic training at Fort Jackson, near Columbia, South Carolina. Selected to stay for eight additional weeks of special training in survival techniques behind enemy lines. Never finished; course was terminated because it was found to be too expensive. However, all the men selected for this special training, about 600 of us, have our official records stamped: "Qualified for Survival Behind Enemy Lines." Words to that effect. Qualified? Never finished the course, probably wouldn't last two days. This is the army, don't bother us with details. Boom, I'm sent immediately to the famous spit-and-polish Mighty Seventh Army in Germany. Gonnsenheim, little town outside Frankfurt. Big logo over the main gate: "Born at Sea/Baptized in Blood/ Crowned in Glory." One of those deals. I get there, I ask around, I go, "How do you get transferred out of this outfit?'' They look me up and down, they go: "*Nobody* gets transferred out of the Mighty Seventh, soldier!'' Words etched in stone.

Three weeks later I get transferred out of the Mighty Seventh to the Second Armored Division in Bamberg. Month later I'm ordered to the front, as it were, Neustadt, smack on the Russian-patrolled East German border. Naturally, with my bona fide special qualifications for survival behind enemy lines, I draw twelve-hour shifts with other lucky hotshots patrolling the wide-open border in a couple of Jeeps and armed with carbines and Colt .45s. If we spot any movement, like a column of Russian tanks speeding at us with cannons blazing, it's no sweat, we just radio for our own tanks to move up. Of course, by that time we'd be baptized in blood and crowned in gore. Spent nineteen months there, rose to the rank of sergeant and patrol leader. I'm of German-Irish ancestry, so I looked forward to seeing something of my fatherland. Saw a lot of the border. Even saw some Russians. Kids like me. Fired at us occasionally with their popguns to break the monotony.

Spain, that was something else. Autumn of 1973, Catherine and I spend two weeks on the island of Majorca. NYPD function, Emerald Society. Complete disaster from day one. We arrive en masse, 150 detectives and our wives, find out the hotel screwed up, overbooked the joint, absolutely no rooms available. Only one clown in the hotel speaks English, he suggests we make arrangements with tourists already in the rooms, see if we can get them to share. I go up to this guy, I introduce myself, I inform him very quietly and politely that in the event he can't find a room for Catherine and me, I'll have no logical alternative but to turn the matter over to my friend Brendan Thomas, who's standing there wild-eyed, six-foot-four, 220 pounds of angry anthropoid ape, who specializes in rearranging the bone architecture of people's faces. We get our private room. Brendan and his lovely wife Margaret (Liz Taylor with chestnut hair and hazel eyes) also get a private room. Others are left to their own diplomatic devices. Next two weeks make Alcatraz look like Fantasy Island. Weather's dreadful, nowhere to go, nothing to do,

and the food—well, there's no other word for it, the food
sucks. Majorca's supposed to be celebrated for its lobsters.
Tell you what, these lobsters look like they died from an-
orexia nervosa.

That's the extent of my European experience. Looking
forward to England. Brendan says it's civilized, even though
they talk funny.

We arrive more or less on time, 8:35 A.M., but air traffic's
a bit heavy and we go into a holding pattern due west of
Heathrow. Sunny day, Monday, April 26, I'm still in the
window seat, I'm looking down at green and brown geometrical patterns of farmland. Brendan says he thinks we're cir-
cling over Eton, Windsor, and Runnymede, all southwest
bank of the Thames. Finally get clearance to land, touch
down smoothly at 8:47, taxi to terminal 3, gate 29. Chief said
we'd be met at the gate by a New Scotland Yard detective
named Charles Lawson. Grab our hand luggage and garment
bags, step off the plane, only two people are standing to the
side of the boarding bridge, both attractive young ladies.
One's a short, dark-haired girl in a Pan Am uniform and ID
badge; other's a tall, smartly dressed brunette whose eyes dart
to us, seem to find their mark. She steps over to me smiling.

"Excuse me, are you Mr. Rawlings?"

"Yes."

"I'm Detective Sergeant Charlotte Lawson. Chief Superintendent Kellogg asked me to meet you and Mr. Thomas."

I shake her hand. "Appreciate it very much. How'd you
recognize me?"

"Your Chief Vadney gave us detailed descriptions." Ushers me to the side, shakes hands with Brendan, introduces us
to the uniformed lady, Mary Glass, Pan Am Special Services.

"Welcome to the U.K.," Glass says. "Have a pleasant
trip?"

"Excellent," Brendan says.

Off we go into a long hallway crowded with passengers. I
exchange small talk with Glass, she's more my size, very
bright and personable lady. Brendan chats up Lawson, she's
at least five-eleven, mid-twenties, quite well endowed. Typical of the chief to give us the name Charles Lawson, transpar-

ent mistake for the Duke: *Female* detectives in Scotland Yard? Ya gotta be *kiddin'!*

In the huge, modern, spotless Immigration Hall, non-British passengers are standing in long lines leading to a series of desks. Mary Glass escorts us to a desk at the far left side, no line at all, speaks to the Immigration officer. Brendan and I hand in our landing cards and passports, me first. "Good morning, Mr. Rawlings; how long do you expect to be in the U.K.?" Couple of weeks. "And are you here for business or pleasure?" Business. "Thank you very much; hope you enjoy your stay." Get our passports stamped, Lawson flashes her ID, whole routine takes maybe thirty seconds. Straight ahead, down a flight of stairs into the Customs Hall, enormous, modern, spotless, about twenty-five gleaming carrousels, many surrounded by passengers. Glass leads us to carrousel 7 with the lighted sign "Pan Am 102." We're the first from our flight, luggage hasn't even arrived.

Goes like that, we feel like real VIPs. Glass has other passengers to meet, wishes us luck, we thank her. Brendan reaches in his breast pocket, for a horrible second I think he's going to tip this lovely lady, I nudge him hard in the ribs. Gives me an indignant look, takes out a cigar. Glass leaves, Lawson goes off to grab a spotless brown luggage "trolley," they're in plentiful supply, something you'd never see at JFK unless it had a uniformed man behind it with his hand out. Civilized people, these Brits. Ten, fifteen minutes later we have our two suitcases, we're on a first-name basis with Charlotte, we're wheeling our trolley under a big green sign that reads—this is no shit—it reads: NOTHING TO DECLARE. Big red sign to the left reads: GOODS TO DECLARE. Out we go, nothing to declare, I can't believe this. We could be wheeling out fifty kilos of heroin here, whatever, nothing to declare. Charlotte tells us they spot-check, but still. This is civilized stuff, they actually trust people here. Imagine something like this at JFK? No way. Forget it. Guilty till proven innocent.

Charlotte's car is a light-gray 1982 Hillman. Looks very small, but our suitcases, carry-on luggage, and garment bags fit snugly in the "boot" (trunk) and it seats four, so Brendan has plenty of room to stretch his legs in back. From the minute Charlotte puts it in gear and pulls out into heavy traffic, we know we're in the presence of a superb driver. Fast hands, sharp reflexes, excellent peripheral vision, sound judgment, this kid's got it all. Makes me feel secure because I don't really trust many drivers. Glad we didn't have to rent a car and try this ourselves; fighting a jet-lag while attempting to drive on the left side of the road from the right-hand seat and shifting with the left hand doesn't bring happy thoughts.

Still, the M4 is a super divided freeway and we roar due east past miles of farmland, cows and horses standing in the distant mist, past Osterley Park and Chiswick, into West Kensington where the M4 becomes Talgarth Road, changes to Cromwell Road around Earl's Court. Now Cromwell becomes Brompton Road heading northeast into the Knightsbridge-Belgravia area, elegant living and luxury stores, and there it is off to our right, the block-long Harrods, even I've heard about Harrods, reminds me I promised to buy Catherine a gift in there. Continue northeast to the end of Brompton, Hyde Park is straight ahead, trees pale green in the early spring, now a right into Knightsbridge itself, east past Albert Gate and Apsley House, then she takes the roundabout at Hyde Park Corner, hangs a left into Constitution Hill, and ahead to our right is the north wing of Buckingham Palace. Out front, Charlotte does a complete circle around the Queen Victoria Memorial so I can get a good view of the main entrance and forecourt. Palace is bright white in the sun and looks much larger than its pictures. Royal Standard is flying from the roof, meaning the Queen is in residence today. It's only 9:35, too early for the Changing of the Guard.

Back to business, this isn't the scenic route, it's the most direct route from the airport to the Yard. Now Charlotte heads south on Petty France into Broadway, and suddenly we're looking at a modern skyscraper straight from Manhattan: New Scotland Yard. Glass and concrete reaching for the sky; can't even see the top floors from the car. First few stories are surrounded by steel scaffolding that provides a "street bridge" over the sidewalks to protect pedestrians. What's happening? Charlotte's a bit embarrassed about this.

Building's only fifteen years old but already the concrete slabs that support each horizontal span of six adjoining windows are beginning to crack. Small fragments of concrete periodically fall to the street. Architects and engineers are attempting to correct the problem and estimates run to millions of pounds. Not a very pleasant subject for Charlotte, she obviously has a great deal of pride in the Yard, but she tells it like it is.

We leave our luggage in the car. Appointment with Chief Superintendent Kellogg is at ten, so we're about fifteen minutes early. First thing I notice, security around here is very tight. Both revolving doors to the lobby are guarded by officers in immaculate dark-blue uniforms and caps, clean white shirts, black ties, shined shoes, even their buttons look freshly polished; wish certain uniformed NYPD officers could see these guys. They don't check ID outside the doors, they merely observe who's entering; each is equipped with a walkie-talkie and a "truncheon" (billy). Lobby is a large, brightly lighted rectangular area with a long reception desk manned by three civilians.

Charlotte flashes her ID at the desk, makes a quick phone call. Superintendent Kellogg is in a meeting; he'll come down to sign our passes personally at ten. She asks us to wait in the little lounge area to the far right, she'll join us upstairs. We go over, sit on one of the blue couches in the lounge area, watch the steady stream of men and women come through the revolving doors. Uniformed guards are posted at the wide marble entrances to the two banks of elevators. Every employee must show his or her ID before entering the elevator areas; every visitor or messenger must have a pass issued at the desk. After five minutes Brendan and I think we can distinguish between clerical workers and detectives by the manner in which they show their ID. They all have identical thin leather card holders, none have metal badges like us. Clerical workers open their leather holders long before they reach one of the guards, then hold the ID in plain sight as they pass. Detectives, both men and women, all smartly dressed, invariably wait till the last split-second before flashing the ID.

Another five minutes and I'm getting restless. Near the
long glass wall opposite the reception desk is a prominent
marble stand holding two adjoining glass display cases. I get
up, stroll over, take a look. Glass case to the left has a round
opening in the top and a tall "eternal flame" burns inside;
case to the right holds a thick book opened to the middle,
apparently filled with names. An inscription is chiseled into
the marble stand dedicating the eternal flame to the memory
of members of the Metropolitan Police Force who lost their
lives in the service of their country during both world wars.

Shortly before ten o'clock a tall muscular man with longish
gray-white hair walks briskly toward us wearing a dark-gray
three-piece suit and dark tie. His deeply lined face reveals
stress and fatigue but he manages a smile as he approaches.

"Detectives Thomas and Rawlings?"

"Yes, sir."

"Yes, sir."

"Ashley Kellogg; sorry for the delay."

We stand, shake hands, exchange greetings as he escorts us
to the desk. Now he has to fill out an individual pass for each
of us in triplicate, which we have to sign. Next we're on an
elevator to the sixteenth floor, devoted primarily to CID's C
Department, and into the Cl area, Serious Crime Branch.

Kellogg has a modest rectangular office overlooking Broadway. Fluorescent lighting, white walls with tastefully framed
lithographs of nineteenth-century London street scenes, fitted
gray carpeting. His desk, covered with piles of neatly arranged folders and papers, faces away from the wide windows; there are four visitors' chairs, two small tables, and a
low bookcase. Brendan and I take the two chairs to the left of
his desk. Instead of sitting behind the desk, he selects a chair
against the wall directly opposite us.

"Tell me," he says smiling, "does Chief Vadney still
conceal that tape recorder under his visitors' chairs?"

"Yes, sir, I'm afraid so," Brendan says.

He joins us in soft laughter, crosses his legs. "Delightful
man, Vadney, I've known him for—oh, it must be eight, nine
years now. We've worked together on numerous cases both

here and in New York. Any chance he might get over for this one?"

"There's a strong possibility," I tell him. "He has a personal interest in this case, wants us to keep in close touch."

Kellogg's blue eyes sparkle warmly at the thought of a Vadney visit. Glances at his watch now, speaks in his usual rapid clipped accent: "Monday mornings are particularly hectic around here, I have another meeting at ten-thirty, so we might just as well get on with it. Naturally, we're well informed about the details of the robbery; it received a great deal of publicity here. Quite an extraordinary case indeed. I gather from Chief Vadney that you have good reason to believe Miss Alvarado may have entered this country within the past three or four days, is that correct?"

"That's our assumption," Brendan says.

"Yes. Now if you'll brief me on specifics, we'll see to it that you receive all necessary assistance—manpower, vehicles, special equipment, anything you might require. Have you managed to narrow her possible whereabouts to a specific area?"

"Epping Forest," I tell him.

"Ah, Epping Forest. That's northeast of Central London, very large area. Well, then, initially we might have you liaise with local officers in Epping Forest. Because, let's be fair, the people who know the area best are the local officers, particularly those who've been there a long time. I mean we know Epping Forest well because we use it for various types of exercises. It's not an easy area from the standpoint of investigation because it's so big and some parts are difficult to get to. Only one main road goes through it. Do you have anything more specific, the name of a road or the nearest village?"

"Yes," I tell him. "We're looking for the home of Miss Phyllis Waring."

He frowns. "The home of—?"

"Miss Phyllis Waring. I believe she's lived there since about nineteen thirty-eight."

Kellogg sits back, hesitates. "Yes, we're all quite familiar with Miss Waring. You realize, of course, you're talking about the *owner* of the North Star Diamond?''

"Yes, sir."

"Miss Waring is a very old lady. Eighty-two, I believe, and a recluse at that. As I understand it, she hasn't been seen in public for many years."

"That's our understanding, yes."

"Well, there's no problem in finding the house itself, it's called Pretoria House, very large estate. But, frankly, I'd be very loath to—go in and disturb the old lady's privacy. Unless we had compelling evidence that it was necessary."

"We don't want to go in," I explain. "We just want to do surveillance on the house."

He looks relieved. "I'm sure that can be arranged without any difficulty whatsoever." Then, after a pause: "Forgive me, but I can't understand the connection. Why would this Alvarado woman—?"

"We don't know," Brendan says softly.

"But you have good reason to believe she's there?"

"Yes, sir," I say.

"Very strange indeed."

"Miss Alvarado's a strange woman," Brendan says.

Kellogg nods, glances toward the window. "So is Miss Waring, as you'll doubtless find out."

# 11

THE NEAREST PUB is just a few doors away from the Yard on Broadway, called the Feathers, famous old Victorian haunt straight out of Sir Arthur Conan Doyle. You stand in front of this elegant place with its polished marble pillars, gracefully arched windows, elaborate geometrical moldings on the upper floors, then glance up to your right at the huge modern skyscraper of New Scotland Yard that's already starting to crumble, makes you wonder if space-age architects got beauty confused with burglary. Not that our NYPD headquarters is any better; architects on that one got progress confused with prisons. Anyway, Charlotte Lawson takes Brendan and me to the Feathers for lunch about 11:45 and the ground-floor area is already jammed. We go up the narrow spiral staircase to the Princes' Bar (they call this the first floor) and manage to get a table in one of the recessed windows. First English pub I've ever been in, this is a real education. Now we're in the 1880s for sure, dark varnished woodwork, stained glass windows, heavy carved ornaments, Tiffany-type lamps that used to be gaslit, tends to make Rosie O'Grady's Pub pale in comparison, but of course that's Irish, what do you expect? Beginning to get crowded up here too, strictly self-service.

I go up to the mahogany bar, wait my turn, order "three steins of beer, please." Bartender gives me this look, says,

"Y'want *steins*, gov, go to Germany; 'ere we only got *pints*."
Live and learn. Back to the table, sip our pints, pick up on
the clientele, ranges from construction workers to tweedy
Yard detectives. Charlotte looks over the menu, decides
Brendan and I have to experience an authentic British dish,
happens to be the special, hot homemade steak-and-kidney
pie. Brendan's buying, he ambles up to the food bar, I get a
chance to talk with Charlotte, clear up some questions.

Originally, Chief Superintendent Kellogg selected her to be
our temporary partner because he knew we were after a
young female suspect who's also an alleged killer, and Charlotte happens to be the best young female "shot" (as they
call officers trained in firearms) in the entire Yard. Now that
he knows we plan round-the-clock surveillance on a home in
Epping Forest, he assigns Charlotte to us on a more or less
permanent basis. Reason? She grew up in Woodford (where
her parents still live), a suburb of London that's about five
miles south of Honeylane Plain in Epping Forest where the
Pretoria House is located, so she has a working knowledge of
the general area, including the nearby town of Waltham
Abbey where we'll probably be staying.

"Question," I ask her quietly. "Are you carrying?"

"Yes."

"What type weapon?"

"Smith and Wesson thirty-eight."

"What model?"

"Thirty-six. Chief's Special, two-inch barrel."

I smile, shake my head, take out a cigar. "Happens to be
exactly the same weapon carried by the majority of NYPD
detectives, me included."

"It's standard issue for Yard detectives now. Mind you,
we don't own them, we don't normally carry them."

"So I hear."

She takes out a cigarette, I light it, she keeps her voice
low: "Actually, we started out with the Walther three-eighty
PPK. Discovered it had a tendency to jam under certain
climatic conditions."

"That's the trouble with automatics." I light my cigar, sit

back. "Tell me about yourself. How long you been on the force?"

"Five years. I joined the Cadets at seventeen, I was admitted to the force at eighteen-and-a-half. That may seem young to you, I know your minimum age requirement is twenty-one, but our whole educational system is vastly different from yours, as I'm sure you know. I received the usual fifteen-week training course at Hendon, then I was posted to the station in Woodford for the required two years' probationary period. When I passed the final examinations I immediately applied for the CID and asked specifically for assignment to C-One."

"Why C-One?"

Glances at me a bit sharply. "Why not?"

"No, I'm curious. Why Serious Crime?"

"Why? Because, obviously, apart from Special Branch, it's the most exciting and challenging branch in the Yard. Quite frankly, I enjoy it. And, modesty aside, I have every qualification considered essential for the job. Intellectual, physical, and emotional. Does that answer your question?"

"Completely."

When she smiles, takes a drag on her cigarette and looks away, it occurs to me for the first time that this is a very classy young lady. Let me explain exactly what I mean. First impression, stepping off the plane, I'm aware of this tall, attractive brunette, fashionably dressed, period. Then something happens. Soon as she introduces herself as a detective—snap!—I'm looking at her from an entirely different perspective. I'm not in the baloney business, never have been, so I'll say this straight. Charlotte identifies herself, questions flash through my mind instantly, I can't help it: *Will I be working with her? How much experience does she have? Can I trust her with my life?* That last question may seem dramatic or exaggerated, but I assure you it's not. It's probably the single most critical question that any cop, male or female, with any real street experience at all, asks himself or herself immediately under similar circumstances. You meet a potential partner, from that moment on you're not consciously looking at that person as an attractive or personable male or female, you're looking at a professional cop. And you're asking questions.

Thanks to Chief Kellogg and Charlotte herself, all significant questions are answered except the life-trust one, which I have no way of knowing short of an actual combat situation. So I'm sitting back now, enjoying my pint and cigar, and I'm really starting to look at this kid for the first time. Classy young lady, think I'm going to like working with her. Reminds me in some respects of Terri Krzczek, young detective from the Nineteenth, remember her? Same sort of classic features, high cheekbones, flawless complexion, ultrafeminine voice, but of course Charlotte's about five inches taller and the British accent tends to give an illusion of sophistication beyond her years. To my ear, anyway. If Terri looks like she just stepped out of a Pepsi ad, Charlotte just stepped out of an ad for Schweppes tonic water. Curiously refreshing.

Brendan comes back with a tray, serves the homemade steak-and-kidney pie in little brown casserole dishes, nice and warm. We clink our pints, "Cheers!" Dig right in. Absolutely delicious, I'm beginning to like this kid more every minute.

After lunch she takes us back to the Yard and up for a visit with C7, technical supporting unit, where she signs out for most of the standard surveillance equipment we'll need: Separate high-powered binoculars for day and night; two Nikon cameras; three telescopic lenses (200-, 300-, and 500-millimeter); a dozen rolls of Kodacolor ISO 400 for day; a dozen rolls of the new Kodak Technical Pan for night; and three walkie-talkies. Lastly, Transportation supplies a dark-gray 1980 Triumph TR7 and a dark-brown 1981 Jaguar XJ6 Sedan, both automatic, that can be exchanged for a wide variety of other makes as frequently as we require.

Charlotte pulls her Hillman into the underground garage, we transfer our six pieces of luggage into the Jag (her favorite car), and when she slides behind the wheel of this thing, you know it's pure enjoyment. I ride with her, Brendan takes the TR7, he's experienced on the left side of the road.

Off we go about 2:15, Charlotte leading at a moderate speed. First stop has to be her flat, 34 Fitz-James Avenue,

West Kensington, opposite direction from where we're going, but she has to change and pack. Arrive around 2:35, tree-lined narrow street, quiet residential neighborhood, all parking spaces are taken. She double-parks in front of the building, motions for Brendan to do the same. Jumps out, says, "Ten minutes tops," and you know she means it.

Brendan and I get out, light up cigars, admire these sleek sets of wheels, freshly washed and waxed, Yard goes first class all the way. Charlotte's "block of flats," as she calls them, occupy the corner of Fitz-James Avenue and the North End Road, relatively fashionable area. Rectangular flagstone courtyard gives way to what appears to be an old, distinguished brick building—all five stories and three sides completely encased in steel scaffolding! Disease must be contagious. Now we see crews of workmen are sandblasting the old brick façade, repairing the ornate balconies, replacing drainpipes, patching the roof. Not too pleasant for tenants who stay home all day. Here's one white-haired old witch on the balcony of a fourth-floor flat, she's screaming bloody murder at one of the workers for spilling something on her flower boxes. Brendan laughs, says softly, "Give 'im 'ell, luv!"

Less than ten minutes pass, Charlotte walks briskly through the courtyard in a chic tan suede jacket and designer jeans, clutches a shoulder bag, carries a matching suitcase. Tells us we're in luck: She called the famed Welsh Harp, one of the few inns in all of ancient Waltham Abbey, managed to reserve two rooms, both with private baths! True luxury awaits us. In we get, off we go amid the fragrance of genuine leather upholstery and purring engines.

Getting to Epping Forest from Central London, you take A106 northeast through Hackney, Leyton, Wanstead, get on the A104 at Whipps Cross, follow it through Woodford, and you're in the heart of the Forest itself. As Charlotte drives, she tells me just enough basic history to make the pale-green scenery intriguing: Epping Forest stretches over 6,000 acres and includes some of the oldest trees and plants known to man. Evolved over some 10,000 years; archaeologists have evidence that human beings lived in this forest around 8,000

B.C. Takes you back. Although the Romans, Saxons, and Normans all played a part in changing the forest over the centuries (it was once 60,000 acres), it's still one of the few surviving examples of medieval woodland management. Beats the hell out of Muir Woods.

We take a left at the little town of Wake Arms, head northwest on A121 through Honeylane Plain (where the Pretoria House is) and arrive in Waltham Abbey about four o'clock. Welsh Harp is in the little market square here, two-story inn dating from the fifteenth century, painted white with dark vertical timbers and a sloping slate roof. One thing I notice, far left side of the second floor is listing badly, almost dangerously, over the passageway that leads to the parking lot in back. Hope that's not one of our rooms up there, I wouldn't sleep a wink at that angle. We drive carefully through the passage (a Caddy would never make this mother) and from the parking lot we have a good view of the huge 922-year-old stone church that gave the town its name. Charlotte says it was built by King Harold in 1060 and it's the oldest and most complete Norman church in the country. End of history lesson, but it gives you pause to consider this magnificent thing was standing here five-and-a-half centuries before the Pilgrims landed at Plymouth Rock. King Harold was killed by the Saxons in 1066, Charlotte adds, he's buried out back, like to see his grave? Not after steak-and-kidney pie, thanks, maybe tomorrow.

After checking in (Brendan and I got the listing room, now we know why there were vacancies), we get right to business while there's still daylight. Pile in the Jag, Charlotte drives us back to Honeylane Plain, about two miles southeast, to make our first pass on the Pretoria House. Turns out to be in a sparsely wooded residential area, Blackweir Lane, roughly half a mile south of A121.

Drive past slowly on the narrow asphalt road. In an area of sedate old Victorian mansions, the exterior doesn't seem to stand out in any respect but size, primarily length. Seen through the bars of a black wrought-iron fence easily ten feet high and topped by barbed wire, the house is four stories of red and gray brick, tall windows and balcony doors framed in white stone, and the steep slate roof holds ornate garret windows and multiple chimneys. In soft afternoon light the third-floor windows are like mirrors reflecting the new leaves of two stately elms flanking the pillared entrance. Heavy wrought-iron gate appears to be the only entry to the graveled circular driveway, but the drive branches off to the right and disappears behind the house, maybe to a garage.

Directly across the road is a little area of birch and elm trees, followed by another mansion set way back among trees and shrubbery, followed by another small wooded area. Not exactly ideal for surveillance from the relative comfort of a car, but you could always hide the vehicle somewhere and observe from the woods. I can visualize myself sitting out on a limb for my eight-hour shifts, binoculars and Nikon at the ready. Charlotte continues up the road about a quarter-mile, turns around with the help of a driveway, back we come for a second pass, but we're concentrating on the opposite side of the road. Past the little area of birch and elm directly opposite the house is a long driveway leading up to an old stone house atop a knoll; two cars are parked outside. Beyond that, another patch of woods. Seems to rule out surveillance from a vehicle. Wait a minute, Charlotte has an idea. Turns left at the next crossroad, Southworth Hill, sure enough we're climbing a short hill. Levels out, next hill is much steeper. No houses along this road, woods becoming more dense. Levels out again, Charlotte hangs a sharp left into an unmarked narrow dirt road through the trees. Clearing up ahead, farmland, we're obviously on private property. Look down the two hills to our left, we're catching glimpses of Blackweir Lane between clusters of trees, runs roughly parallel to the dirt road. Continue ahead maybe fifty yards, now we can see the back of that old stone house on the knoll; beyond and below to its right, fair to middling high-angle view of Pretoria House. Charlotte stops here, I grab the binoculars, get out, take a look. Not bad at all: I can see the gate, part of the circular driveway, most of the front entrance and, from this elevation, a gravel parking area out back near the garage. Made in the shade for surveillance, except of course we're trespassing on somebody's farmland. No house or barn in

sight, just three or four acres of freshly plowed furrows in
long neat rows, spring planting, don't know what crops.
Well, if Farmer Fosdick finds one of us parked here with
binoculars and cameras, we can always say we're birdwatchers.
Birdwatching is big in Britain, he'll buy it all the way:
Birdwatchers from New York, you say? Yes, sir, we're looking
for the strange and elusive Alvarado Pussy.

Back to Waltham Abbey, now the jet-lag is beginning to
catch up to us in a hurry. Time is of the essence, as usual, so
Charlotte volunteers to take the first surveillance shift, 8:00
P.M. to 4:00 A.M. Brendan and I flip a coin for the next, he
loses with a groan, draws 4:00 A.M. to noon.

Cocktails about six downstairs in the Welsh Harp pub at a
table near the giant stone fireplace, bathed in the soft glow of
candlelight and a crackling fire, this is real fifteenth-century
stuff. Next, at Charlotte's urging, delicate prawn cocktails in
a tangy sauce, followed by medium-rare roast beef and York-
shire pudding, hearty burgundy in an ancient carafe; basic
menu here hasn't changed in three centuries. Almost embarrassed to pay the tab with my American Express card; elderly
waiter accepts it with resignation. Plastic is the price of
progress.

Next morning dawns bleak and chill in the sagging old room,
feel like a dizzy Norman king. Vaguely remember Brendan's
alarm going off at three, poor devil. Take a leisurely hot bath
in this enormous old tub supported by iron claws. Water tank
for the toilet is suspended from the ceiling and operated by a
long pull-chain. Separate faucets for hot and cold water, have
to fill the sink to shave because the hot water's actually
steaming. White turtleneck, blue blazer, gray trousers, wend
my way down the narrow stairs to the pub for breakfast.
Order bacon and eggs, black coffee, English muffin. Elderly
waiter gives me this look. "Y'want English *muffins*, mate, go
to America; 'ere we only got *toast*." Probably still upset
about the plastic.

Figure Charlotte will sleep till about noon, I'll be off in the
Jag to relieve Brendan by then, so I decide to take a stroll
around town. First stop, Barclays Bank in Market Square,

first chance I've had to exchange currency. Exchange rate today is 1.74, not bad; $100 U.S. buys 57 pounds, 47 pence. Next stop, Bookends, just across the street from the Welsh Harp, to buy a map or guidebook of some kind. Exterior is deceptive, quite a large place, same basic architecture as the inn, excellent selection of hardcovers and paperbacks. I'm the only customer in the store at this hour, so the owner comes over, gives me his undivided attention: Scholarly, bearded, middle-aged man, balding, rather thick rimless glasses that magnify his blue eyes. Tell him I'm from New York, staying at the inn, want to tour the town, interested in guidebooks. Wind up with two little tour booklets, both with maps, one full-color brochure on the abbey itself, and a larger booklet on the history of Epping Forest.

As we're walking to the cash register counter in the middle of the store, I notice one of the hardcover nonfiction best sellers on display is *Pretoria and the North Star* by Aubrey Davis. Pick it up, look it over; handsome Oxford University edition with a black-and-white photo of Sir Charles Pretoria on the jacket.

"Popular book?" I ask.

"Oh, yes, quite." He hesitates at the cash register, waiting to see if I'll buy it.

I leaf through it. Center section has a selection of photos including several of Miss Waring and one of the Pretoria House. "I read excerpts from this, published in another book. Very interesting."

"Yes, indeed. Actually, it caused quite a scandal here, the newspapers in London made the story something of a cause célèbre, the tabloids, you know."

"That a fact?"

"Yes. All in the most dreadful taste. That was several years ago, of course, nineteen-eighty, I believe. It became the number-one best seller in the country the very first week it was published."

"Because of the scandal?"

He frowns, thinks about it. "Initially, yes. No question that had a lot to do with it initially." Reaches in the pocket of his brown herringbone jacket, takes out a black leather tobacco pouch and slender pipe. "But quite frankly, in retrospect, the truth is—in my judgment anyway—the truth is, it's really quite an extraordinary biography in its own right. I mean, in all fairness, the illicit love affair occupies only a very small portion of the work itself. Granted, that's what caught the public's fancy, of course. But the proof of the pudding, it's really stood the test of time now, hasn't it? Two years later it's gone to many more printings and it's still very much in demand. It is, after all, the definitive biography of Sir Charles, none of the others compare to it in sheer primary sources of research."

"Still on the best-seller lists?"

"Oh, no. No, at least not in London, not in the *Times*, it's been off for—perhaps a year or more. But here in this area, for example, it's still a very good seller indeed. Particularly during the summer, the tourist season. As you may know, Miss Waring happens to live in Epping Forest."

"Didn't know that."

"Oh, yes. Just several miles southeast of here, in Honeylane Plain, to be precise. Sir Charles willed her his summer estate there, the Pretoria House, magnificent place." Fills his pipe by scooping it around in the pouch. "Unfortunately, tourists have been driving there the past two summers, droves of them, driving there, stopping in front, taking snapshots, you know, making a bloody nuisance of themselves. Well, apparently that's coming to an end now, apparently the estate is being put up for sale."

"Really?"

Nods, takes out a box of wooden matches, lights the pipe, lips making a soft sucking noise. "Yes, it's a shame."

"She's selling it because of the tourists?"

Thick billows of smoke obscure his face. "No, no. The rumor is—and I can easily accept this—the rumor is, Miss Waring simply cannot afford the upkeep now. Can't say it surprises anybody in this day and age, inflation being what it is. I mean, she's always had to employ a full-time staff for one thing. On an estate that large—twenty-two rooms, twelve acres of grounds out back—the maintenance costs alone must

be positively staggering. Gardners, house servants, kitchen
help, chauffeur, the lot.''

"Sounds like 'Upstairs, Downstairs.' "

He smiles, pipe smoking nicely in his clenched teeth,
pleasant aroma. " 'Upstairs, Downstairs,' precisely. Victorian,
aristocratic standards. Except that she's paying nineteen eighty-
two prices. I mean, imagine just heating a place like that six
months a year. Imagine the property tax alone!''

I hand him the book. "Think I'll take it. I understood from
the excerpt I read that Sir Charles left her a great deal of
money, plus ownership of the North Star.''

"Quite true." He adds up the five items quickly, rings up
the sale. "Twelve pounds seventy-five." Takes my twenty
pound note. "Sir Charles left her very well off indeed, but
one has to remember that was some forty-four years ago."
Hands me my change. "Seven pounds twenty-five, thank you
very much."

"What about the North Star?"

"Yes, well, that's a story in itself. As I understand it, the
insurance premiums had been escalating at an alarming rate
over the past twenty years or so. As the value of the diamond
itself continued to increase. I believe, if I remember cor-
rectly, Sir Charles took out trustee-account insurance on the
diamond through Lloyd's of London in the amount of two
hundred fifty thousand pounds in the late nineteen-thirties. To
cover premiums of five thousand pounds a year for some fifty
years. Well, as I understand it, that initial premium has now
more than quadrupled. Ridiculous, really, twenty thousand
pounds a year for insurance. Little wonder, Miss Waring was
more or less forced to put the diamond up for auction in New
York, as you probably know."

"Yes. It was stolen, I read about it."

"Stolen along with eleven other stones from one of your
finest galleries. Greatest diamond robbery in history, according to the papers. But I'll tell you something." Places the
five books in a paper bag, hands it to me. "Callous as it may
seem, I believe it was a blessing in disguise for the old lady. I
mean, she's kept her premiums strictly to date all these
years—or I should say the trustee has—and the stone's cur-

rent value, according to the papers, is two-point-seven-five million pounds. Now, here's the big question: If the New York auction had in fact taken place, who's to say that any individual or any organization, however large, would actually have submitted a bid anywhere near that amount? Who's to say the diamond would indeed have been sold at all?"

"I see what you mean."

"You see? But of course it's all academic now, isn't it? I mean, Lloyd's will surely honor the claim for the full amount, following the normal waiting period."

"So the lady's worries are over."

"It would appear so, yes. Unless there are extenuating circumstances. For example, she may already be in serious debt. But certainly not to the tune of two-and-three-quarter million pounds."

"But the house is definitely for sale?"

"On the market fairly recently, yes. Of course, with the interest rate being what it is, I expect prospective buyers are few and far between. The real-estate market here is terribly depressed. I understand it's the same in the States."

"Oh, yes. Would you happen to know the real-estate agent?"

"The—for the Pretoria House?"

"Yes."

Removes his pipe. "Yes, it's an exclusive listing with a local firm, Jeremy Kirby. Might you—? If you don't mind my asking, might you be interested yourself?"

I smile, shake my head. "Not me, personally, but it's a—maybe it's a happy coincidence. I'm here with two business associates. We represent a New York client who's interested in real estate in the general area of Epping Forest. That's actually why we're here; just arrived last night."

"I see."

"We represent Walter F. Molars, president of the New York philanthropic foundation of the same name. Within the next year or so he wants to move his family and domestic help to an estate in this general area."

Raises his eyebrows, puffs on the pipe again. "Well, by all means, you should pay a visit to Mr. Kirby. He's right in the square, I'll show you." Leads me to the front of the store, points through the window. "Jeremy Kirby, just near Barclays Bank."

I shake his hand. "Thank you very much."

Off I go, feeling every inch the distinguished representative of the Walter F. Molars Philanthropic Society. Real-estate office is small but relatively modern compared to most buildings in the square, big spotless windows with display shelves holding several dozen photos and descriptions of residential properties under the logo:

### JEREMY KIRBY
The 'Real' Estate Agents

Maisonettes to Mansions

One of the photos in the window, prominently placed, is that of the Pretoria House, impressive high-angle shot, obviously taken from a helicopter. Lengthy description written in typical British understatement. Asking price: £750,000. A steal.

In I go. Modern décor, oil paintings of local landscapes, large framed detail maps of surrounding areas, two teakwood desks on opposite sides of the room, left one occupied by a smartly attired, diminutive, middle-aged blonde lady who's talking on the phone; other desk is empty. She smiles, motions for me to take a seat, finishes the call quickly. Turns out to be Mrs. Elizabeth Kirby, wife and partner, her husband's out showing a property. Offers me a cup of coffee, delightful Irish-English accent, soft-spoken, eloquent. As I explain the whole Walter F. Molars bit, her eyes seem to widen involuntarily. Asks me to fill out a standard questionnaire, gets on the phone immediately.

Comprehensive questionnaire; I fill it out carefully. Today it's standard operating procedure for NYPD detectives to carry at least one set of false identification cards, usually a New York State driver's license and a Social Security card, officially cleared by the respective state and government agencies. My phony cards are in the name of John Phillip Gaulrapp. Strong, solid German-Irish name, happen to like it.

Mrs. Kirby has to talk with several people before she reaches someone with authority. Bottom line, Miss Waring is temporarily indisposed, but she's already given Mrs. Kirby virtual carte blanche to show the place to any individual or group she deems to be acceptable. Representatives of the Walter F. Molars Philanthropic Society are obviously in that select category. Just a moment, please. Holds her hand over the mouthpiece.

"What time would be convenient for you, Mr. Gaulrapp?"

I shrug. "Whatever time's convenient for you."

She shrugs. "This morning?"

"No problem."

Glances at her watch. "Shall we say—eleven o'clock then?"

Glance at my watch. "Excellent."

# 12

CHARLOTTE OPENS HER DOOR CAUTIOUSLY, chain-lock secure, in response to my knocks at 10:05; no telephones in these ancient rooms. Kid looks good without makeup and less than six hours sleep, curiously refreshed. I hand her a cup of black coffee, ask her to get dressed in her Sunday best and meet me in the downstairs pub at 10:45 sharp, I'll explain everything. Looks at me with these penetrating dark-blue eyes, says, "I'll be there." Believe it. I go down, take a window-table in front, order another coffee. Place is empty except for the elderly waiter and a kitchen crew getting geared up for the lunch crowd. Sun is finally out, warm yellow shafts slant through the old lead-framed diamond-shaped panes. I light up a cigar, sip my coffee, take advantage of a chance to read short sections of *Pretoria and the North Star*. First I study the three black-and-white photos of Phyllis Waring, all circa 1920 according to the captions: (1) At a sidewalk café in Paris with her table companion cropped out; (2) in a swimsuit at a beach in St-Tropez with her blanket companion cropped out; (3) formal head-and-shoulders three-quarter profile, young oval face with mischievous dark-brown eyes, almost perfect teeth, small dimples, framed by long, dark, thick hair. Photo in the one-piece swimsuit reveals more than adequate breasts, unusually slim waist, extremely attractive legs. Vivien Leigh she's not, at least not in these shots, but biographer Davis's description of "hauntingly beautiful" is right on target. Look her up in the index, Davis devotes maybe thirty-five pages to her illustrious love affair that began when she was all of seventeen. Background is somewhat sketchy but enlightening:

Born Phyllis May Waring on March 30, 1900, in the small resort of Hove in southwest Sussex on the English Channel near Brighton, she was the youngest child and only daughter of Edward Thomas Waring, a butler, and Ada Georgiana Grant, who became a "court dressmaker" after marriage. She had two brothers, Cyril (1894–1968), and Roderick (1897–1960).

In 1907 the family moved to Cheltenham, a resort in north Gloucestershire, where Miss Waring attended school until the age of sixteen. Although she expressed a strong desire to study medicine, financial considerations made this impossible. Instead she was trained to be a beautician and hairdresser, serving a three-year apprenticeship in Cheltenham.

It was during this period, in the summer of 1917, that she first met Sir Charles, then forty-five, who was on an extended holiday with his family in Cheltenham. Although the specific circumstances of their first encounter are not known, letters from family and friends confirm that Sir Charles was "abruptly called back to London on business on August 22," leaving his family at the resort. He did not resume his holiday until September 6. Miss Waring's two-week holiday began and ended during the same time; her letters to friends and family were postmarked from London between August 24 and September 2.

In the summer of 1918, Sir Charles and his family took their holiday in Paris; Miss Waring wrote to friends from the same hotel where the Pretorias were staying, the famed Le Bristol on fashionable Faubourg St. Honoré. The following summer Miss Waring spent two weeks at an exclusive resort in the Cap d'Antibes where Sir Charles and his family had rented a villa. By that time, of course, the affair was common gossip among the British aristocracy.

When Miss Waring became a fully qualified beautician and hairdresser in 1920, she left home to accept a position in Torquay, Devonshire, a resort on the Channel. True to form, Sir Charles and his wife spent the summer there. In the autumn Miss Waring accepted a better position at a salon in Croydon, north Surrey, but remained only a few weeks before her appointment to a managerial position at London's prestigious Katté salon, situated on Threadneedle Street between the Bank of England and the Stock Exchange. Before the spring of that year she moved into a comfortable home in Woodford Green, Essex, deeded to her by Sir Charles, and commuted to London daily by train. . . .

Goes on into the delicious understated details of their torrid and at times "tawdry" (guess he means "kinky") affair, 1921–1938, then launches into somewhat sensational but carefully documented facts and faces concerning her—wow! —various new assignations with distinguished gentlemen friends throughout the 1940s; at least she had the decency to observe the obligatory two-year mourning period after Sir Charles hopped the hearse. Biographer Davis sure did his homework; look forward to reading the sordid research.

Charlotte shows up several minutes early in a quietly elegant soft-blue figure-flattering inspiration of Yves Saint Laurent, looks every slender inch a dignified British representative of the Walter F. Molars Philanthropic Society. I fill her in on the details, she's delighted. Now we discuss poor Brendan. No question we could reach him with the Yard's high-powered walkie-talkies, but why not surprise him, astound him, pump a little adrenaline into his otherwise drab morning shift? I can see his eyes now as Mrs. Kirby's sleek limo or whatever glides around the circular drive and Charlotte and I emerge into the bright April sunlight. I'll turn toward the hills, of course, maybe try to give him a subtle signal with a selected finger. Hope he has the Nikon ready.

Arm-in-arm we stroll across the sunny Market Square, arrive punctually at eleven. Introduce Charlotte to Mrs. Kirby, they chat a bit, seem to hit it off at first Yves-drop. Now, ready for this, Mrs. Kirby casually removes a cordless telephone receiver from her desk, pulls up the antenna, dials a number, asks the chauffeur, who happens to be named Trevor, to come 'round for us, thank you very much. Out we go, up it rolls, turning heads in the square, must say even I'm

impressed with this touch, happen to know something about
British cars from listening to Jim Mairs over the years. Mairs
would call this *nouveau*-classic, but it's a sight to behold:
Mint condition shell-gray 1972 Rolls-Royce Silver Shadow
four-door saloon, eight cylinder ninety-degree V-unit with
overhead valves, fully automatic transmission, four forward
speeds and reverse through epicyclic gears, independent front
and rear suspension, two-speed automatic height control for
rough roads or heavy loads. Shell-gray uniformed Trevor
opens the rear door, we slide into red leather upholstery of
the finest English topgrain hide, matching red deep-pile carpets, facia panel and door garnish rails of walnut veneer,
padded capping rail covered in black leather, vanity mirrors
for the ladies.

Off we glide past gawking commoners. Care for a tiny
pick-me-up? Don't mind if we do. Mrs. Kirby touches a
button, walnut panel opens, out slides a fully equipped bar,
Waterford decanters and glasses, silver ice bucket and tongs.
I do the honors, gin and tonic all around, sculptured lemon
twists. Civilized motoring. Mrs. Kirby turns out to be a
veritable Epping Forest history book, constant line of understated chatter. Fine with us. Over the highway and through
the wood, to grandmother's house we go. Arrive about 11:10,
greeted at the wrought-iron gate by a distinguished silver-
haired man in banker's gray uniform and spotless white gloves,
Exeter would piss green with envy.

"Good morning."

"Good morning. I'm Mrs. Kirby, we have—"

"Yes, madam, you're expected. Miss Waring is in the
sauna room at present and asks not to be disturbed, but you're
cordially invited to view the rest of the house and grounds at
your leisure."

"Thank you very much."

Through the gate, around the circular drive, tires crunching, stop under the stately elms at the pillared entrance.
Distinguished silver-haired butler in banker's gray uniform
and spotless white gloves waits for us on the narrow sidewalk, opens our door.

"Good morning."

"Good morning. I'm Mrs. Kirby, we have—"

"Yes, madam, you're expected. Miss Waring is in the sauna room at present and asks not be be disturbed, but you're—"

"Yes, we know, thank you very much."

I slide out, glance around, select the approximate spot on the hill where Brendan surely sits bug-eyed behind the binoculars (or camera by now), flabbergasted, squirting his knickers with any luck. Just before turning to join the others, I push back an invisible lock of hair from my forehead with the quick flick of a rigid middle finger.

Butler opens the tall solid-oak door, Mrs. Kirby leads the way along a lengthy oak-paneled hallway, footsteps echoing, finally pauses at the top of a short flight of steps leading down to one of the most gigantic and lavishly furnished living rooms I've ever seen. Actually, as Mrs. Kirby explains in hushed tones, it's called the ballroom, which is essentially what it was under its original owner just after the turn of the century. We stand silently for a moment; no one's in the room. Long thin ribbons of sunlight slant from high windows to touch leather couches, luxurious armchairs, statues, paintings, glass tables holding art objects that reflect the sunshafts. We walk down the steps, guarded at floor level by two "knights" in gleaming full-plate sixteenth-century armor. Mrs. Kirby resumes the chatter:

"The room itself is fifty feet by thirty-five feet; appears a great deal larger, doesn't it? As I understand it, the entire room was constructed originally in Italy for some titled aristocrat or other, then dismantled and shipped over in numbered pieces. As you can see, the walls are paneled in solid oak, the floor is inlaid teak, the fireplace is marble, made in Italy." Cranes her neck: "The ceiling was hand-carved and hand-decorated, also imported piece by piece from Italy."

I stroll over to see the painting above the huge fireplace. It's Picasso's original *Femme Nue Endormie*. To the left, in the corner, is a kinetic sculpture titled *Domino Machine*, by Gordon Barlow. Behind the white couch directly opposite the fireplace is a long narrow table holding a glass-topped stereo complex that's easily fifteen feet long. Charlotte goes to the north wall, looks at a painting that even I recognize at a glance, Alfred Leslie's *Playboy of the Western World*. I walk over to take a closer look; as I do, Mrs. Kirby rolls back a large section of the wall to reveal a projection room with two modern thirty-five-millimeter movie projectors covered by clear plastic. She tells us the wall on the far opposite side rolls back electronically to reveal the wide-angle theater-sized screen.

Tour of all four floors and twenty-two rooms takes well over an hour, then she's set to show us the grounds. I tell her I'm sure the twelve acres are more than adequate for Mr. Molars. Now we'd like to see the downstairs pool area; we're certain Mr. Molars will want a first-hand report on that.

Mrs. Kirby shrugs, smiles. "As you know, Miss Waring's in the sauna room down there."

I glance at my watch. "It's been over an hour, Mrs. Kirby."

"Well, you heard the gentlemen at the gate and door."

"All right then," Charlotte says agreeably. "Let's skip the sauna room entirely, shall we? Just show us the pool area and we'll be on our way."

She frowns. "The sauna room adjoins the pool."

I frown.

Charlotte frowns. "Surely the door will be closed."

"This *is* distressing," Mrs. Kirby says quietly. "Miss Waring left very specific instructions not to be disturbed. I really can't go against her wishes."

Charlotte checks her watch, speaks softly. "Mrs. Kirby, we have another estate to see at one o'clock this afternoon in Wake Arms, then still another near High Beach at three. Wednesday through Friday are booked solidly and we'll be leaving this particular area Saturday morning. Our assignment is to view each estate in its entirety."

Mrs. Kirby hesitates, glances away; the commission on a £750,000 sale does tend to give one pause, especially in a flat market.

I clear my throat quietly. "If the pool's under repair at the present time, we can easily—"

"Oh, *no*," she snaps. "No, no, the pool is fine, the pool is absolutely—breathtaking."

Charlotte checks her watch.

I check mine. "Mrs. Kirby, I think we've taken up enough of your time. You've been very kind and we appreciate—"

"Wait a minute," she says decisively. "We'll take a quick peek at the pool."

At the northwest corner of the ballroom near the stereo library (that has literally thousands of albums and tapes), we descend a narrow flight of stairs, go through a heavy door, and emerge into the pool area, which I can only describe as mind-blowing: You step into a pleasantly warm, distinctly South Seas atmosphere complete with white coral formations, exotic and fragrant plants and trees, giant Polynesian statues, and a contoured swimming pool forty feet long with a cavelike opening at water level leading, Mrs. Kirby explains, to a hidden "grotto." Also points out an underwater window at the deep end of the pool and tells us it's part of a lower-level bar where one can watch the swimmers. If one cares to.

Door to the cedar-paneled sauna room is open; nobody in there, to Mrs. Kirby's great relief. There's an adjoining sunlamp room, game room, gymnasium, even a small bowling alley. Shows us the game room first, a plush and thickly carpeted L-shaped area with a handsome billiard table in the center, flanked by a total of eighteen electronic video games, Pac-Man included, of course. As we're walking around the pool deck to see the gym, we hear a soft splash from inside the hidden grotto. Apparently the only way you can get out of there is to swim underwater through the coral cavelike opening, and a woman is doing that now. We watch her slim figure in the lighted water, bent by the waves, coming up slowly in a white cap and white one-piece swimsuit.

She surfaces, a deeply tanned, dark-eyed, distinguished looking lady, swims to the edge nearest us, gives us a brief, polite smile. Relatively tight-skinned oval face, almost perfect teeth, a trace of dimples, appears to be in her mid-fifties, tops. Voice is calm, but not exactly friendly: "Mrs. Kirby, what can I do for you?"

Kirby's flustered. "Miss Waring, I'm—terribly sorry, I—thought you'd be upstairs by now."

Light from the water flickers on Miss Waring's face as she squints up at us. "Hello, I'm Phyllis Waring."

Charlotte and I squat down, shake her hand, which I note is quite wrinkled and veined, and introduce ourselves. Seeing this lady's remarkably attractive face-lifted features at close range sends an ice-cold shiver from my neck to my asshole.

"Magnificent estate," Charlotte tells her softly. "Beyond question the finest we've seen so far."

"How kind of you to say so." Miss Waring glances around, smiles just a bit wistfully. "To be perfectly honest, I'll be very sorry indeed to leave it. Still, it can't be helped. Please, now, all of you go in the game room and I'll join you in a minute."

Charlotte and I exchange a fast glance, follow Mrs. Kirby into the game room. Several minutes later Miss Waring comes in wearing a pale-blue terrycloth robe and thong sandals, brushing her long, dark, thick hair, coloring difficult to detect, obviously not a wig. Has all the graceful movements of a relatively young woman; hands and feet alone betray her age. Truth is, if she were wearing gloves and shoes, it would be virtually impossible for strangers to guess anywhere near her true age. As a trained observer, I'm fascinated, I admit it, I find it hard to keep my eyes off her.

We all stand around the billiard table now, talk quietly, give Miss Waring the basics of who we represent, what we're looking for, our general timetable. Charlotte does most of the talking at this point: Consummate actress, superb con artist, totally believable liar with the inherent ability to embellish a story with exactly the right combination of fact and fiction. All very low-key, of course. In a word, this kid has all the critical talents needed by a successful detective. Or a crook.

Miss Waring offers us a drink; we accept. At the bar, she consults a little booklet that lists the stereo selections by number, picks up a plastic gadget that looks like a telephone dial, touches several numbers. Soft classical music fills the room and pool area. It's odds-on she hasn't had a serious prospective buyer since the estate went on the market, because now she gives us a personal tour of the gym, explains the equipment in some detail, shows us the small bowling alley, the sauna room, the sunlamp room. Tells us she uses all of these facilities on a daily basis and according to a very rigid schedule: One hour of fairly rigorous exercise in the early morning, followed by an hour of leisurely swimming, a half-hour sauna, then a nourishing breakfast; five minutes under the sunlamp protected by a special sunscreen lotion recommended by her dermatologist; half an hour in the game room to maintain good hand-eye coordination and have some fun; bowling alley's reserved for the afternoon or early evening, sometimes alone, sometimes with friends, always a full tenpin game of ten frames, her present average is 207.

Each time we come out of a room I glance at the cavelike opening to the hidden grotto. Finally I ask her about it.

She laughs quietly, gives me a wink. "Not quite as mysterious as one might think, I'm afraid. Actually, it's just a private little pool surrounded by a series of coral ledges with cushions."

"Must be great for parties," Charlotte says.

Laughs again, raises an eyebrow. "I daresay it's seen its moments over the years. Come along, I'll show you the lower-level bar."

As we're making a turn at the deep end of the pool, she shows us adjoining men's and women's bathrooms, complete with showers, then an equipment storage closet with floor-to-ceiling shelves of neatly folded swimsuits for guests in a variety of sizes and colors, monogrammed towels and terrycloth robes, snorkel masks, flippers, even basic scuba gear; a laundry basket on the floor holds several used towels and one article of wrinkled white sportswear that catches my eye.

Heavy door in the far corner opens to a black wrought-iron circular staircase. Down we go. Lower-level bar is straight out of Ian Fleming, exquisite décor, pleasantly air conditioned, indirectly lighted, intimate little booths and tables

with candlelamps, and the soft stereo is on in here too. We sit
in comfortable leather armchairs at the bar, munch on cashews, look through the big rectangular window at the lighted
turquoise water and the mouth of the hidden grotto to the far
right. As Miss Waring pours another round of drinks, I
swivel, look around for a bathroom. None in sight.

"Miss Waring, where's the nearest bathroom?"

"I'm afraid you'll have to go back up to the pool deck."

"Please excuse me, I'll be right back."

Hop up the circular staircase, through the heavy door, into
the warm South Seas climate, straight to the equipment storage closet. Reach into the laundry basket, push the used
towels aside, fish out the article of wrinkled sportswear: A
white short-sleeved jumpsuit, low upright collar, big front
zip, red-lettered label on the breast pocket reads *Saint Germain*.
Remembrance of things past: First week in April, 200 East
Eighty-fourth Street, get off the elevator at nineteen, Tara's
waiting for us in an open door to the far right, identical
jumpsuit; kid's eyes are red, hair's a mess, looks like she's
been out all night. Remember that?

Relatively popular brand name in the haute couture bou-
tiques these days, New York, London, Paris, right? I stand
there with the jumpsuit in hand, watch the reflection of the
water tremble over the soft white material. Slim elastic waist
would certainly fit Miss Waring, length is just about right
too. Somewhere in the back of my mind I'm trying to pin-
point exactly why I can't seem to visualize this lady in this
particular garment. Wordless but strong gut feeling. Modern
and fashion-conscious as I'm sure she is, this lady simply
wouldn't wear this item, wouldn't feel right in it. Why?
Don't know, going on pure instinct. Now I examine the
inside label just below the collar, white letters against a red
background:

Jean St. Germain

Paris

Reverse Side for Care

Reverse side gives washing instructions, English to the left, French to the right, international symbols in the middle. Last line to the left reads: Fabric Made in America. Fabric happens to be listed as 100 percent cotton. Logical assumption, fabric was shipped to France for manufacturing by Jean St. Germain, finished product shipped to a variety of countries around the world. No other labels or tags to indicate where it was sold. Now I smell the collar carefully: No perfume or cologne or sunscreen lotion discernible to me. Examine the collar for traces of makeup: Pale yellow discoloration from sweat, little ring-around dirt, no makeup visible to the naked eye. Take a close look at the bottoms of the straight, hemmed legs: Slightly dirty, possibility of some shoe polish. Lastly I inspect the perineal area: No runs, drips, errors. Hang the jumpsuit on the edge of the basket, reach in, pull out the towels: Three large ones, all fairly damp. Unlikely that Miss Waring used all three before greeting us, but normally she does her leisurely swimming in the early morning after her exercise routine, so three towels don't necessarily prove anything. Toss the towels back in, then the jumpsuit. Start to turn away, glance at the jumpsuit one more time. It's just too young. Maybe that's the gut reaction I've been feeling. Regardless of hair tints and face lifts and suntans and exercise schedules, this trendy French fashion just seems to me to be too young for this elegant old lady. Presumptive reasoning, I know, since I've only observed her for maybe ten minutes, but I tend to trust my gut instincts.

Now I glance at the cavelike entrance to the hidden grotto. Reflections from the water move over the white coral. Questions: What was the old lady doing in there? Was she alone? Is it conceivable that I might be standing just fifty feet or so from Tara Alvarado? If so, is it illogical to assume that I may never again have such a fortuitous opportunity to corner her? Two alternatives come quickly to mind, each with obvious pros and cons: (1) Change fast into one of the guest swimsuits, frog into the grotto, settle it here and now; if I do, Miss Waring and/or Mrs. Kirby will almost certainly see me, of course, and our neat little covers are blown; (2) patience and shuffle the cards, maintain our surveillance, return at least several more times, hope for a break.

As the man says, you gotta know when to hold 'em, know when to fold 'em. Based on experience, I opt to fold 'em this hand, odds just aren't good enough, too much to lose. Go into the men's room, flush the toilet, go back to the lower-level bar. It's now 12:35, we have another appointment at one, we're running behind, have to move on. Don't want to appear too anxious first time around. Miss Waring understands perfectly, very graciously escorts us upstairs, points out a few features of the living room that Mrs. Kirby didn't know or neglected to mention.

Then, on the way to the front door, my attention is drawn to a small red light up on the dim landing, opposite side of the hallway from where we entered. As we walk down the hall I see the source of the light is a little glass case on a pedestal containing the delicate statue of a horse. Miss Waring leads us over to it, stands on the opposite side. Her face and hair are bathed in the light.

Her voice is very soft. "Lovely, isn't it?"

"Yes," Charlotte says. "It's a strange light."

Miss Waring nods. "The horse is a holographic projection."

"Really?"

"Yes. *China Horse*, by Gordon Barlow."

I shake my head, look at it closely.

"Surely you've seen one before," Miss Waring says.

"Just in department store windows, never this close."

Keeps her voice very low. "It's a three-dimensional image stored on a high-resolution photographic plate, exposed with a laser. When one develops the film and lights it with another laser, it recreates the image in space."

Looks absolutely solid, like any other statue. Thought crosses my mind the old girl might be putting us all on; she gave glimpses of a very dry British humor in the bar. I have to smile.

"I know," she says. "It's difficult to believe at first."

Charlotte's smiling now. "So, actually, the horse itself isn't there?"

"That's correct."

As Charlotte and Mrs. Kirby laugh quietly, I walk around all four sides, my face right next to the glass, then I look at it from the top. Hell of an optical illusion.

Miss Waring taps a fingernail on the top of the case. "If you removed the glass and tried to touch the horse, you'd see. If I turned off the holographic projector and snapped on the hall lights, you'd see. The process is the most accurate three-dimensional illusion of reality ever discovered. The man who developed the theory of holography received the Nobel Prize for Physics in nineteen seventy-one, Professor Dennis Gabor of England."

Still difficult to suspend belief in what my eyes are seeing as a totally solid object. Miss Waring reaches around the pedestal, presses a switch, and the red light in the glass case vanishes instantly, leaving us in semidarkness. We hear her thong sandals flapping on the bare floor, then a click, and the overhead lights blaze on. I blink in the sudden brightness, look at the glass case. Statue's gone. In its place is a plate of smoky glass with gray-green swirls. As so often happens when your senses deceive you, we find ourselves laughing. I walk around the case again, inspect every inch. Little horse is gone; or, rather, it had never been there as a solid reality.

Miss Waring comes back, leans down, gazes into the empty case. She's on the opposite side again and I watch her through the glass. She pushes back her long dark hair. Her eyes seem like a little girl's.

"This is my favorite art object in the house," she tells us, almost confidentially. "I turn it on every once in a while just for fun, just to remind . . ." She hesitates, wets her lips.

"Beg pardon?" I ask softly.

"Oh . . . just to remind myself of something."

I wait, then: "May I ask of what?"

"Oh, it's just . . ." She straightens up, glances away. "Perhaps some other time, when I'm in a better mood."

"I understand."

She gives me this look, almost as if she's afraid she's hurt my feelings. "All right?"

"Certainly."

We follow her to the door in silence. She opens it herself

before I can come around. A soft yellow triangle of sunlight
moves slowly across the floor, becomes a dappled rectangle;
she remains in the shadow of the door. Outside, the butler
and chauffeur are leaning against the shell-gray Rolls-Royce,
talking, smoking; they straighten quickly, drop the cigarettes,
adjust their ties.

Charlotte and Mrs. Kirby chat briefly with the old lady,
thank her for the unexpected treat of such a warm personal
tour. I go last, take her small hand in both of mine.

"We'd like very much to come back."

"Please do, Mr. Gaulrapp. I'd like that too."

"It's been a genuine pleasure to meet you."

In shadow, her eyes seem suddenly sad, and for just a
moment the taut tan face resembles a painful mask. Then she
smiles, giving a glimpse of the near-perfect teeth, obviously
capped, and revealing just a trace of the dimples. "I assure
you, the pleasure has been mine."

Out we go. Butler opens the door smartly, helps the ladies
in, bids us a safe journey, closes it with a soft but solid click.
I glance back and what I see is frozen in my mind: A slim,
dark-haired woman in a pale-blue terry-cloth robe has just
stepped into partial sunlight, dwarfed by the huge oak door,
right hand held up now in a graceful gesture of goodbye.

We move slowly, quietly away, around the circular driveway, and I watch her through the rear window. She remains
almost motionless. I like this strange, remarkable old lady.
Honestly like her. But I can't help wondering what it would
be like, the reality rather than the illusion, if one could
somehow see it now, at eighty-two years of age: The face
behind the mask.

# 13

WE'RE ALL BACK AT THE WELSH HARP, surveillance has been interrupted for about an hour, but we figure it's worth it, we're way ahead of the game, now we need to pull some strategy together. Call the chief about 2:10 P.M., 9:10 A.M. New York time, bring him strictly up to date. Although the discovery of a Saint Germain jumpsuit similar to one owned by Tara Alvarado isn't exactly the kind of hard-on evidence we'd like to report to a man who's still up to his ass in alligators, he seems ecstatic. A half-swing broken-bat Texas-League dying quail looks just as big as a powerhouse line-drive wall-banger in the box score, especially if you're salivating to jump a jet to international fame. Makes a decision on the spot to grab an evening flight: Pan Am 102, departs Kennedy 8:45 tonight, his time, arrives Heathrow 8:25 tomorrow morning, our time. "Stay put, continue surveillance round-the-clock, Little John, stink-on-shit; call Kellogg, tell him I'm on my way." *Bang*. Sit there with the receiver in my hand, can't help smiling. Case is practically solved. Walter Fosdick Molars. On his way.

Must be an omen of good fortune, because when Charlotte calls Chief Superintendent Kellogg to fill him in, he gives her a rundown on the Yard's own initial investigation (less than two days) that helps piece together at least a part of the puzzle:

Phyllis Waring has two daughters, both believed to have been fathered by Sir Charles Pretoria, although never officially recognized—Wendy, fifty-four, and Felicity, forty-eight. Intelligence on Felicity is relatively comprehensive: Born April 6, 1934, Woodford Green. Graduate of St. Mary's Convent, Warwickshire, and Glenarm College, Essex. Employed as assistant to fashion editor of *Vanity Fair* magazine, London, 1953–56; junior ground hostess and ticket agent, TWA, London, 1956–60. Married British free-lance journalist Patrick New, April 2, 1957. One daughter, Ann, age twenty-four; married British stockbroker John Hill, June 1, 1978, separated same year; employed as flight attendant, British Airways, 1979 to present.

Yard's intelligence on Miss Waring's eldest daughter Wendy is still incomplete: Born March 27, 1928, Woodford Green. Graduate of St. Mary's Convent, Warwickshire. Employed as junior officer and children's hostess for steamship firm Union Castle Line, London, 1954–57. Married June 21, 1956. More to come.

I ask Charlotte to call British Airways' personnel department, identify herself, attempt to get the present home address of Mrs. Ann Hill as part of a routine investigation. She does: 200 East Eighty-fourth Street, New York. Bingo. Alvarado's roommate. Now we can start to make some educated guesses. Based on experience, we know only too well that uniformed crew members and flight attendants are the least likely groups to encounter any difficulty whatsoever in two key aspects of international travel: (a) Boarding the flight itself, whether working or "deadheading"; and (b) getting through customs and immigration.

Our first guess follows the most logical line of reasoning: Tara Alvarado, armed with a forged U.S. passport (relatively easy to obtain in New York), a forged British Airways ID card, a standard British Airways flight attendant's uniform, and the savvy protection of four-year veteran Ann Hill, had the carte blanche capability to illegally enter and exit London at will, no questions asked.

Second guess: Since the robbery took place Monday, April 19, same day Eddie Lopata was killed, we think it's a safe assumption that Alvarado and Hill holed up in New York for at least three or four days, maybe longer, depending on Hill's work schedule. Since weekend flights are generally more crowded, let's say they boarded a London flight Saturday, April 24; they would have arrived Sunday, just two days ago. Hill is based in New York, of course, so if it's a short layover she'd probably stay at the crew hotel in London, along with Flight Attendant X. Long layover, she might reasonably be expected to see grandmother in Epping Forest, or even stay with her, in which case Flight Attendant X might reasonably be a house guest.

What's the British Airways' crew hotel in London? Charlotte says quite a few crews stay at the Sheraton Park Tower in Knightsbridge. Gets on the phone, asks for the assistant manager, identifies herself, tells him she's conducting a routine investigation, wants to know if a British Airways flight attendant by the name of Mrs. Ann Hill is registered. Like the kid's style. Couple of British Airways crews are registered, negative on Mrs. Hill. Nice try. Now she calls Heathrow Immigration, identifies herself, asks if Mrs. Hill was listed on the manifest of any British Airways flight during the past three days. Immigration officer takes a few minutes to check it out. Affirmative: Mrs. Ann Hill is listed on the manifest of British Airways Flight 338, Saturday, April 24.

Only logical alternative we have is to concentrate on the Pretoria House. I'll start the next eight-hour shift at 3:30 this afternoon, but before I leave I ask Charlotte to make two more phone calls: First to the Yard's C7 unit to request a high-priority rush order for three sets of engraved business cards, conservative type face, under the firm name of the Walter F. Molars Philanthropic Society, 1032 Fifth Avenue, New York, NY 10028 (nonexistent address), each set personalized with our individual names and titles: Charlotte A. Lawson, Special Assistant to the President; John P. Gaulrapp, Executive Vice-President; Walter F. Molars, President. Brendan gets aced out of the cards, but he understands; whenever

we're viewing the property he'll have to be on surveillance.
Charlotte's assured the special order will be rushed through
Harrods on a confidential basis, twelve cards to each set,
delivered to her at the Welsh Harp by Yard courier Thursday
afternoon.

Final call: Since Charlotte told Mrs. Kirby we were booked
solidly Wednesday through Friday and planned to leave the
area Saturday morning, I ask her to phone Kirby around 4:30,
tell her how impressed we were with the property compared
to the others we've seen, and lay the groundwork for a
possible visit by Walter F. Molars himself. She'll turn on the
charm, explain that Mr. Molars is scheduled to be in London
on business later this week and, based on our initial reports,
might very well want to view the mansion personally; can this
be arranged?

Just after three o'clock I speak to the elderly waiter in the
Welsh Harp pub, order a ham and cheese sandwich to go,
plus two large containers of black coffee. Next I transfer the
binoculars, camera, lenses, film, walkie-talkie, and three of
Brendan's cigars from the TR7 to the Jag, take off about
3:15, arrive at our spot on the dirt road high above Blackweir
Lane some ten minutes later. Binoculars seem to give an even
better perspective of the mansion and grounds than I remember from yesterday. Surveillance has always been one of the
most difficult parts of any case for me. Absolutely dread it.
Still, being out in the fresh air on a sunny hilltop in Epping
Forest beats the hell out of Manhattan streets. I get out
the Nikon, try the 200-, 300-, and 500-millimeter lenses,
sip coffee, smoke Brendan's cigars, keep the motor idling
as I listen to music and news on the stereo's wraparound
speakers.

No activity at all during the remaining daylight hours. Sun
begins to set beyond the distant hills of trees to the west, land
colors seem to intensify for a while, become almost luminous, then the light softens very gradually. With the oncom-
ing night, the air becomes cool and damp and I'm more
aware of sounds from the deep forest to the southeast. I turn
off the radio and engine, listen to the steady drone of cicadas
begin to dominate staccato sounds of birds and frogs. Forest

smells become heavy, spring wildflowers, pine cones, sorrel, and something that resembles the familiar odor of night-blooming jasmine. Soft shades of yellow appear in the rear windows of the old stone house on the knoll below to my left. No streetlights along Blackweir Lane. Occasional cars pass now, people returning from work, headlight beams flicker behind trees that border the narrow road. About 7:10, signs of life from the Pretoria House: Ground-floor front and side windows throw pale gold rectangles across the gravel drive and well-kept lawn. I focus the binoculars on the front windows; white lace curtains obscure the rooms. During the next half-hour, a few lights go on in second- and third-floor windows; again, white lace curtains make viewing impossible. Time for my ham and cheese sandwich, big event of the night. Bread is fresh, generous slices of ham, Swiss cheese, lots of mayonnaise, just a hint of mustard, crispy lettuce. Beefeater martini would be nice, but I settle for cold black coffee. Enjoy every minute, top it all off with a richly aromatic Dutch Masters panetela. Far off in the distance to the northwest, a church bell tolls the hour: Eight slow, solemn bongs. Could it be coming from the ancient stone bell tower of Waltham Abbey itself, some two and a half miles away? Doubt it. Would've kept me awake last night. Last peal seems to linger and echo in the chilly air.

Short time later I'm startled to see headlights, brights up, approaching on the dirt road behind me. Instinctively, I reach under my blazer to the small of my back. No gun. Feel extremely vulnerable. Close my electric windows fast, lock the doors. My hand goes to the key in the ignition. I wait, watch the headlights in the side-view mirror; they move slowly past on my right. Car stops directly opposite mine. In moonlight, it seems to be a limo of some kind, has the lines of an old Bentley. Driver in a dark suit and cap emerges from his righthand seat, leaves the lights on, walks around the rear of the car, opens the back door, reaches in to help someone out. Now he escorts a woman in a dark fur coat over to my door. I'm in the right-hand driver's seat, I'm squinting, but I can't see her face clearly. Driver taps his white-gloved fin-gets on my window. I touch the electric lever, roll it down about an inch.

"Yeah?" I snap.

"Mr. Gaulrapp," the lady says softly. "It's Phyllis Waring."

It sure as hell is. I hesitate, then roll the window all the way down. She smiles, extends a black-gloved hand. I shake it, but I'm speechless. Swear to God. Speechless. Doesn't happen often, but I can't think of a damn thing to say. Only thing I can think to do is smile. Weakly.

"I think we should have a talk," she says.

"Of course." I start to open the door.

"No, no, I'll come around."

Chauffeur ushers her around to the front passenger door. I unlock it, he opens it, helps her into the seat.

"Please wait for me in the car," she tells him.

"Yes, madam."

"Turn the lights off and make certain the windows are closed."

"Very well, madam." He closes the door.

She waits until he's back in the limo, lights off, windows closed. Three-quarters of her face is in shadow; her mouth, chin, and neck are white in moonlight. Now she clutches the fur coat to her neck, keeps her voice very low. "Mr. Gaulrapp, if that is indeed your name, I believe the time has come to speak candidly."

"Fine with me."

"I rise at five-thirty every day." Glances at her lighted house down the hill. "This morning, from my bedroom window on the fourth floor, I saw a vehicle parked in this very spot." Turns, looks directly in my eyes. "By moonlight. Saw it very distinctly. About an hour later, at sunrise, I studied the vehicle through binoculars. A modern sports car, a Triumph, I believe. I observed it, on and off, for the next several hours. During that time, a tall heavy-set man got out, holding what were obviously high-powered binoculars, and began observing my house and grounds. Nothing else. Not the countryside, not my neighbors' houses. Mine. Mine alone."

I wait, then: "Why didn't you call the police?"

"Let's not beat around the bush, shall we? I know why he was here. I know why you and Miss Lawson came to view the house this morning. I know why you're here now. As a matter of fact, I've been expecting you. It's a relief to me, finally, that you're here."

Again I wait, study her motionless lips in the soft moonlight. When she continues, her lips seem to move in painful isolation from the rest of her deep-shadowed face:

"Are you familiar with Shakespeare, Mr. Gaulrapp?"

"A little."

"Have you ever seen *Macbeth?*"

"Some years ago, yes."

"A few lines come to mind that seem somehow appropriate to what I'm about to tell you: 'If you can look into the seeds of time, / And say which grain will grow and which will not, / Speak.' Do you recall those lines by any chance?"

"I'm afraid not."

"Act One, Scene Three." Shakes her head slightly, lips tighten. "Those lines would make a splendid epitaph for my gravestone. I have two daughters, Mr. Gaulrapp, as I'm sure you know by now, if you've done your homework. Both born out of wedlock, of course. The eldest, Wendy—we've always called her that, her real name is Gloria Vivien. When she was a baby, she was crying in her crib one day and the nurse we had leaned over the crib and shook a finger at her and said: 'You can stop that crying now—Wendy!' God, I can remember it so vividly. From that time on, Charles and I always called her Wendy. She always resented the name, at school she used to say, 'My name is *not* Wendy, it's Gloria!' Forgive me, I'm digressing. At any rate, Wendy was an absolutely beautiful little girl. Exquisitely beautiful, if I do say so myself. Center of attention, of course. When she was six years old, Felicity was born. And, for a time, Wendy was the most protective, patient, loving sister one could possibly hope for. Simply idolized the child. For my part, I treated each of them as equally and fairly as humanly possible. Whenever I gave anything to one—affection, chocolate, a toy, whatever it was—I would give exactly the same to the other. Clothes, trips, parties, education. Affection, love, money, exactly the same. So I don't know how it happened. I honestly don't know. It must have been genetic. A recessive gene. That's as near as I can come to explaining it."

"I'm not sure I—understand."

She continues in a kind of soft monologue, almost oblivious to me. "Yes. That's what I've always said. That would also explain the incredible gift, the genius for music. God knows it didn't come from Luís. He could barely carry a tune, Luís, never played a musical instrument in his life. Who knows, perhaps it came from my side of the family, although I doubt it. I seriously doubt it."

"Excuse me, Miss Waring, but who's Luís?"

"Luís Alvarado, Wendy's former husband. Forgive me, I was digressing again. In nineteen fifty-six Wendy was married to Luís Díaz Alvarado, a naturalized American of Spanish descent, who was then an instructor in Spanish literature at Columbia University in New York. The following year she gave birth to their only child, Tara Maria."

Automatically, I shift in my seat to face her more directly.

She nods. "So now we get down to it, don't we, Mr. Gaulrapp?"

"Yes."

"Tara Maria Alvarado." She crosses her arms, holds herself, as if she's suddenly cold. "She was born in New York. I never even laid eyes on the child until she was twelve. Except in photographs, of course, which told me nothing except that she was a rather stunning dark-haired, dark-eyed child. Oh, I'd receive the odd thank-you note for birthday presents, Christmas gifts, that sort of thing. Meticulous printing, then handwriting that resembled an adult's by the time she was ten. Finally, Wendy and Luís took her to London in the summer of—I believe it was nineteen sixty-nine. Yes, that's right. She was twelve then. Nothing could have prepared me for—adequately prepared me for that visit. They stayed almost two months. Precocious? God! I didn't know the meaning of the word before I saw that—that child in action. I beg your pardon, 'child' isn't the right word. Not even close. At twelve years old, Tara was—she conducted herself like an adult in almost every sense of the term. Talked like one, dressed like one, acted like one. She'd grown up with adults, spent her entire childhood surrounded by adults. Intellectual adults, at that, in the Columbia University community. Faculty members, the only people they knew, the only friends they had. Academicians, pure and simple, if you know what I mean. Ivory tower academicians, serious scholars, insulated from the outside world. Luís was—I always said Luís was like some absurd character from a Cervantes novel. If you think Don Quixote tilted at windmills, Mr. Gaulrapp, I assure you he was a veritable pragmatist compared to Luís. I mean, the man would sit there in my living room and recite whole passages from *La Galatea* or *Novelas Ejemplates*, verbatim from memory, impeccable English translation. Positively electrifying to his colleagues, I'm sure. I'm sure he was the life of their parties, as it were. Quite frankly, I found him an insufferable bore. So did Wendy, finally, after twenty-one years of marriage, the last few apparently being a nice imitation of hell. They were divorced in nineteen seventy-seven. By that time Tara was in her third year at university, she'd long since moved out of that madhouse.''

"When did you see her next?''

"Tara?''

I nod, watch her lips carefully.

Miss Waring glances down at her lighted house again, takes a deep breath, exhales with a sigh. "In May of nineteen seventy-eight Tara graduated magna cum laude from the University of Miami's School of Music. A gifted pianist, something of a musical genius according to all reports. Thanks in no small measure to Wendy, I might add, who forced her to practice five to six hours a day from the age of five. Disciplined the very spirit out of the child long before she had reached the age of reason. At any rate, Tara graduated and returned to New York to live with her father for a while. Abruptly, she announced that she would not pursue a musical career after all—I could have predicted that years ago—and began studying to become a professional photgrapher, of all things. Wendy had been back in London for nearly two years then, she had a flat in Chelsea, she was living on what little remained of her trust-fund inheritance from Charles. Tara's twenty-first birthday was approaching—July seventh, nineteen seventy-eight. In this country, Mr. Gaulrapp, a person's twenty-first birthday is an extremely important event, among the most significant in one's life. I understand it's less so in America."

"It's a major event, but probably not as important as it is here. I don't know enough about your country to make an intelligent comparison."

She gazes at me in silence for a moment. "I like you, Mr. Gaulrapp. You're not a pretentious man. But to continue, Tara's twenty-first was rapidly approaching. Wendy was severely depressed, not having seen her daughter in almost three years, so she came to me and we put our heads together and arranged for a gala twenty-first birthday celebration for Tara at the Dorchester. Tara arrived here in mid-June. They both stayed at Pretoria House, along with Felicity and Patrick, who had graciously planned their holidays around the celebration. So it was a real family get-together, the first one in many years. Felicity's daughter Ann and her husband John couldn't stay at the house, but they attended the party."

"Excuse me, Miss Waring, I have a question. Did Tara photograph the North Star during that particular visit?"

"Yes, she did."

"Sorry to interrupt, but I was curious."

"Of course. I understand." She wets her lips, draws the collar of her coat closer again. "I realize only too well that I have a rather pronounced tendency to digress from the point. I'm afraid it's one of the prices one pays at my age, Mr. Gaulrapp. Every bit as frustrating as arthritis, I assure you, but not quite as painful."

"I understand."

"In any event, yes, Tara prevailed upon me to let her photograph the diamond while she was here. She sat me down and explained that she intended to specialize in photographing precious stones and various objets d'art, so I agreed without hesitation. It hadn't—actually, it hadn't been photographed since I received it in nineteen thirty-eight, the year Charles passed away. He had it photographed for insurance purposes, of course, and I'd seen pictures of it in a few books and magazines, but that was in the early nineteen-thirties when color photography wasn't nearly as perfected as it is today. So, of course, I knew it would be a valuable addition to her portfolio. I've always—the family thinks I'm foolish, but I've always kept the diamond in the house, in a very large safe I bought especially for it, along with many other jewels Charles gave me over the years. I must say, Tara did a remarkable job. She photographed two whole afternoons, a total of perhaps eight or nine hours, every imaginable angle. The most extraordinary one, in my opinion at least, was the—she created what appeared to be a small mountain of my other jewels holding up the North Star. God, the refraction of light, it was absolutely splendid. Did you happen to see that one?"

"Yes. To me it was—dreamlike is the only word that seems to fit. Something like a blue iceberg on another planet."

"That's the one. Excellent analogy, I never considered that particular image. Yes, it was dreamlike. It was used for the cover of the Heritage Gallery program, you know."

"Yes, I saw it."

"My solicitor, Mr. Cavallo, obtained a few advance copies from the gallery and gave one to me. Quite extraordinary cover."

"Miss Waring, before you continue, would you mind if I asked you a few questions?"

"Not at all."

"Did Tara Alvarado have any influence at all in your decision to auction the diamond?"

"None whatsoever. It was a decision I made in concert with my solicitor, my barrister, and my accountant. All of whom suggested that I should seriously consider the possibility of putting it up for auction as long ago as nineteen seventy-six, as I recall. The most influential opinion of all was that voiced by my accountant, Mr. Martin Blaustein, who had been Charles's own accountant for many years. Toward the end of nineteen eighty-one, it became quite clear to us all that it was a matter of urgent financial necessity."

"I see."

"It's a very long story and I won't trouble you with it. As you undoubtedly know, Charles saw to it that I was placed in a sound financial position before he passed away. He was a very generous man indeed, Mr. Gaulrapp. Unfortunately, two key factors combined over the years to gradually threaten the integrity of that position: My stubborn penchant for maintaining the standard of living to which I've become accustomed in Pretoria House; and of course the almost unbelievable escalation in the rate of inflation that has effectively crippled this country in the more recent past." She purses her lips, then gives a small, slow, ironic smile. "Another factor, laughable in retrospect, is that none of my distinguished financial consultants really expected me to live as long as I have. To put the whole matter as succinctly as possible, Mr. Gaulrapp, I've been drawing on my capital for a very long time now and I'm afraid it's time to pay the piper. We had a family conference about this, we discussed it quite openly."

"When Tara was here?"

"Yes. That was in fact the last time the family, such as it is, had the opportunity to actually get together, listen to the unvarnished truth from my financial people, and consider the various remedies that might be taken."

"Including the possibility of an auction?"

"Certainly. That was one of the prime considerations. According to Mr. Blaustein, if the North Star could be sold at auction for anywhere near the market value—remember, this was nineteen seventy-eight—we could pay all our creditors in full and avoid the most unpleasant alternative of all, selling Pretoria House itself and many of its furnishings. However, Mr. Blaustein and Mr. Cavallo cautioned us not to be optimistic about the prospects of actually finding a buyer for the diamond at auction. They were both of the opinion that the so-called market value of the stone was grossly inflated and unrealistic. I was inclined to agree with them. I was also emotionally disinclined to part with the diamond for reasons I'm sure you understand."

"Of course."

"So the idea of an auction was put on the back burner, so to speak. Until last year. Something unexpected had occurred, the ramifications of which were quite surprising. To me, to my consultants, to the whole family. A great deal of publicity had been generated by the publication of a definitive biography about Charles.''

*"Pretoria and the North Star."*

She hesitates. ''Yes. Have you—read it?''

''Just a few sections.''

''Actually, you should read the whole book, Mr. Gaulrapp, it's quite well done. At any rate, the point I'm getting at, the book was published in nineteen-eighty, became a best seller, ignited an almost unbelievable amount of—I believe the term is 'mass-media' attention—and Mr. Cavallo was suddenly inundated with requests from journalists, ranging from the sublime to the ridiculous. Over the course of that year, one solid fact began to emerge with rather startling clarity: A great many people were interested in the North Star. All requests for information, photographs, whatever, were politely turned down, of course. But after a year had passed, Mr. Cavallo began making some discreet inquiries on his own—I didn't know about it—to some of the better-known rare jewel merchants in London, Paris, and New York. You must understand that Mr. Cavallo has always been a rather conservative gentleman, the kind of solicitor who tends to reserve judgment until he has more than ample evidence at his command. Well, he finally came to me last year, in the summer it was, we sat down over a glass of sherry. And he calmly announced that something unusual had taken place concerning the market value of the diamond. Apparently the book and its attendant publicity—most of it utter rubbish, by the way—had in some inexplicable way captured the imagination of a vast number of people indeed and had somehow elevated the North Star itself to the unlikely position of a—God, I hate to use the word—'legend.' I was in the possession of a legendary diamond. Well, we had a good laugh about that, I assure you. Incredible how these things come about, isn't it? The serious part of all this was his considered opinion, based on discussions with a cross-section of rare jewel merchants, that if we should decide to put the stone up for auction at such an opportune moment, it might very well fetch its actual market value—the amount for which it's insured. Which would more than solve my increasing financial problems. Reluctantly, after a great deal of reflection, I instructed him to proceed, to begin the business of arranging such an auction.''

"Do you recall when he finalized plans for the auction? Approximately, the month?"

Her lips remain motionless for maybe twenty seconds; then: "I believe it was November. Yes, that's correct. Last November."

"Are you aware that Tara Alvarado started showing her portfolio to the Heritage Gallery last November?"

"No. No, I didn't know that. To the best of my recollection, the very first time I knew she had any connection with the gallery was about mid-January. Wendy called in mid-January to say that Tara had landed a job as the gallery's official photographer. I was delighted for her. I didn't have even the slightest notion of what was going on in the girl's . . .'' She shakes her head, sits back, three-quarters of her face in shadow again. "No, that's not true. That's not true at all. I knew. Or, rather, I should have known. I should have remembered."

"Remembered what?"

Her lips tighten slightly. "We had—conversations, Mr. Gaulrapp. Conversations when she was at the house that summer, the summer of her twenty-first birthday. She was here for almost two months, so there was ample time. I was concerned about her because she seemed depressed. I used to watch her wandering around the grounds, photographing, always alone. Photographing flowers, plants, birds, trees, small animals. She seemed to be such a quiet, lonely, introspective youngster. So I tried to get to know her a little better. I honestly tried. She wouldn't have anything to do with the rest of the family, avoided her mother like the plague, so I tried to have little conversations with her now and again. To let her know that I liked her and wanted to be her friend, that's all. Our talks were so—difficult at first. Very stilted, very—uncomfortable. And then, as the weeks went by, a month, I don't know, she began to respond to me in her own way. Gradually. She seemed to understand that I wasn't prying, wasn't criticizing, wasn't trying to give advice. That I accepted her for who she was, not who she was supposed to be. That I genuinely liked her and cared about her and her career. *Her* career, the one *she* wanted. She responded because I think it occurred to her that we actually had a lot in common. At her age I was every bit as defiant and independent. Anybody who didn't like it could go to hell. And I was a loner too, of course, I knew all about loneliness, I knew how that felt. So, to make a long story short, we responded to each other, we began talking about all sorts of things, we even talked about Charles, and I hadn't done that for a very long time. We decided that she should photograph the North Star for her portfolio. She insisted that I watch, so I did, I sat there and watched through both afternoons. She shot it inside, on the floor, in natural light from the windows. And on the last afternoon, when the sun was soft and warm, slanting in nicely to give ideal refractions, she finished her final roll of film and said something that touched me very deeply. So deeply that I wept. God, I remember that moment so vividly. She was on her knees on the floor, wearing her old jeans and a T-shirt, face sweating, hair a mess. She was rewinding that final roll of film, staring at the North Star, lost in thought. Her hand slowed, then stopped abruptly. When she finally spoke, her voice was so low it sounded like a different person. She said, 'I know how much this diamond means to you. I've never been in love, but I've often tried to imagine how it must feel. When it's the real thing and you both know it.' Then she turned to me, saw that I was suddenly in tears, and her eyes filled too. 'Phyllis,' she said, 'I swear to God, no matter what happens, nobody is ever going to take that stone away from you as long as you live.' That was what she said.''

I wait, then speak softly. "Where is she now, Miss Waring?''

"She's been in the house since Sunday evening.''

"Where's the diamond?''

"All the diamonds she stole are in my safe.''

"Is she armed?''

"Yes."
"Does she know we're here?"
"Yes."
"What does she want?"
"She wants to meet with you."
"Where and when?"
"In the house. Alone. Tonight."

# 14

I FOLLOW THE BENTLEY LIMO down the hill with my brights up so Miss Waring and her chauffeur can't see that I'm using the walkie-talkie: "B or C, come in; B or C, come in." Static. It's now 8:16, Charlotte has the shift starting at 11:30, she's undoubtedly asleep; I figure Brendan's in the Welsh Harp pub and he's got the walkie-talkie with him. As the Bentley makes a right turn into Blackweir Lane, I try again, louder this time. Within a few seconds Brendan's voice booms back loud and clear: "B here, B here!" Music to my ears. "B, Operation Molars is blown. Just finished meet with Miss W on hill. I'm now following old-model Bentley limo, plate Paul-Mary-William, to house for planned meet with armed subject Miss A. Copy?" Static. "Armed subject Miss A?" Static. "Affirmative. Request outside cover immediately. Alert Kellogg. If I don't call by nine—repeat nine—come get me. Copy?" Static. "Copy, J. On our way." Bentley slows, headlights turn left, distinguished silver-haired chap opens the heavy gate. In we go. As I start turning into the circular drive, I glance in the rear-view mirror. Gate is being closed. Around we go, tires crunching, I keep my brights on as we glide through the gold rectangles of light thrown by the front windows. Before we arrive, the big oak door opens and out comes the butler. I stop behind the limo, kill the lights and motor, grab my walkie-talkie, step out. Butler escorts Miss Waring into the house; I follow. He closes the door, she thanks him, dismisses him for the evening.

Our footsteps echo as we walk along the hall and down the short flight of stairs into the enormous softly lighted living room. As usual, Miss Waring speaks quietly:

"Tara asked to see you alone in the pool area. Is that all right with you, Mr.—excuse me, what is your actual name?"

"Rawlings. Detective John Rawlings, New York City Police."

"Detective Rawlings. Is that all right with you?"

"Yes. Any idea what she has in mind?"

"The way she explained it to me, I believe she merely wants to open a line of communication. I think that's how she worded it."

"I see."

"I should tell you, Detective Rawlings, the girl has been acting somewhat irrationally since she arrived."

"Irrationally?"

"Decidedly irrational behavior. Actually, she arrived in this country Saturday morning with her cousin Ann Hill, as you probably know. They stayed at the Sheraton Park Tower for one night. Ann had her standard twenty-four-hour layover and left for New York on the eleven o'clock flight Sunday morning. She called me from Heathrow to say that Tara was asleep at the hotel and had been sleeping for some twenty consecutive hours. She begged me not to call the police, she warned me to stay as far away from Tara as possible. Detective Rawlings, to be perfectly honest about it, I simply didn't know what Tara was going to do at that point. Neither did Ann. The fact of the matter is, she'd terrorized Ann into helping her escape to this country. Ann said she was frightened for her life. I can understand why. When Tara arrived here unannounced Sunday evening, she was on the verge of hysteria. She'd climbed the fence, she'd gained entry to the house by breaking a rear window. I was very frightened indeed. I did exactly as I was told. I opened the safe, locked the twelve diamonds inside, and accompanied her to her bedroom—'her' bedroom she called it, the one she had that summer, the summer of her twenty-first birthday. I accompanied her to the bedroom, I sat and talked with her while she unpacked her one small suitcase. She had a revolver in the suitcase."

We pass the stereo library and pause at the northwest corner of the ballroom near the stairs to the pool area. Miss Waring glances down at the heavy door to the pool, holds herself, lowers her voice even more:

"We talked for perhaps two hours. During that time her moods fluctuated from exaggerated feelings of elation and optimism to severe depression. Over and over she kept returning to the theme that she'd kept her promise to me: No one would ever take the North Star away from me as long as I lived. I tried my very best to reason with her, but to no avail."

"All right, you've done everything you could, Miss Waring. I'll talk to her now."

"The girl is obviously ill."

"Does she have the gun with her?"

"I don't know."

"Where will you be while I'm with her?"

She glances into the living room. "I don't—know. I suppose I'll go up to my bedroom. Fourth floor."

"How can I reach you?"

"There's a telephone intercom system for every room. There's one in the pool bar. My number is four-zero-one."

"Let me alert you to something. Within minutes now, several detectives will park on the road directly outside the gate." I hold up the walkie-talkie. "If I don't call them by nine o'clock, they have instructions to come in after me. They're armed, of course. You could help considerably by posting a man at the gate, ready to open it if that becomes necessary."

"I'll make a call right now. I'll also leave the front door unlocked."

"Thank you."

"Please do me one favor, Detective Rawlings. Please do your utmost to avoid force if at all possible. I know you have a job to do. I know how difficult it may be. But try to remember you're dealing with a girl who is obviously quite ill.''

"I'll try."

She glances down and away; her eyes look sad in the tight-skinned face. "Despite everything, I love the girl. I honestly do."

"I understand. You go ahead now. I'll give you a call as soon as I can."

"Thank you." She turns, walks back through the living room, still holding herself in the fur coat.

I take a deep breath, grip the walkie-talkie firmly, walk down the narrow flight of stairs, open the heavy door. Warm and fragrant South Seas atmosphere, exotic plants, flowers, trees, statues. Stereo is on in here, soft piano music, vaguely familiar classical piece, what is it? Jim Mairs would know. He'd also know better than to get himself in a vulnerable situation like this, unarmed. Glance around. Stroll along the deck to the left, footsteps sound hollow on the coral slabs. I'm very much aware of the open doors of the rooms flanking the pool: Bowling alley, gym, sauna room, sunlamp room, game room. All are dark. Tara could be in any one of these rooms watching me, maybe sighting a gun at my head right now. I continue down to the shallow end, clear my throat, test my voice:

"Tara?"

Nothing.

"Tara, cut the crap, huh?"

Nothing.

Glance at my watch: 8:23. Once again my attention is drawn to the far side of the pool and the cavelike entrance to the hidden grotto. Reflections from the water flicker across the white coral. There's about a two-inch space between the water and the curved top of the passageway. Ordinarily I'm not given to compulsions, quite the contrary, but now I begin to experience this strange impulse, combined with a more logical feeling of flat-out curiosity, to find out what's actually in there. Truth is, I've been a cop virtually all my adult life, but I've only had the opportunity to do a few things on the job that I'd call relatively flamboyant, glamorous, James Bond-type maneuvers. What the hell, you only live twice. Anything is better than standing out here in the open.

Off I go, back to the deep end, turn left, straight ahead, then right, past the men's and women's bathrooms to the equipment storage closet. Open the door, floor-to-ceiling shelves of neatly folded swimsuits for guests, variety of sizes and colors, monogrammed towels, terry-cloth robes. Laundry basket on the floor is now empty. Flip through the swim trunks, grab a size thirty-four in navy blue. Quick change takes maybe twenty seconds, dump my clothes in the laundry basket, I'm ready to go. Pick up the walkie-talkie, only link to the real world, step to the edge.

Lower myself quietly into the water, walkie-talkie held high, water is pleasantly warm. Silent one-arm breast stroke to the mouth of the grotto. I can see dim colored light through the two-inch space, but that's it. Hold the walkie-talkie in the space, submerge my head, glide through calm as Mark Spitz, surface with a very soft splash. Area is creatively track-lighted from the high coral ceiling. Long thin shafts of reds and blues needle down, crisscross, sparkle on an elliptical lagoon-type pool here surrounded by a miniature Roman amphitheater of relatively steep coral ledges. Dreamlike atmosphere is somewhat destroyed by soft stereo music from speakers somewhere off in the dark.

When my eyes adjust I see the figure of a woman sitting on the edge of the fifth ledge, the top one, legs dangling. Smoking a cigarette. Can't see her face yet, but she's nude. I swim to the edge directly below her, hold on. Silence except for the quiet piano music. Five seconds. Ten. Now she moves the cigarette to her lips, takes a drag. Face lights up just enough. My voice echoes slightly:

"Hello, Tara."

"Rawlings, you asshole, so glad you could make it."

"Hear you want to talk."

"That was the general idea. Figured it'd take you five minutes to get enough balls to come in here. Took three and a half."

"You're under arrest, Tara."

"Is that a fact?"

"Want to hear your rights?"

"Want to hear how you can be a wealthy man, John? A millionaire?"

"Never really wanted that."

"Bullshit. All you have to do is swim out of here. Tell the others you never saw me, I pulled a decoy, escaped while you were in the house. We'll make it cash, John. Any way you want it."

"No way. One thing I can't figure: You seemed to have everything going for you in your life, Tara. What made you pull a stunt like this?"

"Happen to love the old girl."

"Insurance money?"

"That, too, sure. Five million, you kidding? She needed it. She needed it both ways."

"Can't believe you killed Eddie."

"He was *filth*, Rawlings. A vicious fuckin' *animal*. If you knew what he did to me the night of the robbery you'd understand. He didn't *deserve* to live. He deserved to have his fuckin' *brains* blown out. Take my word for it. Case closed."

"Miss Waring thinks you're ill, Tara. Seriously ill. You agree with her?"

She blows smoke into the dark, watches it flash through the narrow shafts of red and blue. "You mean *sick*, Rawlings. *Ill* is too classy a word for what I've got. Yeah, I agree with her. I'm sick, I know fuckin' well I'm sick, I've been suffering from specific mental sickness most of my life. One thing *I* can't figure: *You*. As a trained observer, a real pro, I'm surprised you didn't pick up on at least some of the more obvious symptoms *long* ago."

"Good point."

"You dropped the *ball*, Rawlings."

"Yes, I did. Obviously."

"What'd you do, chalk all this weird shit up to my IQ?"

"I suppose so. I suppose that was part of it."

"You suppose so. Oh, God, yeah, that's—typical. Absolutely typical, right on the money. You *suppose* so. Want the truth for a change? Want a raw piece of the *truth?* The truth

is, you're supposed to *know*, Rawlings. You're supposed to
be *trained* to know. You're supposed to be *paid* to know. The
truth is, you and Thomas and Vadney, all of you, you went
*along* with all this shit, you *bought* it, you ate it *up,* all the
lies and deceits and decoys and Oscar-winning performances
I was slinging at you because—the truth now, the real raw
truth—because it was infinitely *easier* for you to do *that* than
it would've been to do the opposite: To work with your
*intellects*, you collective intellects. To take the cigars out of
your mouths and the martinis out of your paws and sit down
and really *think*. Think it *through*. To turn the problem on its
head and examine it from a fresh perspective and come up
with a few ideas that might be marginally *creative*. Like I
did, like I was doing, over and over, constantly. To match
*wits* with me instead of going along with the flood of incredible *shit* I was feeding you. You had dozens and dozens of
opportunities to do that, opportunities up the ying-yang, right
up to the minute of the robbery. Why didn't you *see* that?
*Why?* You know as well as I do, all of you, but you'll never
admit it to yourselves. *Why?* Because the answer to that
question is much too painful. *Why?* Because it means you
would've had to admit you'd been conned. You would've had
to say, Wait a minute, we've been all *wrong* here, we've
been attacking this from the wrong *angle*, we've been asking
ourselves the wrong *questions*. Yeah. Yeah, and why's that?
Maybe you haven't bothered to stay current on modern *techniques*. Maybe you're too complacent, too cock-sure you're
right, too—too *experienced*. Experienced in the *old* ways.
The black-and-white old *ways*, old *days*, old *clichés*. Ever
think of that, Rawlings?''

"Yes. Yes, I have."

"You could've *stopped* me, y'know that? If you'd used
your brains instead of your macho cockiness, you would've
seen through the whole scam. A few of the lies—not all, but
a few—were so fuckin' transparent I—I swear to God—I was
astonished. Appalled you didn't call my bluff: Flabbergasted
you didn't pick up a signal of some kind. Know what I think?
The *truth?* I think you've had it, Rawlings. I think you've
bought it. I think you've been in harness too long. I think

you're too *old*. I think you're too *outdated*. I think you're a fuckin' *anachronism*. You should really hang it up while you can still do it with some semblance of dignity. Before it gets—embarrassing. Ever think of that?".

Pretty good shots. Essentially cheap shots, but well aimed. In the pause, I'm almost tempted to say what I feel, to lash back, to launch a diatribe of my own, but then common sense takes over. I take a deep breath. The single most important fact of all, the fact she neglected to include, is painfully self-evident as we look at each other in the unreal light: I wasn't smart enough to stop the robbery, but I was smart enough to track her down. Now, obviously, she's desperate, or she wouldn't have called the meet. So I don't feel angry at what she just said. By and large, I've gone past that emotion in this racket. Long since. Still, given the circumstances, one of her statements stays with me, hits deep, because of the way she said it: "You could've *stopped* me, y'know that?" Tone of her voice was close to a plea, as if she was saying: *You could've helped me.* Can't seem to shake that idea. That really gets to me. I have a feeling I'll carry that one around a long time.

Now she continues quietly: "One thing I'll say for you, I'll give you one thing, you're an *honest* cop, Rawlings. You're not for sale. Not at any price. Who knows, maybe in the long run that's better than being a modern, computerized, scientific whiz-kid cop. Although I have my doubts. The scientific whiz-kid probably could've stopped me. Who knows?" Her face lights up as she drags on the cigarette. " 'Miss Waring thinks you're ill.' Jesus wept. If it wasn't all so naïve, so inept, so *old*, it'd be hilarious. But for your information, Rawlings, to set the record straight, 'Miss Waring' happens to know something about my particular 'illness' because *she's* been treated on and off for the *same* particular 'illness' most of *her* life. Yeah. Did you know that? Did she—volunteer that information? Did you guess that? Why the hell do you suppose a beautiful woman like that has chosen to be a *recluse* all her life? Want a label, feel more secure with a label? The technical term is manic-depressive psychosis, ever hear of that? Lovely affliction, lots of laughs. Psychotic reaction marked by—the classic symptoms are severe mood swings: Confidence, euphoria, fantastic schemes, wild flights of the imagination; and at the other extreme, periods of deep depression. When you're genetically predisposed to develop the condition, like me, the mood disturbance often occurs with little or no provocation. They call it 'endogenous' depression. Manic and depressive symptoms alternate in cyclical patterns, separated by extended periods of remission. 'Miss Waring thinks you're ill.' *Hah!* Sorry, Rawlings, but sometimes you—I see you got your walkie-talkie with you, huh? Nifty. You got a backup team ready to move in, right, Scotland Yard at the ready?"

"That's—"

"Armed to the teeth, right?"

"Yes, they are."

"What time is it? How much time we got?"

Turn my watch to the light. "It's now—about eight thirty-five. We have roughly twenty-five minutes."

She tucks her legs under her, laughs softly. "Before they blast their way in and rescue you from the mad-dog killer, huh?"

"Your words, not mine. You're the one wanted to talk. You looking to deal?"

"Yeah, I was. Deal number one was for you to swim out of here D-and-D. No way, you never really wanted to be a wealthy man, and all shit like that there. Let's see now. Deal number two coming at you: Eleven diamonds in exchange for the North Star. More than fair. You simply say you couldn't find it. Huh?" She waits, then imitates my voice: "Don't know, Tara. Can't promise you anything, of course. Have to check it out with the chief."

"Not bad. You're forgetting one small detail."

"Yeah?"

"Eddie Lopata."

"Ah, yes, of course, how forgetful of me. Fast Eddie. Mr. S-and-M himself. Intriguing juxtaposition of abnormal personalities: *Sick versus Sick*, all rise, please. Want the irony? My original game plan was to offer him all the other diamonds, all eleven, as his share. All I wanted from the start

was the North Star. Much better than a fifty-fifty split, I'm
sure he would've accepted with enthusiasm. As it turned out,
I never made the offer. The night of the robbery, when
he—did what he did to me, seven hours of torture, I decided I
was going to blow his fuckin' brains out the very first
opportunity I had. That may or may not sound sick to you,
Rawlings, depending on where you're coming from, but I can
honestly say I don't regret it. I'd do it again. I'm just sorry I
didn't get a chance to make it more painful for him. He died
instantly. That was far too merciful for him. What I really
wanted to do, I wanted to shoot him in the scrote and watch
him bleed to death slowly, screaming for help, but I didn't
have that luxury, I couldn't risk it. By the way, I was in
complete control of my mental faculties when I did it. So, in
all honesty, I couldn't plead temporary insanity."

"That won't make any difference, Tara, in my judgment.
With your history of mental—trouble. You'll be hospitalized.
You'll never go to prison."

"I'm quite well aware of that. What you don't know,
Rawlings, what you have no way of knowing, is that I have
absolutely no intention of spending the rest of my life—or
any part of it for that matter—in a mental institution."

"You know as well as I do that you'll have no choice in
the matter. That determination will be made—"

"*That* determination will be made by *me*, Rawlings. By *me*
and me alone. Now *you're* forgetting." She reaches down to
the cushion on her ledge, picks up a small revolver. Points it
away from me, flashes it through a thin shaft of light so I can
get a better view. Looks like a snubnosed .38, but I can't be
sure.

"Forgetting what?" I ask softly. "I knew you were armed
before I came in here. What're you going to do, kill me? Go
ahead. That won't change anything, you know that."

"You ever visit one of our celebrated mental hospitals?"

"Yes. Several."

"Uh-huh. Good. Then you know." She places the gun on
the cushion, takes another drag on the cigarette. "Warehouses. Brutal, disgusting warehouses. Human rubbish piles
of modern medical science. Anybody who's actually seen

what goes on in those degrading hellholes knows. If you're not a lunatic or a virtual catatonic when you're committed, you *will* be within the first year of confinement. Steady diet of strong antidepressants. Treatment? They don't know where to begin. Psychiatry is still a primitive science at best, less is known about the human brain than about any other major organ. Even shrinks admit that openly. The only significant difference between so-called mental hospitals today and the stereotypical insane asylums of fifty years ago is the modern antiseptic atmosphere. Cruel and unusual punishment? Shit. Life on death row is a blessing by comparison. Take my word for it. I'm not guessing. I know."

"Maybe you'll get lucky, Tara. Always the possibility you might be judged sane to stand trial. If so, you might get a shot at death row."

"Yeah, *life* on death row. Know how many people are waiting in line?"

"In the U.S.? Close to a thousand, last I heard."

"One thousand one hundred and thirty-seven, including thirteen women. Thirty-eight states still have the death penalty, including New York. But nobody's been executed in our gallant state since the fried Eddie Lee Mays at Sing Sing in nineteen sixty-three. Rawlings, you're supposed to be something of an expert on the criminal justice system in New York, tell me why? Why won't they fry 'em any more?"

"Never claimed to be an expert, but I'll give you an opinion. It's not a rational issue these days, it's an emotional issue."

"Uh-huh. Know the *real* reason? The *truth?* Our criminal-justice system has been rendered virtually *impotent* over the years by well-meaning bleeding-heart groups like the Civil Liberties Union. Know how they used to execute people in the U.S., in the old days?"

"Hanging."

"Hanging. Hanging was standard for more than two hundred years. *Public* hanging. Murderers, for the most part. Now that had drama, Rawlings, that had flair, that had impact. Then, in eighteen-ninety, the great state of New York came up with a far more sophisticated, humane method of execution—or so the public was told—the world's first electric chair at Sing Sing. Over the next seventy-three years, exactly six hundred and ninety-five people were executed in that chair, almost all murderers. Unknown to most of the public, who didn't *really* want to know anyway, was the fact that in *each* case the executioner had to pull the lever *four* times. Each time, two thousand volts shot through the victim's body, causing the eyeballs to bulge and finally *burst*, then—thanks to the metal cap—literally broiling the *brains*. Sophisticated? Humane? Me, I think that *stinks*, Rawlings, if you'll forgive the metaphor. I think they should've stayed with hanging."

"Lot of people agree with you."

Tara stands now, stretches her arms over her head luxuriously, bathed in the soft bands of red and blue. Takes a final drag on the cigarette, flicks it high out over the water, watches it tumble end-over-end, flashing through the shafts. "Which brings me to the *real* reason for this meeting. The *truth*. I murdered a man in cold blood, Rawlings. I admit it. I feel no remorse for doing it. I believe I have the right to be legally tried, convicted, and executed. I deserve that. Obviously, our criminal justice system has been rendered incapable of carrying out that responsibility. So, after a great deal of reflection, I've decided to do it myself."

I start to climb out of the water.

"*Stay where you are!*" She grabs the revolver, holds it with both hands in a combat crouch, points it down at me. "*Back in the water! Now! Move it!*"

I lower myself back in, try to keep my voice calm. "Tara, for God's sake—think. Think what you're doing."

"I *have* thought about it. I've thought of practically nothing else since I saw Thomas up on that hill this morning."

"You accused me, him, all of us, of not really thinking, not thinking problems through, not using our intellects. Aren't you guilty of the same thing now?"

She keeps the gun pointed directly down at me, two-hand grip, arms stiff. "Follow my logic, asshole: If I'm dumb enough to surrender to you, what happens then? I'll be taken back, charged, indicted, arraigned, held without bail, sub-

jected to weeks of psychiatric examinations, judged legally
insane, and sent to a mental hospital to rot. That's not an
educated *guess*, Rawlings, that's a *fact*. You *deny* that?''

I hesitate, glance away, try to come up with something to
hold her attention. She moves quickly to the far left side of
the ledge, picks up a white object that looks something like a
life preserver, steps out on a small coral platform that's
apparently used for diving. Turns to me, gun in her right
hand. The white object isn't a life preserver. It's a small coil
of thick white rope with a hangman's noose. I can see the
long part of the rope now as she yanks it taut; it's tied to the
ceiling, far out from the platform.

"Tara," I hear myself saying. "For the love of God, don't
do this. Please don't do it."

Her voice softens now, gives a slight echo from the new
position, sounds almost tranquil. "You see, Rawlings, I thought
*this* problem through, didn't I? I used my intellect. Actually,
the truth is, I've rigged this rope a thousand times in my
imagination, in my dreams, since I was a child. I know about
hanging. I've studied the subject." She uses her left hand to
place the carefully constructed noose over her head and around
her neck, then begins the methodical task of pushing her hair
outside the rope in graceful, routine movements. "It's easy if
you know what you're doing. There's a certain cold, precise
science to it. In judicial hanging, the condemned is allowed
to drop six feet—I have exactly six feet of slack here—so the
sudden dead-weight jerk of the rope breaks the neck. However, that's not the clinical coup de grace, as most people
think. The base of the tongue is forced into the back of the
throat to block the air passage; the large blood vessels supply-
ing the brain are abruptly shut off, and the vagus nerves and
carotid arteries are compressed, causing the heart to stop.
Unconsciousness and death follow very quickly."

I begin to feel the hard accelerating beat of my heart. I try
to speak but I can't. I try to climb out of the water but I feel
almost paralyzed. Still holding the gun, Tara calmly tightens
the rope with both hands, then stands quite still, arms at her
sides. Dim reflection of the water moves over her nude figure

now, poised high above me. For just a moment, she resembles a statue.

"Have you ever touched the North Star, John?"

I try to answer no, but I can't.

"Have you ever held it in your hands? Do you know how that feels? To hold a fragile little piece of eternity?"

The next few minutes are difficult for me to describe with any real degree of accuracy because the images have long since become a recurring dream, some parts vivid, others blocked from even subconscious recall, most movement transformed into a frustrating series of slow-motion flashes, sequential but fragmented. I invariably experience the dream in the early hours of the morning during the deepest part of sleep and wake up in a cold sweat. To the best of my recollection, here's essentially what I visualize and hear:

I'm in the warm water, looking up at Tara's nude figure on the diving platform of the fifth coral ledge. In slow motion, she tosses the revolver out into the darkness over the water. I wait for the splash. It never comes. I hear the distant pounding of my heart—two beats, two beats, two beats. I climb out of the water slowly, laboriously, clawing at the first coral ledge. She holds her arms out straight *You could've stopped me* in a high-dive posture and stands motionless. I try to yell at her, scream at her, but my voice makes no sound. I climb the second ledge now, scramble over cushions *I think you're too old* and reach for the third ledge. She bends her knees slightly, goes up on her toes, pushes off, arms reaching high in the dark, body lifting slowly, gracefully. I keep watching her, use all my strength to *I think you're too outdated* hook my right leg up over the third ledge. Her body flashes upward through delicate, trembling, crisscrossed shafts of red and blue, stops frozen at the apogee of the dive. Stumbling, falling, rushing toward the fourth ledge, out of breath, out of strength, shaking, exhausted. Now she begins the downward angle, arms and legs straight, body sleek, dark hair blowing back. Down, down, thick white rope losing slack so slowly, *I think you're a fuckin' anachronism* unraveling in crazy circles so slowly. Fingers scratching, clawing, bleeding now, pulling my weight up the fourth ledge. No sound when the rope goes taut: Body turns, flips slowly, the sharp midair somersault. Dark hair rises in long thick strands, unfolding, standing straight now. Far, faraway sound of a child crying. Warm blood on the coral next to my face.

*Have you ever touched the North Star, John? Have you ever held it in your hands? Do you know how that feels? To hold a fragile little piece of eternity?*

# 15

CHIEF ARRIVES 8:25 NEXT MORNING, he's got Jerry Grady with him, they're met at Heathrow by Chief Superintendent Kellogg himself, briefed on the evening's events. Yard helicopter is waiting, whisks them straight to Epping Forest, a distance of some twenty-five miles as the crow flies, ETA Miss Waring's big back lawn about 8:45. By now the circular drive is jammed with police cars and vans, the house is crawling with distinguished detectives, Blackweir Lane is a gridlock of press vehicles, horns honking, tempers teetering, and the ladies and gentlemen of the media are crowded outside the bobby-guarded gate politely demanding a news conference, earliest possible, thank you very much indeed. In a word, we have the makings of a real circus here, panoramic aerial view fit for a duke, as the chopper swoops in from the west and booms over the house. Brendan and me, we're out on the back patio when the bird touches down. Soon as the chief climbs out in his Burberry trench coat, we whip out our cigars. Should be quite a show. Grady's got his Nikon out, of course, recording everything for posterity: Molars cracks another biggie nut case.

Chief heads straight for me in the bright April sun, ignores my outstretched hand. Left eyebrow arches, holds a beat, lowers fast. Sky-blue eyes narrow to dark slits. "Rawlings, refresh my memory, huh?"

"Sure try, Chief." I bite off the end of my cigar.

"Seems to me I had a phone conversation with you just yesterday. You recall that?"

"Sure do." I spit the end on the patio.

"Yeah? Well, maybe I'm not going senile after all. Now, correct me if I'm wrong, but didn't you indicate to me that you had this house under surveillance?"

"Sure did." Now I light the cigar.

He nods, grins, shakes his head. "Now, correct me if I'm wrong, but I seem to recall giving you explicit instructions to sit tight on this broad, to wait till I arrived. That sound basically correct to you?"

"Sure does."

"Point I'm getting at, Rawlings, you just couldn't do that, could you?"

"Circumstances made that—"

"Couldn't obey a direct order!"

"Circumstances made that impossible, sir."

"That a fact? Seems to me we've had this problem with you before, mister. Talk to you later. Where's the body?"

"Swimming pool."

We all go inside. On telephone instructions from Kellogg late last night, the body was not to be touched until Chief Vadney arrived and was afforded the opportunity to observe the scene himself. Detectives from the Forensic Science Laboratory were allowed to recover the revolver from the pool and to photograph the body from a variety of angles, standard procedure, but that's all. Tara's still hanging.

Brendan and I lead Kellogg, Vadney, and Grady through the huge living room where the butler is serving coffee and tea to at least a dozen detectives, courtesy of Miss Waring, who finally retired to her bedroom about an hour ago. Charlotte waves to us from the sofa facing the fireplace. She was up with us all night, handling the phones, escorting the parade of Yard people to and from the pool, tape recording my statement, transcribing it, typing it up, and completing other necessary paperwork. She looks like she's had it now, but she gets up quickly, greets Kellogg, asks if she can be of further assistance. He thanks her for all she's done, orders her to go back to the inn and get some sleep.

A bobby stands guard at the top of the stairs leading to the pool area. Kellogg tells John not to admit anyone else until we're through. Down we go, through the heavy door, into the warm and fragrant South Seas. Chief utters a low whistle, stands by the deep end of the pool, shakes his head slowly as he looks at the white coral formations, giant Polynesian statues, exotic plants and trees.

"Holy jumped-up Jesus," he says.

"Extraordinary," Kellogg allows. "Quite extraordinary. I've heard about this, but I must say I never imagined—I always assumed the stories were exaggerated."

"It's another world!" Grady says. "Another fuckin' *world!*" Starts taking pictures, using his strobe now.

"So where's the body?" Chief asks.

Brendan points to the cavelike opening. "She's in there, gentlemen. Private little pool. We'll have to change to swimsuits."

"Swimsuits?" Chief asks.

Brendan shrugs. "Yeah, well, I mean we don't *have* to, Chief. I mean there's nobody around, we can go in bare-ass if you'd rather."

Chief hesitates, frowns, looks Brendan up and down. "Bare-ass, Thomas? *Bare*-ass?"

"No, I mean it's just—just a suggestion, y'know?"

"Thomas," Chief says quietly. "You're in England now, huh? *England.* Not an Irish bog, okay?" Glances apologetically at Kellogg, gives him a small molar-shower. "Kid's been up all night, Ashley, y'know? Little off the wall at this point, just ignore it, huh?"

Kellogg manages a weak smile.

"If you'll follow me," I tell them, "guest bathing suits are stored over here."

We walk to the storage closet, footsteps echoing, select swim trunks in our sizes. Brass has its perks: Chief goes into the men's room to change, Kellogg goes to the ladies' room, pauses, knocks politely before entering. Brendan, Grady, and I change on the pool deck, rankless wretches that we are.

I glance at the closed men's room door, turn to Brendan, do my imitation of the chief very softly: "Bare-ass, Thomas? *Bare*-ass?"

Closes his eyes quickly. "Don't. Please."

"Impropriety aside," I say quietly, "man happens to have a big bandage on his bum. Forgot that, didn't you, lad?"

Eyes close tightly, painfully this time. "Oh, shit."

"Exactly the name of his famous list. You just made it."

Couple of minutes later all hands are on deck. I slide in the warm water first, swim to the coral opening. Chief's behind me, doing what looks to be a doggie-paddle, possibly in deference to his injury; I try not to notice. Kellogg's next, then Brendan; Grady's last, camera held high. I go under, glide though, surface, swim to the edge. It's too dark to see Tara clearly, but I asked the lab men to leave one of their high-voltage lanterns for us on the first ledge. It's there. Chief surfaces, paddles to the edge near me, followed by Kellogg and Brendan. Grady has a little trouble getting the Nikon and strobe through the two-inch space; Brendan goes back to help him. We wait for our eyes to adjust before climbing up on the first ledge. I go first, walk carefully to the lantern, pick it up.

Before turning it on, I glance up at Tara. Her slim nude body is seen mostly in dark silhouette against the delicate track-lighting, touched by only two or three long thin pin spots of red and blue. When I snap on the lantern and move the strong beam to her body, it's still something of a shock, and I've viewed it several times now: Her figure flashes bright white in the semidarkness, almost luminous, like a marble statue suspended in midair over the pool, just above my eye level, long dark hair covering her entire face and neck. But that's not all. Apparently, when her neck was

broken in the sudden jolt, her involuntary reflexes caused her
to reach instantly for the noose that was in fact choking her to
death. Whether her hands completed that instinctive journey
to the neck, and perhaps even gripped the tightened rope, is a
question for the gentlemen in the Forensic Science Lab; that
her hands began the reflex action is beyond question. Both
are poised before her at about breast level, frozen now by the
familiar effects of rigor mortis. But that's not all. The bright
marble statue has assumed a posture that conveys an unmistakable signal to any reasonable viewer: The fingers of her
left hand touch her heart; her right hand extends out more,
wrist gracefully curved, fingers slightly spread, motioning to
us, inviting us to join her. Tell you the God's honest truth:
I've seen a hell of a lot of weird corpses in my career, quite a
few with limbs stiffened in grotesque ways by rigor mortis,
but this one gives me pause. Sends an ice-cold finger clear up
my asshole.

Obviously affects the others in a similar way. They stand
there on the ledge in total silence, four husky figures facing
this glowing midair apparition. Total silence for maybe ten
seconds, and these guys have seen a lot of wild stiffs in their
time too. Finally:

"Weird fuckin' momma," Chief says.

"Bizarre beyond words," Kellogg says.

"Fuckin'-A," Grady says. "Hold the light there, John,
don't move." Flash-click-whine! Flash-click-whine!

"Where'd she jump from?" Chief asks.

I move the lantern beam up to the little diving platform on
the fifth coral ledge, hold it there. Flash-click-whine!

"She had a gun on you, huh?" Chief asks.

"Yes, sir. Tossed it in before she dived."

"She actually did a—like a high dive?" he asks.

I make the lantern beam bounce up and down on the diving
platform, swing it up in a high arch, swoop it down to the
body, add a fast jerk at the end. Soft laughter from Brendan
and Grady.

Chief hesitates, then: "Rawlings, without the vaudeville,
huh?"

Goes like so. Grady takes a lot more shots for the media, including some of the chief and Kellogg with Tara's body hanging behind them, between them (side angle of Tara), gazing up at her from the water (rear view of Tara), da-da. I'm the lighting engineer, Brendan's the stage manager, Chief's the director and co-star. Kellogg gets in the spirit of things, makes an offhand observation that Tara would be a smashing addition to Madame Tussaud's. Dry British humor. Chief nods, thinks on it, says, "Who the fuck's Madame Tussaud?"

When we finally finish and swim out into the big pool, here's a young bobby waiting for us on the deck.

"Chief Superintendent Kellogg," he says. "I have a message from Miss Waring, sir. The lady requests a private meeting with you and the Americans before the press conference. She suggests the lower-level bar of the pool might be the most convenient place."

"I see," Kellogg says. "Did she specify a time?"

"At your convenience, but before the press conference, sir."

Kellogg climbs out of the pool, looks at his watch. "The press conference is scheduled for ten o'clock; it's twenty past nine now. Please tell Miss Waring we'll be happy to meet her in the bar at nine-thirty, if that's convenient for her."

"Yes, sir."

"And please keep everyone out of here until we're finished. That includes the Forensic people."

"Yes, sir." Bobby salutes, walks briskly to the door.

We each grab a guest towel from the storage closet, dry ourselves, get dressed. When Kellogg and the chief relinquish the bathrooms, Grady, Brendan and I go in to comb our hair. Before we go down to the meeting, the chief and Grady take a long look at the big underwater window of the lower-level bar. Nothing surprises them about this place any more. "Straight out of *Playboy*," Chief says.

I lead the way, open the heavy door in the far left corner, look down the dark wrought-iron circular staircase. Feel for

the light switch, snap it on. Hold the door for the others.
Clank, clank, clank, down and down we go, round and round
we go. Kellogg opens the door to the bar, feels for the
switch. Click. In we file, amid low whistles from the chief.
Soft indirect lighting, pleasant air conditioning, intimate little
booths and tables. Chief places his Burberry coat over a
chair, strolls over to the black padded-leather bar, sits in one
of the comfortable black leather armchairs, looks through the
rectangular window at the lighted turquoise water. Flash-click-
whine! Grady's having a ball.

Chief finds the bowl of cashews, begins munching, turns to
us. Looks almost British in his brown tweed jacket, white
shirt, ultraconservative tie, gray V-neck sweater, gray trousers. Glances at his Astronaut Moon Watch. "You guys hear
the one about Ben Brown?"

We tell him no.

Smiles, pops another cashew in his mouth. "This big
animal of a pro football tackle walks into the men's room at a
fancy restaurant, goes over to take a leak. Men's room attendant's on duty, little fag, he gets the soap out, starts runnin'
the water, gets the towel ready. Can't keep his eyes off the
big dude's tool there. Big dude finishes up, tucks it back,
comes over to wash his hands. Little fag looks up at him,
says, 'Man, you is really *big;* how *tall* is you?' Dude sneers
down at him, growls, *'Seven-foot-four!'* Fag says, 'Man,
that's really *big;* how much you weigh *in* at?' Dude growls,
*'Three hundred eighty-five pounds!'* Fag says, 'Man, that's
really *big.'* Hands him a towel, says, 'If you don't mind my
askin', how——how big is you between the *legs?'* Dude dries
his mitts, glares down at him, throws the towel in the sink,
growls, *'Nine inches hangin'!'* Fag says, 'Man, that's *really*
big.' Says, 'Please tell me your *name,* so when I see you on
TV, I can tell all my friends I met you.' Dude towers over
him, hands on hips, now he shouts it out: *'BEN BROWN!'*
With that, the fag's eyes bulge out, he sways, he faints flat
on the floor. Big dude gets down, he's shakin' him, he's
slappin' his face, he says, 'Ey, wake up, ya little asshole,
wake up! What the hell's wrong with ya!' Fag opens his eyes

wide, shakes his head, says, 'Oh, man, what you *said*, what you *said!*' Dude goes, 'Whaddaya mean, what I said? All I told ya, my name's Ben Brown!' Little fag's eyes roll back in his head, he says, 'Oh, man, I—I thought you said Ben *DOWN!*' ''

We're all laughing, especially the chief, he's pounding his fist on the bar, eyes watering, flashing every molar in the left side of his head. Now he tries to repeat the punch line, but he can't do it, he can't get it out.

*Click!*

Sounds to me like a deadbolt lock. Hard to tell with all the laughter. I walk to the door, turn the knob. Locked. Somebody just locked us in. I look at the mechanism: Medeco deadbolt. Impossible to pick. Instantly, I look for the hinges. They're on the outside.

"What the hell's goin' on?" Chief asks.

"Somebody just locked the door," I tell him calmly.

"Somebody just locked the *door!?*" he says.

"Yes, sir. We're locked in."

"Ridiculous," Kellogg mutters. Strides to the door, turns the knob both ways, pulls it, pushes it. Knocks hard three or four times. Listens. Face starts to color as he calls out: "Anyone there? I say, anyone out there?" Listens. Nothing. Now he pounds his fist on it, *bam-bam-bam-bam!* "Hello! Can you *hear* me?!" Nothing.

Next, the indirect lighting begins to dim. Very gradually. Like somebody's trying some kind of psychological torture.

Chief jumps to his feet, looks around fast. "Rawlings, any other doors?"

"No, sir, not that I've seen."

"You guys got walkie-talkies?"

"No, sir, we left them upstairs."

"We got a telephone in here?"

I remember. "Yeah, an intercom system." I walk quickly behind the bar, look around for it, find a small white "Princess" type phone on the shelf. I grab it, dial 401, Miss Waring's room. When I put the receiver to my ear, there's no sound whatsoever. I push the disconnect button several times, listen. No sound. I dial the number again, listen. No sound.

"Line's been cut," I say.

We're in semidarkness now. As the lights continue to fade, our attention is naturally drawn to the rectangular window of lighted turquoise water and the coral mouth of the hidden grotto to the far right. Within twenty seconds the room is in total darkness except for the unreal blue-green glow from the window that now resembles a huge empty aquarium or maybe a Jacques Cousteau movie.

"Ashley," Chief says.

"Over here, Walter."

"We'll have to use your service revolver."

"My service—?"

"To blast the lock on the door."

Silence. Then: "Walter, I don't *carry* a service revolver. None of us do, unless the circumstances clearly warrant. You know that."

We all stand around the bar in the glow from the window now, waiting for something to happen, trying to think of something to do. I note the air conditioning is still on, so there's plenty of air; also, if there's enough time we can easily locate the air ducts and determine if they're wide enough to crawl through. I'm just about to verbalize that idea when Grady clears his throat and comes up with a suggestion of his own:

"Chief, as I see it, there's only one exit left."

"Yeah? What's that?"

"The window."

Chief lowers his head to the bar, makes a painful sound.

"We're not that far below the water," Grady says.

"Detective Grady," Kellogg says quietly. "I suggest you, uh, rethink that idea."

"We could break it with a chair," Grady says. "It can't be all that thick."

"Jerry," Brendan says. "Think about it. That water would rush in here like fuckin' Niagara Falls. We'd drown like rats."

Long silence. Can't help but visualize the horrible image of Grady smashing the window with a chair and tons of water exploding in on us. Silence is finally broken by a strange, delicate sound. Soft piano music, barely audible, dreamlike. All of us lift our chins, look up, listen. Volume of the notes increases slightly; it's coming from two stereo speakers situated high in the corners of the room above the window. Gradually I become aware it's the same piano music that was played last night, vaguely familiar, solemn, haunting, what the hell is it?

Kellogg whispers something.

"What?" I whisper.

"Mozart. Mozart's Requiem Mass."

I feel suddenly cold. Look around at the other faces, pale blue-green in the glow, frowning, straining to hear. Moments later, a voice is heard over the music; although the tone is soft, even gentle, it startles us:

" 'If you can look into the seeds of time, / And say which grain will grow and which will not, / Speak.' Remember those lines, Detective Rawlings?"

"Yes, Miss Waring. Can you—can you hear me?"

"Very clearly indeed."

"*Macbeth*, wasn't it? Act One, Scene Three?"

"Precisely right. Excellent memory, Detective Rawlings. But then, as I've noticed, you have a relatively rare gift, whether you're consciously aware of it or not. Rare in this day and age, at any rate. You have the patience to actually *listen* to people. Really listen. I appreciate that quality, I must say, it's refreshing. It gives one the impression, however illusory, that you're genuinely interested. That you *care* about people. Even doddering old people like me, who drift off into ad nauseam digressions. Remembrances of things past. When all that's important, it seems, is the present. And the future."

I wait. Then: "Miss Waring, where are you?"

"In the game room. Surrounded by the electronic revolution, as it were, standing at the console of a very modern electronic communications system. Ironic, isn't it, that we've

devised such elaborate and sophisticated methods of com-
municating with one another, whilst, at the same time, we've
somehow—"

"Miss Waring, this is Chief Superintendent Kellogg, Scotland Yard. May I ask—"

"Good morning, Chief Superintendent. How marvelous
of you to interrupt at such an opportune moment. Do you
recall the three words of advice that Flaubert gave to
Maupassant?"

"Why, no, I can't say—"

"He said: 'Don't state; render.' You've done exactly that.
You've rendered the point I was trying to make. Rendered it
in a far more forceful way than I could have stated it.
Congratulations, sir."

Kellogg frowns, clears his throat. "Miss Waring, may I
ask a question?"

"By all means."

"Why not come down and join us? You have my personal
guarantee that we'll all give you our undivided attention."

"I have my reasons for not joining you, Chief Superintendent. Reasons that will become quite clear to you in a matter
of minutes. I ask your indulgence. In the meantime, please
accept my apologies for having locked you gentlemen in. I
thought it necessary. Let me hasten to add that you're not in
any danger whatsoever."

In the pause, the Requiem Mass seems very faint. Chief
reaches into the inside breast pocket of his tweed jacket, takes
out his Sony TCM-600 tape recorder, places it on the bar,
presses the record button.

"First things first, gentlemen," Miss Waring says, sounding sharp, clipped, businesslike. "The robbery. 'The Great
Diamond Robbery,' as the press has quite accurately described it. It was my idea from the very beginning. I con-
ceived it, I planned it, I orchestrated it, and I very nearly
got away with it. I was on the phone with Tara in New
York every day for well over three months. That can be
easily verified, of course. I initiated the calls in all instances
so there would be no record on her phone bill that could

be traced to me. Tara was a very willing accomplice, cooperative, obedient, even creative when circumstances demanded. But on the whole she merely followed my directions. I was quite pleased at the outcome. Until I read the press reports stating that she had—rather, she was alleged to have—murdered Mr. Lopata. Murder wasn't part of my plan, gentlemen. It was to be a victimless crime. There was never any intent to physically harm anyone. I explained that to Tara over and over again, right from the beginning. Mr. Lopata was to be given the eleven other diamonds as his share. I wanted no part of them. The very first question I asked Tara when she arrived here Sunday evening was: 'Why did you kill him?' She told me why. She provided enough of the disgusting details to satisfy my necessity to know her justification for such an appalling act. In my opinion, it was not even morally justified, and I told her that. In my opinion, there is no justification, moral or legal, for the killing of another human being, with the sole exception of self-defense. Such was not the case in this instance. In any event, despite everything, I loved Tara like one of my own daughters, and I was saddened that she decided to take her own life. Not surprised, not in the least, but saddened. You see, gentlemen, I believe that all of us have the inherent right to take our own lives, providing we do not physically harm others by so doing. That inherent right should be intuitively obvious to any rational human being. Legal opinions to the contrary are patently absurd. For reasons sufficient to me alone, I intend to take my own life in a few moments, and I'll tolerate no legal or moral arguments or impediments. As a realist, I've already taken the necessary precautions, as you see, to preclude such interference, however well meaning it may be.''

"Miss Waring?" Kellogg says.

Pause. "Yes."

"I appeal to you in the name of God to stop and consider what you're—"

"Oh, shut up!" she snaps. "I'm simply going to end my own life, Chief Superintendent Kellogg. I've had a long, full life, I've enjoyed it for the most part, and I've decided it's time to stop now. I appeal to *you* in the name of God to stop appealing to *me* in the name of God. Now, gentlemen, down to business. You'll find the eleven other diamonds in a red jewel box on the dresser in my bedroom, fourth floor. I trust you'll return them to their rightful owners. As for my own belongings, I've left a legal will, of course, it's in the possession of my solicitor and executor, Mr. Robert M. Cavallo, who was also the executor of Sir Charles's will. What remains of my estate, after all creditors have been duly paid in full, will go to my two daughters, Wendy and Felicity; all my worldly belongings, as the saying goes, with one exception: The North Star. As I am, after all, a selfish individualist, as well as an incurable romantic, I have instructed Mr. Cavallo to provide for the disposition of my body in the following manner, quote: With the North Star fixed securely in my hands, I desire to be sewn up in a clean white canvas sack such as the one selected for Sir Charles Pretoria, and dropped overboard in the Atlantic, southwest of Land's End, at the precise location where Sir Charles was dropped, to wit: Exactly six degrees longitude west of Greenwich, fifty degrees latitude north of the equator, so that my bones may rest not far from those of Sir Charles, end quote."

"Miss Waring?" Kellogg tries again.

She ignores him now, but her voice softens. "Insufferably romantic, I realize, but Charles and I agreed on the spot many years ago, gentlemen. He kept his part of the promise, now I intend to keep mine. The method I've chosen is simple, painless, and almost instantaneous. During the war, during the dreadful bombings, after I sent Wendy and Felicity away to boarding school and was left alone, a neighbor gave me a single capsule of potassium cyanide, to use in the event of a dire emergency. Very kind and thoughtful gesture, I thought. I've kept the cyanide capsule all these years. I have it in front of me now. One bite is all that's required. The time is now nine thirty-eight. I've asked the uniformed officer who guards the stairs to the pool to please come down to the lower-level bar at exactly nine forty-five and help me back up the stairs. As he'll see when he arrives, the key to the bar is in the lock. Soon enough, gentlemen, you'll be free. So will I.''

Soft chords of the Requiem Mass replace her voice. Five seconds. Ten. Chief looks at me. Grady looks at Brendan.

"Miss Waring?" Kellogg calls.

Five seconds.

"Miss Waring!"

Five seconds. Ten.

I look out the window. There's a shadow on the water directly above. Figure stands quite still, then wavers.

It happens so suddenly that all five of us jump back in automatic reflex: The body of Miss Waring plunges straight down through the water, feet first, facing us, so close to the window that her hands, clutched to her heart, actually brush against the glass. Thick streams of bubbles gush from her open lips, her eyes are wide, her long hair trails above. Down, down, all the way, face and hair descend below the window. Now we see her again in the slow backward fall, hair moving down and away from the face obscured in bubbles, hands losing the object pressed to the heart: In turquoise light, it absorbs the blue, becomes blue, flashes deep blue as it tumbles up from her grasp, spins alone for a moment, then seems to pulsate slowly, rhythmically, as it continues its dreamlike journey. Down, down, slow-motion, all the way *Have you ever held it in your hands?* to the bottom to touch its shadow; bounces softly, turns, flames, finally comes to rest *Do you know how that feels?* near its owner's small body, just inches away from her outstretched hand, palm up, slender fingers curved *To hold a fragile little piece of eternity?*

That night at the Welsh Harp pub, Brendan, Charlotte, and me are having after-dinner drinks at a window table, the chief's tipping a few with Kellogg and Grady at the next table, the ancient jont is packed with townies, Yard detectives, boys and girls of the media, everybody seems to be having a ball, all laughing and talking about the much-postponed press conference, what a real animal circus it turned out to be, grossly uncharacteristic for the British fourth estate, or so I thought. Not so, Kellogg informs us after an unbelievable hour of attempting to orchestrate more than a hundred scuffling reporters and photographers from Fleet Street's ten major dailies, eight major Sunday papers, including tabloids so hungry for sensation and circulation they make our own *News* and *Post* seem like tame spin-offs from the *Times*. Talk about *paparazzi*, they call them "monkeys" here, and I can understand why. One of these clowns, strangling in the only necktie he owns, ignites a near riot when he punches a BBC cameraman in the mouth for getting in his way. That's when the press conference ended, by the way; Kellogg and Vadney had to literally shove their way out of the middle of this crazy mob. Vinnie Casandra and his boys are saints compared to these scumbags.

Naturally, most early evening editions of papers around town are sold out, but the chief manages to grab one, *The Sun*, tabloid with the largest daily circulation in the country, and coverage in this one is typical. Two front-page pictures (courtesy of Jerry Grady): To the left we have a positively grisly full-length side-angle shot of Tara hanging stark white in the darkness; to the right we see a somewhat blurred closeup of Phyllis Waring's wide-eyed, open-mouthed face on the floor of the pool. Tasteful headline, too:

### TARA HANGS;
### PHIL FANGS!

Granny was mastermind!

All of which puts me off tonight, even makes me angry, although I'm trying to get in the spirit of things here. Difficult to do, because I don't like the British press, I don't appreciate humor that callous. Freedom of the press? Sure.

But there should be self-imposed limits. Competitive free enterprise? Fine. But simple common decency should be a factor in editorial decision making. I don't care what the arguments are, I don't care if it's the wave of the future; this kind of journalism sucks. And I could kill Grady for giving them those shots.

I'm sitting here tonight, I'm looking out through the old lead-framed diamond-shaped windowpanes, and I'm thinking: Maybe what Miss Waring said about me is true, and maybe it's a fatal flaw in this racket. I *did* care about her. Deeply. I *do* care about people. Certainly more than I did when I first pinned the shield on twenty-seven years ago. That's strange because, generally speaking, the opposite becomes true for most cops. Does caring about people in a case cloud your vision? Maybe what Tara said about me is also true. Maybe I *am* too old, too outdated for this line of work. Maybe I should hang it up, draw my full pension, go out and get one of those nine-to-five corporate security jobs where they pay those big bucks; Catherine and John certainly deserve better than I've been able to give them. When the front page of a tabloid gets to me, slams me in the gut, something's seriously wrong. Why does it hit me so hard? Why does it hurt so badly?

Charlotte's voice seems to come from a distance: "Are you all right, John?"

I turn, try to smile. "Me? Sure."

"You look so—I don't know—angry."

"Angry? No. No, I guess I'm just—I'm very tired."

Brendan finishes his brandy. "We've been up better'n twenty-four hours, Johnny. I'm calling it a night. Kellogg wants us in his office nine sharp." He stands, kisses Charlotte on the cheek, slaps me on the shoulder as he moves to the chief's table to say good-night.

I sip my brandy, smile at Charlotte. In the soft gold of the candlelight she looks calm and rested, lovely as ever.

"What is it, John? Tell me."

"Nothing important."

"Yes, it is. What are you angry about?"

"I feel old."

She frowns. "Old?"

"Yeah. I don't know. When the chief showed us the front page of that paper, it got to me. Ten years ago, even five, I think I would've laughed out loud."

"You cared for those people, didn't you?"

"Yes, I did."

"You cared whether they lived or died."

"Yes. I did."

"That's nothing to feel—old about. That's nothing to feel angry about."

"How did *you* feel?"

She pushes back her hair, thinks about it. "We're told over and over that we simply can't afford to get involved on an emotional level. But we do. Many of us do. Not on all cases, of course, but enough to have an impact on us. We care because we can't help but care. We care because we're dealing with human beings and we see part of ourselves in them. Many of us care, John, and age has nothing whatsoever to do with it. When I got back here this morning, I had a very strong drink, went upstairs, got into bed, and I wept. I wept, and I wasn't ashamed to do that. The real danger, I think, is getting hardened to the point where you really *don't* care. That's when you should feel old. That's when you should seriously consider getting out of this business, and the sooner the better."

I stare at the candle. "Remember our first talk?"

"At the Feathers Pub, yes."

"Remember I asked why you selected C-One?"

"Yes."

"You shot back that you enjoyed it, that you had every qualification considered essential for the job—intellectual, physical, *and* emotional. Remember that?"

"Yes."

I hold up my glass. "Tonight you just proved it."

She clinks glasses, smiles. "Rawlings, you're a pisser."

Now, depending on where you're coming from, that may seem like an inappropriate toast from a bright young Scotland

Yard detective, but I assure you it hits home, it makes me feel ten feet tall. As we drink to it, the anger fades, and for some reason I feel a hell of a lot younger. Tell you what, it's the best compliment I've had all day.

## About the Author

John Minahan is the author of numerous books, including the Doubleday Award novel *A Sudden Silence* and the million-copy best-seller *Jeremy*. An alumnus of Cornell, Harvard, and Columbia, he is a former staff writer for *Time* magazine and was editor and publisher of *American Way* magazine. Mr. Minahan and his wife are currently living in Miami. He is the author of the first novel in this series, *The Great Hotel Robbery*, also available from Signet.

## Thrilling Reading from SIGNET

(0451)

☐ **THE EMERALD ILLUSION** by Ronald Bass. (132386—$3.95)*
☐ **ON WINGS OF EAGLES** by Ken Follett. (131517—$4.50)*
☐ **THE MAN FROM ST. PETERSBURG** by Ken Follett. (124383—$3.95)*
☐ **EYE OF THE NEEDLE** by Ken Follett. (124308—$3.95)*
☐ **TRIPLE** by Ken Follett. (127900—$3.95)*
☐ **THE KEY TO REBECCA** by Ken Follett. (127889—$3.95)*
☐ **TOLL FOR THE BRAVE** by Jack Higgins. (132718—$2.95)†
☐ **EXOCET** by Jack Higgins. (130448—$3.95)†
☐ **DARK SIDE OF THE STREET** by Jack Higgins. (128613—$2.95)†
☐ **TOUCH THE DEVIL** by Jack Higgins. (124685—$3.95)†
☐ **THE TEARS OF AUTUMN** by Charles McCarry. (131282—$3.95)*
☐ **THE LAST SUPPER** by Charles McCarry. (128575—$3.50)*
☐ **FAMILY TRADE** by James Carroll. (123255—$3.95)*

*Prices slightly higher in Canada
†Not available in Canada

---

Great Horror Fiction from SIGNET

*Prices slightly higher in Canada
†Not available in Canada

**Buy them at your local
bookstore or use coupon
on next page for ordering.**

## Recommended Reading from SIGNET

## JOIN THE *SIGNET MYSTERY* READERS' PANEL

Help us bring you more of the books you like by filling out this survey and mailing it in today.

1. Book Title: _____

2. Using the scale below, how would you rate this book on the following features? Please write in one number from 0-10 in the spaces provided.

| POOR | | NOT SO GOOD | | | O.K. | | | GOOD | | EXCEL-LENT |
|------|---|---|---|---|---|---|---|---|---|---|
| 0 | 1 | 2 | 3 | 4 | 5 | 6 | 7 | 8 | 9 | 10 |

*RATING*

Overall opinion of book ....................... _____
Scene on Front Cover ....................... _____

3. What are your two favorite magazines?
   A. _____
   B. _____

4. Do you belong to a *mystery* book club?
   (   ) Yes          (   ) No

5. About how many mystery paperbacks do you buy each month? _____

6. What is your education?
   (   ) High School (or less) (   ) 4 yrs. college
   (   ) 2 yrs. college          (   ) Post Graduate

7. Age _____    8. Sex: (   ) Male  (   ) Female

9. Occupation: _____

Please Print Name:_____

Address:_____

City: _____ State: _____ Zip: _____

Phone #: (        )_____

Thank you. Please send to New American Library, Research Dept., 1633 Broadway, New York, NY 10019.